Copyright © 2025 by Sherilee Gray

Edited by Karen Grove

Proofread by Judys proofreading

& Shelley Charlton

Cover Designed by Natasha Snow Designs

www.natashasnowdesigns.com

All rights reserved.

No part of this book may be reproduced in any form or by any electronic or mechanical means, including information storage and retrieval systems, without written permission from the author, except for the use of brief quotations in a book review.

This is a work of fiction. Names, characters, businesses, places, events, locales, and incidents are either the products of the author's imagination or used in a fictitious manner. Any resemblance to actual persons, living or dead, or actual events is purely coincidental.

ISBN:

978-1-0670019-5-7 (Epub)

978-1-0670019-6-4 (Print)

BAD MAGIC

HELLHOUND HEAT SERIES

SHERILEE GRAY

CONTENT NOTE

BAD MAGIC contains scenes that include extra large penetration, knotting, blood, gore, violence, explicit sex.

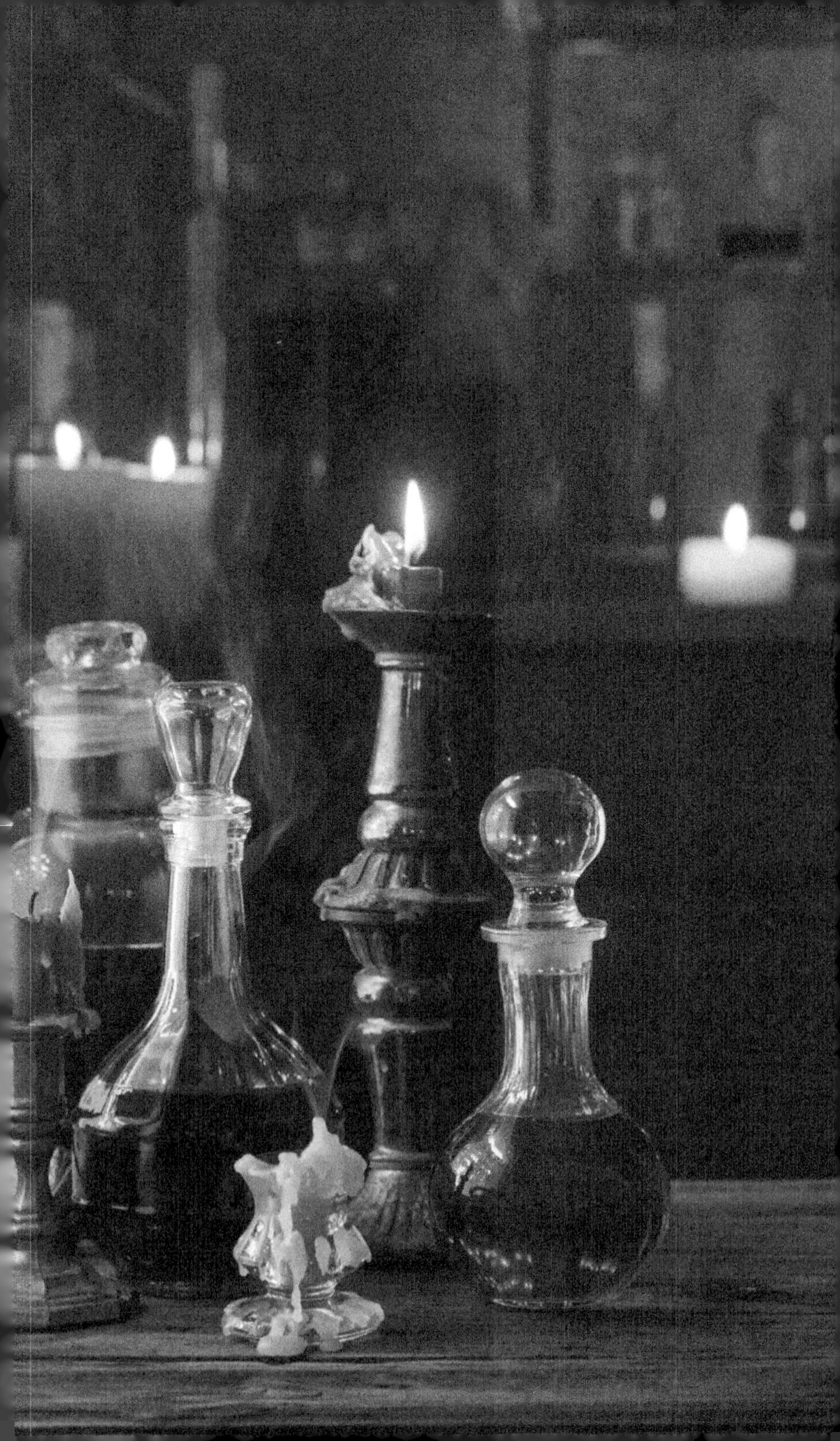

PROLOGUE

Sutton

THE CHEMIST SLICED into me again. I screamed until I tasted blood. The twisted monster cut deeper into my flesh as I thrashed. Something gave inside my abdomen as he tore one of my organs from my body. A wet thud sounded as he dropped it into the dish beside him.

I didn't know how long I'd been here. My only reprieve was blessed unconsciousness, at least until he healed me, bringing me back so he could start his "experiments" all over again.

He'd broken through our coven's wards, invading our home, then had singled me out. I needed this to end. I'd rather he kill me now than suffer another moment of this horror. Shadows creeped in at the edges of my vision, and I thanked the goddess that the terror and the agony would finally stop, even if it was only for a little while.

Numbness slowly traveled through my body, and I let darkness take me away.

A low, deep voice reached out, wrapping around me, pulling me back from the murky depths. My eyelids were weighted, my body bound tight from terror, but as that voice called to me again, warmth spread through my veins, and the terror slipped away.

I was okay.

The comforting scent surrounding me told me that everything would be okay now.

My skin tingled, heating where the monster had sliced into me. Still, my eyelids, my limbs, were deadweights, and there was no talking past my raw, swollen throat.

More voices reached me now, but the one closest still murmured to me, and every time it stopped, there was another wave of those warm tingles.

"Fucking wake up, Sutton."

Actual words. I could make them out now. *Woo-hoo.* Go me.

"Come on. Open your eyes."

I recognized that growly voice. If only I could open my eyes, or better yet, my mouth, and tell him I was awake.

More tingles, more warmth.

Prince Charming. The arrogant hellhound who had snatched me from the street and taken me to see Fern when she'd been hurt. Yeah, that voice. His scent. That was definitely Jagger.

As the numbness slowly thawed, I realized what was causing the tingles. The hound was gently licking my wounds to get them to start healing. He was growling low as well, almost constantly now.

I tried to open my mouth again, but my lungs were being crushed and my heart was in a vise. I desperately struggled to drag in a breath.

"Sutton needs a healer," Jagger growled.

Then everything went dark again.

Two weeks later

The darkness of my room closed in, and I struggled to draw breath. The Chemist's face, those black latex gloves, the scalpel, it was all flashing through my mind on repeat, and I couldn't make it stop—like a twisted Ferris wheel that I couldn't get off.

Snatching up my phone, I hit Fern's number. She understood. My friend knew what I was going through. He'd hurt her first. He'd hurt her so many times.

"Sutton?" Her voice was calm, gentle. "Breathe, babe, slow and steady. You're okay. He's gone. He's dead. You're safe now."

I didn't reply, I couldn't, only managing a pitiful whimper before I hissed. It pissed me the hell off that he was still here in my head, even though I knew I was safe. Having Fern right there on the phone helped me slow my breathing and pull it together enough to finally speak.

"Th-thanks," I whispered down the line, then squeezed my eyes closed. "Fuck...sorry." She'd been through far worse than me, for far longer. She was also newly mated, and here I was waking her in the middle of the night to drag her back into Hell with me, like some walking, talking, physical embodiment of her trauma, forcing her to relive it all over again.

"I'm here for you, day or night. You don't need to apologize to me, not ever." She was silent for a moment. "If I hadn't—"

"Don't," I said, feeling even worse now. I had to stop doing this. It wasn't fair to her. "Don't you dare blame yourself. You did nothing wrong, and neither did I. That twisted fucker did this. This is all on him."

"Yeah," she whispered after a beat of silence.

The last two weeks had been one step forward and four back. I wasn't the only one who'd been hurt when The Chemist had broken into our coven house. Phoebe, my other best friend, had been badly hurt as well, and the rest of the coven had been magically bound and locked up. Thankfully, we'd had the best healers in the city come and tend us. If it wasn't for Agatheena, a well-known witch who practiced dark magic, and Fern's newly found great-grandmother, I wasn't sure I would have survived.

The growl of an engine rumbled in the distance.

Anticipation filled me, and I shoved back the covers, easing my still weak body out of bed, and shuffled to the window.

A big, black bike rolled to a stop. The rider—tall, broad...huge—swung his well-muscled leg over the seat and climbed off.

Jagger.

"Charming just showed up," I said.

When I'd first met him, he'd been the complete opposite, so I'd called him Prince Charming. The name had stuck.

The hounds were taking turns watching the house. Yes, the danger was over, but they offered to do it anyway, while the coven healed mentally and physically after the horrors that happened here.

"Is that okay?" Fern asked.

I blew out a shaky breath as Boo, my sweet familiar, landed on my shoulder and, tucking in his bat's wings, pressed his soft head into my neck. "Yeah. Now that he's here, I'll be able to sleep." Jagger seemed to be on guard duty more often than not. I guess he was the unlucky one who kept drawing the short straw, but I had to admit, I only really slept when he was here. The other hounds were great, but Jagger was the only one who made me feel truly safe. The fact that he was super freaking arrogant and kind of cold didn't seem to matter.

"I'm glad. Has he spoken to you yet?"

"No, not since..." I swallowed audibly. Not since he'd held me in his arms, licking my wounds and begging me to *fucking wake up* in that rough and desperate voice of his. "He just stands out there, scowling, then leaves early." I blew out another breath, and this time it didn't come out as shaky. Win! I studied his chiseled features and handsome face. "Why does he come here if it pisses him off so much?"

"I think what pisses him off is what happened to you and Phoebe, not that he has to be there. Hounds really don't like it when females are mistreated."

"Right," I said, not believing a word of it, well, except for the part about hounds being protective of females. He looked like he'd rather be anywhere but here. I fought back a yawn and failed. "I think I'll try to sleep now."

"Night, Sutton."

"Night, Fern."

One week later

. . .

The sound of Jagger's bike echoed up from the street, and I took my first deep breath all day. Yes, I knew what his bike sounded like. They all sounded a little different, and I'd figured out which one was his since he was here more than the others. His bike sounded deeper and resonated through my chest when the growl of the engine filled my room in the dark.

As I always did, I shoved back the covers and went to the window. He was leaning against his bike. I waited for him to pull his phone from his pocket and settle in for the next several hours like he usually did—instead, his head tilted back and his glowing eyes, that were currently hellhound gold, gazed up at my window.

I froze. Could he see me here in the darkness? I held my breath, my feet cemented in place.

Jagger didn't look away. When his hound was in check, his eyes were a stunning shade of green but could also change to bright red when he was pissed off.

Step back.

But before I could, he crooked a finger at me.

Did he really want me to go down there?

He did it again.

I quickly stepped back. He did, he wanted me to go down there. *Crap.*

I swallowed, my mouth as dry as hell. *Get it together.* If the surly hound had something he wanted to tell me, at the very least, I owed it to him to go down there and listen.

I shoved my feet into my pink fluffy boots, and Boo stirred. "I'll be right back," I said as I slid on the long yellow cardigan I used for a robe. I shut Boo in before he could follow me, then headed downstairs. My heart raced as I opened the front door and stepped outside for the first time since everything had happened.

Jagger watched me walk along the path, striding forward to meet me with that swagger of his turned all the way up to peak swag.

We both stopped with the tall iron gate between us at the end of the garden path. "Hey," I said, feeling awkward and shy and...weird. I hadn't stood face to face with him, talked to him, since that awful day, and even then, he'd been the only one talking.

"How you doing, Sutton?" he asked, taking in my face, before his gaze slid over my hair. He breathed in deeply through his nose before his gaze carried on down my body. His jaw tightened, as if he were seeing each wound under my cardigan, each slice carved into my body by a madman, all over again.

"Um...yeah, okay, I guess." I could pretend I was tough, but he'd see right through it, and I'd never been the type of person who felt the need to pretend I was okay when I clearly wasn't, and besides, he deserved the truth from me. "Nights are the hardest."

He did that jaw-tightening thing again. "Yeah?"

I nodded, chewing my lip. Yep, this was totally awkward. I didn't want to talk about that night, but I needed to say this. "I want to...to thank you, Jagger, for what you did for me that day and...and now. When I know you're out here, I can actually sleep."

His eyes, that had returned to moss green, reignited like a fire had been lit behind them. "You don't need to thank me," he said, then looked away for a moment, his chest expanding on a rough breath before he looked back.

The silence stretched out between us. I wrapped my cardigan around me tighter. "Was there, um...something you wanted to tell me?"

A muscle at the side of his jaw twitched. "I'm needed in

Hell. You won't see me out here anymore. I leave in the morning. Didn't want you to think..." He looked lost for words. "I wanted to reassure you that you'll still be safe, that my brothers will be here as long as you need them," he said gruffly.

Alarm raced through me, hard and fast, like ice water had been pumped into my veins and was overflowing through all the wounds covering my body, spilling at his feet.

The level of dismay I felt was irrational, but there was no stopping it, and because of what he was, he had to feel it. No, he didn't have much of an emotional range, but a hound understood fear when he sensed it, and the way his head jerked back, I knew I was right.

"What's going on, Sutton?" He was frowning deeply.

"Nothing."

"You're afraid." He looked around us, as if there was an enemy closing in and he was ready to tear their head off. He turned back to me when he realized there was no threat, and his brows shot up. "Are you afraid of me?"

My face burned with embarrassment, but I sure as heck wouldn't let him believe I was scared of him. "I'm not afraid of you, the opposite in fact."

That glowing gaze bored into me. "Spell it out," he demanded.

As annoying and blunt as he could be, it didn't change the fact that he deserved the truth. This male had literally saved my life. "You...you, ah..."

"I what?" he said impatiently.

My irritation flared. "You...*specifically*, make me feel safe, okay?" I huffed out a breath. "I have no idea why, it's not like you're all charm, right, Charming?" I said and rolled my eyes. "But that's the truth of it, and I don't... I don't want you to go, all right?"

He stilled, and his shoulders seemed to grow wider under his jacket while he studied me some more. Finally, he grunted, the growly sound lifting goose bumps all over my skin. "I have to go. Lucifer's orders."

I nodded and bit down on my lips when stupid, humiliating tears sprung to my eyes. *What the hell was wrong with me?*

Jagger didn't miss those either. His eyes actually widened, and he looked ready to run for the hills. "Don't you fucking cry," he growled out.

"I'm not going to cry," I fired back as tears spilled over and slid down my cheeks. "Why would I cry over you leaving? That's ridiculous." More tears fell as a horrified Jagger watched on. "And you can't order me not to cry, Charming. It doesn't work that way."

"I don't do tears, female."

"Well, I don't cry. It's just a...a psychological response to you saving my life. My brain obviously associates you with safety, that's all. Your voice and your...your scent was the first thing I became aware of after it happened." Oh gods, did I just say his *scent*! "Don't look at me like that—"

"Like what?"

"Like you want to throw up."

"Hounds don't throw up."

"Well, lucky you." I kind of thought I might throw up myself. Another round of tears slid down my cheeks. There was no stopping them now.

Jagger jerked back again. "What the *fuck*, Sutton."

I tried to mop them up with the sleeve of my cardigan. "Just ignore it."

"How the fuck am I supposed to do that?"

"Stop cursing at me." Now I was trembling. "You're leaving, aren't you? Just go."

His fingers curled around the iron bars of the gate. "My brothers will still be around," he said again, looking as awkward as I've ever seen a hellhound look.

"I know."

"The danger's over."

"I know that too. I mean, logically, anyway."

He cursed again, standing there with a strange look on his face for probably a full minute, then he shrugged off his leather vest, hooked it on the gate, and reached back, dragging off his T-shirt.

I blinked at him in shock. His wide, ripped, and tattooed chest was perfect in every way. Muscles, so many muscles that were defined as if he'd been sculpted by one of the masters, and with just the right amount of chest hair. My cheeks burned hot and my mouth went dry. "What are you doing?"

He put his leather vest back on, then shoved his hand, and the T-shirt, through the bars at me. "Take it."

"What? Why?"

His monster biceps bulged. "Pups feel safer when they're surrounded by their parents' scent. It might help?"

"I'm not a pup, and you're not one of my parents," I said, and my parents had never made me feel safe.

"I know that," he said, grinding his teeth. "I'm thinking the same principle could apply here?" He shrugged a gargantuan shoulder. "Fucked if I know, Sutton. You're the one who mentioned scent. So maybe having something with mine on it will help while I'm gone?"

He was literally giving me the shirt off his back to get me to stop blubbering, and pathetic as I was, I took it from him. "Fine," I said, barely stopping myself from pressing it to my nose right in front of him to test the theory. "Is that all you wanted? To tell me you're leaving?"

His gaze lit up again, switching from green to gold as he jerked up his chin.

I hugged myself tighter. "I appreciate everything you've done for me, Charming." Why did this feel so awful? Why was the thought of him going so painful? The words, *don't leave me*, were dancing on the tip of my tongue. "Look after yourself," I mumbled instead.

"You, too, babe," he said as I spun away and rushed back inside the house.

Still, he didn't leave, he stayed until the sun came up. I knew that because I couldn't sleep, not when my stomach was churning and the thought of him leaving made me feel physically ill. I'd lain there, wearing his shirt, surrounded by his scent, while I listened for the sound of his bike taking him away—like some obsessive fangirl.

It finally came when the rest of the house stirred, starting their day.

There was a pull in the center of my chest when the rumbling growl of his engine starting, reached me from outside. The hideous feeling inside me spiked viciously, and before I knew what I was doing, I'd shoved back the covers, and not caring that I was only wearing his shirt, tore out of my room and down the stairs.

Flinging the front door open, I ran along the path. Jagger's head jerked my way as I reached the gate. He was sitting on his bike, and my heart slammed in my chest as I punched in the security code and opened the gate.

He stood, swinging his leg over the bike and frowning. He started toward me as I ran at him.

"What's going on—"

I slammed into his chest, wrapping my arms around his

massive body, clinging to him. I didn't know what the hell I was doing, but I had to do it. I couldn't stop.

"What's going on? Are you all right?"

I shook my head.

"Look at me," he ordered.

I shook my head again.

He took my face in his hands, tilted my head back, and his intense green eyes searched my face. "Are you hurt? Talk to me," he growled.

Something built in my chest until it was unbearable, and before I realized what I was going to do, I lifted to my toes and slammed my lips against his. Jagger froze, going rock solid as fire—no, fireworks—exploded between us. *Oh my gods*. Goose bumps lifted all over me, my scalp tingled, and my belly heated.

One of his massive arms banded around me, and he gave me a rough squeeze, and his lips finally moved, just once, a gentle press, then he lifted his head.

My breath was shaking when I looked up at him. I couldn't read his expression, but his eyes *glowed*. His hand lifted, and he ran his fingers down the side of my face, over my hair, fisting it lightly, then released me.

He said nothing, but his chest was heaving and his nostrils were flared as he stared down at me, a rumble rolling from him.

I'd kissed him. I'd kissed Jagger. Just a touch of lips really, but it was the best kiss I'd ever experienced.

I stood back as he swung his leg over his bike. "Take care, Sutton," he finally said, his deep voice full of grit.

Then he revved his bike and roared off down the street.

As the sound of his engine grew distant, the only way I was able to soothe the feeling of loss inside me was to fist the shirt at my chest and lift it to my nose again.

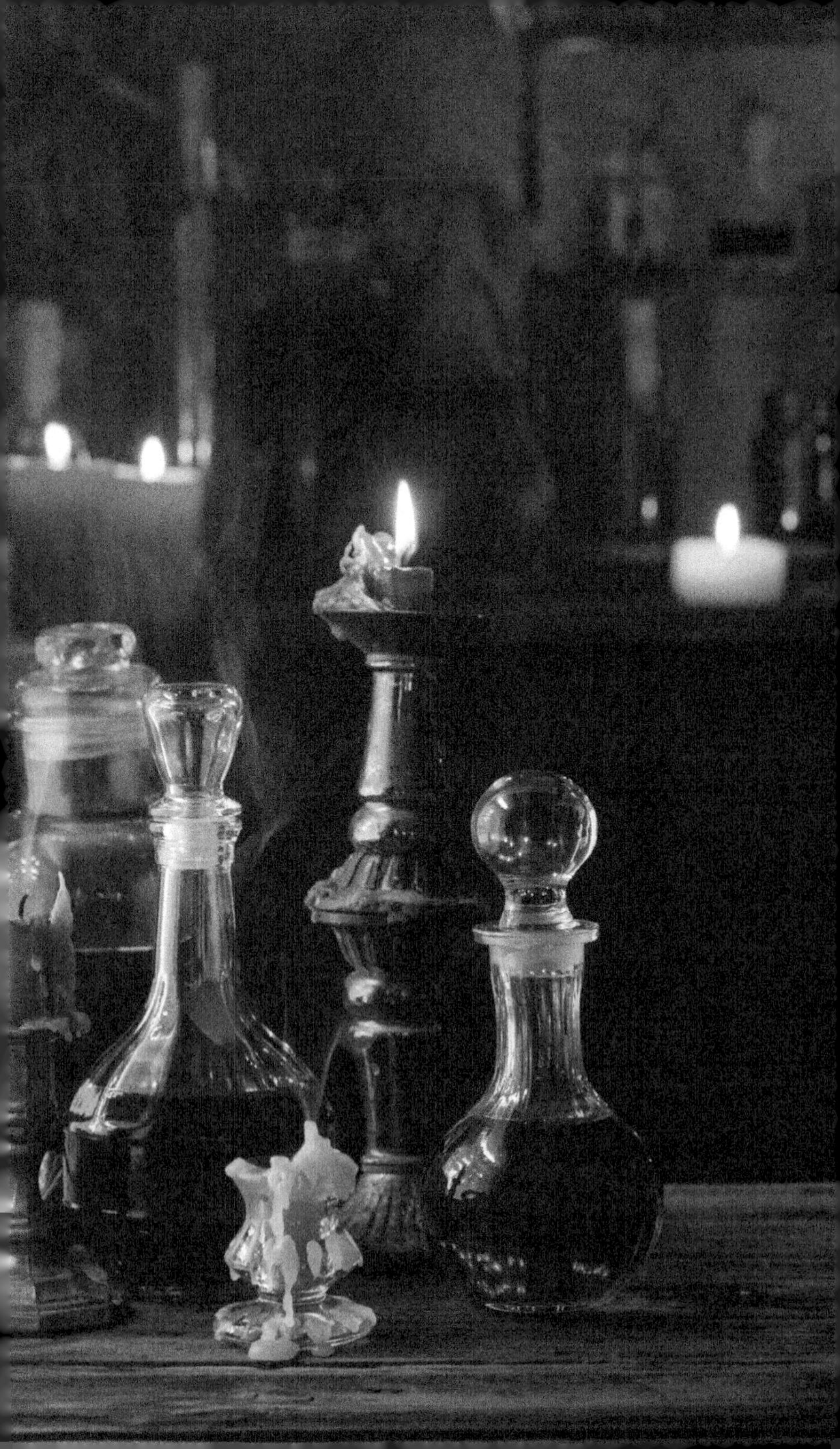

CHAPTER ONE

Sutton

LAUGHTER ECHOED THROUGH THE TREES. I hung back, watching from the shadows as coven Ellis filed out of their cemetery.

A pang of pain, followed by a rush of anger filled me as my mother and father, my sister, aunts and uncles and cousins, all together, enjoyed a midnight harvest. Cemeteries were places of great power for a coven. Everything here held magic—the dirt and grass, the gravel on the path, every herb and flower, it was all useful. Magic never left a witch completely, not even when we died. The bones of our ancestors continued to pump magic into the earth, which was why we grew large herb gardens in our cemeteries, so when harvest time came, we were well stocked with powerful ingredients for potions and elixirs.

The clink of the iron gate closing rang out and their chatter slowly faded as they walked away.

Running my fingers down Boo's back, I left my hiding

place behind one of the garden sheds and watched them drive away. Sensing my spiraling emotions, my tiny familiar used the hooks at the ends of his delicate bat wings to climb higher and snuggled under my hair.

"I'm okay, Booboo," I whispered as I made my way through the headstones and over to the main herb garden.

I had a shift tonight, ambulance duty, and I needed to top off my supplies. We had a small cemetery behind Ashborne house, but it wasn't as old and nowhere near as powerful. If my family knew I still had access to this place, they would've dragged me before the witch's council and demanded severe punishment. But since my mother had cut me out of their lives like a festering wound, they'd all but forgotten I ever existed.

Apparently, having demon blood tainting the coven was a big no-no. And maybe if I hadn't transformed into an *ugly fucking monster*, my cousin Bonny's words, when I used my healing magic, then *maybe they would have been able to pretend I was normal*, said to me by my aunt Julia as my stuff was being tossed out of the house, I would have been here with them tonight.

My father, upon learning I wasn't biologically his and that his wife had been unfaithful, decided it was too much work to leave her, or even really fight about it, and instead pretended I never existed. He always had been lazy. So yes, they were cold and mean and, more often than not, just awful, but I'd been young, and they were my family. They'd left me alone, unprotected, scared. That rejection, and what came after, had shaped who I'd become.

So, no, I wasn't with them, and I never would be again. Instead, I skulked around in the shadows and stole what I needed. A literal thief in the night.

I used to pray to the mother every night, begging her to

make me like them, to take my demon blood away, but of course the goddess never answered. There was no changing what I was.

I twisted the heavy gold engraved ring on my thumb as I approached my grandmother Bity's headstone. She'd given it to me before she died, when I'd broken into the house to see her on her deathbed. The spell she'd engraved in it meant I could bypass the Ellis wards and take what I wanted.

Crouching, I ran my hand over the smooth stone. "Hey, Gran." I pressed my palm to the earth and felt her familiar power vibrating through the ground, and my heart squeezed. "I miss you."

She'd been the only one in my family to love me as I was.

Shoving down the pain, I quickly grabbed my hand shovel and jar. I filled the container with dirt, then rushed to the herb garden, where I took what I needed, more than I'd usually risk taking, but harvest night was always the best time to come because they never noticed anything missing.

It just really freaking sucked seeing them all together, even if it was only from a distance—and even if they were all awful.

Nope. Shove that down as well.

Quickly packing everything in my bag, I slung it over my shoulder and headed off, pulling my phone out as I walked. I typed a message to Jack, asking him to swing by and pick me up for our shift, then sent a group text to my coven, telling them to let me know if anyone heard from Luke tonight. He hadn't been home in almost a week, and that wasn't like him.

I'd been living rough when I'd been introduced to coven

Ashborne. Phoebe had offered me a place to stay, and the witches there had welcomed me with open arms. They were all like me, born with mixed blood, and they'd quickly become my family. They were all I needed.

I hit send and my eyes were drawn to the Nightscape message notification that popped up.

My heart did a little leap as I clicked it open.

Jagger had followed me on the app a couple months after he'd left for Hell. I'd been the only person he'd followed then, and I still was.

He didn't always reply to my messages—okay, I messaged him every day, and he replied like once every couple of weeks, and it wasn't really a reply, more a request for another picture because he *wanted to see for himself that I was okay*. That was a lie, though. He'd followed me on Nightscape and had sent me that first message, for one reason only, something that I'd tried to tell myself to forget, that it couldn't be true, even when everything in me screamed that it was.

The truth was, that after he'd left, I started to think that Jagger and I were mates.

There'd been no other explanation for the way I felt.

Why else would his scent calm me the way it did? Why else couldn't I stop thinking about him? What other reason could there be for the way my body reacted when we'd kissed. This wasn't just some infatuation, I felt it on a level that hadn't existed before I'd met him. Instincts, demonic ones, had roared to life, screaming that he was mine.

I'd known who he was the moment our lips touched. I'd felt it with every part of me. If I were honest, I felt something the day he snatched me off the street and took me to treat Fern when she'd been injured several months ago.

But despite how sure I'd been, I'd still asked Agatheena

what she thought when she'd come to check on my injuries the last time. The powerful, dark witch had looked at me with that piercing gaze, and said, "Of course he is, you nitwit!" Along with a few other things, but she'd definitely confirmed it.

Jagger had to feel it too. Why else had he come to say goodbye that night? Because he felt this insane connection between us as well, and the only reason he hadn't admitted it was because there was nothing he could have done about it. I'd still been recovering, and he'd been forced by Lucifer to go back to Hell to do his lord's dark bidding, or whatever the heck it was they did down there.

We'd both been playing it cool because neither of us wanted to make it harder on the other. Okay, maybe I hadn't been as cool, blubbering all over the place. But I knew that's why he always grouched and acted indifferent with me, because starting anything up before he left was impossible. I got it, and it sucked.

But I knew from Fern that it was really hard on males to stay away once they found their females, so I'd said nothing. I sent him the pictures he asked for, and I'd resigned myself to wait until he came back, when we could finally be together.

I clicked open my Nightscape messages and my heart sank. Not Jagger. Some invite to a retro house music, dance party. I tapped Jagger's name anyway. The last message was from me, yesterday, telling him about the new healing oil I'd been working on. Above that was a picture of me in shorts and a tank top, standing in front of the bathroom mirror. My hair was crazy, and I was pulling a silly face. There was also dirt on my arms and a smudge on my cheek after working in our little cemetery's herb garden all day.

He'd looked at it but hadn't commented, which was

standard Jagger. In a week or so, he'd ask for another picture, then vanish again. I had no idea what he was doing in Hell, something that obviously kept him very busy, and I mean, *it was Hell*, maybe the Wi-Fi was patchy?

I smiled. Everything would work out in the end. It was fated after all.

Shoving my phone in my bag, I got in my car and headed for home.

I'd been through some not so great things in my life, but I was still here. I'd survived. I chose to be happy every day, to push through, to soldier on. Staying positive, seeing the good in people, that was how I'd found my new coven.

Sure, there'd been another bump in the road with the attack, but now the fates were finally on my side.

I'd been through the worst.

Now it was time for the reward.

·)))·●·(((·

"Roll him to his side," Jack said as he pulled the tube from the young shifter's throat.

"What on earth is going on?" I said as I hovered my hand over his abdomen, firing up my magic.

Jack shook his head. "This is the third one tonight."

The younger male coughed and groaned. At least he'd make it. We'd lost the overdose patient we'd treated earlier. My powers let me see anything relating to a person's well-being, physical or mental. No, I didn't see pictures as such, but for a moment in time, I was in a patient's head. I could feel what they were feeling, but in an abstract way, a way that conveyed the full scope of their condition and the circumstances surrounding it without actually crippling me from the pain they were experiencing. Unfortunately, the mental sides of things—what someone suffered and how it affected them—managed to reach me, especially if it was particularly bad. "He took the same drug as the others. He thought it was safe. He just wanted a good night out."

"Idiot," Jack muttered.

Yep. Poor pup.

Jack Connors was a demi-demon—in other words he was half human, half demon—and had been helping demons, shifters, and others in Roxburgh for a long time. He started off working in a human hospital, intercepting cases that involved demi like him, then shifters and witches and anything not human. There'd been a desperate need for a hospital of our own. So Jack had opened a clinic and got the ambulance service up and running, and he'd been the one to hire me. Jack was awesome; no, I hadn't felt that way when we first started working together. I may have referred to him a time or two as a giant douche-canoe. But I realized after getting to know him, he hadn't had it out for me, he just really freaking wanted the clinic and ambulance service to work.

Jack's phone lit up. "Another OD." He cursed. "Dogwood Park."

Crap. I eased our patient back, rushed to the front of the ambulance, and jumped in the driver's seat. We'd have to drop him off afterward.

"He's secured," Jack called. "Go go go."

I tore off at breakneck speed. Dogwood Park was an old industrial area that'd been purchased by a bunch of wolf shifters. They'd subdivided it into large plots, like several acres each, and had been demoing the old buildings. The plan was to turn it back into forestland and build luxury cabins for local shifters with ready cash to buy and enjoy their own piece of paradise.

And right in the middle of it all was the arena. Another new venture that had taken off. It was in an old converted warehouse and now held fights every Wednesday night. Those attending could fight or bet on their favorites and, hopefully, make a nice chunk of change at the end of the evening.

The ambulance was called there almost every Wednesday, where we patched up the idiots who went to get their asses kicked. Usually, those fighting were fast healers, but we'd had a few touch-and-go moments. There were also a lot of broken bones and dislocated joints, and those had to be set quickly or there was a risk of them healing out of alignment.

As soon as I sped into the parking lot, someone waved us over. A crowd had gathered outside the main entrance. I jumped out and rushed over to assess the situation.

The female was foaming at the mouth and convulsing. This was no fighting injury. "We'll need to pump her stomach," I called to Jack.

He grabbed what we needed and ran to join me, and we got to work.

Thankfully, once we got the drugs out of her, she seemed okay, but we needed to get her to the clinic ASAP.

Jack secured our new patient on the gurney. "I need to get these two transferred."

"I'll wait here, there could be more," I said. Both stretchers in the ambulance were full, and if someone else got hurt, we'd have no room to transport them.

"Yeah, probably a good idea the way tonight's going. You'll be okay?" he asked.

"Yeah, fine."

Jack took the Taser from the glove compartment and

handed it to me anyway. "Don't hesitate if someone tries to mess with you."

"You know I won't." Though that had never happened. Everyone who came here seemed to recognize the uniform now, appreciated what we did, and stayed out of our way, which was the only reason Jack was cool leaving me.

"As soon as I drop them off, I'll head back."

"I'll be fine," I said again, grabbed the pack we kept stocked with supplies out of the back of the rig, added a few extras from my own bag, and slid it on.

I jumped down, shut the doors, and headed into the warehouse as he drove away.

The place was packed as always, and loud. Cheers mixed with music blared through the room. Mainly wolves, crows, bats, and a few other breeds of shifters came for the fights, but there were always demons as well, and a handful of vampires came most weeks.

Scanning the room, I spotted Rome and Lothar, beers in hand, watching the action going on in the cage; several other hellhounds were there as well.

A demon of mixed breed, by the looks of him, and a crow shifter were currently fighting, and going by the number of lines tattooed on the side of the crow's head, and the grin on his face, he was toying with his opponent. No one was usually stupid enough to take on the crows, besides the hounds that is. The demon must be new here.

I scanned the room, looking for anyone who might need my help as I made my way over to Lothar. We spent a lot of time at the hellhounds' clubhouse now that Fern was mated to Relic, and when Jagger came back, I'd be there even more.

My heart did a stupid flutter, and I couldn't contain my grin when I stopped beside Loth. "Hey," I called.

He looked down at me, then behind me. "Where's your backup?"

I smiled wider. Hounds were emotionally stunted, yes, but they really were protective of females. Probably because they didn't have any. Female hounds weren't a thing, only their male offspring were hounds. Females took after their mothers. "He's taking some patients back to the clinic," I yelled over the music. "He'll be back soon."

Roman patted me on the head. "What up, shorty?"

By the looks of him, he'd already fought, not because he was bruised or anything, but because there was blood that I doubted very much was his smeared on his knuckles. The groupie beside him pressed her boobs against his arm and narrowed her eyes at me.

I ignored her. "Thought I'd stop by to say hey. I'm just doing the rounds—"

"Medic!" someone yelled from the cage.

I spun around. "Crap."

The crow stood back, splattered with blood and utterly calm, while the demon lay on the floor, sliced in several places, his leg at an odd angle and an arm that was obviously dislocated. The crow had gone easy on him—the demon was still breathing.

"Medic!" I yelled, trying to push through the crowd. "Let me through."

Suddenly, I was airborne, big arms lifting me and shoving the crowd aside. "I got you," Rome said, getting me where I needed to go with ease and planting me on my feet.

The cage door was open, and I rushed in and quickly got to work setting his break and getting Rome to help me pop his shoulder back in, while I stopped the demon's bleeding and used my magic and healing oil to jumpstart his own healing abilities.

When I was done, his friends came and carried him away, and I got out of the cage so they could hose away the blood for the next two fighters.

Idiots. Seriously, absolute imbeciles, all of them. I didn't get the appeal of any of this.

Over the next half hour, I patched and set bones as needed. Jack had obviously been held up, but so far there'd been nothing I couldn't handle.

I made my way through the crowd and spotted Luke. Relief washed through me. He was our youngest coven member, sweet, impressionable, and a little gullible. He hadn't been answering my calls the last week, and I'd been getting worried. I assumed he'd been staying at his girlfriend's place. What the hell was he doing here? He better not try to get in that cage; he'd get his fool self killed. I waved at him, and I was positive he'd seen me, but instead of coming over, he took off.

What the hell?

I started after him, when someone grabbed my arm. "Please, can you help my friend?" A male was slumped against his side, pink foam gathering around his mouth.

Shit. Another one. "Put him on the ground. Get back!" I yelled at everyone closing in around us. I was checking his airway when Jack arrived. Thank the goddess.

"We need to pump his stomach." I grabbed what we needed from my bag.

Jack inserted the tube, and I dipped my head low, letting my hair fall forward to cover my face—and my transformation—as I attempted to draw the residual poison from him with my magic.

Something hit my shoulder, and I was shoved back.

My cousin Bonny stood over me, a look of disgust on her face. "Get your filthy fucking hands off my boyfriend."

She pointed at Jack. "You save him, but that gross demon freak doesn't touch him."

Jack looked up at her, and I could tell he was about to tell her to fuck off. I know my cousin, though, and that would only set her off more. No matter what she thought of me or me of her, we needed to save this guy.

I lifted my hands. "It's okay," I said to him.

By the look on his face, Jack didn't agree. I stood, stepping back while the guy's friends held him down when his convulsions got really bad.

"We need to get him to the clinic," Jack yelled.

They lifted him, and I followed, rushing for the ambulance. They got him on a stretcher, but even from a distance I could feel his life force weakening. "We're losing him," I called to Jack.

"Do your thing, Sutton," he said and headed for the driver's door.

My cousin grabbed my arm. "I said you can't fucking touch him," she all but shrieked.

"Then he dies," Jack bit out. "You either let Sutton work on him, or you should say your goodbyes now."

Hatred burned from her eyes, but she finally nodded and followed me into the back of the ambulance. Jack shut the doors after us and jumped into the driver's seat.

I held my hands over him, using every bit of healing magic I could to keep him alive while we sped from the parking lot and along the main road, leading us out of Dogwood Park. The whole way, I felt Bonny's magic crackling around us, ready to attack if anything went wrong. Ready to hurt me because of what I was, as if we'd never played together as children or spent holidays and birthdays together.

"He better not fucking die, Sutton," she said.

I ignored her and kept working as Jack slowed, turning on the lights and siren, cursing as he tried to ease out of an intersection and into traffic, but no one was letting him through.

That's when I heard the rumbling sound of an engine so familiar, so comforting, as unique to me as the male who rode that particular bike. I looked up in time to see it round the corner into Dogwood. The rider looked up, and I was positive he saw me before he opened up and tore down the road, heading toward the warehouse.

Jagger.

Jack pulled out, stopping traffic, and gunned it.

That was Jagger. I was positive.

Excitement filled me. He was home.

He was finally home.

CHAPTER TWO

Sutton

I CHECKED MY HAIR AGAIN, smeared on some lipstick, then hustled back into the bedroom to slip on my shoes. Heels. I only wore heels on special occasions, and tonight was a very special night.

It hadn't started off special, the things Bonny said had wormed their way under my skin, but then I'd seen Jagger and I hadn't cared anymore what she had to say. We saved her boyfriend, and I'd left the clinic without another word to her.

I'd thought about my family enough for one day, so shoving tonight's interaction to the back of my mind, I smiled wide. My nerves were going wild, but they were excited nerves. Good nerves.

Hands trembling, I ran them down my dress. It was floaty, short, and skimmed my curves in a subtle but sexy way. The bright yellow dress was new, dotted with sunflowers that made me happy, and I loved it.

I went back to the bathroom and added my necklaces, slid on my rings and the little peridot cauldron studs I bought the month before, then fussed with my hair again. Jagger liked my hair. He'd never said it out loud, of course, but every time we'd been in the same room, his gaze would drift over it, and he did this thing where he'd draw in a deep breath. I braided a thin, green velvet ribbon, almost the same color as Jagger's eyes, down the side. I gave my outfit one last look in the full-length mirror and smiled.

"You've got this," I said to my reflection.

Snatching up my bag, I hefted it over my shoulder. I'd filled it with some extra things in case I was away for a few nights. When Fern and Relic mated, she vanished for several days. Hounds were possessive and, once they found their mates, completely obsessed. Jagger had been forced to stay away from me for several months, he'd want me close now.

I assumed Lothar or Roman had told him earlier tonight that I was at the fights, which was obviously why he'd gone there. I'd texted Fern when I got home and told her I'd seen him. She said she was at the clubhouse waiting for Relic, that the hounds were in some meeting, which was obviously why Jagger wasn't here with me now. Warrick, their alpha, must have called them in.

I could message him, but I wanted to surprise him. I'd be there waiting when their meeting finished.

My entire life I'd been insecure. Being brutally rejected by the people you loved and trusted the most in the world did that to a person. I didn't need to fear that from Jagger. He was my mate. I'd tried so many times to tell myself I was wrong, to not get my hopes up, but even with all the trauma I'd been through, all the hate and rejection because of my demon blood and the way it made me look when I used my magic—there was no ignoring the truth.

Jagger was mine, and I was his.

I had nothing to fear from him.

The fates had chosen him for me, and for the first time in my life, I had nothing to be afraid of. Yes, it helped that Agatheena had confirmed it, but even if she hadn't, the truth had been there—I'd just had to listen, to surrender to my own intuition. Jag wanted me too. That's how mates worked. I'd watched Relic pursue my friend. I'd witnessed him break down her walls, and I watched them fall in love.

Now it was my turn.

It was my turn to be loved and cherished. It was my turn to be the most important person in someone's life.

I quickly texted Fern to tell her I was heading to the clubhouse and not to tell anyone. My friend knew the truth. She hadn't said it outright, but she wasn't as subtle as she thought.

Slipping on my coat, I slung my bag over my shoulder, then carefully lifted Boo, who was snoozing, hanging from his perch, and I placed him on my shoulder. He crawled in more snugly, and I grabbed my keys and headed out.

When I pulled up to the clubhouse thirty minutes later, I was greeted by Brick. He opened the gate for me, and I lowered the window to say hi. He leaned in, and the young hound gave me a cocky wink.

"Hey, Sutton," he said, flashing his dimples and a good dose of sharp canines. The kid was a flirt.

I laughed, feeling breathless and honestly a little faint, but gods, joyful. I don't think I'd ever used that word in my life. "Is Fern still here?"

"Yeah. I'm just waiting for War to send my replacement for guard duty, then I'll join the party."

"Party?" I looked toward the clubhouse. The doors were thrown open, and I could see it was full of people and, yeah, could hear music.

"Jag's back. His brothers wanted to welcome him home." He gave me another grin. "So, you want to hang later? I'll come find you."

Okay, I wasn't expecting a party, but I guess they started after the meeting? I shook my head at Brick. "As lovely as your offer is, I already have someone to hang with."

"If you change your mind, I'm not hard to miss." Giving me another flash of those dimples, he stepped back.

He wasn't wrong, Brick was only twenty, but he was huge, definitely one of the larger hounds in the pack. I parked, grabbed my bag, got out and, taking a deep, steadying breath, strode up to the main doors.

The place was crowded. Friends and family of the hounds, mainly witches and shifters, were already here partying.

I searched the room, but I couldn't see Jagger. Gods, what if he'd come looking for me right after the meeting and we'd missed each other—

The crowd in front of me parted.

There.

My heart did a wild thud in my chest when I saw him.

He was standing with Lothar and Warrick at one of the tall tables. Relic stood opposite him, Fern under his arm. Goddess, the excitement was bubbling from me now; I was almost giggling I was so giddy. As I got closer, I realized my friend was scowling across the table at Jagger. I frowned, looking between them—and that's when I noticed the female tucked into his side.

Her arm was around his waist.

My steps faltered.

What was he doing? Why was that female touching him? The little girl who had been hurt and rejected so badly screamed at me to turn and leave, to get the hell out of there. But the female who was looking at someone else touching her male forced me to keep walking.

Fern turned then, spotting me. Her eyes widened, and Relic's jaw tightened.

I turned toward Jagger, not at him, though, at the female with her arm around his waist. I couldn't take my eyes off her, and I didn't like the way I felt.

"Sutton," Fern said, rushing around the table to me.

I couldn't look away from the other female, though. I didn't do confrontation. It had my PTSD flaring up in a way that was debilitating for days after, but I couldn't not say something. "I—I'd like you to s-stop touching him." The fact that those words had just come out of my mouth, even stuttered as they were, and that I was envisioning making this she-wolf bleed, told me everything I needed to know. I didn't do physical altercations, I avoided them. I was a healer. I didn't injure, but I wanted to right then. For the first time in my life, I wanted to inflict pain.

"What the fuck did you s-s-s-say to me?" she said, mimicking me and smirked.

"I think you heard me," I said, managing not to stutter this time.

The wolf cringed. "What the fuck is wrong with your face? Freaky-looking bitch," she muttered.

Fern tried to put her arm around me, to pull me away. "Sutton, honey. Let's go down to my den for a bit."

Why was she talking to me like that? She knew the truth. She knew Jagger was mine. She'd been hinting at it for months.

My gaze shot up to Jagger. He wasn't even looking at me, he was talking to another hound.

"Jagger..."

He turned to me then.

"Sutton," Fern said again. "Let's go."

Again, why was she talking like that, like I was some unstable freak she was afraid would flip out.

"Jagger?" I said again, waiting for him to say something, to *do* something.

His brows lowered, like I was the one behaving insanely, like I was the one standing there with someone else, pretending I felt nothing for him whatsoever.

"What are you doing?" I choked out.

His frown deepened. "What are you talking about?"

Fern tried to pull me aside, and I pulled away. "You know. You know what I'm talking about."

"I don't know what the fuck you're talking about, Sutton. Spell it out."

My throat was so dry I struggled to swallow. "You're my mate. We're...mates." The last came out barely audible.

His chin jerked up, and he stared down at me for several moments, then he shook his head. "Female, you're confused."

"I'm not." I gripped the edge of the table. "Your scent... you gave me your shirt, and—"

"I wanted you to stop crying."

"No...that's not what happened. I'm not..." I was struggling to say what I needed to, my words getting all tangled up. "You kissed me, and I felt it, I felt—"

"You kissed me, Sutton," he said low. "I'm not your mate, that's impossible."

Oh gods.

Fern tried to pull me away, and I jerked out of her hold.

He didn't want me.

He was wrong. He was lying. We were mates, I knew we were. He just didn't *want me*.

My *mate* didn't want me.

I forced a smile, because that's what I did. I smiled through the pain, it was how I survived. "I'm sorry," I said. "I don't know what I was...sorry," I said again. "I was confused. I think I...I need to go now." I stumbled back, my heart pounding hard, so hard I felt dizzy. I looked around me through a red haze. My face was still demon, my eyes, my veins, that's why everyone was looking at me. Several wolf shifters were holding up their cameras, filming me and laughing.

"Put those fucking phones down," I heard Relic say.

The crowd closed in, and I lost sight of Jagger. I spun away, running for the door, and tripped in my stupid fucking heels, hitting the ground hard. My bag went flying, all my things, my clothes and toothbrush and all the other crap I'd brought went scattering all over the floor. Boo exploded from under my coat, chirping and flapping above me, terrified.

"Oh, honey," Fern said, crouching beside me and yanking down my dress that had flown up. There was pain, pity in my best friend's voice.

The alpha's mate, Willow, rushed over to help Fern gather my things, as I frantically stuffed everything back in.

I tasted blood. My lip had to be split, and I guessed a couple layers of skin had come off my knee from the old rug. My face burned with humiliation as I scrambled to my feet, calling Boo back to me. He was fragile. Gods, I could have crushed him. He could be hurt.

"You're bleeding. Come with me," Willow said.

I shook my head and held my hand out for Boo, and finally, he came to me. I held him close while he trembled against me. I needed to check if he was okay.

Those females, they were still filming, following me, laughing, cringing at the way I looked. I had to get out of there right the hell now. "No, I—I'm fine. Thank you, though," I said and forced another smile, then spun and ran for the exit, ignoring Fern calling my name as I shoved through the crowd, finally bursting through the door and out to the parking lot.

"You change your mind, babe?" Brick said, walking toward the main doors that I'd just fled through.

I ignored him calling after me as I rushed past and ran to my car. As I started the engine, I tried to catch my breath, dangerously close to hyperventilating. I slid my hand over Boo's little body, and he chirped softly. If he was in pain, I'd feel it. He'd calmed and, thank the goddess, seemed okay. I dragged in another steadying breath, and when I was sure I wouldn't pass out, I looked up. A massive hound was outlined in the doorway.

Jagger.

He was watching me.

I stared back, fighting the tears stinging the backs of my eyes. Oh gods, he didn't want me. *Stuff it down*. Do not cry. Not again. The tears spilled over. *Shit*. I was such a damned idiot. I would never, ever allow myself to be that vulnerable again, not for anyone.

Jagger started toward me, striding across the lot.

I threw my car into drive—the engine stalled.

Fuck. I tried to start it again, and nothing happened. I

spun back to Jagger and his hand was lifted, aimed at me. He'd used his powers to stop my freaking car. I tried again, but the engine was completely dead.

He strode up to my window, and crooked his finger at me to get out. I didn't move, I couldn't. "Sutton, get out of the car."

I shook my head.

The window came down, all on its own.

I gripped the steering wheel. "I want to leave."

His big hands gripped the door through the open window. "What the fuck was that?" He sounded pissed off.

I spun to him, my heart in my throat. "I told you, I was confused. Now can you let me leave?"

He jerked back. "Are you fucking crying?" He thrust his fingers through his hair. "Told you I hate that shit, female."

"I'm not crying because of you," I lied even though it was humiliatingly obvious.

"No?"

"No."

He stared at me, hard. "I'm not your mate."

"Okay," I said.

"Fuck," he snarled. "Not sure where you came up with that bullshit, but there is no fucking way we're mates."

The look on his face was one of utter denial, of outright horror, maybe even disgust at the idea, and I wanted to curl up into a ball and puke. "Got it, Jagger, loud and clear. Can I leave now?"

He stared at me for several more, long seconds, then finally, he let go of my door and stepped back.

I turned my key, and this time, finally, the engine started. Without looking his way again, I threw the car back into drive and tore out, almost taking the gate with me when the hound now guarding it nearly didn't get it open in time.

Oh gods, I felt sick.

I didn't head for home. I couldn't face it. Fern would have called Phoebe by now. She was probably already waiting for me, to check I was okay. I couldn't talk to either of them, not yet. So instead, I headed to the clinic.

By the time I pulled into the parking lot, I was trembling uncontrollably. I practiced my breathing, worked at calming myself down so when I swiped my key card and let myself in, the red haze had gone, my claws had retracted, and I'd changed back. There were a couple rooms here for staff, and thankfully, no one was at the front desk when I walked in, so I didn't have to talk to anyone.

I'd put my phone on silent, but it'd been lighting up since I left the clubhouse. I pulled it from my pocket now and scrolled the texts. All from Fern and Phoebe.

I realized Fern had replied to me after I told her I was on my way to the clubhouse. I'd missed it while I was driving. She'd told me not to come, that it wasn't a good time.

She'd been trying to protect me. To stop me from walking in on Jagger with some other female and, despite what I knew to be true, living his life like I didn't exist. Kind of like he had been for the last few months.

I slid off my coat, putting Boo in the pocket, and hung it up, then lay on the bed. I knew I shouldn't, but I opened Nightscape with a sick feeling in my belly and searched for the female he'd been with. I knew her name. She and the others filming me were regulars at the clubhouse.

I gasped in a horrified breath. She'd posted a video of me. I knew she would. I couldn't stop myself from clicking play. I watched as I stammered, telling the female touching Jagger to stop, while my face transformed, the veins in my neck and cheeks turning black, then pooling beneath my eyes, watching as the whites of my eyes turned black as well, while my irises shone red.

The wolf shifters' commentary played along in the background, calling me a freak and desperate as I told Jagger I was his mate. It even showed me falling, my dress flying up, flashing my new underwear. Blood poured from my lip as Fern and Willow helped me gather all my things.

I couldn't see Jagger, people had crowded in between me and the table he'd been standing at—then a big hand covered the camera and everything went dark, and a gruff voice, one of the hounds, growled at her to get the fuck out and not to come back.

Turning off my phone, I tossed it on the floor, shaking and sobbing as the same words repeated over and over in my head:

He doesn't want you either.

CHAPTER
THREE

Jagger

THE SCENT of Sutton's distress lingered in the parking lot, lifting my hackles and making my stomach churn, and fuck, I barely resisted shifting and going after her.

Why the hell would she say that shit? The little female was confused, still fucked up after what happened to her. That had to be it. The only reason I was fighting with the beast to stay here and not go after her again had to be the sense of responsibility I felt for her.

Being the first to get to her that day, finding her cut up, knowing the taste of her blood from licking her wounds, the scent of her fear, was fucking with me.

"What the fuck was that?" Relic said as he strode out of the clubhouse, Fern right beside him. She looked up at me with eyes that had gone demon, like Sutton's had.

"How the fuck would I know?" I said, letting my hound rattle through my chest and blend with my voice.

"Sutton is my best friend and you—"

I headed for my bike before she could finish and before I said something that would rile the beast. She was as confused as her friend.

Fern ran ahead, getting in my way, and slammed her hands against my stomach. "You will listen to me. You may rank in this pack, but I'm not a hound and you don't get to cut me off and just walk away."

I looked at Relic over her head. "Get your female in hand."

Fern flushed with rage, her fingers curling into fists. "You arrogant piece of fucking—"

Relic lifted her off her feet and shoved her face against his throat, effectively gagging her. "—shit," Relic finished for her. "That's what you were going to say, right, Tink?" Her muffled yes came out loud and clear. "I don't know what the fuck you were trying to prove in there," Relic said. "And only you and Sutton know if you're mates or not, but what you just did, the way you treated her? If you *are* mates, then you have seriously fucked up, brother, you might have fucked any chance of ever claiming her. And if you're not? Then you just hurt a really good female, one who trusted you so much, having you guard her place was the only way she could sleep after that fucker carved her up. That, my brother, was fucking uncool."

His words were like a brutal jab to the sternum.

He eased up on Fern, and she spun to me, her bloodred hair flying everywhere. "You don't deserve her!"

I already knew that, but it was irrelevant, because she wasn't mine.

"You done?" I said to both of them.

Fern squirmed. Relic put her down, and she stormed

toward her car, got in, slammed the door shut and sped out of the parking lot, obviously going after Sutton. Good. Better she not be alone given how messed up she still was.

Relic planted his hands on his hips, watching his mate go. "I fucking hope you know what you're doing," he said, then strode to his bike and went after her.

I got another whiff of Sutton's scent still lingering in the air, and I found myself breathing it deep into my lungs—blood. Not a lot, but she'd been hurt. I noticed her lip was cut, it had to be that.

I shoved my fingers through my hair and looked back at the gate she'd sped through. The female was sensitive, fragile.

Maybe I should have taken her aside when she spouted that mate bullshit in the clubhouse, maybe setting her straight in front of everyone had been the wrong play, but it was too fucking late now. Following her out here and stopping her from leaving, probably hadn't been a good idea either. I'd just wanted to try and make her see the truth, for her own good, but I got the feeling I only made it worse. I breathed deeply again, taking in what remained of her scent. Had her lip been split before she came here? I hadn't noticed it or smelled the blood when she first came to the table.

"Fuck." I curled my fingers into tight fists as the uncontrollable urge to go to her and find out why she was injured slammed into me again.

Instead of getting on my bike, though, I got in my truck, ignoring the urge that wouldn't fucking go away and the weird sense of responsibility I'd felt for her since I lifted her off that gurney, unconscious and cut up, and I stomped on the gas, heading for Oldwood Forest.

I'd been gone a long time, and I needed to hunt. Stalking deer would be productive—and would distract me from thinking about the way Sutton had stood there in her pretty yellow dress covered in flowers, her cheeks pink and eyes bright, looking up at me in expectation. It would stop me from thinking about all that wild honey-blond wavy hair, with its little braids or how soft it looked.

Yeah, the female was beautiful, sweet, had a scent that drove me fucking wild, but I wasn't her mate. That didn't mean I didn't want to fuck her, because I did, which was why, for the last three months, every time I relived that soft kiss, I'd had to curl my fingers into a fist or shake them out when a visceral memory of the way her hair felt against my palm forced its way into my mind.

It was a hound thing, no big deal. My beast loved the texture of her hair. It was the same reason I'd visited her in her room at night when she was still recovering all those months ago, when no one else was around, and why I couldn't stop myself from running my fingers through it, why I'd pressed my nose to it and breathed her in.

I craved touch, like all hounds, and I liked the way Sutton felt. That's all.

))) ● (((

The crackling of the fire reminded me of Hell and eased some of the tension in my gut. My hunt had been successful. I'd taken down two stags, field dressed and hung them. I should take them back to the clubhouse chiller now, but they'd be fine overnight, with how cool it was.

I'd been looking forward to sleeping in my own bed for the last three months, and here I was sleeping on the forest floor instead.

Maybe because every time you'd thought about sleeping in your bed, you'd envisioned Sutton in it with you.

Snarling under my breath, I shoved my jacket beneath my head and tried to get comfortable. No wonder she was confused. With the way I wanted to fuck that female, I had to be throwing out mixed signals.

I rolled to my back, and tried to shove Sutton from my mind. I should at least try and stay alert. There were demons all over this forest, even if they wouldn't dare come near me. Maybe if they snuck up and tried to take my head in the middle of the night, they might be able to kill me, but then the entire pack would descend on the forest, and that wasn't something they'd ever risk.

My hand automatically reached for my phone, and before I could stop myself, I did what had become my nightly ritual, scrolling through the photos Sutton had sent me while I was away. I'd tried to keep contact to a minimum, but I'd done it for her. She'd admitted she associated me with safety. I thought getting her to send me a pic every now and then, just that small amount of contact, would make her feel safer. I felt responsible for her. I hadn't meant to lead her on or make her think we were more than we were.

She'd cried when I told her I was leaving, what the fuck was I supposed to do?

Bullshit. You were feeding your perverted little addiction.

"Fuck." I rubbed my hands over my face. Yeah, I'd studied every inch of her in those photos over and over again, and when I was in bed at night and couldn't stop thinking about her, thinking about how she'd feel under me, I'd stroked my cock to them, imagining that's exactly where she was.

Fucking her wasn't a possibility now, though, and I

could admit, after that kiss, I'd been hoping to spend some time with her, that maybe she'd want to have some fun, but that couldn't happen now, not after tonight.

But maybe we could go back to her sending me the odd pic, to her sending me those long messages about what she'd been up to during her day? I'd liked reading those. I'd looked forward to them.

I had smelled blood on her. Not much, but she had been hurt. Would she reply if I asked her to show me a picture, if I told her I needed proof she was all right? Would she send me a photo even now? She'd been upset. The scent of her distress still hadn't left me.

I rubbed at my chest. Sutton was pissed at me now, sure, but I could manage this fucked-up situation. I could manage Sutton's emotions. She'd get over what happened at the clubhouse, and I could control my animal need to fuck her. I could do both for as long as I needed to, just as long as she kept sending me those photos.

My thumb hovered over my phone. I just needed one more picture, then I'd leave her alone. Then I'd be done.

Jagger: *Pic? Smelled blood on you. Is it just your lip? Need proof you're okay.*

I hit send and waited.

The little icon with a picture of Sutton and her familiar dropped down beside the message, letting me know she'd seen it.

Three little dots appeared.

She was doing it. I blew out a rough breath as the tension making every muscle in my body knot eased up a little.

A message popped up, not a photo.

Sutton: *Sorry, Charming, you can source your wank-bank pics elsewhere from now on.*

Then a picture did pop up, but it was of her hand—flipping me off.

Nothing about her response was Sutton. She wasn't aggressive, she wasn't quick to temper, and when she did get fired up, it was awkward because that just wasn't her nature. I understood anger, and right now that's what she seemed to be feeling. Why? Yes, she'd been upset when she'd left the clubhouse, but I hadn't done anything wrong. Relic said I hurt her feelings, but she said herself she was confused.

The photo vanished, again, followed by the message.

She'd deleted them. That didn't surprise me, despite what happened between us. Sutton was too sweet to send something like that—

"What the fuck?" The photo she'd sent me a week ago vanished as well, the one with her standing in front of the mirror, making a face. That was one of my favorites.

Then the next vanished, and the next.

One by one her photos and messages disappeared. I jumped to my feet, my heart pounding, my stomach clenching tight. Her little updates, telling me about her day, what she'd been doing, how work was going, they were all being deleted as well. Shaking my phone, I roared at it, stabbing at the screen, as if that could stop what was happening. She was deleting them all, months' worth of messages and photos—until there was nothing left.

Until she'd taken everything she'd given me away.

A pounding filled my ears as blood flooded my extremities. I curled my fingers into tight fists when my skin flushed hot. My chest, it felt weird—there was pain. I couldn't breathe. I couldn't fucking swallow.

What the fuck was wrong with me? Why did I feel this

way? Why did I feel any-fucking-thing? They were just photos—they were just silly fucking messages.

If that's all it was, then why did it feel as if I were coming apart, as if my world had been torn out from under me?

)))·◐·(((

It was barely daybreak when I rolled up to the little cottage on the outskirts of Linville, only a short ride from the clubhouse.

Grabbing the bags from the back of the truck, I strode up to the front door. I'd cut most of one stag into steaks, and a few larger pieces for roasting. There was enough here to last a good long while.

The sound of a guitar, of Lenny's soft voice singing, stopped abruptly when I knocked.

A moment later, the curtains twitched, and one big brown eye peered at me through the small gap. I lifted the bags. "Venison. Thought your freezer might be getting low?" Lothar said he'd keep an eye on the place, and it looked like he'd taken care of the yard while I'd been gone, but the skittish little female was my responsibility, no one else's.

The curtain dropped, and her light tread could be heard through the door as she approached. "Okay...uh, thanks," she said through the wood.

She wasn't going to let me in, she never did. I put the bags down in front of the door, planted my hands on my hips, and looked at my boots, knowing she'd be watching me through the peephole and not wanting to freak her out by staring back. "You need anything else, Lenny?"

"No, thank you."

I nodded. "Okay, babe, you got my number if you need anything, yeah?"

"Yes."

"I'm gonna head off, but you call if you need me."

Silence.

With no other choice, I got back in my truck and headed to the clubhouse. The garage was already open when I pulled in. Relic and Fender were sipping their morning coffees and getting ready for work. I got out, lifted the second stag from the back of the truck, and carried it behind the workshop to the walk-in chiller to hang it.

When I came back around, Fender was looking down at his phone, scowling.

I heard someone say Sutton's name through the speakers.

"What are you watching?" I said, closing in on him.

His scowl lifted to me. "Someone from Draven's pack posted this on Nightscape." His scowl deepened. "What the actual fuck, man?"

I snatched his phone, then thrust it back. "Make it play from the start." I didn't know how to work all this shit. Maybe if I did, I could have stopped Sutton from deleting all those photos and messages or saved them somehow.

Fender tapped something on the screen and handed it back, and I watched as Sutton stood at the tall table, looking at the female beside me with her arm around my waist. Sutton's veins turned black, her eyes shifting, now swirling red and black.

"I—I'd like you to s-stop touching him." Her voice broke, shaking, and I could see the rest of her was as well even on the small screen.

"What the fuck did you s-s-s-say to me?" the wolf said, mimicking Sutton.

I growled.

"I think you heard me." Sutton squared her shoulders a little.

The wolf screwed up her face. "What the fuck is wrong with your face? Freaky-looking bitch."

I sucked in a sharp breath. I'd been too busy trying to wrestle down my hunger for her when she walked up, and the blood that had been rushing through my fucking ears had blocked everything out. I hadn't even heard the wolf say that shit.

I watched the rest unfold, while I just fucking stood there and let Sutton be disrespected, humiliated, in front of everyone. While Fern tried to lead her away—when she'd looked up at me again.

"Jagger..."

Every muscle in my body jerked at her voice saying my name through the speaker. Fern tried to draw her away again while Sutton looked at me with wide eyes.

"Jagger?" she said again. I fucking hated the look of betrayal on her face. "What are you doing?" she rasped.

"What are you talking about?" My voice rang out.

Fern tried again to pull her away. "You know. You know what I'm talking about."

"I don't know what the fuck you're talking about, Sutton. Spell it out."

Her pretty, swirling red eyes sliced through me. "You're my mate. We're...mates." Her voice was a barely there whisper.

My shock was obvious. "Female, you're confused."

"I'm not." She shook her head. "Your scent...you gave me your shirt, and—"

"I wanted you to stop crying."

"No...that's not what happened. I'm not..." She was stuttering, flustered. "You kissed me, and I felt it, I felt—"

"You kissed me, Sutton," I said to her. "I'm not your mate, that's impossible."

My fingers curled into a tight fist as her expression went from betrayal to horror, then devastation. Loyalty, anger, and lust may be the extent of my emotions, but Lucifer gave us the ability to recognize others, to understand them, and I wanted to take my own fucking eyes out.

A smile curled her lips, and I realized that wasn't Sutton's smile, it didn't reach her eyes, it didn't make her whole face light up. "I'm sorry," she said. "I don't know what I was...sorry," she said again. "I was confused. I think I...I need to go now."

She stumbled back, looking around while people stared at her, laughed at her, while the wolves filming her talked shit about her. And I did nothing.

"Put those fucking phones down." That was Relic.

Sutton spun away then, running for the door. The crowd had closed in, and I'd lost sight of her at that point, but then again, I'd forced myself to look away.

I snarled viciously when I saw what actually happened after she ran. She'd tripped, hitting the ground hard. Her familiar had exploded from her coat, while she lay there, her dress tossed up, her bag sliding across the floor, her things going everywhere, clothes, underwear, a toothbrush.

She'd packed as if she'd planned to stay.

Then it hit me, she thought she'd be staying at the clubhouse—with me.

I was growling continuously now, and there was no stopping it. I didn't like the strange sensations inside me, or the physical responses that came with them, like I was burning up, like I was in someone else's body and mind. No, I fucking hated them.

Fern and Willow helped her up and gathered her things, while the female filming laughed and said a bunch of shit about how Sutton looked.

Then I saw blood drip from her lip to the floor, more when she stood, from her knee.

Willow said something, and Sutton held out her hand, her familiar finally coming back to her, then she glanced at the camera, then back to Willow and shook her head.

That's how her fucking lip was split open. Then she shoved her way through the crowd and ran out to the parking lot.

Rage pumped through me. In the end, my instinct had insisted I go after her. I'd told myself I'd just see if she was okay, instead I'd yelled at her while she'd cried, like a fucking deranged asshole. Now I couldn't work out if I was more pissed off at the wolves who'd filmed and posted that video, or myself.

No, I wasn't her mate, but she hadn't deserved that.

The beast slammed against my psyche, trying to break free, the roar in my head so loud that my fucking bones rattled. What the *fuck*? Why was I so messed up over this little female? It didn't make sense.

Fender pried his phone from my tight fist, then shook his head at the way it was now crushed on the sides.

"Brother, I thought you and Sutton—"

"Don't fucking think," I snarled and strode away before I took all this rage out on the wrong person.

The truth was, if I could have a mate, if things weren't so fucked up and I could have what War and Relic and Dirk had, I'd want that with her. That's why I'd stormed after her, that's why I'd stopped her from leaving and acted like a giant prick, because she stirred something inside me, made me feel things, want things, that should be impossible—things that fucking terrified me.

Because if I could have a mate, I'd want it to be Sutton.

A mate wasn't something I'd ever wanted, though, for several reasons—and I'd made a deal a long time ago to ensure that I never found one.

That's how I knew Sutton wasn't mine.

It was impossible.

CHAPTER
FOUR

Sutton

"I'm okay, Boo." My sweet familiar was pressed against my cheek, trying to comfort me. He'd been doing that a lot lately and had sought me out when I got home this morning. He should have been asleep. I rubbed my hands over my face. Gods, last night was one big hideous blur. My brain's way of trying to protect me, I guess, and I would've been happy to keep it that way. Unfortunately, there was now video evidence, not only filling in the blanks in my memory but making sure that everyone else on Nightscape had every single gory detail of my humiliation locked in their minds as well.

My mother, and the rest of my estranged family, would have definitely seen it by now.

It was too awful to think about. Too painful. Too... everything.

Stop. Don't go there.

I would not waste time thinking about the people who didn't want me in their lives. Nope, I'd focus on the people who knew the real meaning of family. My coven, my friends.

That's when I remembered seeing Luke at the Dogwood fights last night. He was alive and well, thank the goddess, so why wasn't he answering my calls? And why the hell had he run from me?

It didn't make sense—unless he was in some kind of trouble.

There was a tap on my door. I glanced up as Phoebe poked her head in.

"How you doing?"

"Rejection's my middle name, remember?" I said, then made a silly face. "All good here." I'd just gotten off the phone with Fern checking on me again as well.

"Don't joke about that, Sutton, what he did—"

"He made his choice, and I'm making one as well. I'm not going to cry into my pillow about him. I'm not going to let his choice break me. I don't need a male, I have you, and Fern, and the rest of the coven. That's all I need." And maybe if I told myself that enough times, then eventually I'd believe it.

"I can stay," she said. "We can hang out."

The others were packed and ready to leave for the conclave, something Luke had been seriously looking forward to. He'd been excited about it for months. It was the first year we'd been invited. He was a little anarchist, and he couldn't wait for our coven to walk in and take our rightful place among the others, and hopefully piss a few people off. Especially now that Fern was mated to a hellhound. Relic had agreed to going along as protection. I'd, of course, imagined Jagger going as well. *Stop.*

"I love you for offering, but I'll be working the whole time anyway." I'd told everyone that Jack needed me to work, which was a lie. I'd already taken the days off to go to the conclave, but despite all my big talk, I wasn't in the mood for company, but most of all, that video...that's what had changed my mind. I couldn't face my mother, knowing she would have seen it. Someone would have recognized me and relished showing her. My sister probably.

Phoebe's eyes were soft. "I don't like the thought of you here alone."

"I'll be fine. I could do with a little me time."

Pheebs gave me a look that said she didn't believe me, but she didn't push. "I don't like leaving without Luke either, but he's still not answering my calls." Her lips tilted down.

"I saw him last night. So I know he's okay. He's probably just decided to go to the conclave with his girlfriend. You know what he's like. He can only focus on one thing at a time."

Phoebe laughed. "Yeah, you're probably right." She pulled me in for a hug, then gave Boo a pat. "We're about to leave, but if you get lonely, call, and I'll come straight back."

"I promise, I'll be fine. Just have fun, okay?"

She squeezed me tighter. "Love you."

"Love you too."

I followed her down the stairs and waved everyone off, forcing a smile that felt utterly wooden. I closed the doors as they drove off, and the stifling silence closed in around me. I was in pain, I could recognize that, but I would survive it. I'd get through it.

I'd spent a good portion of my life waiting, hoping the people who were supposed to care about and protect me would realize they were wrong and they'd love me back—it never happened.

I wasn't going to waste time hoping that Jagger would change his mind and want me. That was a fool's dream. It wasn't going to happen.

He'd had three months to decide what he wanted, and how he would communicate that to me when we were finally face to face, and he chose to act as if I didn't exist. As if I were imagining what we were to each other. Maybe I was wrong, and he didn't feel it, but how could he not? To me, the pull between us was *huge*, all-encompassing. When our lips had touched...yes, it was cliché, but the earth moved.

Yet rather than just talk things through with me, in private, he'd chosen to publicly humiliate me. Then to act like nothing had happened, and have the gall to ask for another photo? That hadn't just been messed up, it had been cruel.

So, I was done. I decided I would choose the people who chose me a long time ago. And that was enough. It would be enough.

Since I'd lied to Phoebe about working the next few days, I'd occupy myself in other ways, like figuring out what was going on with Luke. Maybe I was right and he'd show up at the conclave. At least I hoped so. But until I knew for sure, finding him was my number one task. Then I could yell at him for worrying me.

I took the stairs, heading up to the second floor, and strode down the hall to Luke's bedroom. Usually, I wouldn't dream of invading his privacy, but the moment he ran from me, and then continued to ignore my calls and texts, his privacy became forfeit. He was in trouble. I was certain of it.

Walking in, I turned in a slow circle, then screwed up

my nose. It smelled like gym clothes and smelly running shoes.

Luke was twenty-two, and like the rest of us, he had been rejected by his coven when his mixed blood had made itself known. I'd found him on the streets five years ago, skinny, grubby, and selling drugs on a corner for another witch.

Luke was a healer like me. He was talented, funny, smart, and I loved him like a little brother. The more time he spent away, the more I got this feeling that something wasn't right. I felt it in my bones. Yes, Luke was easily distracted, and he was known to ignore calls and texts, especially when he was with Evie, his girlfriend, but never from me, and if he didn't answer immediately, he always called back the same day.

His bed was unmade, his laundry basket overflowing. His dresser was cluttered with odds and ends, receipts, body spray, and the awful aftershave he bought when he first met Evie. His computer was in the corner, and I leafed through the papers he'd scribbled notes on beside it. A stack of herbology books was there as well. Nothing jumped out at me. The books were standard for what we did. I had all the same ones. I'd helped him source them when he first came here and asked me to help him get a deeper understanding of his gift. I'd been teaching him so that he could eventually work at the clinic as well.

A notepad was on the floor, and I picked it up, flicking through the pages. Nothing was written on it, but I could feel indentations on the top page. Grabbing a pencil from the jar beside his monitor, I did what I'd seen private detectives do in movies and rubbed the side of the lead lightly over the top.

Success.

It was a list. "What do we have here, Lukey." I ran my finger down the page. The first few ingredients listed were pretty standard stuff, but the rest... "Shit." Were not.

These were all things Fern sold in her store, Malicious Brew. Witches who veered toward the darker side frequented my best friend's establishment, and I immediately recognized the last five ingredients on the list. They were all things Fern stocked, but she stored them in the back because they were too dangerous to put on the shelves. They were also ingredients she'd told me were missing when she'd done her stock inventory—an inventory that Luke had volunteered to help her with.

"What the hell are you up to, Luke?"

Fern's store had been broken into just as she and Relic got together, and she'd had no idea what, if anything, had been taken. When she finally found the time to go through her inventory, she'd been surprised anything was missing at all, because the goal of the break-in had been to send a message, to scare her, and not to rob the place.

I closed my eyes and rubbed my temples, then looked around more closely. My gaze was drawn to something black and glossy poking out from under his bed. I grabbed it cautiously. People hid all sorts of things under their beds, and there were certain things I had no interest in knowing about him. Thankfully, it was only a notebook. On the black cover was a hand-drawn symbol in silver ink. I flicked the book open and cursed.

Recipes for different potions—potions he most definitely should *not* be making—were carefully detailed on the pages. But what had the hair on the back of my neck lifting were the annotations written beside each ingredient, additions that when combined, changed each ingredient in a way that would alter its cellular makeup and its purpose.

When used, or taken, it would react in a completely different way than it was originally used for.

Luke was making drugs.

That little idiot was making fucking drugs!

I needed to find him, and fast.

My gut had been trying to tell me he was in trouble, and I'd let this thing with Jagger throw me off. I'd ignored my gut. Now Luke was incommunicado and, going by the evidence, doing something seriously stupid.

I rushed back to my room, slid on my jacket, and grabbed my bag. "You need to stay here," I said to Boo.

He chattered unhappily.

"Be a good boy and look after the house while I'm gone. I promise I'm okay, and I won't be late."

I lifted him from my shoulder and put him on the iron headboard, then rushed out the door. Boo exploded into the air and flew past me, clicking and chirping the whole time, making it clear he was not happy about being left behind again.

"Boo, stay. I'll be back soon."

With one last squawk, he flew up to the light and hung there upside down, watching me walk out the door. No doubt he was planning to stay there and nap until I came home.

Warmer weather was on the way, but it was still cool at night, and I wrapped my jacket around me and jogged to my car. I headed to Evie's house first. She hadn't been home the other times I'd stopped in looking for Luke, but it was worth another try.

She wasn't home, though, so I quickly wrote a note and slid it under her door, telling her to call me ASAP, then headed off to the last place I'd seen Luke, the Dogwood fights.

Fight night was yesterday, which meant the usually packed parking lot and crowded building was empty when I pulled up.

Grabbing the flashlight from my glove compartment, I shoved it in my bag, slung it across my chest, and headed toward the huge, deserted building. I wasn't sure what I was looking for, but Luke had been here last night, so it was a good place to start.

The door was locked, of course, so I made my way around the building, searching for a way in. I aimed my flashlight at the windows around the back and noticed one ajar. "Bingo."

Shoving over a nearby steel drum filled with trash, I heaved it back up so it was upside down. Doing a quick search of my surroundings, to make sure I was still alone, and more than a little pleased when I confirmed that I was, I used a crate to climb onto the drum. Dragging the window open, I wriggled half of my body through.

The scent of blood, sweat, and aggression hit me straightaway. I lifted my flashlight and searched the room. They used this space as a locker room by the looks. There was a bench seat directly below me. *Handy*. Sliding the flashlight back in my bag, I hitched my knee on the windowsill and maneuvered my body through the tight space, so I could drop to the bench feetfirst and not break my neck.

My boots hit the wood with a *bang* that echoed through the room. I froze, listening again to make sure I was on my own. When everything remained silent, I climbed down and headed along the hall, checking the other rooms that I passed. All were empty or had a random piece of furniture in them, but nothing that screamed *clue!* Though, honestly, I wasn't sure what would qualify as a clue. I was hoping my gut would help me out with that.

I carried on along the hall and into the main room. The cleanup crew hadn't been through yet, and litter covered the floor. Empty bottles and plastic cups cluttered surfaces and overflowed from more steel drums, and a couple of bloody towels sat abandoned on the blood-splattered floor of the cage.

Why would Luke come here? Was he really that stupid? Selling drugs in a place like this was pure insanity. Getting caught selling, on land owned by shifters, was asking to get torn to shreds.

I shone the flashlight around the room. Nothing of note caught my eye. What the hell did I think I'd find here? This was a stupid mistake. I started back the way I came, lighting up the floor as I went so I didn't trip on anything—then something caught my eye.

I crouched, picking up a small piece of black cardstock, a tiny envelope with a familiar emblem drawn on it in silver. I opened it, but there was nothing inside. I quickly took Luke's notebook from my bag. The emblem was the same. I sniffed the envelope and recognized a handful of ingredients immediately. "You little idiot." Real fear filled me now that I'd confirmed what he was doing. This was bad.

Oh gods. All the overdose emergency calls Jack and I had gone to. Had they taken the drugs Luke made? I stood and shoved the small envelope into my pocket.

"Who's in here?" a growly voice called.

Shit.

A light was shined in my eyes, and my flight instincts kicked in before I could think about it. I bolted, sprinting for the locker room. A growl rolled through the room, followed by the pounding of heavy boots behind me.

Pumping my arms, I leaped onto the bench seat and dove for the open window—my ankle was grabbed and I was yanked back down so hard that my ribs collided with the side of the bench a second before my head slammed into it.

Hissing, I struck out with my claws that had extended all on their own, long and black and pointed, while my arms flailed like windmills. The male roared, cursing as I scrambled to my feet and bounded back up on the bench and all but dove through the window.

My shoulder slammed into the ground on the other side, hard. I tried to drag myself back up and screamed. My arm was useless, hanging limply at my side. Groaning, I forced myself back to my feet and, trying to hold my dislocated shoulder steady, ran for my car.

Snarls and growls echoed around the parking lot. I spun. Wolves, a lot of them, had me surrounded and were closing in. I fumbled for my keys, and they slipped from my fingers, hitting the ground. Before I could scoop them up, I was grabbed around the waist and slammed into the hood.

My fear turned me into a feral creature. My eyes were a red haze as I went wild, hissing and fighting, trying to slice my captor with my claws.

The wolf fisted my hair and slammed my head against the hood, then wrenched it back. "What the fuck are you doing here, demon?"

Blood poured from my nose and lip, the slice in it reopening. To them I was all demon, and they were going to kill me for it. If I couldn't explain who I was and why I was here, they would tear me to shreds—and even if I did explain, they might still kill me.

The wolves had been warring with the feral demons in Oldwood Forest, forcing them back, fighting to regain the territory they'd lost a long time ago. To them, I was the enemy. I was just another demon encroaching on their home.

The wolf curled his fingers around my throat and spun me to face his pack mates. Their glowing eyes stared back, filled with fury and hatred, their chests heaving, veins bulging, all of them out for blood.

"Speak, scum," he snarled. "Or I'll fucking make you speak." He shook me roughly. I tried to unlock my jaw, but fear had me frozen, had thrown me back several months, to the basement of our coven house, trapped by another monster who wanted to hurt me—who had hurt me.

"Put her in the van," he growled.

CHAPTER
FIVE

Sutton

I HAD no idea where they were taking me.

The wolf who'd grabbed me held me now, totally mobile as we bumped along a dirt road, heading toward the goddess only knew where.

"Ugly demon bitch," he said low. "Either you talk, or I make you fucking scream."

I tried to unhinge my clamped jaw to speak, to explain what was going on, but the fear was just too great. I was in a full-blown panic attack, and all I could do was sit there paralyzed, trying to breathe, while this wolf told me over and over how much he despised me for what I was, and how much he was looking forward to hurting me because of it.

When I was afraid, there was no holding back my transformation, and I knew my eyes were glowing red in the back of the van, that my nails were still black claws, and my veins also black in stark contrast to my pale skin. The combination was more than a little disconcerting to look at, and the half dozen pairs of glowing wolf eyes watching me with equal amounts of hatred and disgust told me exactly how they felt about my appearance.

One of the wolves stood suddenly and rushed to the doors at the back of the van, looking through the dirty windows, and cursed.

"We've got company."

"Who—"

The deafening sound of motorcycles rumbling around the van was suddenly so loud it was like they were on top of us.

"Why the fuck are hounds following us?"

My heart slammed against the back of my ribs a moment before the van was hit by something heavy. The large vehicle abruptly jerked to the right, fishtailing a moment in the mud before the rear of the van swung into a large tree, stopping it in its tracks.

"What the fuck—"

The door shrieked, the steel groaning a moment before it was torn off completely, then it went flying, crashing somewhere in the forest.

I sucked in a stunned breath.

Standing in the now gaping space, illuminated from behind by moonlight, was Jagger—and at least two other hounds.

Jagger was naked, his tattooed chest heaving and his face contorted with rage and traces of his hound. "Get your fucking hands off her *now*." The last roared, his voice a deafening force that had me shrinking back and lifted goose bumps all over me.

No one moved.

Jagger snarled. "Now, wolf, or I will send you to Hell screaming."

The wolf abruptly lifted his hands, releasing me, then shoved me hard toward Jagger, like I was some deadly poisonous creature. My shoulder popped back into place from the force, and I managed to bite back my shriek.

Jagger grabbed me, hauling me out of the back of the van, and I could feel his heart pounding hard against mine as he held me to him in a viselike grip.

Warrick strode forward, and the alpha hellhound's eyes were blazing red. "What the fuck are you doing with this witch? Does Draven know this is how you treat females?"

At the mention of Draven, the wolves' alpha, the male who had held me in the van, flinched, his unease so strong even I could smell it.

"She's no witch," the wolf fired back, then spat on the floor. "She's a fucking demon. Look at her. We have every right to deal with demons encroaching on our territory, in any way we see fit."

"Wrong on both counts. Not that it matters, but she is more witch than demon, and even if she had not a drop of witch blood in her veins, you would have been making the wrong fucking play, wolf."

"All she had to do was speak up. She chose not to."

"Because she's fucking terrified!" Jagger roared.

He obviously hadn't missed how badly I was shaking.

The wolf's gaze slid over me, uncertainty filling his eyes for a moment before it turned to defiance. "Bullshi—"

Roman grabbed the wolf by the throat, and slammed him to the floor of the van so hard, the steel dented. "Does she look like a feral to you? No, she looks more like the kind of female they snatch for breeding."

"What if she'd been a breeder trying to escape her

demon captors?" Warrick added. "I don't know how you treat females in your pack, asshole, but warning: you do anything like this again, and we will make sure you never do again. Understand?"

Rome shoved the wolf away and turned to me. "You okay, Sutton?"

I nodded, but it was hard with my face pressed against Jagger's throat, his grip not even coming close to easing. If anything, it had only grown fiercer.

The wolf's gaze sliced between me and Roman, then back to Jagger, and it was like the enormity of his situation finally hit him.

His gaze widened in alarm. "I had no idea she was yours. I would never have touched her if I'd known. But come on, man, she broke into our place. Why don't you ask her why she was there? That's something I'm certain our alpha will want to know. We thought she was up to something. I was just trying to defend our territory from the enemy, and she sure as hell looks like the enemy to me with the fucked-up way she looks. She sliced me up with her claws, for fuck's sake. She doesn't look like any witch I've ever seen."

That's when I noticed the deep gouges down the side of his face.

Jagger snarled again, the sound ripping through the forest.

"Now would be a good time to shut the fuck up," Warrick said, then placed a hand on Jagger's shoulder, his red, glowing eyes burning into the wolves. "Get the fuck out of here, now. I'll be calling Draven to deal with you. You're lucky we're letting you leave at all."

The wolf didn't say anything else, but his upper lip peeled back, flashing his canines. Then the wolves started the van and tore off along the dirt track, a shrieking sound coming from the dented and torn-up vehicle.

"Get her home," Warrick said to Jagger, holding his gaze for long seconds. "I'll speak with Draven. Looks to me like some of his pack have gone rogue with that shit."

I was still frozen, and I hated myself for it. I thought I was getting better. I thought I was doing okay, now this had thrown me back to that nightmare, and probably set me back months. Jagger strode along the road we'd driven, not saying anything, just continuing to hold me in a firm grip. His bike was up ahead, and when we reached it, I saw his clothes in a heap on the ground. I could only assume he'd gotten off his bike and shifted so he could smash into the van to stop it.

I refused to let my brain come up with reasons for that, reasons that could give me false hope.

He eased me down his naked body, staring at me with those moss-green eyes of his. "You think you can hang on to me on the back of the bike?"

I nodded. Still struggling to get my vocal cords to freaking work.

"You're bleeding." His hand went to my forehead. "You hit your head?"

I nodded again.

He studied me, his jaw tightening. "You know who's got you, yeah? You know it's me, don't you, Sutton? That you're safe?" His tone was harsh, short, abrupt, a contradiction to the things he'd said and the look in his eyes.

Yes, I knew I was safe. He would make sure no one hurt me. He'd protect me, like he had before, but who would protect me from him? From the damage he could do to my heart and soul? He'd rejected me. He was here now, but he wasn't staying. I had to remember that. My head was woozy. I probably had a concussion. I was struggling to think clearly. I knew I should tell him I didn't need his help, but right then I did.

He hurt you, and he'll keep on hurting you.

"Yeah, Jagger, I know exactly who you are," I said, finally finding my voice.

His throat worked, his nostrils flared, but he said nothing, just quickly dressed, climbed onto his bike, and held out his hand to help me on.

I didn't want to go on the back of his bike. I didn't want to be anywhere near him, certainly not that close. That's what my head was saying, but my heart wanted to stay in his arms and feel safe for a little while longer.

"Just take me back to my car." I'd allow myself that small reprieve from my convictions, just long enough for him to take me to my car, and then I could ignore him again for the rest of my life.

He shook his head. "Someone's already seeing to that. I'm taking you home."

Shit. I turned back to where Rome and Warrick had been, but they were already gone.

With no other choice, I climbed up on the bike behind him and wrapped my arm around his waist, hanging on to his shirt the best I could with the other damaged one. Jagger started the bike, walked it back, then turned and headed out of the forest.

I'd never been on a bike before, and sitting like this, I was far too close to him. My front was plastered to his back. Goddess, I could feel his heat through his leather vest, and the way his upper body expanded with each of his deep breaths.

It was a beautiful torture.

How many times had I imagined this since I realized

who he was, since he went back to Hell. I'd thought about this, especially after Fern shared how much she loved riding with Relic. Now I was finally here, on the back of his bike—but he wasn't mine. This meant nothing, not to him, because he didn't want me.

Because he would never want me.

My head was fuzzy, and my limbs felt weak. Yeah, I was definitely concussed, and I was going to blame that for the stupid, pathetic thoughts rolling through my head.

The worst part was that being this close to him, confirmed what I already knew. Jagger was my mate. There was no doubt, not for me.

Exhaustion was settling in and it was getting hard to hang on, but we were almost at my house. I blinked, shaking my head when shadows began dancing at the corners of my eyes—

My hand slipped from around Jagger's waist, and I started to tilt sideways. One of his big arms shot back, wrapping around me, holding me to him as the bike slowed, then stopped.

He climbed off the bike somehow, scooping me up at the same time, then maneuvered me in his arms. I was too weak and drowsy to protest.

I could hear him talking, but his voice was distant. He was doing a lot of cursing and barking at me to stay awake. Total déjà vu.

He got back on the bike, with me across his lap, my head against his shoulder and my legs over his arm that held the handlebars, then he hooked the other arm around my waist, holding me close. He said something else, but I couldn't understand this time, my mind was buzzing too loudly now, and the shadows in my head were overtaking my vision completely—then everything went dark.

When I woke, I was in my bedroom and Jagger was sitting on the bed beside me. He had a bowl of icy water and a cloth, and he was wiping my face.

"Good," he growled out. "Now stay the fuck awake." He wiped the cool cloth across my brow, frowning. "You got a couple of big eggs on your head, female. You should've fucking told me you weren't feeling right before we got on the bike. You could've fallen off and fucking killed yourself."

Why was he still here? Boo? I searched the room, then spotted him hanging from the light above, watching. He obviously didn't see Jagger as a threat or he'd be dive-bombing him and chirping his head off. "You can go now. I don't need a nursemaid."

He ignored me and continued to swipe the cool cloth down the side of my face. "Not going anywhere until we sort out these wounds and I know you're out of the woods with this concussion. Not like anyone else is here."

He was right. Crap.

Jagger scowled again as his gaze slid over my face. "Did that fucking wolf do all of this damage?"

"Not all of it."

"What the hell were you doing in there, Sutton?" His eyes flashed. "Those wolves were seriously in the wrong, the way they treated you, but you were in their territory, and from the sounds of it, you broke into one of their buildings." His movements turned stilted. He looked agitated. "And with the way you look, when you do your thing..."

My gaze shot up to his. "The way I look? You mean like an ugly fucking demon bitch? That's how that wolf described me. It's how my family saw me too. How about you, Charming? Is that what you see as well?"

His chin jerked back. "No." He snarled a little, then his hand lifted to my hair.

I flinched. And why the hell had I asked what he saw when he looked at me? I didn't care anymore, right?

"I'm not gonna hurt you." His big chest expanded. "You have to know that?" His hand still hovered in the air, and he reached out again, like he was holding out his fingers for a wild dog to sniff. I held perfectly still as he touched my hair. "You got blood all in this pretty hair of yours," he said, surprising me, then did that jaw-tightening thing he seemed to do a lot around me.

Was he remembering the last time he'd seen me with blood in my hair?

"We need to wash it out." He stood abruptly.

"We don't need to do anything. I'll wash it later."

He shook his head, a stubborn look on his face. "Can't fucking look at all that blood in your hair. We're doing it now."

I opened my mouth to argue, but he was already shoving the covers back and scooping me out of bed. "Put me down. We're not doing this."

"Yeah?" He flashed his sharp canines. "Who's gonna stop me?"

He strode into the bathroom, turned on the shower, then shrugged off his leather cut, revealing all that defined, muscled skin decorated with tattoos.

That's when I realized I was in only a T-shirt, one he'd obviously taken from my drawer when we got here.

"You took my clothes off," I accused.

He shrugged. "Needed to see what the damage was."

"You saw me naked?"

His eyes flicked down to mine. "So?"

My face flushed hot. He'd seen the scars; every single slice The Chemist had made in my flesh. Jagger had just gotten an up-close-and-personal look at them, and if he hadn't already stomped on my ego enough to crush me, that would have done it. Nice to have confirmation of just how much the mate that the fates had chosen for me didn't want me. My naked body incited nothing more than a shrug. *Awesome.* I guess, that was better than all-out revulsion.

Jagger stepped unceremoniously under the cool spray, still holding me to him. I shrieked, and he shushed me impatiently, then cradling me in his huge arms, he maneuvered me so my head was under the water.

I lay there, stunned, confused, and despite his indifference to me, aroused as he gently slid one of his large hands over my scalp, feeling for the eggs there and being super careful as he washed blood out of my hair.

A deep rumbling sound rolled from his chest, and I sucked in a breath. The sound was one of satisfaction. I didn't need to be a hound to recognize that. He was utterly focused on his task, like it was the most important thing he'd done, and would ever do in his life. My head tingled as he continued to work his thick fingers through my hair.

Finally, he switched off the water and, still holding me in his arms, stepped out of the shower, before roughly rubbing a towel over my body.

"Lift your arm. Need to get this shirt off."

"What? No."

"Seen it all before, Sutton. I'll close my eyes if you're that worried." Then he carefully eased my injured arm out of the wet shirt, while I complained and struggled uselessly, before whipping it over my head, and yes, his eyes were closed as he rubbed the towel across my chest and down my back, drying the rest of me. He reached back without looking and grabbed the shirt I'd left in here that morning, then carefully pulled it over my head. It was the shirt he'd given me several months ago, when I'd cried that he was leaving. I hated thinking about that now. Loathed it.

I'd also been wearing it when I'd run out the next morning and thrown myself at him, when we'd kissed. No, when I'd kissed him. He'd made sure I didn't get that part wrong, hadn't he? I didn't want to think about that either.

Then I was up again, ensconced in his arms, so he could carry me back to bed.

He laid me down, dragged up the covers, then disappeared into the bathroom. When he returned, a towel hugged his waist, his wet jeans discarded. "You got a dryer?"

Holy hell. I mean, I'd seen him naked less than an hour ago, but I'd been more than a little distracted. His huge frame seemed to crowd my small bedroom. He was basically naked again, and utterly beautiful. I didn't know where to look. "Ground floor, room off the kitchen."

He strode out, down to the laundry room I assumed, then was back again a few minutes later. He went back into the bathroom, then came out carrying another dry towel.

He was headed straight for me. "What are you doing?"

Jagger climbed on the bed, the towel around his hips splitting open dangerously, not that he seemed to care—and pulled me closer so he could use the dry one to wring the water out of my hair. He squeezed it gently, removing the excess moisture, and as he did, he made another one of those satisfied sounds. "So fucking pretty. Love this hair."

I knew he liked it. How many times had I caught him looking at my hair? The way he'd touched it after I'd kissed him that one and only time. But why was he telling me this?

Why was he doing this to me?

He needed to leave. This was too much and, honestly, too painful.

He'd rejected me the night before in front of everyone in the clubhouse, and in a way that was cruel and careless. Now he thought he could just come here and I'd let him take care of me like we were something special to each other? We weren't.

I thought we could be, but I'd been wrong. He couldn't have it both ways. He couldn't look at me like I was nothing and then tell me I had pretty hair.

He couldn't follow me on Nightscape and spend three months asking for photos, then make it clear he wanted nothing from me until his instincts kicked in, telling him to protect his mate because that's what had happened tonight, then expect me to just let him look after me.

No.

That's not how this was going to work. And it wasn't fair for him to think any of this was okay.

CHAPTER SIX

Sutton

I gave him a shove. "My hair's dry enough."

A growl rattled through his chest. "No, it's not. You'll catch a cold."

"Well, then it will be my own fault," I said and pushed his hand away when he brought the towel toward me again.

He dropped his hand, studying me like I was some impossible puzzle to solve.

"I think you should go."

He frowned. "You're concussed and no one else is here. I'm not leaving." He relaxed against my headboard like a stubborn jerk. "How about you tell me why you were at Dogwood? Why did you break into that building?"

His square jaw was like granite, his green eyes piercing through me. If I didn't give him some kind of answer, I knew I'd never get him to leave. "Fine. A member of our coven is missing. I saw him at the fights the other night when I was working. I don't know what I was thinking, that I'd find some kind of clue, I guess. It was a stupid idea."

"Yeah, it was," Jagger said. "Why'd you think you'd find something there? That makes no sense."

"Jeez, thanks, Charming. Now that we've covered what a moron I am, you can get your pants on and leave." Then I remembered I had found something, so not so stupid after all.

"Give me this missing male's details and I'll ask around."

"No, thanks."

His brow lowered. "No?"

"I don't want your help."

He actually looked confused. "I can do this for you."

"I said, no."

"Why are you being unreasonable? You can't do this on your own. It's too dangerous."

"First, who said I'd do it on my own? There are other people I can ask...other *hounds* I could ask if I wanted to." He growled. I ignored him and carried on. "I can do a lot of things on my own. I've been on my own most of my life, as a matter of fact. You certainly weren't there to protect me when I was living on the streets and forced to run from breeder scouts, or when I was attacked while sleeping rough in a park and had to stab some rabid demon in the eye to get away, or when someone beat the shit out of me and stole all my things...or when I found them, hexed them, then stole my things back. No, I got through all of that on my own. I survived. I even survived the monster who broke into this house"—*I survived you leaving me and rejecting me*—"and I plan on continuing to do so. I don't need your protection—"

"Stop talking." His eyes flashed hellhound red as his canines extended and his face contorted with rage. "If you keep telling me the shit that's happened to you, I'm not sure I can hold back the beast."

I held that red gaze. "Why?" I pushed.

"Because I don't like it when females get hurt."

"So, you'd react this way with any female? It has nothing to do with me?"

The muscle in his jaw jumped. "Yeah, I would, but you're—"

"You're full of shit." There was no holding those words in, they just slipped out. "We kissed, and I know you felt it. You felt what was between us."

"Tell me you won't put yourself in danger again. Promise me," he rumbled, ignoring what I said.

I straightened my spine and hoped I hid my wince. "I don't have to promise you anything."

"Yes, you do," he said, his voice now blended with his hound.

"Why do you care?" Confrontation usually made me want to puke, or brought on a panic attack, but not with Jagger, apparently there was no holding back. I couldn't.

He snarled, his chest rising and falling rapidly.

"Or are you too much of a damned coward to admit the truth, even to me, where no one else will hear?"

His nostrils flared, and he literally ground his teeth.

I smiled wide and nodded. "Like I said."

"I...care about you, about what happens to you, that's why," he said, the words sounding as if they were being squeezed out of him. His skin was visibly rolling along his tattooed shoulders as he attempted to hold back his desire to shift. Maybe the part of him that was all hound didn't care about the way I looked or what I was. Maybe the hound was just as confused and angry as I was that Jagger was rejecting his mate.

"Why? Say it," I rasped.

More teeth grinding. "I don't know."

"Yes, you do, but you won't say it because you don't want me. Because you would rather fuck some random wolf shifter. Because you would rather be with any other female than me."

"That's not fucking true and you know it."

"I don't know anything when it comes to you. You run hot and cold. You stand outside my bedroom window for weeks after I'm hurt, then you vanish for three months. You start messaging me while you're away, then you humiliate me in front of your whole pack." I shook my head. "No, Jagger, I don't know."

"I just...I need to know that you're safe. For some reason, I need that. Will you at least give that to me?" he said.

I flinched. Was he really going to pretend he didn't know what we were to each other? That he didn't feel it? This was probably my last chance to get it all out there on the table, so, and unlike him, I refused to hold back. "I don't know if you know this about me, but when you earn my trust, when I love, I do it big. I give everything. I would have given you everything, Jagger, if you'd wanted it. But you don't want that from me, and you won't even tell me why."

He released a ragged breath. "You're wrong. We're not mates, it's impossible. What you feel for me, it's something else."

Impossible? He'd said that at the clubhouse as well. Was the idea of us being mates that awful or unthinkable to him that he refused to even contemplate it? "Impossible? Then why are you here? You won't leave me alone. You're the king of mixed freaking messages. You make me think you want me, so I open myself up to you, then you throw it back in my face. I try to forget you, but somehow, you've strong-armed your way back into my life, for how long, Jagger? Just long enough for me to have hope, before you leave again?"

He shook his head. "That's not what I'm doing."

He was sweating, shaking, his eyes were still scarlet and the veins under every part of exposed skin bulged. The towel around his hips hid nothing, and he was hard, tenting the fabric around his waist.

"You want me. You want to be with me. I know you do," I said, and there was no missing the desperation in my voice.

His nostrils flared. "Yeah, I won't deny I want to fuck you, but that doesn't mean we're—"

"Mates? Fated?"

"Sutton," he growled. "Stop. Stop this before…"

"Before what."

"Don't—"

"Before you lose control? I can see how hard you're fighting it."

He shook his head, hissing through his teeth.

"Why are you here?" I fired at him again.

"Stop," he growled.

I shoved his chest. "Or what?"

With a snarl, he jerked forward, looming over me, panting, vibrating. His fingers curled around the covers, and he snapped them back, so they were no longer covering me, then he slid his hand up my bare thigh.

I froze. "What are you doing?"

"What you want," he said, lips peeled back.

"You're going to mate with me?" I asked breathlessly.

He paused and snarled again, shaking his head like he was trying to clear it. "No, not that."

I wanted to throw up. "You won't make me your mate, but you'll give me a pity fuck to shut me up?" Heat flushed through me, and my face burned with humiliation that quickly grew into anger. Slamming my hands against his chest I tried to shove him off.

He stayed where he was. "Just let me touch you, that's all I was going to do. I'll make you feel good."

I blinked up at him. He was clueless. No, he was cruel. Twisted. "Feel good?" I choked out. "You make me feel utterly worthless."

The look he gave me was one of utter confusion. "No, this is what you want. I know this is what you want."

"You've lost your damn mind. What the hell is wrong with you?"

His hound shone from his red eyes, and his hand actually trembled as he reached for me again. "I'm just... I'm gonna make you feel good."

I shoved at his chest. "I said, no." Boo burst from his spot above us, chirping and swooping.

Jagger gave him no notice and shook his head, his chest heaving as his hands curled around my shoulders, holding me tightly. He was completely lost to animal instinct. "You need this."

No, he was the one that needed this, and he was too deep in denial to see why.

He leaned in, a repetitive rumbling sound vibrating from him as he ran his nose along the side of my throat, causing goose bumps to lift all over my skin. "Fuck," he groaned. "Submit to me."

Pain filled my chest. I couldn't take another moment of

this, not one more second. "Jagger, I rescind all access to house Ashborne," I choked out.

His head jerked back. "Don't you fucking dare—"

"Get the hell out of my house," I said as magic wrapped around him. The combined power of the wards created by the witches who lived in this house, banded around him and forcibly dragged him off my bed, out the door, and down the stairs. Boo flew after him, diving at his head.

I climbed off the bed, grabbed his leather vest, and followed, making my way down to where he stood clinging to the doorframe, snarling and roaring my name. Rushing through the kitchen and into the laundry, I grabbed his jeans from the dryer, then strode back to the door.

"Don't do this," he bit out.

"You've given me no choice." Lifting my hand, I used my power to give him one final shove, forcing him through the open door behind him. He ran back at the doorway, hitting the ward with force. I felt the magic shudder through me.

"Let me back in, Sutton."

"You need to leave, and never come back. You can't have it both ways. You can't reject me as your mate and still demand access to my body." Boo swooped down, landing on my shoulder.

"That's not...that's not what I'm doing." He shook his head violently, like something was buzzing around in it. "That's not, no... I would never..."

Holding his green gaze, I tossed his jeans at him. "If you batter the ward long enough with your strength and powers, you will weaken it, and you will eventually force your way inside. But if you do that, I will never forgive you. If you force your way back into this house and you try to touch me again, you need to get it through your head that it will be *against my will*. I don't want your hands on me, Jagger. I don't want you anywhere near me. As far as I'm concerned, the fates can go to hell right along with you, because this is done. This is over."

Every muscle in his body heaved with his panted breaths. "Sutton, fuck...don't—" He snarled, his upper lip peeling back, his canines flashing.

Jagger was always in control, contained. Right now, his long, dark hair was loose, hanging around his shoulders in a wild mess. Goddess, he looked as feral as I'd ever seen him. All animal. How could he deny what we were to each other after this?

Still panting, he lowered his head, looking at the ground.

I stood frozen, not sure what he was going to do. Would he leave? Or was he about to charge and try to force his way back into my house?

Finally, he lifted his head, and all that I saw in his eyes now was horror. "Sutton...I..." He shook his head again, as if he were trying to regain control over whatever was going on in his mind. "Fuck, I'm so sorry. I don't know what just happened. I would never..." He cursed again, viciously. "I never meant to scare you."

Something blazed in his eyes, something I refused to name. He didn't move, and I knew I had to be the one to finish this, whatever this was now.

I shook my head. "It's better this way. At least now I know who you are. You're not the male I thought you were," I choked out. "Goodbye, Jagger."

Then I shut the door, locked it, and even though I knew he could break through it if he really wanted to, that he could use his powers and his strength and eventually bust through the wards—because he and his brothers had done it before—he wouldn't.

I headed back upstairs and climbed into bed.

This time he wouldn't.

CHAPTER
SEVEN

Sutton

I JOLTED awake when my phone started ringing.

Crap. I'd been trying to stay awake because of the concussion. I quickly snatched the phone off my bedside table when I saw Luke's name on the screen.

Thank the goddess. "Luke?"

"I don't have much time. Please, Sutton, just listen to me. I'm in trouble."

I shoved myself up, wincing when my head pounded and my ribs throbbed. "What the hell's going on? Where have you been? Why haven't you been answering my calls?"

His gulp was audible. "I...I've pissed off the wrong people, Sut, I'm in serious trouble, and I don't know what to do."

The fear in his voice reached me through the phone so strongly that my own skyrocketed. I'd never heard him sound that scared before.

"Okay, Lukey, I'm listening. Whatever this is, whatever's happening, we can fix it. Just tell me what's going on."

"You're gonna be so pissed at me. I didn't mean for it to get this tangled up. It was just supposed to be a way to make some quick money. No one was ever meant to get hurt."

Oh gods. I shoved back the covers and climbed out of bed, gritting my teeth when my bruised and stiff body throbbed. "You can tell me anything, you know you can."

His breath shook. "Some guys at work, shifters, they were talking about the fights, about how they wanted something to give them an edge, you know? I said I could do it, because easy, right? I promised it was safe, that no one would get hurt, that I knew what I was doing... I thought I did, but—"

"You made performance-enhancing drugs?" Yes, I'd already worked that out, but still, I wanted to reach through the phone and wring his freaking neck.

"I thought it'd be harmless, and it would have been if they'd followed my instructions, if they hadn't overdone it." He sniffed. "If they'd just stuck to the dose I gave them, then none of this would have happened. No one would listen to me though. They thought more would make them stronger..." He sobbed, and it broke my heart. "People got sick, they overdosed...people *died*, Sutton." He sobbed harder.

No, we weren't biologically related, but this kid was my brother. The family I was born with wouldn't stop to pick me up if I was dying in the street. Luke, the other people in this coven, they'd do anything for me. Luke had done something seriously stupid, something that would mess him up for the rest of his life, but still, I'd do whatever I could to help him.

"Where are you? Just tell me where you are and I'll come and get you. We'll figure this out together."

Silence fell between us.

"What aren't you telling me?"

He made a choking sound. "The first batch I made, the guys who took it, they did really good, they won their fights. Then this demon took notice. He made an order, a really big order. Not just performance-enhancing but party drugs as well."

Fuck. There were some powerful demons in this city, but they didn't mess with humans, which meant so far they'd managed to maintain their sanctuary status. The Knights of Hell didn't relieve them of their heads, and the hounds didn't drag them back to Hell. They also didn't do anything that drew Rune's attention, the demon Lucifer had appointed as his eyes and ears when it came to the demons above ground, which meant they had free rein and were seriously dangerous.

"I gave them their order, but then people started dying." Another pause. "So I broke into the main dealer's house, and I stole it back."

"You did what?"

"I couldn't let anyone else die because of me. But now I owe them a lot of money."

"Then give them their money back and come home."

He sobbed again. "The money's all gone. I used it to buy the ingredients, then Evie took the rest of the cash, and she's not answering her phone."

That fucking bitch.

"They're gonna kill me, Sut. They said they're gonna kill me if I don't give them their money back. I'm so scared. I don't know what to do."

He was spiraling, and I had to pretend I wasn't because

he needed me. *Gods.* I was so angry at him for doing something so stupid, but he needed me to be strong right now.

"You need to get as far away from Roxburgh as you can until I work out what to do. Lie low until I can get the money together, then we can get you out of this mess."

"It's a lot of money. It's so much money, Sutton."

I had some savings. If I had to use some of it to get him out of this, then that's what I'd do. "How much?"

"Fifty grand. It's fifty fucking grand," he gasped out, sobbing harder.

Holy shit. I sure as hell didn't have that kind of money. "Right…okay. I'll work something out." I had no idea how, but I would.

"I have to go. They could be tracking me. I'll buy a burner and call you when I'm safe."

"Luke, hang on—"

The phone went dead.

Shit. I paced across my room to the window and stared out to the dark street.

Where the hell was I gonna get fifty thousand dollars?

›)》●《(‹

It turned out, drinking didn't solve all your problems.

It also didn't magically help you figure out how to find fifty thousand dollars and save someone you loved from possible torture and death. What it did do, however, was stop you from having an epic panic attack, so I was calling it a win.

I lay in bed, staring at the ceiling, and the longer I stared, the angrier I got. I didn't get angry easily. I tried to be positive, but there was no positive angle in this mess. And who the hell did these assholes think they were, anyway? Luke had been pushed around, cast aside, and had been forced to live on the streets like I had. He'd made a mistake, a really, seriously bad one—*people had died*—but I couldn't let him die as well.

My fingers curled into tight fists. Everyone in this coven had suffered in one way or another. We'd been treated like pariahs, cast aside because of what we were or how we looked—never good enough, never catching a damned break.

I knew that firsthand. My family thought I was disgusting, a blight on their perfect coven. No one talked about the fact that I was born this way, with demon blood, because my mother had an affair with a *freaking demon*! No one cared about that part, oh no, just that I didn't look like them, that my eyes and veins were a huge flashing red light telling everyone what my mother had done, and we couldn't have that now, could we? We couldn't have that shame staining their precious coven.

She literally fucked around and got found out, but I was the one who paid the price for her selfishness. There'd been nights of fear on the streets when I didn't think I'd survive, so much loneliness, years of self-loathing, something I still struggled with, then I found my coven and everything got better—until a monster broke in and cut me up. The fates giving me another giant *fuck you, Sutton*.

And then came Jagger, and I thought, yeah, finally. *Finally*. Something was going to go my way. I'd truly convinced myself that the fates thought, *hey, that Sutton got a pretty rough deal, let's give her something good to make up for all that crap we threw at her*—but, no. Instead, they decided to serve me up a whole lot more.

They dangled that hound in front of me, and just when I thought I was going to get my happily ever after, finally, they snatched him away—but not completely, not straightaway, first they humiliated me, then they made me think he'd changed his mind, *then* they snatched him away for good.

Grabbing the glass off my bedside table, I downed the last of my drink. That one might have been a little heavy on the vodka. I was still seriously tipsy. Well, there was only one answer for that. Dance it off.

I dragged myself off the bed and turned on some music. Boo was in his "cave," a little hidey-hole I'd made him to sleep in during the day. It was basically soundproof, and he didn't stir.

I did an experimental twist of my waist. My ribs hardly even hurt now. *Thanks, vodka, I knew I could count on you.* No one was here to annoy with the volume, so I turned it up. I tried not to think about Luke afraid and alone, or the shit Bonny had said to me the last time I saw her, while I was saving her freaking boyfriend's life—or Jagger in the bathroom with me, washing my hair, or the way he looked standing in the doorway in only a towel. It didn't work and I shivered when I thought about him basically begging me to let him make me *feel good.*

His voice rang through my mind over and over again.

You got blood all in this pretty hair of yours.

So fucking pretty. Love this hair.

He loved my hair. The only thing he did love about me apparently.

My rage shot higher. Well, screw him. I stormed into the bathroom, yanked open the drawer and grabbed out my scissors. He didn't get that. He didn't get to love my hair and nothing else. I wouldn't let him. Grabbing a chunk of it, I cut just below my chin, the sharp blades slicing through the strands easily. Then I kept going, hacking through braids, and the beads I'd threaded through the other side slid off, bouncing on the floor tiles.

I didn't stop until it was gone, lying in a heap on the bathroom floor.

Dragging in a shaky breath, I released a broken sob as the scissors clattered to the counter. Hot tears streaked down my cheeks. This was it, the last tears I would allow myself to shed for that male.

I survived my family and coven throwing me away, I could survive this.

This was nothing, just a blip. I barely knew him. This thing inside that made me feel lost without him, that made me crave him, that made me feel as if my life was over without him, was a trick. It was a biological ploy. Jagger was like a growth, a foreign body that needed to be excised. He didn't belong here with me, no matter what the fates tried to tease me with. They'd made a mistake.

I just had to find a way of cutting him out completely.

Then I'd stop feeling this way. Then this pain would stop.

CHAPTER
EIGHT

Jagger

I STRODE PAST THE PIT, hellfire licking up from the edges and heating my skin.

This was home—maybe this was where I needed to be for a while, until things with Sutton cooled off.

A growl slipped free as I hefted the stag higher on my shoulder, and I tried not to spill the bucket of hot water I carried in the other hand, and strode deeper into the tunnels.

Another growl, low in my chest, rolled from me out of nowhere. I couldn't seem to stop it for some reason. No, that was bullshit. I knew the reason. It was every time I thought about Sutton and the way she'd looked at me before she shut the door in my face, locking me out of her house—which meant I was growling constantly.

I still didn't know how I'd lost the grip on my control so thoroughly.

Seeing her hurt like that. In danger. My control had started corroding the moment I realized she was in trouble.

My snarl bounced off the stone walls on either side of me. Somehow, I'd sensed her fear that night, I'd *known* she was in serious danger. A hound used scent to track, and the animal part of me wouldn't let go of Sutton's, her scent was fucking imbedded deep inside me.

I'd tried to shake off the pull toward her, the sense that she was in trouble, because I didn't believe it. Why would I feel that? How? But a hound never ignored his instincts, and not following where they led me, where her scent led me, was impossible. They'd taken me straight to Dogwood —to Sutton in that fucking van.

After that, instinct had taken over, had driven me to snatch her from that wolf, put her on the back of my bike, and take her home to tend her wounds.

Seeing her afraid, injured, the beast had demanded I take care of her. The beast and the man were one and the same—we were of the same mind in all things—and that part of me wouldn't let me forget the taste of her lips, and now—fuck—there was a growl of *mine*, constantly in my head. Animal instinct was pulling me toward her, making me feel things that should be impossible, my stomach was tight, and my hands fucking shook and my head was full of confusing and persistent thoughts, and I was afraid I knew why.

I'd barely resisted tearing the heads off those wolves. If Warrick and Rome hadn't been there, I'm not sure I could've stopped myself. Yes, those fuckers deserved it, but it would've caused all kinds of problems with Draven and the rest of his pack. I was War's lieutenant, given that position because I could keep my shit tight when I needed to. It was Draven's job to reprimand his pack, but as soon as I'd seen Sutton, afraid and bleeding, I hadn't cared about that, I would have happily started a war.

I thought I had the hunger, the desire for Sutton, under control. I thought that seeing her hurt, licking her wounds, tasting her blood had caused some kind of fucked connection to her, was behind these overprotective feelings I had for her, and that I could easily handle them. I was wrong.

The scent of her blood had roused the beast until that part of me had been shoving against my skin, rolling under my flesh, desperate to take over, to hunt down those who hurt her and put them down.

As soon as I'd run my fingers through all that soft, gorgeous, fucking honey-blond hair stained red, I'd been back in that basement with her. I'd seen her the way I'd found her three months ago, so close to death that she'd almost been lost to all of us.

After that, washing the blood out of her hair, getting rid of the smell, had been all I could think about, and the more I'd touched her, the more I'd smelled her, and the more time I spent with her, the more I lost control—until I was nothing but beast.

Being near her was too dangerous. I couldn't be in the same city, the same house, and definitely not in the same fucking room.

Which meant this wasn't just some protective feelings I was dealing with here, this was something else, something that should not be fucking possible.

Fuck.

Her wounded face, injured, and not just from the beating she'd taken but from the way I hurt her, flashed through my mind.

You're not the male I thought you were.

I gritted my teeth, remembering her parting words, but they were nothing I hadn't deserved.

I finally reached the large steel door at the end of a cave, one that I'd carved out myself several years ago. My blood and sweat were in every gouge along these walls, and in the archway I made for this door. The door itself had been forged in hellfire by my own hands, because it needed to be strong, secure. Safe.

Pressing my hand to the steel, I let my powers pulse through it, allowing the seal I'd created to recognize me. I felt the barrier drop.

Then taking the key from my back pocket, I unlocked the massive padlock and slowly opened the door.

A vicious, bloodcurdling snarl ricocheted off the walls as I stepped inside and shut the door behind me. I turned to the massive hound standing across from me, mouth foaming, black fur matted, and red eyes blazing.

I was the only one who could approach Kurgan. I was the only one he let near him.

The thick steel cuff around his throat was attached to a long, heavy chain, stopping him short so he couldn't attack anyone else who came in here, but he didn't need it when he was with me. He wouldn't attack me.

"Be easy, Kurgan. It's Jagger." I strode closer, lowering the stag to the floor in front of him. "You're okay," I said as his snarls and growls increased in volume.

I hadn't been here for a couple of weeks. I hated staying away so long. Maddox had brought his food to him in my absence, but that meant in all that time, Kurgan had no real interactions other than Mad throwing him food from the door. Only a few of us knew about Kurgan—me, Lothar, War, and Maddox—because Lucifer insisted he be kept a secret.

Holding out my hand, I stepped closer, nice and slow. Sometimes, when I was forced to stay away for longer periods of time, the madness took a firmer hold and only my scent brought him back. His snout wrinkled as his growls increased and his fangs extended, longer than any other hound's I'd seen.

He finally caught my scent and instantly calmed.

"That's it. It's just me." I ran my hand over the matted fur on his head, and he lowered it, letting me scratch him more vigorously. "Eat your supper."

Kurgan ripped into the venison, making short work of the huge stag.

Water trickled down the stone wall in the corner, filling a large basin, giving him a constant supply of clean drinking water, and he drank from it now, washing all that meat down before he finally turned to me and sat on his haunches.

"Got you some warm water for a wash." He didn't like to shift for anyone else—War occasionally, but no one else—so he wouldn't have washed while I'd been gone. I took the rag and soap that I'd tucked into my back pocket and the towel that I'd slung around my neck and put them down by the bucket.

His red eyes came to me, more animal than any other hound I knew, then he tilted his head back and with a painful howl shifted. He did it so infrequently that when he finally did, his shift was slow, like his joints were made of rusted steel needing to be freed up with force.

Finally, he stood across from me, his gaze on the floor, his dark hair just as wild as his fur had been. Kurgan wasn't just the biggest hound I'd ever seen in his animal form but in his human form as well.

Kurgan rarely spoke, though when he did, his voice was

so deep and blended with the beast that he terrified most beings.

He dragged the bucket closer and proceeded to wipe the dirt and blood from his skin with the rag, dipping it in the water, soaping up, and slowly and methodically cleaning himself.

He paused suddenly and turned to me, and his eyes had changed, shifting from red, to green.

I knew what was coming, what he always asked every time I came here.

"Female?" he asked, his voice impossibly deep and rusty.

"Your female's safe, son."

"Meat?"

I nodded. "I took her a stag as well. Steaks and a few roasts and left it on her doorstep. Her house is safe," I said, telling him what I told him every time. "She has blankets, and locks, and your brothers are guarding her—"

He growled another of those bloodcurdling growls, and I lifted my hands. "From a distance, they watch her from a distance. No one's getting close to Lenny, son. I won't let anyone get close to her."

He nodded, grunted, and continued to clean the dirt and blood from his skin.

I sat leaning against the wall, and when Kurgan finished, he did the same. He sat against the wall, his legs out in front of him, ankles crossed, imitating me. It happened occasionally, these moments of lucidity, but again, only with me.

It wasn't supposed to matter. Hellhounds were brothers, all of us. We weren't separated into families, at least those of us not mated. That's not how we were. Lucifer created us—that made us his children, that made us brothers, pack, family, if that was the word you chose to use.

But somehow Kurgan understood on a deeper level that I was his.

That he wasn't Lucifer's creation—that he was mine.

His family.

His blood.

That I was his sire.

Did he know that I was the reason he was broken as well? That it was my fault he was locked away, separated from the female chosen for him? That I'd done this? That he suffered this way because of me?

I was the poison in his veins.

Relic wasn't the only hound to come from Lucifer's experiment all those years ago, but Relic was the only success.

Both Kurgan and Relic were the first hounds born naturally, instead of being created full grown by Lucifer like the rest of us. They were the first pups born without mated parents, since back then none of our brothers had been mated. Lucifer chose me and Lothar to sire the pups and used our seed to impregnate demon females who volunteered for the task.

Relic was born healthy.

Kurgan had been born damaged.

I knew without doubt that I was the poison that made Kurgan this way, because Lucifer had inseminated another demon female with my seed at the same time, and my second pup had been born so sick, he'd only survived a few hours. I'd held him in my arms before he'd slipped away, wrapped in one of my shirts, surrounded by my scent for comfort. Something had cracked inside me when he'd taken his last shaky breath. The handmaids had taken him from me—and emotions I'd never felt before had spilled out, had almost shattered me.

I'd been so incapacitated by what I was feeling, I'd almost lost my mind. The only person I'd spoken to about it was Lucifer. It was a fucked-up time, both me and Lothar hadn't been acting like ourselves after siring our pups. A lot of time had passed since then and memories faded, but I knew for a fact that mating wasn't the only way to force a hound to develop emotions—pups could do it as well—mate or not. I knew firsthand.

Lucifer had fixed me, though. He'd erased those emotions when I'd fucking begged him to take them away, and thank fuck he had. He'd sealed my emotions back up tight so I could function again, but the memory of what I'd felt, had remained.

The memory of loving that pup, of seeing him suffer, watching him die—it was all still there. I hadn't forgotten the way I'd felt about him or Kurgan, and sitting here with him now, I realized those feelings weren't just memories anymore. It wasn't as big as back then, but it was there, like a whisper growing louder.

Kurgan was mine. My son, and that connection burned in the center of my chest now.

Sutton had done that, hadn't she?

She was the reason I was unraveling. Somehow, she was breaking through.

But how? Fucking how? Because there was only one way that could happen, and Lucifer promised that would never happen for me. Locking away my emotions wasn't the only thing I'd asked him to do during that dark time—I'd also asked him to make sure I never found a mate, whatever it took.

I knew what it was to feel everything, all the pain and

grief and hopelessness that came with losing someone you loved. I'd been there, I'd done that, and it had nearly destroyed me. I couldn't have that. Not again.

I rubbed my temples, my fucking head pounding. When I looked up, I caught Kurgan doing the same thing, mimicking me again because he'd been so fucking isolated that he barely knew what the fuck he was. I didn't think he'd even seen himself in a mirror.

His gaze slid between my hand and his, and he wiggled his fingers, then grinned.

"Female?" he asked again, the grin slipping.

Fuck. I wanted to take him out of here so badly, let him free, but if I did, he'd go straight to Lenny and kill her, because that's what he did. He killed anyone, anything, he didn't trust, and being close to Lenny again, along with the mix of those instincts and the desire to mate, and that little female would be dead in minutes.

"She's safe," I said again. "No one can hurt her."

"Meat?"

"She's got all the food she could ever need."

He looked back down at his hand, then back up at me. "I can...get her meat," he said, his voice rusty as hell as he tugged on the chain hooked to the cuff around his throat.

That was more than I'd heard him say in a fucking long time. I shook my head. "You have to stay in here."

He growled. "I'll get her meat," he said again and stood.

"Remember what happened last time you left?" Inexplicably, two years ago he'd sensed her from down here, and he'd busted out of his old cell, somehow found a gateway out of Hell, and gone straight to her. He'd terrified her so badly there was no way she'd ever accept him. Kurgan wasn't capable of that kind of relationship, of any kind of relationship.

He'd freaked that female out so badly she barely left her house now, and if I hadn't gotten to her in time, she'd be dead. I had no choice but to try to make him understand. "You'll hurt her, son."

"No." He shook his head again, his chest and shoulders rolling as the beast pushed forward.

I knew exactly how he felt in this, didn't I?

Kurgan wasn't the right male for Lenny, just like I wasn't the right male for Sutton.

Kurgan didn't know how to control the beast, and if he escaped again, when the bloodlust finally cleared and Lenny was torn to pieces at his feet, he'd be left with the knowledge that he'd destroyed the only thing he'd ever cared about.

Kurgan exploded into his hound, snarling and growling, pawing at the floor and yanking at his chains to get free. To get to Lenny.

I wouldn't let that happen. I would not let him suffer that pain.

No fucking way.

⁂

Lucifer answered the door when I knocked. He was wearing jeans, but they weren't done up. Music was blaring from another room, and he was holding a beer. "Jag, my man, what can I do you for?"

I followed him into his quarters and was hit with the scent of sex. A female poked her head around the door on the other side of the room. "Are you coming back?"

"Entertain yourselves for a while, I have a guest," he said without looking at her.

None of his handmaids were here, they would have

answered the door if they were, but then, they tended to make themselves scarce when Lucifer was in the mood to fuck. They'd be close, though. His warriors were never far from him.

Lucifer sat on the couch and lifted his drink. "Want one?"

I shook my head.

"I have a roomful back there if you want to join in?"

"I'm good, thanks."

He shrugged. "Your loss. So not a social call, then?"

"No." I had to ask. Something was wrong. I was starting to feel again, and I needed to know why. "When I lost my pup, and you took my emotions from me, I asked you for something else."

Lucifer stilled—it was slight, but I didn't miss it.

His yellow eyes locked on mine. "I asked you to make it so I never found a mate, and you agreed."

"I did," Lucifer said.

I breathed out a rough breath. "Okay, then why am I starting to feel again?"

He placed his beer on the table beside him. "I think you know."

I frowned. "No, I don't."

"You have a theory, that's why you're here." Mini, his cat, slinked over and curled into his lap. Lucifer ran his hand down her back. "And fyi, that theory is correct."

I shot to my feet, a growl rumbling from me. "You just said it wasn't possible."

"No, Jag, I confirmed that back then, when you were all fucked up in the head, I agreed to your request."

"Same thing."

"It's not."

"Why?" I bit out.

"Because I lied," Lucifer said casually as he placed Mini on the seat behind him and stood as well.

"You what?" My ears started ringing, and my head spun as I struggled to drag in my next breath.

"Jagger, my brother, you have to know I have no sway when it comes to that shit. That's the fates' business, and I can't meddle with that." He shrugged again. "Back then, the state you were in, I told you what you needed to hear."

I ran a hand down my face. "You can't be fucking serious?"

His expression hardened. I'd veered into disrespectful and needed to get my shit under control, but it wasn't easy.

"I did what I had to. You were ineffective in that condition. You've enjoyed five hundred years of ignorant bliss, plenty of time to get yourself prepared for this."

"I haven't prepared for it, because I didn't think it would ever happen," I ground out.

"Your mated brothers seem happy." He picked up his beer. "I lied to you because I had to. You have a problem with the mate the fates chose for you, take it up with them. Now if you'll excuse me—" He stood and strode off to join his guests in the other room.

Take it up with the fates? That wasn't how this worked.

They didn't change their minds.

I walked out, back into the caves, my mind racing.

Sutton was my mate. Of course she fucking was. Of course, she'd been right.

What the fuck was I going to do?

Mating Sutton would mean releasing the last of the emotion I was still holding back, releasing all that pain, experiencing it all over again. And worse, it would mean feeling all of it while I helplessly watched her grow old and eventually die.

Witches weren't immortal, and Sutton's witch blood was predominant, despite the way she transformed. Hounds could sense immortality, and she wasn't. Her life was finite. Lucifer wouldn't just give her immortality, either, not like he had for War. I didn't have anything to barter like he had had. And unlike Relic and Dirk, my mate wasn't already immortal.

I wouldn't survive making her mine, allowing myself to love her, like I had that tiny pup, only to lose her.

I couldn't watch her age and weaken. I couldn't hold her in my arms while she slipped away.

Knowing I would eventually lose her, I'd always be holding a part of myself back, trying to protect myself from that pain, and she'd resent me for it.

Sutton deserved a mate who could give her everything she wanted. A male who could give her healthy pups and a family.

A primal roar burst inside me.

I could never give her that, and my need to protect her —from me—was just as strong as my need to make her mine.

CHAPTER NINE

Sutton

I LOOKED up as Magnolia walked into the clinic for her shift. There were only so many healers in the city, and we all kind of did a rotation.

The witch was an exceptional healer, and a friend; she was also the alpha hellhound's sister-in-law. I'd been avoiding the clubhouse even though Fern had assured me that Jagger had gone back to Hell for an unspecified amount of time.

I was glad. It didn't hurt *at all*, and I'd keep telling myself that until it stuck. Him leaving again just made it easier for me to forget about that jerk.

"How was your shift?" she asked as I slung my bag over my shoulder.

"The wolf shifter in room seven threw his pudding at me, so that was fun. Apparently, he doesn't like pudding."

A wicked smirk curled Magnolia's lips. "Did he now? I'll be sure to pay him special attention."

I laughed. "I think it's fear. A clinic, especially to shifters, can seem utterly foreign."

"Don't you dare feel sorry for him," she said. "The assholes in this city need to start appreciating what Jack's done for them, what we do for them. They're damned lucky."

"Agreed." I chuckled. "I'll leave him in your capable hands, then."

"How you doing?" she asked before I could walk away. "Haven't seen you outside of work lately."

The video of my humiliation had gone viral. The wolf who'd been standing with Jagger had taken the video down, and I guessed I had Willow to thank for that. Draven, the alpha of the Silver Claw Pack, was mated to Iris, another Thornheart sister, but it had unfortunately been too late. It was already out there and shared thousands of times on Nightscape.

I shoved down the pain and smiled. "I'm fine."

"Glad to hear it." She motioned to my hair. "Love the new look, by the way. It's hot as fuck."

Mags was good people, and I appreciated her trying to make me feel better. "I felt like a change," I lied. I'd been living with the blunt bob for the last week and I still hadn't gotten used to it.

"Well, it looks awesome, even with pudding in it."

My hand flew up to where she pointed, and my hair crunched under my fingers. I groaned.

Mags chuckled. "Enjoy the rest of your night."

I lifted my hand to my hair again as I walked out. Thankfully, Phoebe had been able to fix the hack job I'd done of it when she got home from the conclave. Which I very much appreciated. But I'd kept what had caused me to drunkenly hack off my own hair and what I had learned about Luke to myself. She hadn't pushed when I told her I didn't want to talk about it, but she wouldn't let me shut her out forever. Eventually I'd have to tell her something.

The Jagger stuff I would tell her about when that time came, but what was going on with Luke, well, I wasn't sure that was a good idea, not yet anyway. Generally, bad guys and gangsters didn't like you talking about their "business," and the more people who knew what was happening, the higher the risk to everyone involved. Not that I didn't trust my coven, I did. But I also wanted to protect them.

There was no point freaking everyone out. I had an appointment with the bank in a few days. If I could get a loan, I could get this all cleared up and no one would have to know. Luke could come home, and things could go back to normal.

He'd called the night before last and said he was safe. He just needed to lie low for a few more days, then hopefully this would all be sorted out.

I unlocked my car. My tub was calling me, preferably filled with bubbles. It'd been a long shift with one seriously difficult patient. I just wanted to wash the pudding out of my hair and not think about all the crap in my life—

Someone grabbed my shoulder and jerk me back roughly.

"I'd strongly advise you not to scream," a rough voice said against my ear.

I was spun around and came face to face with a tall male with sharp features and dead eyes. His gripped my shoulder tighter, and my internal alarm bells wailed.

I tried to pull away, but he held on tight. "Let me the hell go."

He grinned, and the sight sent ice sliding down my spine. "Now aren't you a pretty little thing."

My heart pounded out of my chest and fear gripped my throat, but I tried not to show it. "Do I know you?"

"How remiss of me. Let me formally introduce myself. My name is Poe, and I'll be your escort this evening."

"I'm not going anywhere with you—"

"Apologies, I am again getting ahead of myself. We have a mutual friend, you and I, and, well, he's been a very bad boy. My boss would like to have a word with you about this mutual friend, and hopefully we can come to some kind of mutually agreeable arrangement."

"I have no idea what you're talking about. Now you need to let me go so I can get into my car." I tried to pull from his grip.

Poe's fingers dug into my flesh. "Now, now, sweetheart. You're getting yourself worked up. I would highly advise you to stay calm and do what you're told. I'd really hate to have to hurt you." He leaned in closer. "There are only two ways this is going to go down. You either come with me like a good girl, nice and quiet, and we'll all have a pleasant little chat, or we do things a different way, a way that you won't like"—one of his hands slid up the side of my throat—"but I will, immensely." His eyes flashed.

Oh yes, this creep wanted me to do it the hard way. This sick, twisted asshole was enjoying every moment of the power he held over me.

Combat magic, darker spells to cause harm, didn't come easily to me. After all, I was a healer. Those kinds of spells weren't readily in my repertoire. I did have one I'd practiced after what happened to me, but even that was difficult. Regardless, I had to try. If I could get away from him, I could run inside.

I let my magic flow through me, building and growing as best I could in my panicked state while frantically looking around the parking lot for help, for anyone to help me, but there was no one.

"Let's go," he said and started pulling me around to the other side of the car.

It wasn't enough power, not nearly enough, but I fired my magic at him, letting it pulse through me into his hand.

He jerked and growled but didn't release me.

His chuckle grated over me. "That all you got? Aw, sweetheart, I'm kind of embarrassed for you."

I scowled up at him.

Excitement filled his eyes again. "So, I take it we're doing this the hard way?"

There was no getting out of this, and fighting would only make this worse for me. "Fine, let's go see your boss."

"Shame. I was really hoping you had a bit more backbone." He snatched my keys out of my hand, shoved me into the passenger seat, and shut me in. I didn't bring Boo with me to work, thank the goddess, at least he was home safe with Pheebs. Poe got in, started the engine, cranked up the stereo, and tore out onto the street.

I gripped my bag so tightly my knuckles ached as he drove farther and farther away from Ashborne house, taking streets I'd never been down, in a part of the city I'd never ventured to.

I'd expected him to take me to Seventh Circle, where most of the demons above ground were permitted to reside —as long as they toed the line and followed the rules;

namely, don't mess with humans. No killing, torturing, or eating them. If they behaved, they were left to their own devices. Instead, we drove until we reached the edge of Roxburgh and headed for a big old house right out of a horror movie. It was surrounded by acreage and trees that stood like a huge misshapen army of spindly monsters lining the long driveway and ready to pounce.

Gravel crunched under the tires as we rolled to a stop outside the front of the house.

Poe got out of the car, strode around, opened my door, grabbed my bicep, and marched me up the stairs.

The main door opened before we even reached it, and the demon who stood inside was as tall as Poe and just as freaky looking. I didn't know what kind of demon he was, but he had the same dead eyes and sharply angled features. Only when this one smiled, he flashed viciously pointed teeth. Poe had obviously filed his down to appear more human.

I doubted the creepy one staring at me as Poe led me inside ever left this place. He couldn't pass in the human world, not with those teeth.

The walls were a deep hunter green and there were small ornate lamps on the walls, glowing pale yellow and doing little to illuminate the space. My boots thudded against the deep red rug swirled with black and gray. It looked expensive and good if you needed to disguise, I don't know, blood stains, for example.

I shuddered. Whoever lived here was playing at being the Lord of the Manor instead of the demon thug he actually was.

We stopped at a set of doors, and Poe knocked lightly, respectfully, on the dark wood.

A harsh voice called from inside, telling us to enter. The urge to pull away from Poe's tight grip, to run, to get the hell out of there, was hard to control. My flight instincts were in full red alert. Poe opened the door and dragged me in after him.

The room was just as dim as the entrance and main hall but not so dark I couldn't make out its contents. My gaze instantly went to the male standing in front of the fire. His hands were clasped behind his back, and he stared into the flames while the silence stretched out between us. The cold and unwelcoming vibes that filled the room made me tremble.

"What am I doing here?" Panic had settled in, and I was struggling to breathe properly. My vision washed with red and my claws slid from the tips of my fingers as I transformed, I was honestly surprised it hadn't happened earlier.

His head jerked my way, a sneer on his very unpleasant face as if my voice offended him in every possible way.

"Did I say you could speak?" he said, proving I was right.

Poe squeezed my arm tighter, telling me without words to shut the hell up. I did, snapping my mouth shut and biting my lips together. Whoever this demon was, I didn't want to be on his bad side, at least not more than I already was.

He turned his entire body slowly, oddly, as if his joints worked in a different way than any other creature who stood on two legs, before moving toward me with weird, gliding strides that lifted goose bumps all over my body. He didn't stop until he was mere inches away. Looking down at me, with those hate-filled eyes, he smiled.

The sight was utterly chilling.

"We'll get right to the point, shall we?"

I was too scared to answer, so I bit my lips harder and nodded.

He grinned wider, obviously pleased that I'd learned my lesson. "Very good," he said. "Perhaps we can come to an arrangement after all?" He lifted a hand, and I flinched as he took my jaw in his cold, clammy fingers, tilting my head from side to side, taking in my demonic transformation. His gaze slid to my mouth, then back up, holding my eyes captive in his dead-man's stare. "I had been prepared to retrieve what was owed to me in...other ways, but I see now that you're a very smart little..." He flashed his teeth. "Demon. Maybe we won't have to go to such extremes quite yet?"

For once, the way I looked might have actually helped me.

No one had mentioned Luke's name, but I knew that's why I was here, but what this creep thought I could do to help, I didn't know.

"I hear you are a very gifted healer, Miss Ellis?"

I flinched at the sound of my surname. I didn't use it, I hadn't used that name since I was kicked out. It was clear he knew about me. He knew everything about me.

"You taught our young Luke everything he knows," he said, finally saying his name. "But I think we'd be much better off dealing with the teacher rather than the student. What do you think, Miss Ellis?"

He stood over me, waiting for me to answer, I assumed, so I forced myself to open my mouth and speak. "If you could... If you could just give me a few days, I can get the money Luke owes you. I can pay you back, and it will be like none of this ever happened."

The demon chuckled, the sound grating through me.

"Well, now, aren't you delightfully amusing. Sadly, that's not how this is going to play out. Luke has inconvenienced me a great deal. I had suppliers waiting for the product he stole, but then no one wants product that can kill their customers. This has gone past just money, Miss Ellis, this is about my reputation in this city. If I let Luke get away with this disrespect so easily, then everyone will think they can lie and steal from me. We can't have that, now can we?"

"I'm not sure what you expect me to do?" I had a feeling I knew, though, and the only way to leave this place and get home in one piece was to agree to whatever it was he was about to ask. He held all the cards in the situation, all of them.

He slid his thumb along the side of my jaw. "You, my dear, will fulfill the orders Luke failed to deliver, and then you will do the same again, and again, and you will keep on doing it until I feel his debt has been paid."

"I can't... I can't do that," I said, the words slipping free before I could stop them.

The terrifying male's gaze slid to Poe, and he nodded.

"Lars," Poe called.

A moment later, another demon, Lars, I assumed, walked in, dragging Luke with him. He was bruised and freaked out, his gaze wildly searching the room before it landed on me.

"Sutton," he groaned. "I'm so sorry. I—I fucked up, I—"

"He went back to his girlfriend's house, didn't you, Luke?" the demon in charge said. "Silly boy. Now look what you've done."

Oh gods. "What are you going to do with him?"

"Nothing...as long as you do as you're told."

He was forcing me to be his manufacturer. There was no way I could refuse. There was no way of getting out of this.

My life was over. My life now belonged to this demon staring down at me.

"You will keep this arrangement between me and you, and if you tell anyone else, I will know, and your friend here, and your precious coven, will pay for your indiscretion. Do you understand?"

I was suddenly relieved that I hadn't told Phoebe anything about Luke and what he'd gotten himself into. Whoever this guy was, he was powerful, he had connections, and he had money. Not only did he have Luke, but he could get to me, and anyone else in my coven. I didn't doubt that for a second.

"I understand," I choked out.

His hand dropped from my jaw, and I dragged in a desperate breath when he took several steps back.

"You have one week to deliver what Luke owes us. Poe will give you the details and be in touch with a time and location for delivery," he said, then strode to the window and stared out at the night. He turned to me one last time, his eyes locking on mine again. "Do not disappoint me, Miss Ellis. I don't like to be disappointed." Then he turned back to the window, dismissing me.

My legs trembled as Poe handed me a folded piece of paper—the order, I assumed—before I was frog-marched back through that creepy freaking mansion, away from Luke, then dragged out the door, and shoved down the stairs toward my car.

I rushed for the driver's side.

"Looking forward to the next time we meet," Poe said, tossing me my car keys.

Catching them, I got in my car, fired it up, and tore out of there so fast, gravel spat from under my tires.

I slammed my hands on the steering wheel. "Fucking *fuck*. Motherfucking, fucking *assholes*."

I had just become a manufacturer of illegal magical drugs for some twisted demon drug lord—and there was no escaping it.

Not if I didn't want anyone I loved to get hurt.

CHAPTER TEN

Sutton

Three and a half weeks later

I PULLED up outside the Dogwood fights and stared at the building through the rain pelting my window. Lights flashed inside, the sound of cheering muted by the thunder outside.

My knee jiggled as I chewed my fingernail, or tried to, they were all bitten down to the stubs. Here's hoping the wolves who threw me in the back of that van several weeks ago weren't here tonight. That would really suck.

This was my third "delivery," and my heart was slamming into the back of my ribs so hard I was close to passing the hell out. The last two had been relatively easy, quick drop-offs, one at the back of a nightclub, which had felt a bit sketchy but ended up being fine, and the other had been a midnight meeting at a roadside hotel parking lot. After the exchange, Poe had also invited me to try out my product with him, followed by the bed in the room he'd acquired for us. I'd declined and gotten the hell out of there.

Tonight, though, he'd chosen somewhere a lot more public, and he'd also ordered me to look the part. He wanted me to come dressed like a *cage bunny*, his words. I'd wanted to tell him to go fuck himself, but I wasn't the one with all the power in this dynamic.

Forcing down my fear, I grabbed the bag stuffed with a whole lot of drugs, climbed out of the car, quickly locked it, and ran through the rain to the main doors.

The big male guarding the door watched me approach, looking me up and down, and the way he looked at me made my belly feel weird, and not in a good way. I didn't know what the hell dressing like a cage bunny entailed, I hadn't paid attention when I came here for work, but going by the skeevy look on this guy's face, I'd gotten it a little too right.

"What's in the bag, honey?" he asked, reaching for it.

"It's for Poe," I rushed out, like I'd been instructed to.

The guy pulled his hand back quickly and jerked his chin up, telling me I was good to go in.

I pushed the heavy door open and humidity and noise washed over me instantly. How was I supposed to find that asshole in here? The place was packed. Gripping the bag tight, I pushed and sidestepped and wriggled my way through the crowd, searching for him.

Someone grabbed my elbow in a firm grip. Lars, Poe's creepy lackey, scowled at me.

"You're late. Hurry the fuck up." He towed me through groups of people, right across the room and around to the other side of the fighting cage.

I expected him to carry on down one of the hallways or something, definitely somewhere more private. Instead, he stopped suddenly, and I almost tripped over my own feet.

"You're late," Poe's rough voice said close to my ear.

I froze, and he turned me to face him. He was in loose shorts and no shirt. His soulless eyes slid over me, and an appreciative noise rolled from him that made me feel nauseous. "Well, now, look at you. Aren't you a sexy little cage bunny."

I didn't acknowledge his gross comment. "What's going on? Why am I here?"

He shrugged. "Some entertainment before we get down to business. You're going to watch me fight, then we can make the exchange."

"I have no interest in watching you fight. Just take the damn bag so I can leave."

He moved quickly, grabbing me hard and pulling me against him. One arm went around my waist while the fingers of his other hand thrust into my hair. To anyone looking, it might have appeared to be a passionate embrace; in reality, his demon claws had extended, digging into my side, while the ones on the other hand were threatening to gouge my scalp.

"You will watch me fight, like the good little groupie you are, and you will kiss me for good luck before I go in."

My stomach revolted more strongly. "I'm not kissing you."

"Maybe your little friend Phoebe would be more amenable? What do you think, Lars?"

The other demon grunted and licked his lips.

"Do you think she'd do what she was told to protect her friends? Or do you think she'd be selfish and stupid like you?"

I wanted to scratch his awful dead eyes out. "Fine. I'll do it."

He nodded and grinned, flashing those filed-down demon teeth. "Glad you've had a change of heart."

His name was called to the ring all too soon. His opponent was another demon, smaller than Poe but vicious looking. I hoped like hell he'd kick Poe's ass. I'd never paid much attention to the fighting when I came here for work, apart from thinking how stupid it was. Suddenly, I was seriously invested.

Poe turned to the cage, then he scanned the room, before his dark gaze slid back to me. I wanted to shrink away from him, but if I fought it, things would only get worse for me and my coven, so I let him haul me up against him, shove his fingers in my hair, and kiss me.

He nipped my lip, forcing a cry from me, then took advantage, kissing me deeper. I endured it, barely, but the entire time all I could think about was the knife in my pocket, the one I used for spelling, and how badly I wanted to bury it deep in his fucking eye socket.

Finally, he released me and I slumped, breathing deeply through my nose, because bending over and puking was a real threat.

Poe was a disgusting creep, he was forcing himself on me, and I freaking loathed him, but even if all of those things weren't true, my reaction would remain the same. It sounded extreme, but being touched by any male who wasn't Jagger felt wrong in every way.

"Don't move," he said and sauntered into the ring.

Like I had a choice? He faced off with his opponent. Now that I was sure he wasn't looking, I quickly turned away and dragged the back of my hand across my mouth—and my eyes collided with Lothar's.

He was frowning. His gaze sliced from me to Poe, then back again.

Shit.

Then he was on the move, heading straight for me, and there was nothing I could do to stop him. I couldn't leave because it would piss off the demon gangster who was blackmailing me, and I sure as hell couldn't let on to Lothar what was really going in here, not when they still had Luke.

Lars closed in when Lothar strode right up to me.

Loth's narrowed stare sliced through the demon, and he curled his upper lip, flashing fang. "Back the fuck up now or you will regret it, demon," Lothar growled.

Lars bristled, trying to be tough, but there was no missing the real fear in his eyes. All demons were afraid of hellhounds, to differing degrees, and I had to fight my grin when he stepped back.

"Make it quick. Poe won't be happy you're talking to this asshole," he fired at me.

Lothar had already dismissed him completely. "You good, Sutton?" Loth was frowning again, and there was a whole lot more growl in his voice.

"Yep," I said and smiled bright. Lars had stepped back, but he was still listening, and even if I wanted to tell Lothar what was going on, I couldn't. "Just checking out the fights. My ah...friend, Poe, is fighting."

"Friend, huh? You kiss all your friends like that?"

The hound was still growling. "We've just, uh...been on a few dates. It's nothing, you know, serious or anything."

Lothar crossed his big muscled arms over his chest. "That male is bad news, babe, not sure you should be hanging with him."

"Poe?" I forced a laugh. "He's a big softy under it all. I'm fine, honestly."

The concern on his face didn't fade. "Heard you moved out of the coven house. Not sure that was a good play either."

My mouth went dry and my stomach clenched. I'd had no choice. I couldn't prepare drugs there and put my coven in that position, and I couldn't tell them the truth. Distancing myself from them was the only thing I could think of. I'd hurt my friends, but it was for the best. Phoebe and Fern thought it was about Jagger, and I let them believe it because it was easier that way.

I shrugged. "I wanted to go out on my own is all."

"The shit that went down with Jag—"

"I'm not talking about that."

His massive chest expanded and his eyes narrowed. "I know my brother handled things wrong. He fucked up, but, babe, you gotta know he would not be down with this shit. He's protective of you after what happened to you, finding you like he did, and you hanging with that fucker, kissing him, dressed like that in a room full of males, no one here to protect you—"

"You need to stop, Lothar," I shouted over the cheering. "Jagger doesn't care what I do. What he thinks or feels about the way I conduct my life is irrelevant. I don't owe him a damned thing."

The cheering reached a new level, and I turned to see Poe standing over the smaller demon. There was blood everywhere, and his opponent wasn't getting up. Every instinct in me screamed to get in the ring and treat him, heal him, but I couldn't do that either. It would only piss Poe off.

His dead-eyed stare came to me now, then locked on Lothar. *Shit, shit, shit.*

My tormentor strode from the cage and over to me. He hooked me around the neck and tugged me against his sweaty, blood-covered body.

I wanted to retch and shove him away, but instead I stood there like a good little cage bunny, not fighting when he grabbed my chin, and not hissing and scratching when he tipped my head back and kissed me again. I tasted blood and whimpered in disgust.

He released me and tried to stare down Lothar. "You want something, hound?"

"Boy, you better adjust your fucking tone when you speak to me," Loth said, his voice so gravelly it lifted goose bumps across my arms.

Poe was a demon, Lothar was a hellhound. Demon's did not fuck with hounds, not if they wanted to stay above ground. Poe scowled, but sadly shut his mouth. I would have loved to see him get dragged away screaming and bleeding.

Lothar dismissed him, looking back down at me. "You need anything, babe, you got my number, yeah?"

I nodded, then watched as he gave Poe a menacing look before walking back the way he'd come. I wanted to run after him, to tell him what was happening, to beg for his help, but I couldn't. I was stuck.

"What the fuck was that?" Poe bit out.

"My friend, she's mated to a hound," I said. "He just came over to say hi. If I told him to leave, he would've known something was up."

He grunted and, with his arm still around me, dragged me away and down the main hall to make the exchange. Lars followed along behind us. "You tell that fucking hound anything and Luke dies, screaming, understand?"

Bastard. "I understand."

We walked into a room, and Lars shut us in. Poe held out his blood-covered hand and motioned for the bag. I handed it over, and he yanked down the zipper, checking it was all there. I'd adjusted Luke's recipe, making it more stable, but none of it had been easy. Just knowing I could be causing harm was making me physically ill.

He looked up. "Looks good. We want another delivery in two weeks, but this time double."

"Double? That's impossible. The ingredients are expensive. I can't do it."

He held his hand out to Lars, and the other demon handed him a roll of cash. "Tarrant is aware of the cost to you, and because of your good work, going forward you'll be paid."

"Which means Luke's debt is paid, right? So this can end."

"Wrong. It's over when Tarrant says it is. He does understand that Luke left you in a difficult position, though, so he's offering to be more accommodating, out of the kindness of his heart."

Bullshit. He just wanted to make sure he got his drugs. "I don't want your dirty money," I fired back at him, even as fear made my knees weak.

"Either you take it, or you don't, that's totally up to you. But you will be required to fulfill your delivery either way or...do you really need me to spell it out again?"

No, I did not. Reluctantly, I snatched the cash from him, counted out the amount I would need for ingredients, and handed back the rest.

Poe grinned. "You're adorable when you're being all righteous and stubborn."

"Are we done here?"

His gaze slid over me. "For now."

I spun and all but ran from the room. I fought my way through the crowd, avoiding the area where I'd seen Lothar, and finally made it back outside. I wasn't sure I took a full breath until I'd locked myself in my car and was headed back to my tiny studio apartment in the city.

I couldn't keep doing this, and I knew they had no plans of letting me off. I was making them too much money.

I had to find a way out. Somehow, I had to find a way to make this stop.

⸺))🌑((⸺

Jagger

Maddox swung. I ducked, nailing him in the side.

He grunted and returned with one of his own, forcing the air from my lungs.

Maddox commanded our brothers here in Hell for our alpha. War made regular visits, and all of us, except Mad, took shifts spending time between here and the compound.

We'd been sparring for a while, both of us needing to blow off steam. Mad always wanted to fight. Since the loss of his mate, my brother had been carrying around more aggression than he knew what to do with. She'd been taken from him in the most horrific of ways, and he'd come back to Hell afterward with no intention of returning aboveground. His pain had formed a hard shell around him, calcifying to protect him from the truth of what had happened, which was for the best honestly, but now all that remained was rage.

He slammed his fist into my stomach, and I returned with a blow of my own—

"Jag! Phone," Gus called.

I ducked Mad's haymaker and stepped back, waving Gus in. Maddox wasn't ready to stop just yet.

Gus jumped in like the eager pup he was, and I snatched up my buzzing phone. Lothar's name was on the screen.

I hit speaker. "What's up?" I leaped out of the fighting pit.

"Brother," he growled out, and there was a whole lot of noise in the background.

Just from that one word, I knew something was up. "What is it?"

"Your female was at the fights and, Jag—"

"She's an EMT. It's her job." It was on the tip of my tongue to correct him, to tell him she wasn't mine, but that would be a lie. It turned out she was. She always would be, I just couldn't have her, that was the difference.

"Nah, not working. She was dressed to kill, and there with a demon. Poe."

My chin jerked back. "What?"

"Had his hands on her." He made a rough sound. "The demon kissed her, brother."

I was vaguely aware that the sounds of fists hitting flesh had stopped, but I was too busy fighting down my murderous rage to pay much attention. Since Lucifer told me the truth, I'd been working at coming to terms with the realities of it. Reminding myself of why I couldn't have her. I knew Sutton would find someone eventually. I just hadn't thought it would be this soon, and not with a fucking demon. Especially a piece of shit like Poe.

The phone cracked in my hand, dangerously close to smashing to pieces, and I forced myself to loosen my grip.

"You need to talk to her," Loth said. "You need to stop this before she's in too deep with this asshole." Rome said something in the background. "Sorry, brother, gotta go."

We disconnected, and I stood there, fucking frozen, while red-hot rage throbbed through me. I hadn't seen her in a week, but it felt like an eternity. Time moved differently down here. My week would be close to four weeks for Sutton. Had she already given up on me?

That's what you want, asshole.

I growled, the sound as deranged as I felt.

"What the fuck are you standing there for?" Mad snarled behind me.

I hadn't even seen him get out of the pit. "The shit with me and Sutton is complicated, brother. I need to be careful how I play this."

"It's not complicated. She's your female, and she's unprotected. What the fuck, Jag. Go and fucking claim her. Go claim what's yours."

I planted my hands on my hips, while every muscle in my body prepared to fight, to do exactly what Mad said. "You know why I can't do that," I said through clenched teeth.

"Yeah, brother, she is going to die one day, but at least you get to be with her." His nostrils flared. "This pain, this fucking nightmare I'm living in, it means I got to be with Jane. Even if it was only for a short time. She was mine. She loved me, and I know what that felt like. You give that up? You're a fucking idiot," Mad snarled, then strode away.

Fuck.

My muscles tightened, twitching, and I tried to gain some semblance of control. It wasn't working.

I turned to Gus. "Going topside. Let Mad know when he's cooled down."

Gus gave me a chin lift, and I got the fuck out of Hell.

I didn't know what any of this meant? Or what would happen when I got to her. I only knew I had to protect her, and that Poe couldn't fucking have her.

Sutton was mine.

CHAPTER
ELEVEN

Sutton

QUICKLY AND CAREFULLY, I placed the jar I'd just filled with cemetery dirt into my bag, then wrapped the small bunch of Hyssop I'd risked taking in a damp cloth and tucked it in there as well.

Then froze at the sound of voices.

Shit.

The clink of the padlock on the iron cemetery gate came next.

I needed to get the hell out of here. Ducking low, I sprinted for one of the large trees that edged the fence line and tucked myself in as far as I could.

Boo chirped, then poked his head out from my jacket. I held my finger to my lips, and he ducked back.

Laughter carried through the darkness. My mother's. I'd know it anywhere. She laughed a lot, usually at people's expense. Chatter followed. My sister was with her, and another of my cousins—Harriet, by the sounds.

I'd needed ingredients for Tarrant's order, so risked coming back to the cemetery so soon. Now I was going to get caught and hauled in front of the witch's council.

I leaned back as far as I could go as they walked by, trying not to freaking breathe. They were terrible people, judgmental, cruel, but still it hurt. I tried not to let it, but the coven you were born into was part of you, it was in your blood. Being here always felt right, but tonight, standing here, hiding from my own mother, my sister, my family *again*, truly brought home just how unwelcome I would always be. I didn't belong here anymore.

I couldn't stay here and risk getting caught. I had to move. When they were far enough away and distracted, I pulled the hood of my sweatshirt up, slipped out from my hiding spot, and ran for the gate. I was just about there—

"Hey!" my mother yelled.

Oh no.

"Sutton! Is that you?"

"You thieving bitch," my sister screeched.

I didn't stop. I ran until I reached my car parked several blocks away, but my heart didn't slow, not until I was back in my apartment.

Stupid.

I should never have gone back so soon.

They'd make me pay for that.

I was screwed.

))●((

I strained against the gurney, fighting the binds strapping me down, panic filling me. The Chemist pulled on his black latex gloves and picked up his scalpel. The door opened and someone walked in. The Chemist paused as they approached.

Poe stood on the other side of the gurney and held out his hand. The Chemist gave him the scalpel and walked away.

"Now," Poe said, his black eyes dancing with excitement. "Where were we?"

Then he opened his mouth...and howled.

My eyes shot open.

I sat up, heart pounding, then held my breath, listening. The nightmare was awful, and not the first time I'd had it, but it wasn't what woke me up. Something else had.

Shit, had the witch's council come for me already? My mother would have called and reported me for trespassing, I had no doubt. The little studio I'd rented over a cigar shop in the center of the city was warded—still. I listened hard, but everything was silent. I shook my head, on edge after what happened tonight. The council wouldn't come in the middle of the night, not for trespassing, surely.

I forced myself to lie back down.

A howl echoed in the distance, making my heart lurch into my throat.

I shot back up, and Boo stopped chewing the fruit I'd put out for him. I'd heard it in my dreams, hadn't I? That's what woke me. That howl had reached through my dreams. Shoving back the covers, I stumbled out of bed and rushed to the window. Breathing heavily, hand shaking, I eased back the curtain.

I knew who I was going to see before I spotted him, because I realized I felt him close. Somehow, I felt him.

A huge hound sat in the dark street below my window, his eyes still green, glowing up at me.

What the hell was he doing here?

Pain flashed so bright through me, I moaned. Why was

he doing this? Gods. Not again. I battered the pain back with rage, pushing it down as deep as I could get it. Anger was much better, much easier. Much safer.

Dropping the curtain, I strode around my bed, snatched my phone from the bedside table, then stomped back to the window, where I jerked back the curtains and held up my phone. The massive hound blinked up at me, then shifted smoothly, going from four legs to two, black fur giving way to muscled, tattooed skin. Naked, he scooped up the jeans beside him and pulled them on, and then took something from his pocket, his phone.

I didn't want to talk to him. I didn't want to hear that deep gravelly voice, so instead, I messaged him.

Sutton: *Why are you here?*

I watched as he looked down at his phone, reading my message, then head bent, he tapped out his reply. Boo flew over to me, took a look out the window, then obviously unbothered, flew back and carried on eating. My phone beeped.

Jagger: *Loth saw you tonight. Don't want you hanging around Poe. That fucking demon is trouble, understand?*

I knew exactly the kind of trouble Poe was, but what the hell did it have to do with Jagger? He'd made his position clear.

Sutton: *Who I spend time with is none of your business.*

Jagger looked back down, and even from here I could see his shoulders stiffen. He stabbed at his phone screen with those long, thick fingers and my phone chimed again.

Jagger: *It's my concern when you're kissing that piece of shit.*

What now? Oh my freaking gods! My fury shot higher, so hard and fast that I felt dizzy. I couldn't ever remember being this angry. Even when I was kicked out of my coven, I hadn't reached this level of outrage.

I couldn't smile, I couldn't push down all the pain, not this time, not tonight.

He didn't want me, refused to admit we were even mates—and no, I didn't want Poe touching me, and certainly not kissing me, but Jagger didn't know that. He didn't want me, but no one else could have me either? Was that how this was going to go?

He'd been gone close to a month, nearly four weeks of no contact, because I didn't exist to him, I wasn't important —until he thought someone else wanted me?

How dare he toy with me like that. My fingers flew across my phone screen as I typed my response.

Sutton: *Your arrogance is astounding. Seriously something special. I don't know who the hell you think you are? Not mates, right? So who I kiss is none of your business. You made your choice, Jagger. Now you need to back the fuck off and live with it.*

I watched him read my message, then tap another reply, and when he looked up, his eyes had turned red.

Jagger: *My instincts to protect you aren't going anywhere, Sutton, so you're going to have to get used to it.*

I hissed, so incensed I wanted to open the window and throw my phone at his head.

Sutton: *I don't want your protection. Get that through your thick skull and leave me the hell alone. I don't want you. I'm over you completely.*

He read it, typed his reply, then looked back up and flashed his teeth.

Jagger: *You're wearing my shirt.*

I looked down at myself in horror. I was. I didn't even think about it. Every night, I told myself not to, and every night, I couldn't stop myself from putting it on. It smelled of him, even after I washed it, and being surrounded by his scent, it gave me comfort. I hated that I still felt that way.

I would not let him think I needed him, because I didn't. He was the one showing up at my place in the middle of the night. He was the one acting all jealous. Well, he couldn't have it both ways.

My vision turned red, my anger flipping the switch inside me, and I felt as if I was outside my body watching as I tossed my phone on the bed. Then snatching my knife from my bedside table, I yanked the curtains wider. Light from the sign across the street hit me as I climbed onto the wide windowsill.

Jagger froze, his hand still gripping his phone lowered to his side.

Grabbing the neck of the shirt, I lifted my razor-sharp knife and sliced, hacking and slashing it right down the front, destroying the shirt.

Hopefully, he got the message—I didn't want him either, or his fucking shirt.

·))）●(((·

Jagger

Sutton stood on the windowsill, my shirt sliced in two. She yanked it off completely, leaving her in only a pair of underwear. My gaze roamed over her bare skin glowing from the streetlights and highlighting the scars all over her beautiful body as she shoved open the waist-high window.

Scowling, she tossed my shirt at me—then, leaning forward, she lifted both hands, thrusting them out as well, and before I could say anything, not that I knew what the fuck to say anyway, she gave me a double-middle-finger salute, slammed the window closed, jumped down, and jerked the curtains closed.

Shutting me out.

I swallowed thickly. Fuck, my female was a warrior, scarred inside and out from the battles she'd fought and survived—and tonight, she'd never looked more fierce.

I realized in that moment, I was panting, the beast rolling and pushing against my flesh to get free, demanding we go and get her, that we take her home to our den and never let her out.

Coming here was a bad idea, but how the fuck could I stay away? And now that I'd seen her again after being parted from her, I wasn't sure I could leave her again.

My hand was fucking trembling as I quickly typed out another message.

Jagger: *Let me in, Sutton.*

Going in was a bad idea as well, but every instinct in me roared for it, roared for me to get closer to her, right the fuck now.

I waited, but there was no answer.

Jagger: *Open the door. Now. We need to talk.*

Still, no reply came. I strode to the door and tried the door handle, and her ward sent a bolt through me, not strong enough to stop me but strong enough to shock some sense into me.

What the fuck was I doing?

An image of Poe touching her, kissing her, slammed through me again, and I snarled. I hadn't seen it for myself, but my mind was throwing up images and adding some embellishments of its own. Like him stripping my female naked, like him tasting her bare skin—tossing her on the bed and coming down on top of her, of him—

I gripped the sides of my head and shook it with a growl.

Yeah, it was probably a fucking good thing she wouldn't let me in. It was hard, but I made myself step back, away from her door, instead of breaking it down, which is what I really wanted to fucking do right then.

Before I approached her again, I needed to get my shit together.

I needed to think about what the hell I was going to do.

And if I truly thought I could leave her a third time, when everything in me demanded I stay.

CHAPTER TWELVE

Sutton

My breath misted in front of me as I approached the huge multistory building. It was old and terrifying, and the last place I wanted to be, but I was out of options.

I glanced over my shoulder again. Walking around Seventh Circle at night by myself wasn't the cleverest thing I'd ever done, which was why I'd left Boo at home, but I needed help and taking my car was too risky. For obvious reasons, I couldn't go to the hounds or my coven. I couldn't go to anyone who Tarrant or Poe would expect—or could be watching.

If I wanted help, and I did, I needed to go to someone as equally as scary as Tarrant.

People were getting hurt, and I couldn't take Poe's revolting attentions much longer.

Evil kept coming into my life, over and over again. I was trapped in a twisted game of pass the parcel, except it was a scalpel being passed from one monster to the next, all desperate for their pound of flesh. I didn't want to play anymore.

I needed it to stop.

I took in the nearly two-hundred-year-old building. Dark moss had overtaken the stone walls of the massive gothic-style building. I looked up at its arched windows. The place filled me with a horrible awe, every time. It looked like something from medieval England.

Back in the 1800s, it was known as the Sunnydale Insane Asylum. The place had been decommissioned in the early 1980s and was now occupied by demons—and home to the head demon. Rune had been appointed by Lucifer to oversee the demons living in Roxburgh. He'd made this part of the city, now known as Seventh Circle, home.

Rushing through the gate, I jogged past the large shadowy garden, up the main stairs, and stopped outside the wide, heavy doors. Taking a deep breath to steady my nerves, I knocked.

Heavy footfalls sounded on the other side of the door. I really didn't want to have to come here. I'd always made a concerted effort to avoid Rune. He was terrifying, saw too much, was crazy powerful and gave me seriously weird vibes. I always felt as if I wasn't completely in control around him. People dropped their filters, sometimes their inhibitions, when he was in the room. He didn't take control or manipulate you, as such, he just muted the little voice of reason that talked you out of doing questionable things. I always imagined a mini angel and devil on my shoulders when I was near him, only the angel was gagged, leaving the little devil to whisper unchallenged.

But since I had demon blood, I had every right to be in

Seventh Circle, and every right to ask for a meeting with Rune.

The door opened and a demon, a very large one, looked down at me, then his gaze darted behind me and back down. He frowned. "What do you want?"

I glanced over my shoulder, confused, then back and smiled brightly. "I'm sorry for coming so late, but I was really hoping I could see Rune."

He grunted a humorless laugh. "Like you said, you're too late."

"Is he not here? Too late for what?"

He all but rolled his eyes. "For a place in his bed. The spot was filled. You'll need to get here earlier next time." He started to shut the door.

I threw out a hand, stopping it.

The demon scowled, jerking it open. "What the fuck?"

"I'm not here for that. I need help. I need to *talk* to Rune."

He looked me up and down. "What kind of help?"

"It wouldn't be in my best interest to divulge that information to anyone but him." I gripped the strap of my bag tighter. "It's something he'll want to know," I lied. Whether or not he cared enough to help was a crapshoot, but it was a gamble I was willing to take. "And if he finds out I came here and you sent me away—"

"Fine," he grunted and opened the door wider. "But you'll have to wait until he's finished."

Finished with all the sex he was having I assumed. Awesome.

He closed the door, shutting me inside. "Down the hall, take a left at the end, then take the elevator to the top floor. Wait outside. I'll let him know you're here. Whether or not he lets you in is up to him."

"Thank you," I said and headed down the hall, my boots thudding on the cracked and stained linoleum.

"And I wouldn't advise you to get off on any of the other floors. You do, that shit's on you," he said after me.

That didn't sound ominous *at all.*

My nerves shot higher as I rushed down the hall. The vibes in this place were cold, eerie...gods, spooky, and the smell? There was still a background scent of hospital, but there were other, seriously horrendous things mixed in.

I rushed past a lot of closed doors, then finally rounded a corner and got into the ancient elevator. When the doors slid closed, I made sure I hit the button for the top floor, and it shot up, finally bouncing to a stop when I reached the top.

If you told me a few months ago that I would be waiting outside the apartment of the most powerful demon I knew, while he had sex with some random female, I would have called you a stinking liar.

But here I was.

I stepped into the foyer. There was just the one door, so at least there wasn't any confusion. With a groan, I rubbed my tired eyes. Gods, I'd rather be literally anywhere but here.

I had no idea how long a wait I'd have, so I sat on the floor across from the door and tried to make myself comfortable. I wrapped my jacket more firmly around me, to fight off the chill that always lingered in this place. It was like a too-tight icy embrace that you couldn't escape. I shivered, and tried not to think about it. Taking my phone from my bag, I opened Nightscape and, masochist that I'd become, searched *desperate demon gets brutally rejected,* to see if the views had slowed down. They had, a little. At least that was something, I guess, but considering it had been seen by thousands of Nightscape subscribers from all over the world, I wasn't about to start celebrating.

There was also a message from Jagger.

Sorry about last night.

That was all it said. That probably meant he'd left again, that he'd returned to Hell. Good. I hope he stayed there this time. Maybe he'd finally gotten it through his head that what he'd done last night was a massive overstep. That him showing up like he had, telling me what to do, like he had a right to, acting like protecting me was so important to him, like he cared, when I knew for a fact he didn't, was not okay.

My face heated. Maybe my moment of temporary insanity last night, cutting off his shirt and throwing it at him, had done the trick?

Still, my heart hurt just from the thought of him leaving. Gods, a sense of loss filled me to overflowing. My body and mind were at complete odds, and I couldn't take it anymore. *Shove it down.*

Popping in my earbuds, I hit play on my feminine rage playlist, rested my head against the wall, and closed my eyes.

I jolted awake—then shrieked at the massive male-shaped shadow towering over me.

My hand flew to my pounding heart, and I sucked in a breath.

Rune.

He stood there, wearing only a pair of dark pants. His chest was inked and scarred and muscled. He'd been branded in several places—then I realized I was ogling and quickly lifted my gaze, and it locked on to his. His eyes were otherworldly, the color somewhere between yellow and green.

"Sutton, my apologies," he said, his voice resonating all around us. "I didn't mean to startle you."

I had no idea how he remembered my name, but he knew everyone's names, at least those of us who were demon, or in my case, part demon, like some kind of demonic Santa. He could have woken me with kitten licks or butterfly kisses and I still would've jumped out of my freaking skin when I saw him.

"Yes...uh, sorry to, um, loiter outside your apartment."

The elevator dinged, and I turned to see two females, flushed and giggling, getting in.

I turned back to him, taking a steadying breath to withstand how much power flowed from him. Gods, it was heavy and thick and made me hot and cold and trembly inside. I knew showing weakness to this male was dumb, but I honestly didn't have the energy to be strong right then. Which was stupid. This male was Lucifer's sidekick; I doubted he had much empathy to spare, if he had any at all.

He held out his hand, those pale, terrifying eyes sliding over me. "You've been waiting a long time. I'm sure you'd rather talk somewhere more comfortable?"

Reluctantly, I took his hand and scrambled to my feet. He didn't release me, no, he curled his fingers around mine and led me into his apartment. I didn't dare pull away.

His place was the entire top floor of the old asylum and set up as one huge open space, apart from the bedroom and bathroom which were walled off. There were lots of windows, and the night sky twinkled with stars all around us. I'd heard this used to be a rooftop garden that was walled in during the 1950s. It was pretty cool. Definitely not as creepy as the rest of the building.

"It's nice in here. Warm." Unlike the rest of the building.

"Thank you. I like it."

He led me across the room, and I smiled brightly up at him, feeling fully at ease all of a sudden. He lifted my hand and dipped his head, then breathed deep. Scenting me? He made an appreciative sound, all rough and velvety. I liked it.

"Why did you do that?" I asked, and knew somewhere deep inside, I would never have asked that usually, but again, I felt safe right then, relaxed.

Rune grinned, flashing a set of vampy-looking fangs. He wasn't a vampire, though, he was another kind of blood drinker, soul collector, like Fern. "I wondered if you were taken. It seems you're not."

"How do I smell?" I asked and again, somewhere deep inside, I was screaming at myself to shut the hell up, but I wasn't going to, I couldn't.

"You smell like spices, and witch, with just a hint of brimstone. It's delicious."

I lifted his hand and sniffed the back, over the tattoos there.

He chuckled huskily.

I tilted my head back. "I wondered if my demon powers would kick in and I'd be able to recite a list for you as well."

"And?"

"Well, you smell like sex, mainly."

"And what else?"

"Your cologne, it's yummy."

He grinned again. "I don't wear cologne."

"Oh."

He motioned to the couch, and I sat. He sat beside me, draping his arm along the back. "So, are you taken, lovely?"

"No, I'm not. My mate rejected me." My mind yelled at

me to shut the hell up. I ignored it. I felt warm and happy and kind of sleepy.

His brow slid up. "And who is the fool who rejected you?"

"Jagger. He's a hellhound. You probably know him?"

His eyes sparkled. "Oh yes, I know him." He slid his phone from his pocket. "Before we get to the business of why you're here, shall we take a photo and send it to him? Shall we see if we can make steam come out of his ears?"

"What kind of photo?"

"One that makes him jealous," he said, those pale eyes still glittering. "A male who spits in the face of the fates, who rejects such a precious gift, should be made to suffer, don't you think?"

I snorted. "He doesn't get jealous over me. I mean, he showed up when he thought I was hanging with someone dangerous, but it's just the hound in him. You know, like an animal thing, instinct to protect me. It's not actually because he wants me. Anyway, I'm pretty sure he's gone back to Hell. He won't care about a picture. He won't respond."

"Would you like to make a wager?"

"What kind of wager?"

"We send him a photo, and if he loses his shit, you win. If he doesn't reply, I do."

Hadn't he been listening? That was the opposite of what I said. Why would I make a bet I'd lose?

Rune was dangerous, but only to demons who broke the rules. There was no way Jagger would be worried about me being here. I was part demon, Rune was the male in charge of demons in the city. He was no real threat to me, not if I was behaving. "I'll definitely lose, and it'll just hurt again when he proves he doesn't care."

Rune tucked my hair behind my ear and snapped a picture, then held it up. I was staring up at him, my face all flushed and eyes bright, and Rune's tattooed hand was against my cheek.

"He won't reply," I said again. "I don't think we should send it."

"Would you like to hear my terms first?"

I shrugged. "Sure."

He chuckled again. "If he replies in a way that shows jealousy, I'll give you whatever it is that you've come here for, and I won't charge my usual fee. You'll get the friends and family rate, how does that sound?"

"I mean, it sounds great, but it won't work," I said.

His lips twitched. "Don't be so defeatist."

"He literally rejected me in a room full of people. I am defeated." I felt drowsy and rested my head against the back of the couch. "You obviously know I'm right because why else would a demon risk pissing off a hellhound. He could hurt you."

He winked. "Only Lucifer can call me home. The hounds have no authority over me."

"They don't?"

"Nope. And you said yourself he showed up when he thought you were in danger, that it was an animal reaction, right? I'm a powerful demon, you're here all alone. Some would consider that alarming. So you have just as much of a chance as winning here."

I shook my head. "This'll be an easy win for you."

"Only one way to find out."

"What happens if I lose?" I realized he hadn't shared that when he'd given me his terms.

"No friends and family rates for whatever brought you here tonight. Full price."

I didn't know what Rune's *price* was, but I'd come here prepared to pay it, so it wasn't like I'd be losing anything.

"Shall I send it?" he asked, tilting his head to the side.

A sad, reckless, and yes, desperate little part of me hoped Jagger would get jealous. "Fine. Go for it."

He typed something, then hit send. "Now we wait—"

My phone rang.

Rune threw his head back and laughed, a deep pleasant sound that lifted goose bumps all over me.

I checked the screen. "It's Jagger."

"Are you going to answer it?"

Was I? It stopped—then started again. Rune laughed harder.

I got the feeling Jagger would keep ringing until I answered.

I tapped the screen.

"What the fuck are you doing?" he said before I could say a word.

"Jagger?" I said, even though I knew it was him. I felt kind of tipsy, honestly, and not totally myself. "Why are you calling me? I told you to leave me alone."

"Get out of that apartment and get your ass downstairs, now."

"What?" I rasped.

"He followed you here," Rune said and winked.

I remembered the demon looking over my shoulder when I got here. Rune already knew Jagger was out there. "Why did you follow me?"

"Because you're a reckless little idiot who obviously needs protection."

"That wasn't very nice," Rune said.

"No, it wasn't. That wasn't very nice, Charming," I said

to Jagger. "And maybe you should stop talking to me like I'm one of the hounds you order around every day."

"You think Rune is being nice, Sutton? For fuck's sake. Leave that fucker's apartment right the fuck now."

"Stop cursing at me. You're always cursing at me, and Rune is nice." Rune winked. "He's also extremely handsome in a scary, sexy kind of way."

"Thank you, lovely," Rune said, a wicked and highly amused expression on his face. "You're rather beautiful yourself."

Jagger growled, so loud I jumped. "If you touch her while you have her all hopped up on your fucking demon mojo, I'll shred you and deal with the fallout from Lucifer later."

Rune laughed again, dark and gritty. "If you want to wait outside for Sutton until we're done with our conversation, feel free, but we have business to take care of, isn't that right, beautiful?"

"Yep, that's right...handsome."

Rune almost busted a gut laughing, while Jagger snarled, then roared. I heard him through the phone and echoing from outside somewhere at the same time.

He was definitely here.

"I think you should hang up now," Rune said.

"Oh, yes, you're probably right."

"Don't you fucking dare—"

I hung up.

"You won," Rune said.

"I don't know, was that really jealousy? I think it was more just a penis-measuring contest."

Rune grinned wider, flashing his fangs again. "Penis measuring, huh?"

"Yep. I'm not sure I factored at all, honestly. Jagger

doesn't want me, but he doesn't seem to want anyone else to have me either."

"Then perhaps we'll let him stew for a bit?"

I nodded and yawned. "Sounds good."

"So, lovely, how about you tell me why you're here?"

I blinked, and my eyes felt heavy. "Right, of course. The reason I'm here."

Rune sat back and waited, and I forced myself to sit up straight before I fell asleep. "Well, I've got myself in a bit of trouble with a not very nice demon. His name's Tarrant. Do you know him?"

Rune's gaze sharpened. "Oh, yes, I know him. How about you tell me what's been going on?"

I spilled, telling him everything. What Luke did, about Poe and Lars and all the drugs I'd been making for them. I couldn't stop talking even if I wanted to. When I finally finished, he said nothing, just stared at me for a long time, a look in his eyes that made me squirm.

He looked…angry. Really, really angry.

"I'm sorry," I choked out.

His head tilted to the side. "What are you sorry for?"

"I—I don't know. You just look really angry." My stomach was in knots, the vibes pouring off Rune made me want to hide under the nearest piece of furniture and curl into a trembling ball.

"I am angry, but not at you." He rubbed his hand over his jaw. "Do you know my fee for those who come here for favors? Serious ones, like yours?"

I shook my head.

"I'm in the business of collecting souls, Sutton."

My entire body froze. Of course he was. He was a freaking soul collector.

"But I offered you the friends and family rate remember?"

I nodded, while my heart thumped wildly in my chest.

"So instead of your eternal soul, I need you to do something for me."

"What do you want me to do?" I rasped.

He studied me, and I bit my lip to stop the whimper from escaping. "You've already been associating with Tarrant, you're already on their payroll, they think you're one of them."

"They're blackmailing me."

He shrugged. "You're still on the inside, as it were."

"Not really."

"There's only so much I can do when it comes to Tarrant. He isn't your average demon. He's connected, closely related to one of the lords, Beelzebub to be exact. Accusing him of something without proof would not be good for my position here in this city. I'm close with Lucifer, yes, but I'm not a lord. That puts me in a precarious position. I need proof of his wrongdoing before I can make a move, and that's where you come in."

"Proof of the drugs? I can do that easily. I can just—"

"No. Not the drugs. In the eyes of Lucifer, what he's doing isn't grounds for punishment. It's not forbidden. The only criteria for staying aboveground is leaving humans alone. You're not human, and neither is your friend. This isn't something I can get involved with. If I had evidence that humans were somehow involved in his business, though..."

"You think that they are? That he's somehow messing with humans?"

He studied me again, his gaze sliding over my face as if he were looking inside me, assessing if I was worthy of the truth. "I do," he said. "I'm not sure in what capacity, but I think Tarrant has decided he doesn't need to play by the rules. I just don't know what he's doing and since he and I are...well, we're not exactly the best of friends, I can't get close. But you, lovely, might be able to help me with that. You get the proof, and all your troubles will be over."

I chewed my lip. "That sounds kind of dangerous."

"No more danger than you're already in. It sounds like Poe has a soft spot for you, maybe you could use that to your advantage?"

"He makes me sick to my stomach."

Rune grinned again, and a wave of tiredness washed over me. "Yes, he has that effect on people." He winked. "If you do this for me, you can't tell anyone, especially not Jagger. He may have rejected you, but he still has the same instincts to protect you, and that could cause issues." He tilted his head to the side once again. "You have a lot to contemplate. How about you rest for a while and think it over?"

I nodded. That sounded like a really good idea. Especially since I couldn't keep my eyes open. "Okay," I said, and the words came out slurred.

I slumped back, and then Rune scooped me up in his arms and we were moving. He laid me down on a cloud, and I sighed as he pulled something warm and soft over me.

"Night, lovely."

"Night, Rune."

CHAPTER THIRTEEN

Jagger

With a roar, I kicked his door off the hinges and stormed into Rune's apartment.

"Where is she?" I snarled. "She better be unharmed or I'll tear that grin off your face, motherfucker."

Rune sipped his coffee and waved away the demons who'd followed me up here but hadn't dared try to stop me. Wise choice. I would have killed anyone who got in my way.

Rune placed his drink on the table in front of him, stood, then tilted his fucking head for me to follow. It was taking all of my self-control not to shred him into fleshy ribbons. My fingers itched, my claws right there, ready to burst from the tips. I wanted to tear his head from his body and watch him dissolve into dust.

If I did that, though, Lucifer would be pissed enough

that he might stop me from coming aboveground for an unspecified amount of time, keeping me from Sutton. Rune knew it, too, which was why he was probably the only demon in this city not afraid of me or any hound.

Rune walked into the room at the back of the large space and stopped at the foot of his bed. Lying there, curled in a ball and so out of it that she was snoring softly, was Sutton.

I spun to the demon, grabbed him by the throat, and slammed him against the wall. "You used your twisted fucking power and forced yourself on my female?" I felt my features transform, my face partially shifting as my jaw and nose elongated into the hound, my teeth sliding down into sharp points, ready to tear flesh and snap bone.

The grin on Rune's face vanished, and he bared his fangs. He grabbed my wrist, power pulsing from him. He was fucking strong, I knew that firsthand, but he would tire before I did.

"I didn't touch your female, hound. Not in the way you just accused me of. I do not fuck drugged or unwilling females. I do not use my power to influence them in that way, *ever*. If I wanted to have Sutton, I wouldn't have let you inside this building. I would've waited for her to wake, and when my powers had worn off, I would have offered myself to her." He flashed an evil grin. "And since she's been left feeling unwanted and unfulfilled by her mate, I doubt she would have been hard to convince."

"You know nothing." I squeezed his throat tighter, and Rune laughed.

"I know you rejected her," he rasped. "I know you have no rights to that female, not anymore. You gave them up."

I snarled, squeezing his throat harder, so hard any other being's bones would have snapped under my grip by now, and got in his face. "If you come anywhere near her again, I will end you."

Rune pushed against my hold in a show of strength. "She came to me."

I roared in his face. "What did she want with you?"

He said nothing.

"Did you trick her out of her fucking soul?"

"You'll have to ask her that," he said, that self-satisfied look back on his face.

Fury slammed into me, along with an emotion I hadn't felt in a long fucking time, a feeling I did not fucking want —fear. Fear for Sutton. I shoved him away, ignoring his husky laughter as I scooped Sutton from his bed and strode out of the apartment.

I didn't know why she'd come here tonight, but Rune wasn't going to share that information with me. If he'd bartered for her soul, though, nothing would hold me back from straight-up murdering that piece of shit.

Whether or not I'd claimed Sutton as my mate was beside the point. She was mine, and even Lucifer couldn't deny my right to seek retribution.

I held her close as I took the elevator to the bottom floor, snarling at the demons who hovered, following me as I carried her out of the building.

It was the middle of the night, and I only spotted a few demons here and there as I strode along the streets, making my way out of Seventh Circle.

Sutton hadn't roused once, still seriously doped up on Rune's powers. He'd done a fucking number on her.

I'd followed her on foot, so had to carry her to her place a few blocks out of Seventh. I finally reached her door, took her keys from her pocket, and unlocked it. I grabbed the handle, and her ward throbbed through my hand, up my arm, and nailed me in the chest. *Fuck*. I needed to get inside.

I cupped her face. "Sutton, I need you to wake up now." The last thing I wanted to do was force my way through it. I wanted her to feel safe. I wanted her to trust me. I jostled her gently. "Baby, wake up."

She blinked heavily and stared up at me, and as soon as her pretty, sleepy eyes met mine, my heart slammed into my ribs and my fucking knees went weak.

"Jagger?"

"It's okay, you're okay. Need you to let me past your ward, sunshine."

She smiled, and it was goofy and cute and bright as the fucking sun. Yeah, she was still totally fucked up. "Okay," she said and lifted her hand, reaching for the door. She giggled. "Closer, please, driver."

Fucking hell, I wanted to kiss her, badly. I wanted to kiss that gorgeous little smile, taste it. I carried her closer to the door like she asked, and she pressed her hand to it, recited her spell, and included my name, granting me permission to enter. The ward gave, I felt it, like an opening was created in the barrier just to let me through.

I carried her upstairs to her place and let us in—her familiar swooped out of nowhere, diving at my head. I ducked and took in her tiny apartment. The bed was against one wall, a table, a tiny couch, a dresser and a TV, and not much else.

What the fuck was she doing here instead of the safety of Ashborne house?

The bat swooped again, chattering nonstop, trying to protect Sutton, which was illogical but admirable considering his size. Her little familiar was as brave as she was.

Sutton was out of it again, a deadweight draped over

my arms. She felt so light, though, like there was nothing to her. She was a small female as it was, but there was less of her now, like she'd lost weight. I didn't like that.

I didn't want to let her go, but I forced myself to lay her on the bed. She pressed her face into the pillow and moaned before curling up tight. I crouched beside her and slid off her shoes, then pulled her quilt over her.

I took her in, fucking enthralled by the way her thick lashes rested against her flushed cheeks. "What's going on in that head of yours, baby?"

The bat landed on the lampshade above us, hanging upside down, watching.

"Not gonna hurt her," I said to him, unsure if he'd understand. He didn't react when I ran my fingers down the side of Sutton's face, though, so he must have realized I was no threat. I looked back at her and touched her face a second time, desperate for the feel of her, to touch her. I fucking craved her arms around me. I smoothed her hair. She'd cut off all that pretty, soft honey-colored hair. But yeah, she looked beautiful with it like this as well. Running my fingers through the soft strands, unable to resist, I then leaned in and buried my nose against her hair and breathed, taking in her scent.

Every cell in my body fired to life, every nerve ending sparking with pleasure and a sense of rightness. I dragged my nose along her jaw, her throat, groaning at the way her scent deepened where it was warmer.

I rubbed my face against her, the beast in the driver's seat now, and I let myself be taken over by instinct. I let myself give in to the heart of what I was—an animal.

After seeing her in Rune's bed, smelling his scent on her, even if it was only subtle, I needed to wipe it away, suffocate it under my own. So I rubbed my face against her jaw, her throat, her shoulder. I picked up her hand and pressed it to my mouth. My tongue darted out, tasting her skin, and I bit back a growl, forcing myself to release her before I fucking stripped her down to make sure I got my scent on every part of her. That's what the beast wanted. More than anything, the beast wanted every male around to know who she belonged to.

You can't have it both ways. You can't touch her, mark her with your scent, then deny and reject your connection.

Placing her hand carefully at her side, I tucked the covers around her, and just as I was about to step back, she grabbed hold of my hand and pulled me closer. I let her, powerless to pull away from her touch, letting her draw me nearer. She wrapped her arms around my bicep and pressed her face to it, muttering in her sleep.

She rubbed her face against me, like I just had her, and I dragged in a breath to try to control the fierce, contented rumble in my chest. I couldn't move, everything in me refused to pull away, so I planted my ass on the floor beside the bed while she hugged my arm.

Hounds craved touch, and I was fucking blissed out, probably feeling almost as high as she was right then, just from her touch alone. I couldn't take my eyes off her. This was dangerous, allowing myself to give in to this feeling. Allowing her to touch me this way. My emotions, though still few, still stunted, were pushing forward with force.

I couldn't allow that. I couldn't allow it to progress much more than this. I wouldn't survive with my sanity intact at the end of it all. So yeah, this was dangerous for me, but knowing that, even feeling those new burgeoning tendrils of fear because of it, I still couldn't pull away from her. I still couldn't get the fuck up and move away.

I don't know how long I sat there with Sutton clinging

to me, hours, long enough that her familiar had gone to sleep, and I could now see faint sunlight below the curtains—and when she did finally release me with a sigh and rolled to her back, I was fucking panting. My skin was scalding hot and prickled with sweat. I was a hellhound, I thrived on the heat, I walked through hellfire and felt nothing, yet this little female had me sitting here sweating like a mortal.

Blowing out an unsteady breath, I forced myself off the floor and strode to the table. I needed to know what she was up to. There was some mail and a grocery list on the table, but not much else. I worked my way around the small room, searching for—fuck knows what, but something wasn't right.

I opened her drawers and shoved her clothes aside, looking for anything she might have hidden. Nothing. I yanked open the smaller top drawer and stilled. Pretty lace, soft cotton, so many delicate scraps of fabric overflowed the small space. My mind immediately threw up images of Sutton wearing them. I shook my head, trying to shake them away, but they weren't going anywhere. I shoved the drawer closed and turned to the laundry basket. My stomach clenched when I tilted my head back and breathed deep.

I could smell her pussy. Before I knew what I was doing, I picked up the blue pair of panties tucked in beside some jeans, pressed them to my nose, and breathed deeply. I groaned as my cock thickened, straining against the front of my jeans—

"What are you doing?" Sutton said stiltedly behind me.

I spun around, and fuck, her underwear was still balled in my fist, like some fucking panty-sniffing weirdo. *You literally just sniffed them, fuckhead.* Heat washed over me, but different than before. My face was hot. What the fuck was that?

Sutton's eyes widened. "Were you...sniffing my underwear?"

"No."

"You were. I saw you."

I shoved the panties back in the laundry basket. "That's not what I was doing." I crossed my arms. "Something's wrong with you. Something's off, and I—"

"Thought the answer was among my dirty laundry? That sniffing my undies would provide you with all the answers you desperately needed?"

I growled, feeling like a fucking fool, another thing I wasn't accustomed to. "You moved here, you cut your fucking hair, you went to Rune when you needed help and not—"

"You?"

I ground my teeth but gave her a sharp nod because, yes, that's what I wanted. Despite not believing her, then pushing her away, yes, that's exactly what I wanted.

Her brows lifted and she shook her head as she pushed herself up in her bed. "Are you serious?"

There was no anger in her voice. It wasn't raised. I didn't know what she was feeling, I couldn't name it, and that frustrated the hell out of me. When Sutton walked into a room, it warmed, as if the sun followed her around. Looking at her now, that was gone. The warmth was all gone. It made my stomach hurt. I didn't know how to respond to her question after coming to that realization, and I barely resisted rubbing at the ache in my chest.

"I don't know what you want from me, Jagger. I really don't. What are you even doing here right now? How did I get here?"

"Rune texted me you were with him. He used his powers on you, doped you up." His scent hadn't been strong on her, but I wouldn't be satisfied until I heard the truth of what happened from her. "Did he force himself on you?"

"What? No. He didn't harm me." She shoved back the covers and climbed out of bed, then pulled off her shirt, leaving her in only a small tank top that exposed her belly and arms, and I couldn't stop myself from eating up the sight of her bare skin.

"The witch's council prefers not to deal with hybrids like me, and since I have demon blood and Rune has never turned me away, or made me feel less than because I'm not a pure-blooded demon, he's the person I decided to go to." She pulled a clean shirt from her drawer and yanked it on, then her gaze slid to me. "He is the only person I could go to."

"That's bullshit." A growl slipped free.

She huffed out a laugh, but it held no real humor. "Whatever. Look, I have to get to work. You need to leave."

"I can take you. My bike's downstairs—"

"Nope." She turned her back on me, carrying on getting ready as if I wasn't there. "You know the way out," she said, then walked into the bathroom and shut the door.

I didn't want to leave. Striding to the door she'd shut herself behind, I lifted my hand to the flimsy piece of wood between us and curled my fingers into a tight fist, then yanked it back. I wanted to stay here with her, to touch her again so badly, which was why I had to get the hell out of here now.

Somehow, I managed to make myself leave her apartment, but it wasn't easy. I should go back to Hell, that would be the right thing to do, the sensible thing.

But I couldn't do it.

I'd fought as hard as I could. I couldn't fight this pull between us any longer.

I realized I didn't want to. Sutton had little by little stripped my resolve, and she hadn't even tried. Her mere existence had so easily unraveled me.

And honestly, I just wanted her.

I wanted my mate.

Maddox was right. Having her for however long that was, was worth the pain I'd feel when I lost her. But there was a solution for that as well, wasn't there?

The idea solidified as I headed for the door, then someone banged on it, hard. My hackles instantly lifted. They pounded on it again, and I yanked the door open.

A small female stood there, staring up at me with an alarmed expression on her face. She quickly got it together, though, and going by how similar her features were to Sutton's, I guessed I was looking at her mother. She was nowhere near as beautiful, though. Her narrowed eyes and pinched mouth made her look mean. The bitch who had thrown Sutton out, tossing her aside like garbage when she was too young to be out on her own without protection, was scowling up at me. She had two witches with her, both I knew were on the witch's council.

"Who are you?" Sutton's mother fired at me.

I crossed my arms. "No, you're the one who rolled up to Sutton's door, and since I know who you are and what you did to her, I know it was without an invitation, which means I'll be asking the questions. What the fuck do you want?"

She flinched, then puffed up like an angry hen. "Sutton trespassed on our cemetery. She's been stealing from us, the goddess knows how long she's been doing it, and she will answer to the council for it."

I lifted my gaze to the council members, knowing dismissing her would piss her off. "You got proof?"

The female bit her lip. I'd met the male before. Nathan Trotman. I knew him as honest and a friend to Willow's family. He held my gaze as he replied, and it was weighted. "Mrs. Ellis says she saw her." He didn't like the bitch either.

"You saw her? When? What time?" I asked.

"Yes, I saw her. Two nights ago, around eight thirty," she said, looking smug.

"You saw her face?"

"Well...it was dark, but it was her. I know it was," she said, those lips so fucking tight now it looked like she was sucking on a lemon.

"No," I said. "Sutton was with me."

"You're lying!" she squawked.

"You got no proof she was even there, and I'm telling you she was with me. Couldn't have been her. So you need to back the fuck up, and get the fuck gone. That's the fucking end of it." I looked at Trotman. "Anything else, or are we done?"

"We're done. Thank you for clearing that up for us, Jagger."

I gave him a chin lift.

Sutton's mother kept firing accusations as the council members led her away. I watched, not willing to leave until I was sure they'd gone and weren't coming back to ambush Sutton as soon as I left.

"You didn't need to do that."

I turned and found Sutton standing halfway up the stairs.

"Yeah, I did. Your mother's a bitch."

"There were herbs I needed, and I—"

"Don't need to explain to me."

She hugged herself. "Well, thanks...for covering for me." She still wasn't willing to give me an inch, but I got it, especially after just coming face to face with her mother.

"No problem, sunshine. They come back, let me know."

She smiled, like she always did when she was in pain. Trying to hide it from the world. "I told you I can take care of myself."

Yeah, she wasn't ready to give in, and I got that too. My sunshine had been hurt too much in her short life, by too many people, and that included me.

I nodded, then forced myself to leave, giving her the space she wanted, even though all I wanted to do was climb those stairs, pull her into my arms, and tell her I'd always have her back, no matter what.

As soon as I shut the door behind me, I hit Lucifer's number.

"Jag, my man," he answered after a few rings.

I stopped by my bike. "I have a follow-up to our last conversation."

"I'm listening," he said without pause.

"Will you grant Sutton immortality?"

He was silent a beat. "If I do that for you, then I'll have to—"

"You did it for Willow and her sisters. You won't do it for me? I've been loyal to you for over a thousand years, Lucifer."

"You know how this works," he said, his voice hardening. "Immortality isn't something I can give out willy-nilly, I can't just hand it out when someone asks. There are checks and balances, Jag, you know this. There has to be good reason, and you haven't provided me with one."

I knew this, of course, but still I had to ask. "Will you

end my life when Sutton dies? Will you take me out as well?"

There was a long pause. "So you're going to mate her?"

"Yes." I was done resisting. "So will you do it?"

"Are you sure you want that? I'd hate to lose you, Jag. You're one of my children, you know that."

"Yes, it's what I want."

Another pause. "If that's what you truly want."

"It is." I would not live on without her. How I felt now was bad enough, and I hadn't even claimed her in truth yet.

"Then the deal is done."

Lucifer ended the call, and I shoved my phone back in my pocket.

Finally, I could breathe. For the first time in a long time, I could fucking breathe again.

Now I just had to get Sutton to forgive me.

·)))·●·(((·

Sutton

This is so stupid. You're going to get yourself killed.

I'd agreed to Rune's deal, but what choice did I have? I was out of options. Luke could already be dead, and if he wasn't, he was probably wishing he was, and I couldn't live like this any longer.

I hid among a large group of human females and, staying low, watched as Lars strode through the warehouse.

My only option was to get intel for Rune. He was the only one who could help me, the only one with the power to get me out of this nightmare. Luke and I wouldn't be going home until we were free from Tarrant.

Which meant I was currently following Lars. He kept walking, weaving through the crowd, while retro house music throbbed through the room. A DJ stood on a stage at the front, and people danced all around me while lights flashed.

I watched as the demon checked out the room filled with both other and human. Every now and then he'd stop, say something to someone dancing, and nine times out of ten, there was an exchange. He was selling, and though I couldn't see what he was handing over, I knew it was mine. Guilt filled me. I'd made it, and it was as safe as I could get it without losing effectiveness, but if anyone got sick, or hurt, or worse because of me, I wasn't sure I could live with it.

That's when I spotted a group of demons standing against the wall not far from him. They were scoping out the room, paying special attention to the people Lars had just sold drugs to. What the hell were they doing? What were they waiting for?

A moment later, I saw a female veer to the side, stumbling, and like a well-choreographed dance, one of the demons swooped in, flung her arm around his shoulder, and, smiling and laughing like they were old friends, led her toward the exit.

Oh fuck.

They were with Lars, he drugged people, and they were taking them from the warehouse to gods only knew where.

Head down, I rushed up behind him, hooked my foot around the demon's leg, and tripped him. They both went down, causing a commotion. I ducked and rushed for the exit, and not sure what else to do to stop them, I yanked my keys from my bag and used them to break the glass on the fire alarm.

The siren wailed a moment later, and the lights came on less than a minute after that. The music stopped and everyone ran for the fire escape. I scanned the room, watching the demons and their prey. And, thankfully, people began to notice in the light that their friends were worse for wear, and they were helping them leave. I couldn't be sure if they were all human or not, but at least some of them were, I was sure of it.

If I wanted real proof, I probably should have let them take one and followed, but I couldn't live with what might happen, especially if things went wrong. That didn't sit right with me, so instead I found a place to hide just outside the warehouse. I ducked in among the overgrowth, along the tall fence surrounding the building, and waited so I could follow Lars and his demons.

The place emptied out quickly, and I searched for Lars.

I froze.

Jagger strode out, head and shoulders above everyone else.

You have got to be shitting me. I hadn't seen him in there. I had no idea he was following me. But why else would he be here?

He stopped outside the door, tilted his head back and, eyes closed, scented the air. His head swiveled my way immediately, eyes narrowing on my exact location.

Fuck.

His massive body changed direction, turning and striding straight for me.

My cover was blown. Staying crouched in the bushes was pointless. What the hell was I going to tell him? Rune told me not to tell anyone what I was doing.

You don't owe him an explanation.

No, I didn't. I didn't owe him anything.

He stood up to your mother, he covered for you.

I hadn't asked him to do that, he'd taken it upon himself, and now he was apparently stalking me. With nothing else to do, I stepped out from my useless hiding place and straightened my spine as he closed the space between us.

CHAPTER
FOURTEEN

Jagger

Sutton's eyes flashed red when I reached her.

She wanted to hit me over the head with a heavy stick, and I wanted to drop to my knees and beg her to forgive me. I wasn't sure that was the right play though. I'd hurt her, repeatedly. It would take more than that to win her back, if it was even possible at all.

But right now, her safety was more important than anything else.

"Why are you here alone?" I asked, my gaze sliding over her. "And why were you hiding in there?"

She drew in a deep breath, her eyes rolling upwards as she looked to the parking lot behind me. "Why do you think, Charming?"

"I don't know, that's why I'm asking you."

"I was trying to avoid...this," she said waving a hand between us.

"You were hiding from me?"

Her jaw lifted. "Well, yeah. I know this is hard for you to get through your head, but I don't want to see you, and I don't want to talk to you."

I could hear her heart thudding in her chest. Her cheeks were pink and her hands trembled slightly. Even if avoiding me was her goal, she still felt the pull between us.

"Let me take you home. It's not safe here," I said, choosing not to address what she'd just said, that wouldn't help an already tenuous situation. A situation that I'd created, yes, but even I knew talking about all the ways I'd let her down wouldn't help my cause.

"Nope. I'm not going anywhere with you." She shook her head and gave me another of her humorless laughs.

I scowled, clenching my fists. "Tell me what you're thinking." The demand slipped free before I could stop it.

"You really don't know?"

"No."

"Are all hounds as emotionally stunted as you?"

"Yes." Though, I wasn't as stunted emotionally as I had been several months ago. Not even close.

"Fine. Let's do this, one more time."

I frowned. "Do what?"

"Again, I will ask you, what the hell do you want from me, Jagger? You made your feelings and wishes, when it comes to me, *crystal clear*, yet, here you are, *again*, inserting yourself into my life, meddling, interfering, following me around and messing with my emotions. I have to know, are you purposely trying to be cruel? Or are you just this clueless?"

I jerked back, her words a fucking gut punch. "Cruel?" She thought I was being cruel. The mere notion made me feel ill. "I would never hurt you, Sutton. Never." The words came out rough, harsh—fuck, my voice shook.

She crossed her arms, her pretty eyes sad as they traveled over my face, then finally landed and held mine. "But you *are* hurting me. Every time you pull this shit, you're hurting me."

I shook my head in denial, not wanting to believe it but seeing the truth in her gaze all the same.

"Yes," she said. "Yes, Jagger."

"I was wrong," I said, my voice like rusted steel.

She crossed her arms, frustration on her face. "About what?"

I curled my fingers into tight fists at my side. "All of it. I...I didn't know, and I was wrong about fucking all of it, Sutton."

⟨⟨⟨ ● ⟩⟩⟩

Sutton

No.

No fucking way. He couldn't mean what I thought he meant. He couldn't.

"Shut the hell up!" I fired at him. "Stop talking and walk away." I turned to leave, and he grabbed my arm.

"You need to let me explain."

I pulled out of his hold. "I don't need to let you do anything, and honestly, I don't want to hear it." My lips trembled and my heart was a cold lump in my chest. I couldn't do this. The pain was just too deep. He'd hurt me too fucking much.

"Sutton..." He cupped the side of my face. "Please."

I jerked back, spun away, and ran. He could catch me easily if he wanted to, and I was surprised when I made it to my car without him stopping me. Jumping in, my gaze flew to my rearview mirror. He stood right behind me. So close, he could touch the trunk. He didn't though. He just stared back, a pained look in his eyes.

No. I didn't care about that look or what it could mean.

He'd shredded me, over and over again, and now he thought he could just say *he was wrong*? And all would be forgiven? That I would just forget how the male I was supposed to be able to trust most in this world broke me, rejected me so publicly, without a care or thought for my feelings? Or how he'd walked away twice, making it clear he didn't want me?

No fucking way.

Starting the car, my heart pounding, I tore out of the parking lot. Traffic was heavy with everyone leaving, and I knew Jagger was still following—gods, I felt him close. I glanced in my rearview mirror again. There. He was striding along the street.

He ducked behind a building and I lost sight of him, then a few minutes later, I passed him on the side of the road. This happened repeatedly. He chased me, vanishing, then reappearing, stepping out from behind a building or bus stop, or the wooded area that edged the other side of the road.

When I finally pulled up outside my apartment, the dark street was quiet. There weren't any bars or restaurants, and mine was the only apartment on this block.

I got out of my car, gripping my keys tight in my hand. I scanned the pavement, then across the street—Jagger stepped forward out of the shadowed eave of a store.

My heart slammed in my chest as I stared back at him. "I want you to leave. I want you to go away and don't come back," I called out.

He was breathing heavily, and as he took another step forward. I took one back.

He stopped abruptly and shoved his hands in his pockets. "Can't do that, Sutton. I tried, but it's no good."

My eyes stung, but I refused to let the tears fall. "I'm asking you to leave me alone."

His green gaze lit up like a light had been switched on behind them. "Don't you understand? I can't. I can never leave you alone."

I spun away, unlocked my door, and ran up to my apartment, closing myself in.

He didn't mean it. He said he *couldn't*, that he'd *tried* to leave me alone. In other words, he didn't want to be here, but instinct was forcing his hand.

He didn't want me, what he was feeling had nothing to do with me. If the fates had matched him with another female, he'd be standing outside her door right now.

My heart couldn't take another rejection, not from him, and I sure as hell didn't trust him to protect it.

What he was offering wasn't enough.

It was too late.

He was too late.

)))●(((

Sutton

I opened the door at the bottom of the stairs and almost

tripped over a box. What the hell? My name was written on top with black marker.

I searched both sides of the street. No one was nearby. It was late, the night after my run-in with Jagger, and all the stores around me closed. Leaning back, in case something burst out of it, I flicked back the top flap with the toe of my boot—and blinked down at its contents.

Herbs. Bunches of them. Held together with different-colored ribbon, like a box full of gorgeous flower arrangements, but better.

Crouching, I took a better look. Well, shit. These were rare varieties, and almost all of them out of season, so seriously expensive. I scanned the street again. No one was watching me.

My phone vibrated in my back pocket, and I pulled it out. A Nightscape notification from Jagger. Against my better judgement, I opened it.

Jagger: *Thought you could use them.*

I stared down at the message, then back up. Was he watching me? I had to assume he was. After his altercation with my mother, the way he'd defended me, covered for me when I'd been seen stealing herbs, he'd obviously realized how much I needed them. I could use them, honestly. I had an order I still needed to fulfill, and time was running out. There were several herbs in this box that I'd been struggling to source.

With a huff, in case he was still watching, I picked up the box, carried it up to my apartment, put the arrangements in water, then locked the door and headed back out.

Yes, it was a nice thing to do, but if he thought buying me herbs was enough to get me to forgive him, he was wrong—because this wasn't about forgiveness, it was about trust. Jagger didn't seem to understand that, though.

I got in my car and headed to the clinic, and while I drove, I worked at clearing my head. I needed to be focused, people's lives depended on me. But it was an impossible task. I worried about Luke constantly—was he okay, were they hurting him? Then there was Rune and what he wanted me to do. I'd called him last night, after my confrontation with Jagger, and told him what I saw at the dance party. He wanted to get together soon for a debrief and would call with a time. Considering what happened at our last meeting, I wasn't all that fired up for a repeat—and then there was Jagger and his sharp one-eighty.

I gripped the steering wheel. My life was a mess. Add in Fern and Phoebe calling and texting all the time, checking on me, worrying about me, and being unable to share with them why I was acting this way, and I was a female on the verge of a freaking breakdown. Literally.

My phone chimed and I glanced down at it.

Poe.

My stomach rebelled, gripping hard. Shit. I wrenched the car to the side of the road, shoved the door open, and threw up. My nerves were getting the better of me. I was jittery, on the brink of a panic attack, just...fucking terrified, all the time. Hand trembling, I grabbed a takeout napkin and wiped my face. Then took a swig of water from my bottle, spat it out, then dug around in my bag for some gum, before forcing myself to pick up my phone.

Poe: *Tarrant wants an update, meet me before the fights.*

Why did he need a face-to-face meeting for that all of a sudden? Probably so he could torment me some more, the creep.

Sutton: *Everything is on schedule. I'm working tonight, so meeting up is impossible.*

I knew what would happen next. He'd demand I do as

he said. Maybe it was a stupid thing to do, no, it definitely was, but I couldn't deal with him, or Jagger, with any of it right then, so I turned off my phone and shoved it in my bag.

CHAPTER FIFTEEN

Sutton

"Something you want to tell me?" Magnolia asked, looking over her shoulder as we rushed into the warehouse and were instantly hit by the sounds of a bloodthirsty crowd.

Jagger had trailed the ambulance on his bike all night. He hadn't approached, but he'd been there, watching from a distance.

"Nope," I said and pushed my way through a group of shifters. "If he wants to behave like a big stalker, that's up to him."

Mags huffed a laugh. "Seems to be the hounds' MO."

"What? Follow a female around until they finally give in?"

"Yep," she said, shoving, then scowling up at a male who'd stepped on her foot. "You close to giving in yet?" she asked, grinning.

"I'll never give in."

"Uh-huh." She didn't sound convinced. "Oh shit," she said, her eyes widening when we finally made it to the cage.

A call had come in a short time ago for someone who'd been badly hurt, and we finally got a look at our patient. A young wolf shifter lay in the cage. He'd tried to shift, to help his healing, but he was too badly injured to make the shift. He lay there screaming, a horrifying mix of skin and fur, of animal and human limbs. And standing off to the side was Poe, a nasty smirk on his face and hands covered in blood. He'd done this. Fucking bastard. His gaze slid to me, and his eyes were bright with glee as he bounced on the balls of his feet, energized by the damage he'd caused.

He winked.

I quickly looked away, and Mags and I got to work.

"You're going to be okay," I said and pulled out one of my new healing elixirs. I held the back of his head. "You need to drink this. It'll numb the pain long enough to finish your shift, okay?"

He groaned but nodded.

"What the fuck are you giving him, demon?" one of the wolves snarled at me from the sidelines. "Don't touch him with your dirty fucking demon hands." He was one of the wolves who'd thrown me in that van that night.

Magnolia shot to her feet. "What did you just say?"

He immediately realized who she was and flinched. Magnolia was not only his alpha's sister-in-law, she was also mated to a crow, one of the deadliest beings you could encounter. "Yeah, that's what I thought," she bit out. "Now sit down, asshole, and shut the fuck up so we can save your pack mate's life."

His jaw was tight, but he dipped his head and quickly looked down.

"That's it," I said to the young wolf. "Drink it all."

He finished, and a second later, he literally sighed in relief a moment before he finished his shift. His wolf lay on his side panting, and I held my hand above him, running it over his trembling body while I spelled, forcing my magic inside him to start his healing.

"Nice work," Mags said. "Your elixir, that's some good stuff. You want to trade recipes? I have a kickass balm."

I smiled up at her. "Thanks, and yeah, that'd be cool."

She waved the wolves in, and they lifted the drowsy wolf.

"Take him home, he needs lots of rest, but bring him into the clinic if you're worried."

The wolf jerked up his chin and they left.

"No worries, asshole, you're totally welcome," she muttered behind his back.

I gathered my supplies, and we got out of the cage so they could hose away the blood.

"Idiots," Mags said.

"Complete morons. So, I take it Bram doesn't fight? I've seen crows here before."

"That'll be his brothers. They like to come here and freak everyone out and assert their dominance now and again. Bram knows better than to pull that shit."

I laughed. "He's already won you, he doesn't need to impress anyone else?"

She grinned. "Exactly."

Poe was watching me closely. It was only a matter of time before he came over. "Shall we split up? See if anyone else needs treatment, then meet back here?"

Mags hitched her bag higher on her shoulder. "Sounds good. See you back here in a few."

As I expected, Poe intercepted me before I could get far,

grabbing my arm. "Stick around, I made the final round. I'm back in the cage next."

"I'm a bit busy, actually," I said and tried to pull away.

We were right beside the cage door, and he dragged me along after him, stopping just before going in. "We clear?" he asked Lars for some reason. Lars nodded. "Good, now make sure she stays put," he said, and the demon moved in behind me, blocking my way as Poe hooked me around the back of the head. "Need my good-luck kiss, Sutton."

I automatically jerked my head back.

Poe snarled, his claws sliding out against the back of my head, slicing skin. He jerked me forward, leaning in to force his kiss on me—

A thud shook the ground directly behind me.

Poe looked up right before a hand appeared out of nowhere and slammed into the demon's forehead, snapping his head back sharply, stopping his lips from meeting mine.

Fuck.

Poe snarled and charged forward. Jagger rounded me, and slammed his fist into Poe's stomach, sending him flying back and landing hard on the cage floor.

I stared in shock as Jagger grabbed Lars by the throat. "Touch her and die," he growled, then he strode into the cage with Poe, kicking it shut behind him.

Poe jumped to his feet, fury in his eyes as he bounced around and jerked his head from side to side, ducking and weaving. Jagger barely moved, just turned slowly, waiting.

Poe threw a punch, and Jagger grabbed his fist and twisted the whole arm with one subtle move, dislocating bones. Poe screamed and Jagger closed in, slammed him against the cage by the throat and snarled in his face. "You touch her again, I will tear you apart. Understand?"

Oh no.

Fuck.

Jagger then proceeded to beat the fuck out of him, tossing him around the cage like a chew toy. Poe was battered, bleeding, with more broken bones than I could count.

Jagger smashed his sledgehammer-sized fist into Poe's face one last time, and the demon went down, hard.

"Holy shit," Magnolia said beside me.

I hadn't even realized she was back.

Holy shit was right. Jagger had just made my life even worse than it already was. Poe knew I had friends among the hounds, and he'd think I was behind this. He'd blame me for it. If they didn't take it out on me, Luke would be the one to pay, and they'd make sure I knew.

Jagger stood over him, breathing hard, nostrils flared, teeth bared as the announcer named him the winner. He shoved the cage door open and started toward me.

"We need to get in there," I said to Mags.

She ran in, and rushing in after her, I shoved Jagger's bloody hand away from me when he grabbed my arm. Heat flashed through my body, my pulse spiking wildly. This display, this...this freaking pathetic pissing contest...could have just cost Luke his life.

"Poe? Can you hear me?" I said as I ran my hand over him, using my powers to see inside his body, cataloging all his injuries.

He wheezed, a rattling sound coming from his chest.

"Broken ribs," Mags said.

"Yeah, and he's shredded a few internal organs." I continued to hover my hand over him, whispering my spell and wincing when I snapped each bone back into place.

Poe screamed, arching against the mat. He'd see this as

a display of weakness, and there were witnesses. Lots of them. Males like him didn't like being seen as weak. If he didn't want to kill me over this, then me making him scream in front of this crowd would do it.

But I had no choice. The bones wouldn't knit back together correctly if I left them alone. Poe was a fairly powerful demon, his healing would have already started. If I didn't do this now, they'd have to be rebroken so they could be put back in the right alignment.

Lars crouched beside me. "You're fucked," he said, for my ears only.

⟩⟩⟩·●·⟨⟨⟨

Jagger

Sutton worked her magic, healing the fucker who'd just tried to kiss her. What the fuck was going on?

Why was she helping that male?

She'd pushed my hand away when I'd tried to stop her from going in the cage, and she wouldn't even look at me now.

Another demon helped Poe up, bearing his weight and leading him away. I straightened as Sutton and Magnolia walked out.

"Sutton—"

She walked right past me, as if I didn't exist. I followed after her. I'd shown her how strong I was, that I could protect her. Why was she angry? She hadn't wanted that demon to touch her, no way. Impossible.

"Sutton," I said again, calling after her.

My fingers barely grazed her arm, and she jerked it

away like I'd electrocuted her. "Back the hell off," she snapped.

"Maybe give her some space," Mags said, her gaze sliding between us.

Space? There had been more than enough space between us. I didn't want fucking space.

What had I done wrong? I showed her I was a worthy male, that I was strong. I was the alpha's lieutenant. I could give her what she wanted. I was ready now.

I grabbed her arm again, not letting her pull away. "I don't understand. Why are you angry with me?"

She stared up, her eyes big and round and hurt.

I shook my head, the pain in her eyes like a dagger in my chest. "I was protecting you." Fuck, it was an apology, for the stupid things I'd said and done.

"I don't want your protection, Jagger," she said, finally speaking to me. "That's not your job."

Anger shot through me. "Then whose is it? That fucking demon?"

She rubbed her temples, her eyes flashing red. "Mine! I protect myself." She shook her head. "I don't need your kind of protection, it only makes everything worse..." She slammed her mouth closed and shook her head.

"What do you mean?" I said, taking a step closer.

"Just leave me alone." She strode away, Mags hot on her heels.

Leaving her alone wasn't an option. I strode out into the parking lot as they got in the ambulance and I started after her.

My phone rang, and I yanked it out of my pocket. "Yeah," I said distractedly, watching as Sutton drove away.

"Need you back at the clubhouse. Brick's gone missing," War said.

"What do you mean, missing?" If we needed to find him, we could, by his scent alone.

"He left the clubhouse last night and still isn't back. That's not like him. The pup always lets his mom know if he's staying out. He knows how she worries. But we're not getting anything, brother. Not even Dirk or Elena can pick up his scent."

Fuck. If the pup was invisible to us, to his parents, that meant he was being hidden from us. We'd know if he was dead, Lucifer would have told us. Someone had him, someone powerful. "Anyone know where he was headed?"

"A female, not one who comes to the clubhouse, one he met in the city. We got no other details on her."

Not good. "On my way."

I got on my bike and tore out onto the street. Witches, demons, shifters of all kinds, except maybe crows, all could be caught and held against their will and used for their powers or strength. Hounds were left alone, we were too old, too strong, too hard to conceal, and no one wanted to tangle with Lucifer. So if someone was hiding him from us, it was someone with some serious power behind them.

When I pulled into the clubhouse, everyone was already there. I strode over to War. Dirk stood with him. Willow stood beside Elena, trying to comfort her.

"Anything?" I asked.

Worry etched Dirk's face and he shook his head.

"This isn't like him," Elena said, eyes full of fear.

"Who's he tight with?" We were brothers, and we were here for each other, but Brick was only twenty, still a pup, and he had to have friends more his own age.

"He texts Gus a lot. They hang when he comes above ground," Dirk said.

Gus was one of a new batch of hounds Lucifer created,

born full grown like the majority of us but definitely still considered a pup. They looked physically about the same age, and he was definitely more on Brick's wavelength.

"I'll call him, see if he can tell us anything about this female."

War nodded. "Good thinking." He shook his head. "We let you down," he said to Dirk and Elena. "We should've kept a closer eye on him."

We weren't used to having pups around. Besides Kurgan and Relic, who were born and raised in Hell, we hadn't had that many pups. There were others mated, who stayed in Hell, brothers who had already mated and lost their females long ago to old age, their female children as well. Brick was one of the first pups with mated parents born out of Hell. We'd never had to worry about it before, and I guess that gave us some blind spots.

I scrolled to Gus's number as I walked to a quieter spot.

"Jag," he said in a voice that was more hound than man. Living in Hell all the time did that to a male.

"Brother, you heard from Brick?"

"Negative."

"You know anything about the female he's been spending time with?"

"Only that she lets him mount her regularly." There was a pause. "And that she has blond hair, big tits, a nice ass, and a tight—"

"Anything besides the way her body looks?"

"When she orgasms, she's extremely loud," he said matter-of-factly.

I shook my head. Gus and Brick were opposites in every way. Created by Lucifer as Gus was, he hadn't learned social cues like the rest of us had to, how to mimic emotion and blend in with humans. He was as emotionless as the rest of us were—or in my case, had been. Brick, on the other hand, being born to mated parents who both had the full scope of emotions, he'd never experienced the way most of us had lived. "You know where his female stayed? A name?"

"Serena."

"Anything else?"

"He mainly just told me how it felt to mount her."

When we got Brick back, I needed to have a talk with him about this shit. He was a hound, he was big, we all were. Lost to lust, he could hurt a female. Not all could take a cock our size, definitely not humans. "She a shifter?" Shifters were made to take big.

"He mentioned running in the forest with her, so I can only assume she is."

We ended the call and I hit Draven's number, the alpha of the Silver Claw pack.

"Jag," he answered.

"You seen Brick at the keep lately?"

"No, what's up?"

"He's missing. You got a female out there named Serena?"

"No."

"You know of any with that name, packless, living in the area?"

"No females I know of with that name. If there was, one of our males would have sniffed her out."

"If you hear anything, let me or War know, yeah?"

"Will do." He was quiet a beat. "We good? Had a conversation with War, heard a few of my pack got rough with your female?"

"We're good, as long as you dealt with that shit." Draven was a good male, a tough but fair alpha. If he hadn't been those things, we'd have a problem.

"I'm still dealing with it. That shit does not fly with me. Won't happen again, I assure you."

"Appreciate that."

We disconnected, and I strode back to War and Dirk and told him what I knew, which wasn't a whole fucking lot.

"We'll search in shifts," War said. "I'll lead the first shift, you stay here with Rome and Fender and guard the females and pups. Keep everyone in the dens. We'll switch when I get back."

"Sounds good."

His gaze slid to my hands, still covered in Poe's now dried demon blood. "That's a lot of blood, brother, anything you need to tell me?"

"Nothing to report."

He held my gaze, then nodded. "You know where I am if you change your mind."

I lifted my chin and waited while Willow kissed her mate goodbye, then I ushered her and Elena down to the dens. Not that Willow needed protection. The female could kick ass.

Once everyone was situated and Rome and Fender were on guard duty, I headed to my den to wash that fucker's blood off. The females wouldn't like it, and I didn't want to scare the pups.

Reaching back, I tugged off my shirt, then turned on the shower. Now that everything was quiet, Sutton filled my mind once more. She never left it, though, did she? Even when I was trying to fight our connection, deny it, she was always there.

I pulled my phone from my pocket and was about to put it on the bathroom counter when I got a proper look at myself. There were a few scratches on my side and shoulder from Poe's claws, but they'd already healed and only red streaks remained. There was plenty of blood spattered across my tattooed skin, up my forearms and some streaked across the side of my throat, though. None of it was mine.

I didn't know how to please Sutton. I didn't understand what she needed from me, and I doubted I'd know how to give it to her even if I did. But I could give her this—I could protect her. The blood on my skin, from the male who dared touch her, who dared touch what was mine, filled me with pride.

Not sure what the fuck I was doing, but needing to do it for some reason, I opened the camera and snapped a picture. She said she didn't need my protection, but that wasn't true, and deep down I had to believe she knew it as well. She needed me. She needed me to be this for her.

Clicking open the Nightscape app, I opened our messages, the only one there now was the one I'd sent her that morning, after delivering the herbs to her. Did she like them? I had no idea. I hoped she did. I wanted to make her smile. I wanted to make her happy, to give her something she needed. So she wouldn't have to steal from the Ellis coven cemetery, anymore.

Attaching the picture, I thought about what to say. I liked seeing pictures of her, so I had to assume she'd like seeing one of me. She'd sent me so many over the three months I'd been away, and she'd always written something cute or silly to go along with it. I wasn't capable of either of those things. I didn't know how to be funny. I wasn't like Relic. I tried to think of what he might say, then something Sutton had messaged me popped into my head. She'd been angry at the time, yes, but it was definitely something Relic would find funny, something he wouldn't hesitate in sending to his mate to make her smile or laugh.

I quickly typed out the message. I stared down at it. Would it piss her off? She was already angry at me. Anything was worth a try at this point, right?

I hit send, and a weird feeling filled my stomach. Fuck. I was nervous. That's what this sensation was. I'd never been nervous in my life.

I stared down at the message, focused on the icon with her profile picture on it sitting beside my last message, letting me know she'd seen that one. There was a little yellow dot beside it, letting me know she was on the app now. I was literally holding my fucking breath—

The icon dropped down beside the picture I'd just sent.

She'd seen it, and my message.

I waited, my fingers curling and uncurling at my side. The seconds ticked by, then turned into minutes.

The yellow dot vanished.

She'd gone.

Heat washed over me, not for the first time. I'd made the wrong play. I'd fucked up again. This female had me in knots, had me fucking sweating, and—I looked at my face in the mirror—blushing. I was a motherfucking hound, lieutenant of this pack, I did not blush.

Slamming my phone down on the counter, I stripped and got in the shower.

How the fuck was I going to get through to her?

How the fuck was I going to win her back?

CHAPTER
SIXTEEN

Jagger

"You know what this is about? Why Lucifer asked us to meet him here of all places?" Lucifer didn't leave Hell often, for several reasons, this had to be something big.

War strode down the long hall beside me and Lothar. "He didn't share much, only that he might have a bead on Brick." His gaze slid my way. "You gonna be able to keep your shit tight?"

I raised a brow.

"I hear you and Rune got into it last time you were here?" he said.

My fingers automatically curled into a fist just thinking about how I found Sutton in Rune's apartment. "He used his demon powers on my female, had her in his bed. He's lucky I didn't rip his fucking head off."

His brows shot up. "Your female? Worked that out, have you?"

I straightened under War's all-seeing alpha stare. He didn't outright call me a blind fucking moron, but it was implied with just that look. "Yeah, I worked it out."

"And Sutton?"

"She'll come around."

War shook his head as we got into the elevator. I hit the button for the top floor. "Brother, you better have begging at that female's feet at the top of the list of shit you'll have to do to win her over. The way my dove tells it, you'd be lucky if she ever speaks to you again."

Lothar grunted his agreement. "Never seen a male fuck shit up as badly as you."

Didn't I know it.

War nodded. "What's your game plan? You'll need one."

I didn't want to talk about this. I felt like a damned fool, but I needed all the help I could get. "I got her some herbs, rare varieties, expensive."

"What else?" War asked.

My lip curled. "I beat the fuck out of that demon who touched her."

Loth nodded. "Showed your strength that you could protect her. Nice. Now you need to get her in your bed, show her you can take care of all her needs." He grunted again. "Make her come, feed her, keep her safe. She'll come around."

War turned to us, one of his "new" looks on his face. Since he'd mated and now felt all the fucking things, he gave us these looks, especially when we talked about females. "No wonder hardly any of us are fucking mated. The fates were obviously hoping we'd evolve. They apparently got sick of waiting."

"Well, what do you suggest?" I fired at him, and hoped I didn't sound as fucking desperate as I felt.

"Talk to her. I know it's hard, 'cause you're not there emotionally yet, but try to make her understand the reasons for what you did, and for your sake, I hope you have a fucking good one for rejecting her like that. Then apologize as many times as it takes for her to believe you mean it."

The elevator stopped and the doors slid open. We strode up to Rune's apartment door. "I'll try to do it your way."

"It'll work," War said and knocked.

It swung open a moment later, and Rune greeted us with a steely glare. "Gentlemen." His gaze slid to me and his lips curled up, flashing fang. "Jag."

I bit back my growl and gave him a good look at my extended canines.

"Lucifer," War said, cutting off the insult I'd been about to fire at that piece of shit.

Lucifer sat on the leather sectional, looking relaxed. Ursula stood behind him, and she gave us a chin lift in greeting.

"Hey, Urs, you on your own?" Loth asked, taking in the room.

The handmaids nearly always came in twos when they were out and about and guarding Lucifer, and Roxy was always the warrior she paired up with.

"Nope," she said, her gaze sliding to the bathroom door as it opened.

"You should come to one of our girls' nights," Roxy was saying as she walked out, petting a little bat that rested in her hands—I fucking stilled—when Sutton followed her.

Roxy spotted us, and her wide smile instantly lit up her lovely face. Sutton on the other hand seemed to freeze, her step faltering before she quickly looked down and followed Rox around the couch to stand with her and Ursula.

Rune followed, and the prick leaned in and said something low in her ear.

"Take a step back, motherfucker," I snarled, the words bursting from me before I could choke them down.

Sutton's head snapped up.

"I'll remind you whose home you're in," Rune said, his now black eyes on me.

"How about you open one of those windows for me, Rox, and we'll see how well Rune can fly." My gaze slid to Sutton. "Come here." The demand was impossible to hold back, and as soon as I said it and saw the look on her face, I knew I'd made a mistake.

I felt War's stare as Sutton blinked over at me, cheeks bright red. I'd surprised even him. I got it. I didn't do shit like this, but then I'd never been in this situation before either.

"Now, Sutton." Again, even as I said it, I knew it was the wrong thing to say.

War, shaking his head, told me I was right. I was fucking things up...again, but I wanted her away from Rune right fucking now. Lucifer asked him something, but the buzzing in my head drowned it out. My entire focus was on my female and her proximity to that fucking arrogant demon.

She straightened her shoulders, fury radiating from her. "I've already told you, I'm not yours to order around."

I was done talking. I strode toward her.

She took a step back, her eyes widening.

It was almost enough to make me stop in my tracks, but Rune was still too close to her. As I closed in, the alarm on her face switched back to anger. Before I could reach her, she'd transformed completely. Her eyes were red, her veins black, her nails now claws—then she surprised the fuck out of me and ran at me.

Her hands slammed into my sternum. "How fucking dare you tell me what to do!" she yelled. "After the shit you pulled last night, beating the fuck out of Poe like that. For what? To prove something? You have no idea what a mess you made for me."

I dragged in a furious breath. "Poe?" I growled. "You're angry I fucked up Poe? Why are you so concerned about that demon?" I loomed over her, my fingers itching to grab hold of her. "Are you fucking him? Is that it? Do you want him?"

Her beautiful red and black swirling eyes widened. "No," she said, shaking with rage. "I hate that asshole."

"Right," Lucifer said, clapping his hands and standing. "I can see where this is headed, and as entertaining as it would be, you can hate-fuck on your own time. We have business to discuss."

I turned to him. "What does it have to do with my mate?"

"I'm not your mate," Sutton snapped.

Lucifer's bright yellow gaze slid to her, and her mouth slammed shut. He then turned back to me. "If you will save this lovers' tiff until later, that's what you're about to find out."

Sutton stepped away, and it took all my willpower not to snatch her back. Her familiar chirped and wriggled, and Rox handed him back to Sutton, who tucked him under her jacket, and I forced myself to turn to Lucifer and give him the attention he demanded.

"Looks like we have two issues right now. The first?

Brick's missing." His jaw tightened. "No one fucks with my hounds. Whoever took him is dead."

"I'm killing them," Roxy said, her pretty eyes alight with vengeance.

She looked and sounded like the sweetest female in the world. She also adored pups and could kill a being in a thousand different ways without hesitation or remorse.

"That's not decided yet," Lucifer said to her.

She pouted. "You know how I feel about the pups, Luci. If anyone's hurt Brick"—rage contorted her features, not something you saw very often with this particular female—"I'm going to strip the skin from their body and fillet their flesh."

Lothar made a weird sound, shifting from foot to foot, and her gaze sliced to him and her cheeks turned pink.

"Enough," Lucifer said, stepping forward, blocking Lothar from her view. His gaze sliced to me. "The second issue we have is a few demons behaving badly."

I wanted to demand what he was talking about but rolled my shoulders and forced myself to wait for him to finish in his own time. This was Lucifer's show, and no one rushed him.

"We haven't heard about this," War said.

"Because I was dealing with it," Rune said.

"But," Lucifer said, "after Rune told me his suspicions, then War called and told me about Brick, my Spidey senses got all tingly. Brick and this demon issue are linked. I can feel it, here." He cupped his balls.

"What does this have to do with Sutton?" I said, unable to wait any fucking longer.

"She got herself in some trouble, didn't you, lovely?" Rune said to Sutton. "And she came to me for help"—his gaze slid to me—"since there was no one else she could trust."

My snarl burst through the room. "What trouble?" I said and took a step toward Rune.

War grabbed my shoulder.

"Stand down, Jag," Lucifer said easily. "Let Rune speak."

I wanted to rip out his tongue, not listen to him talk about my female as if he *knew* her, as if he knew her better than me. She was mine. Sure, I'd fucked up, I'd gotten confused. But I wasn't confused anymore.

"Sutton is being blackmailed by Tarrant. Poe is the demon she reports to. He's Tarrant's right-hand demon. As we know, he deals directly with manufacturers, is his enforcer, and does wet work when necessary."

"What the fuck? You're being blackmailed?"

She wouldn't look at me.

"Sutton," I growled. "What does he have on you?"

"One of her coven members was cooking for him, providing him with drugs, the kind only a witch could provide. He made a bad batch and tried to pull out of the deal. He owed Tarrant a lot of product. Long story short, her coven mate is being held by them, and they'll keep him alive as long as Sutton continues to fill their orders."

Adrenaline pulsed through me and I fucking saw red. "Easy fix, I'll send Tarrant back to Hell."

"He's not breaking any laws," Lucifer said. "Well, that we know of."

"Sutton is my mate, that should be enough."

Rune made a tutting sound. "That's not what I hear, and besides, Sutton and I made a deal. She gets evidence that Tarrant's breaking our laws, and I put him down and free her friend, isn't that right, lovely?"

"Yes," she said, still not looking at me.

"Poe's taken an interest in her, one that could be easily exploited to get the information we need—"

"No fucking way," I said, my voice all beast. "I don't give a fuck about your deal."

Lucifer's hand shot up, and he pointed at me. "Quiet," he barked. "I'm losing my fucking patience with this." His gaze bored into me. "If Sutton's your mate, then why the fuck aren't you mated?" I opened my mouth to respond, but he kept talking. "The way I hear it, you rejected her, and in doing so, forfeited any authority you have over her and this situation. I know you've changed your mind on that front, but she made a deal with Rune, and that shit is binding. You know that as well. He's a soul collector. Be grateful he didn't take her fucking soul instead of just asking her to get intel."

Rune smirked. "Thank you—"

"And you can shut the fuck up as well," Lucifer said to Rune. "You knew how this would mess with Jagger. You know how territorial hounds are. You could've blown this whole operation messing with Jag's female, mate or not." Lucifer took a deep breath. "This is a delicate situation. Tarrant is Beelzebub's nephew. My lords' confidence in me is already on shaky ground after Relic's drama with his female, discovering Lukan the way they did. They feel I failed them, and they're right, but there are...things on the horizon..." His face transformed, a flash of his true face broke through, for just a moment, something that rarely happened. "Let's just say I may need them, and pissing one of them off now, without proof, will cause me serious problems later on. Sutton is in a position to get that proof for me and, I believe, find Brick as well as another missing hound in the process."

"Another hound's missing? Who?" War growled.

"No one you know," Lucifer said, an odd look on his face.

What the fuck?

"I'm the alpha, I know every hound in my pack."

Lucifer's yellow eyes locked on War's. "We'll talk later."

War dipped his chin, but he looked pissed.

"Sutton will do what is asked of her, but since I see now that Jagger has strong feelings in regards to her safety, he'll shadow her."

I didn't want her anywhere near this, but there was no stopping it, not when Lucifer ordered it. At least this was something I could do to make sure she stayed safe.

"I don't need his help," Sutton said.

"You don't get a say in this," Lucifer said to her. "Not only do you have demon blood, you chose to use it to call in your favor with Rune. You've put yourself on this path. Jagger will be shadowing you, and you'll deal with it." His eyes glittered. "You might even enjoy it."

Her face flushed red.

Lucifer turned back to me. "But if you fuck this up in any way, Jag, I will summon you back to Hell and lock you up until this is done."

"I won't fuck it up," I said and hoped like hell I would keep hold of my control.

"Good. Getting both hounds back is of the utmost importance."

Who the hell was this other hound?

"On that note." Lucifer waved War over, taking him aside.

Roxy moved to stand with Sutton, talking quietly with her, and I strode over.

"Keep your cool," Lothar said, following me.

Sutton looked up when I reached them, her chin set.

"Shadow me if you have to, Charming, but don't expect anything else."

I thought about what War said, and instead of growling and demanding she let me close, that she forgive me and submit to me, like I wanted her to, I tried something else. "I'll do whatever you need to win your trust back."

She blinked up at me. I'd surprised her. Good.

"That was nice," Rox said to Sutton. "See, he's trying. Hounds are big softies really, well, most of them. They just don't know it 'cause they're all emotionless and stuff, and that sometimes leads to them doing really stupid or hurtful shit." Her eyes darkened as they lifted to Lothar. "Hey, Loth. How's it going?"

"Good, sweetheart," he said, pulling her in for a hug. He gave her a squeeze and kind of screwed up his nose and leaned away, then awkwardly patted her back as he untangled himself from her.

I'd seen him do that before around Roxy, fuck knew what his problem was? He seemed to seek her out, then couldn't get away from her fast enough.

"You know anything about this mystery hound Lucifer's talking about?" I asked her.

Her face went blank. "I can't talk about that."

"You sure about that?" Lothar asked, staring down at her, his expression intense, until he winked.

Yeah, he knew the handmaid had a crush on him, and going by the grin he was now flashing her, he obviously wasn't above using it.

Her eyes narrowed. "I'm not a fucking moron, Lothar."

He frowned. "I know that, Rox."

"If you think a wink or a grin from you is enough to get me to betray Luci, then you don't know me at all. Some of us don't so easily betray the people we're supposed to love," she said cryptically, then turned to Sutton. "I'll text you, and we can hang soon, yeah?"

Sutton nodded and watched as the little warrior strode away to stand with Ursula. Rox said something to Urs, and Urs narrowed her eyes at Lothar as well.

"What the fuck did I do?" he muttered.

I had no idea, all I cared about was Sutton, who still stood beside me. Having her this close and knowing she would be for the foreseeable future, I finally felt as if I could breathe for the first time in days.

Sutton's phone chimed, and she pulled it from her pocket—and paled.

"What is it?" I asked, barely stopping myself from snatching the phone out of her hand.

She looked up, fear in her eyes. "It's Poe. Tarrant wants to meet with me."

>)) ● ((<

Sutton

"When?" Jagger's voice was like he was gargling gravel.

This wasn't going to work. Lucifer had made a seriously bad call assigning Jagger to shadow me. After the way he'd reacted to Poe touching me last night, and seeing Rune near me today, it was obvious there was no controlling him.

I looked up at his handsome, stubborn face. "I'll tell you, because I have to. But if you get Luke killed because you can't control yourself, I'll never forgive you."

His gaze locked on mine, and heat swirled through me so fast, it was hard not to squirm. "I can control myself, Sutton."

My belly went all weird. "I hope you're right."

"I am. Luke's the guy from your coven, the one Tarrant has?"

"Yes, though he's more like family." He was standing way too close, so close, I could feel the heat radiating from his body, and yeah, I was getting a serious lungful of his scent. Comfort. He smelled like comfort. His scent soothed me instantly, like it always did.

Well, your nose is a freaking liar. Stop smelling him!

He nodded. "Look, I'll admit my control around you can be...shaky, but it's only because I want you so much," he said, again shocking the hell out of me. "But now I know that keeping a handle on it is what will keep you safe, you have nothing to worry about because your safety is all I care about."

Of course *now* he knew all the right things to say. Had he been practicing in the mirror? I bit my lip as the picture he'd send me last night flashed through my mind. He'd been shirtless and covered in Poe's blood. I'd stared at it for way too long. He could have sent it without any kind of written message, and I would have understood what he was trying to say. *I'll make anyone who fucks with you bleed.*

But then I'd seen his actual message.

A picture for your wank bank.

I had to assume he was trying to be funny, but Jagger didn't do funny, so I could only assume he was just being an asshole again. But that didn't feel right, either, not now anyway. Which took me back to him trying to make me laugh.

Add that to the box of herbs, and there was only one assumption I could come up with. It was his weird way of trying to say he was sorry.

Then again, assumptions were dangerous. Sometimes

they ended in utter humiliation—and a viral video of you being rejected, falling on your face and flashing your undies.

I looked back down at my phone and fear washed through me as I read the text again. "They want me to report to Tarrant in an hour."

His jaw tightened, but he nodded. "Wait here."

I watched as he strode over to Lucifer and War, said something, then strode back to me.

"Let's go."

I headed for the door and felt his hand touch my lower back, guiding me through it. Tingles immediately danced down my arms and zipped through my lower belly. I rushed ahead to break contact because it was too much.

I couldn't believe this was happening. I'd been trying so hard to avoid him, and now I was forced to take him with me every-freaking-where I went.

The fates really were evil bitches.

CHAPTER SEVENTEEN

Sutton

Gripping the steering wheel, I glanced in my rearview mirror.

We'd dropped Boo off at home, where he'd be safe, and Jagger was now in his hound form, running along the tree line as I took the creepy driveway up to Tarrant's enormous house.

I quickly went over in my head what I'd say. All I could do was hope they bought it. If they knew Jagger was my fated mate, even if we weren't mated, they'd kill Luke and cut their losses. No way would they want a hound that close to their operation.

No, the best way out of this was getting the evidence Rune and Lucifer needed, then let them move in and sort things out. Without proof, Luke was just collateral damage. Tarrant would carry on doing what he was doing, I'd lose my friend, and more people would get hurt if they started production again with someone who didn't know what the hell they were doing.

I glanced in my rearview mirror again as I pulled up in front of the house. Jagger had vanished into the trees. I still thought him coming with me was a terrible idea, but at the same time just knowing he was close helped ease my fears.

The main door opened as I got out of my car, and Poe stood there, his black eyes burning into me. He was still bruised and his breathing was shallow. I wasn't surprised. After the beating Jagger had given him, even his naturally fast healing hadn't managed to repair all the damage done to his body yet.

I did my best to slow my erratic breathing, to stay calm. My fear would only excite them more. Tarrant and Poe were like rabid animals. To them, fear was similar to the smell of a fresh kill. It made them want to tear their prey to pieces. I needed them to let me talk, and to believe me. Luke's life depended on it.

When Jagger spoke to Lucifer before we'd left, he'd commanded Jagger to stay back, to only intervene if I was in mortal danger. I had to prevent that any way I could. There was just too much at stake, not only for me but for Lucifer as well, and I did not want to get on the king of Hell's bad side.

Poe gripped the back of my neck when I reached him and pressed his lips to my ear. I stiffened and prayed to the mother that Jagger kept his composure.

"You've got some explaining to do, witch," he grated.

"I know," I rushed out and forced myself to look up at him with wide eyes. His face was way too close to mine, and so was his mouth, but Rune was right, this creep had a thing for me, and I needed to take advantage of it. To get this done, I'd have to use his attraction to me. It might be the only way to get out of this meeting without a full-blown war breaking out. "I'm sorry, Poe, that you were hurt. Let me use more of my healing magic to help you."

His gaze searched mine, and he sucked in a breath, then winced. "Are you trying to fuck with me? Because that would be a seriously stupid thing to do."

"I know it would be, and I think you know me well enough to know I'm not stupid," I said, not breaking eye contact.

He stared down at me for several long minutes, like he was trying to burrow into my skull and read my mind, to work out if I was lying or not.

"Do you want to work your magic on me, sweetheart?"

"Yes," I said, lying through my teeth and feeling more than a little nauseous even thinking about what I might have to do.

He grinned. "Let's see if you survive first. If Tarrant decides you're not a traitor, then we can talk about you putting your hands all over me."

I nodded, and still gripping the back of my neck, he shoved me forward and through the foyer toward Tarrant's office.

"I really hope you're not," Poe said as he shoved me through the door.

Tarrant was in front of his desk, resting against it. There was a plate piled with raw and bloody bones beside him, and he was studying his claws. They were fully extended, and as he looked up, he used one to pick at his teeth.

"What do you have to say for yourself?" he said, his icy voice searing down my spine. "What is your relationship with that hound?"

"I don't have a relationship with him. I know them through friends, that's all. They can be...protective when someone's brought into their circle." I wrapped my arms around myself. "I told them to back off. To stay out of my business. They won't do anything like that again."

"And I'm just supposed to believe you? Anyone getting near my business who isn't invited makes me very unhappy, Sutton, you must understand that."

"I do, and I promise. He won't interfere again."

Tarrant straightened and closed the space between us. "I'm not sure I believe you. I have eyes everywhere, and it's not the first time you've been seen with hounds. They spent a great deal of time outside your coven's house a few months back."

"I can explain that."

"You better."

"Our home was invaded by a witch, a bad one. He tortured me and another member of our coven." I quickly explained everything that happened as best as I could. "The hounds are protective of females and with the close connection—one of their brothers is mated to one of our newest coven members—they decided to guard the house while we recovered, that's all."

"I really want to believe you," Tarrant said. "Killing you would be such a waste of talent. You've made me a lot of money." He waved a hand at someone behind me.

Then Poe turned me to face the door as Lars dragged Luke in with him. He looked rough, tired, but unharmed.

"There are ways of getting the truth, but since your hands are far too valuable, we'll use Luke here as proxy," Tarrant said. "Sit him over there."

There was a chair by the window, and a small table beside it.

"Luke?" I choked out.

His gaze locked on mine. "I'm okay. No matter what,

just tell them the truth. I'll be alright. No matter what," he said again while he held my gaze.

He had no way of knowing what was going on here, but he knew his life and mine was at stake, and he was telling me to let them hurt him, if I had to.

I bit my lip when it started to tremble. "Please, don't hurt him. I'm telling you the truth."

"There's one way to find out." Tarrant looked at Poe. "Do it."

Lars moved behind me then, gripping my jaw and forcing me to look as Poe pulled out a knife, grabbed Luke's hand, and held it down on the table.

"All you have to do is tell me the truth about your connection to the hounds, and you save your friend's finger."

"I told you the truth."

"If you lied to me, you need to admit it now or he loses a finger."

"I told you the truth," I said again. "Please don't hurt him," I pleaded, even though I knew these males had no mercy inside them.

"You've got until the count of three," Poe said.

"I can show you the scars, the ones that witch gave me."

Tarrant paused, his gaze sliding down my body.

Lars loosened his hold, and with my heart beating madly, I lifted my shirt, showing him the jagged scars across my abdomen.

Tarrant studied them, then licked his lips. "Well, now, aren't they pretty." Then he turned to Poe. "I think she's telling the truth, don't you?" He used his claw to pick at his teeth again, then shrugged. "But I think we'll do it anyway, as a deterrent."

"No! Please."

Luke sat utterly still, his eyes squeezed shut. Lars had me in a tight hold, again forcing me to watch. Poe looked up at me as he brought the knife down, severing Luke's pinky finger.

My friend screamed, and I tried to pull away from Lars, but he tightened his hold even more.

Poe looked to Tarrant.

The older demon nodded and turned to me. "I'm going to believe you, for now, witch, but if I find out you were lying to me"—he pointed at Luke—"he dies, painfully, understand?"

"I understand."

Lars released me, grabbed Luke, and took him away, then Poe grabbed my arm and led me from Tarrant's office, closing the door behind him, but instead of leading me to the front door, he headed to the back of the house.

He was going to take me up on my offer. *Oh shit.* "Where are we going?"

"There's a room back here where you can work your magic on me," he said, and my stomach churned.

My mind raced, trying to think of what the hell to do. I needed to get Poe on my side, but I was only willing to go so far to do that.

He led me into a room. A spare room by the looks of it. There was a dresser and a bed and not much else. Certainly nothing personal.

"Do you live here?" I asked anyway, attempting to keep him talking. If he was talking, he wasn't plotting sick things that involved me. I doubted this male could multitask.

"Occasionally, but I have a place in the city where I spend most of my time."

He turned and slid his hands up my arms. "Okay, sweetheart, where do you want me?"

"If you could lie on the bed, I'll work on your ribs. They hurt the most, right?" I said as I worked at keeping the revulsion off my face at having his hands on me.

"I can handle pain," he said, his eyes sharpening.

"Oh, I know, but there's no need to suffer when I can take the pain away." Pretending not to hate him while he still had Luke's blood on his hands wasn't easy.

His eyes stayed on mine, and he tugged off his shirt. I wanted to gag. Instead, I dipped my gaze as if I were shy. He swaggered over to the bed and climbed on, lying on his back.

I moved to the side of the bed and rubbed my hands together while I called my magic forward. I was a healer, and though it wasn't in my nature, that didn't mean I couldn't intentionally cause pain, I just chose not to. Hurting felt wrong in every way to me, but I had the power to manipulate broken bones. I could snap them back into place, which meant I could force them out of alignment as well. It was delicate work, someone untrained could, for example, crush Poe's still healing rib cage. Yes, harming someone felt wrong, but right then I wanted to, badly.

I held my hands over his abdomen, while he stared up at me with hungry eyes and his dick strained behind the zipper of his jeans. When I was done, he was going to push for more from me. The idea made me sick to my stomach.

You could kill him.

I could. If I used every last drop of my power, I could cave in that rib cage, fracturing bones and impaling his organs, while he thrashed and screamed. I could take that knife from the sheath at his hip, the one he used to cut off Luke's finger, and while he struggled to breathe, hack off his head.

I moved my hands over him, seeking out the damage,

the weak spots not fully healed. They'd be so easy to rebreak. With just a little push of my magic at first, that's all it would take, then a bit more.

"Can you feel the warmth?" I asked Poe.

He groaned in a way that was purely sexual, arching a little, his eyes closing. "Yeah, fuck. That feels good."

Something moved outside the window. I searched the shadows. Jagger stepped forward, huge and inked and utterly naked. His lips were peeled back, his fangs extended, and like he could read my mind, he shook his head. *Don't kill him.*

If I killed him here, if I made him scream in agony, others would come running. I'd be caught, Luke and I would be killed, Jagger would burst in here, and all hell would break loose between the demons and the hounds. He could get hurt as well. This was bigger than me. There were other lives at stake. I had to rein in my emotions and stomp down the burning rage inside me.

Instead of breaking him, when I sent him a rush of power, I whispered a spell that had the same effect as sedation. "You might feel drowsy as the healing magic works to knit your bones together," I said.

His eyes opened, and he shook his head, but it was already taking effect. "Don't wanna be drowsy, Sutton," he kind of slurred as he grabbed his dick and squeezed. "Got other plans...for...you."

He passed out.

I didn't stop. I didn't want to take away his pain, but he'd be suspicious if he woke and his ribs were still badly injured. I healed them as best as I could and continued to chant my sedation spell. He'd be out for the rest of the night with how much magic I'd used on him.

Jagger was still watching, and goose bumps prickled all

over me. He jerked his head to the side, telling me it was time to go. He was right.

Lars walked in. "What are you still doing here?"

I jumped and spun around, my hand flying to my chest. I sucked in a deep breath, not wanting to show my panic. "I was working on Poe's ribs. They'll be much better when he wakes, but he'll sleep heavily the rest of the night."

Lars looked over my shoulder at his friend, eyes narrowing. Poe was breathing heavily, obviously still alive. Not the pile of ash I'd wanted to leave behind.

He waved me forward. "Fine, let's go." He grabbed my arm and marched me back through the house, shoved me out the front door, and closed it.

That was more than fine with me. I rushed to my car and tore out of there.

When I reached the end of the long driveway, I looked back and Jagger was again in his hound form, following me. When I was sure no one was around, I pulled over to the side of the road. He shifted as he approached the passenger side, opened the door, grabbed his jeans, tugged them on, and got in beside me.

"Okay?" he asked.

"No." I was far from okay. "They cut Luke's finger off."

"There was nothing you could've done to stop it."

I nodded, but I was shaking as the adrenaline and fear began to seep from my body, leaving me cold.

"There was nothing you could do, Sutton," he said once more. "He's alive. That's all that matters."

I nodded again, glancing his way. His expression was strained, the tendons and veins in his neck bulging. He was struggling with his control right then for some reason, and if I hadn't looked at him, I wouldn't have known, he'd hidden it so well.

"Are you about to go hound in my car or something?" I said. It was easier to talk about him than what I just went through.

"I'm good."

"You look about ready to Hulk out."

The hand resting on his knee, squeezed into a tight fist. "You were just in a house with demons who not only could, but wanted to hurt you. Poe touched you more than once, and I can still smell his stench on you, Lars's as well. So yeah, I'm struggling with my control because the urge to go back there and turn them all to ash is fucking with me pretty hard right now."

"You need to stop saying things like that." I couldn't take it. I was trying hard to be strong. I couldn't let myself trust the things he was saying. His instincts were leading him, not some imaginary feelings for me. He thought he wanted me now, but what about next week, or next month?

"It's the truth, Sutton," he said and shifted in his seat so he was facing me more. "What I did, what I said—"

I wrenched the car to the side of the road. "I need to go to work. You'll need to go hound and run the rest of the way."

"Sutton—"

"I'm going to be late." I risked another glance his way. "And I'll be going straight home after my shift and staying there, so I won't need your protection."

He sat there for several long seconds, the silence ticking by. Finally, he nodded and turned to get out, but then he looked back. "I know you're a warrior, sunshine, I've seen the fucking scars, but you don't need to do it all alone anymore. I'm here now, and I've got you."

I stared at him in shock, my blood rushing through my ears.

"No matter how long it takes," he said, green eyes holding mine, "I will wait for you." Then he got out and shut the door.

I sped back out onto the street as fast as I could.

My heart thudded in my chest as I shook my head and gripped the wheel tight. They were pretty words, but they didn't wipe clean the hurt he'd caused, and honestly, I wasn't sure anything could. *He left me*, more than once, he fought the truth because he never wanted this, and he sure as fuck never wanted it to be me, and I told myself that over and over again. Because knowing it, unfortunately, didn't stop me from wanting him.

CHAPTER EIGHTEEN

Jagger

Kurgan ignored the deer I put in front of him and paced his cell.

He was wound up, full of aggression. I'd come here after making sure Sutton was home from her shift, locked and warded inside her place. He'd been back to almost feral when I walked in.

"Take a breath, son. Everything's okay. You need to calm down." The last time he was like this, he'd worked himself up until he almost decapitated himself trying to get free.

His head lifted, his red eyes burning into mine. "Female," he snarled and gripped the metal cuff around his throat. "Mine."

I could tell there would be no calming him. Grabbing my phone I texted War. He was the alpha. Occasionally, his command, his dominance could break through and get Kurgan to stand down. I hoped like fuck it worked this time.

"She's safe," I said again.

He shook his head. "I protect her." He pointed a finger at me. "Not you. Mine. Not yours."

"Lenny's yours, son. Not mine."

His eyes didn't leave mine as his lips peeled back, then he opened his mouth and let loose a deafening roar. His fists, with nothing else to hit, made contact with his own chest before he spun and slammed one into the stone wall, causing dust to rain down.

Fuck.

He ran for the door and was slammed to a jarring stop when he ran out of chain. The steel cut into his throat, and he roared again, grabbed the chain and yanked, trying to tear it from the wall. My heart slammed into the back of my ribs. Steel forged in hellfire was unbreakable. He'd shred all the flesh from his hands before he broke that chain.

"Kurgan," I barked, my voice breaking. "Stop."

He ignored me, losing it completely. Pain sliced my chest. All I could do was fucking stand there while my son, so desperate to get to his mate, risked fucking killing himself.

War's knock on the door came about ten minutes later. I opened up and he stepped inside. Kurgan strained and snarled, blind to anything but his instinct to get free.

"You know what started this?" War asked.

"No."

"You think Lenny's in heat and somehow he can sense it?"

I hadn't considered that. She was a fox, it was possible. "Maybe."

"Stand back," he said. "It's better if he doesn't see you. I want all his attention on me."

I stepped back into a shadowed corner and hoped like fuck this worked, but if Lenny was in heat, I doubted our chances.

War took several deep breaths, his body growing in size as his muscles flooded with the power of his alpha beast. His face partially shifted, his mouth and jaw becoming hound, then he clenched his fists, drew in another deep breath, and roared, the dominance so loud, the power of it forced me to lower my head as well.

Kurgan paused, but he didn't stop. *Fuck*. He was too lost, as close to being completely feral as I'd ever seen him.

"Stand down," War roared, his voice all beast, all alpha.

Nothing. Kurgan didn't even pause this time.

Blood covered the chain now and dripped from the cuff around his throat, sliding down his chest and dripping on the floor. My gut clenched tight, and my fucking throat ached. If he died, I would never forgive myself.

There was only one other option I could think of. I hated it. But I wouldn't lose Kurgan as well.

☽☽☽●☾☾☾

Sutton

I startled awake when someone knocked on my apartment door. There was no way of getting to that door unless you somehow got through the one at street level, which meant getting through my ward. And mine was the only apartment up here. No one should be on the other side of that door.

I reached for my knife.

"Sutton?" a rough voice called.

Jagger. I blew out a relieved breath. "What are you doing here?" I called back.

The sound of the lock turning, disengaging, came next. I shot to my feet, standing on the mattress and staring at the door in shock. I knew hounds had powers, but I didn't know they could do that.

The door swung open and Jagger strode in.

"How did you get through my ward?"

His gaze slid over me, down my bare legs and back up, then he was striding over to a pair of jeans draped over my desk chair. He thrust them at me. "Put these on."

"What? No. Answer my question."

"You gave me access when I carried you back from Rune's. You were so fucked up on his mojo you obviously forgot."

I had. I'd completely forgotten. He could have come in here any time he wanted, but he hadn't. "Okay, but that doesn't explain why you're here?"

"I need your help." He shoved his fingers through his hair. "Someone...important to me is hurt, fuck, he's out of control. I need you to do what you did with Poe. I need you to sedate and heal him."

I frowned. "I don't understand—"

"We're running out of time. Please, just...will you come with me?"

"Okay." I'd never seen Jagger like this. He was really worried, maybe even afraid. I quickly pulled on my jeans, shoved my feet in my boots, and grabbed my jacket. Slinging my bag strap over my shoulder, I reached for Boo.

"Better he stays here, safer."

Okay, shit, what was I about to walk into? I kissed Boo

on the head, promising I wouldn't be long, then followed Jagger downstairs. Instead of going to his bike, though, he took my hand and led me down an alleyway.

"Where are we going?" I looked around, but no one was there.

"He's not here." He lifted his hand and pressed it against the brick wall. His hand glowed, and the brick beneath it vanished before my eyes. A portal. "He's in Hell."

I took an abrupt step back. Jagger's hand was still around mine, and his fingers tightened, stopping me from retreating completely.

"Nothing and no one will hurt you. Do you trust me?"

Did I? With my heart...the answer was still no. But this wasn't about that. This was about my safety, and in that, yes, I did. I trusted him completely. I nodded.

"It's okay," he said. "I'll keep you safe."

I nodded again and reluctantly let him lead me through the now swirling portal. I was a healer. If someone needed me, I went and I did what I was born to do. Ignoring someone in need wasn't something I could ever do.

Jagger strode briskly through tunnels, leading me deeper and deeper into Hell. The demon blood in me felt as if it were being drawn forth, as if that part of me knew we were home. My vision turned red before it settled back to normal. I lifted my hand and my nails had extended into claws, every vein on my hands, and everywhere else on my body, I was guessing, was now black.

Jagger stopped outside a large steel door and turned to me. When he got a look at me, at the way I'd fully transformed, he sucked in a breath.

Yes, look at your ugly mate. Bet you're glad you never claimed me now, huh?

"I have no control over it," I said. "It's being down here.

I can't make it go away. So if it's gonna freak out whoever's behind that door—"

"You're fine as you are," he said, but there was a weird look on his face.

I ignored it. I knew I was hideous, but there was nothing I could do about it. So I straightened my spine. "So, who's behind the door."

"A hound, his name's Kurgan. He's unstable, broken in ways we don't know how to help him. Sometimes, he loses control and hurts himself trying to get free. I need you to sedate him, and heal him as best you can." His thumb slid over the back of my hand. "Can you do it without getting too close?"

"I should be able to get enough sedation magic into him to calm a little, after that, I'll need to get closer."

Jagger looked grim but nodded. "You don't approach him unless I say you can, yeah? And if we can't physically contain him after that, you don't approach him at all."

"Okay."

As soon as Jagger opened the door, I was hit by a blood-curdling roar. The room had to be completely soundproof. Warrick stood on one side of the room, and the one making all the noise, on the other. He was huge, the biggest hound I'd ever seen. His black hair was long and wild, his skin streaked with blood, his own by the looks of it. It dripped from the iron collar around his throat and from hands that were basically stripped back to bone as he tore and yanked at the chain attached to the wall.

I dropped my bag and slid off my coat. Raising my hands, I stepped forward. The hound spun and dove in my direction. Jagger hooked me around the waist and stepped back, just out of the wild hound's reach.

The massive hound stared at me with red eyes, huffing

and snorting each breath, while he snarled and foamed at the mouth.

"Female," he roared in a garbled voice. "Mine."

Jagger's grip on me tightened. "No, son, mine." His deep voice resonated through me and made my belly swirl. "You've distracted him. Do it now," Jagger said against my ear.

I let my magic build and sent a rush of it at the hound whose eyes burned into me.

He made a pained sound that lifted goose bumps all over me. It was one of pure agony, but his pain wasn't the physical kind. I pushed more magic into him, reaching deep.

He moaned and stumbled to the left, then dropped to his knees, but continued to push forward against the cuff around his throat with enough force that blood poured from him onto the floor.

"Don't stop," Jagger said.

He was seriously drowsy, and I risked reaching out and placing my hand on the top of his head as I fired another burst of magic into him.

Jagger grabbed for my arm at the same time as the bleeding hound's own hand snapped up, latched on to my wrist, and wrenched me from Jagger, throwing me to the floor.

He leaned over me, snarling in my face. Jagger and Warrick dove on him as he dipped his nose to my throat and scented me again. His head jerked back, and he shook it as he gnashed his jaws.

"Lenny," he roared.

I wasn't who he wanted. I grabbed his massive shoulders—while Warrick and Jagger tried to pull him off me—

and pumped him full of power while reciting my spell more forcefully.

He jerked and fought against it, but then finally, he slumped, and Jagger hooked him around the chest so he didn't fall on top of me, rolling him away.

Kurgan lay on his back unconscious, and I lay beside him, trying to catch my breath.

"Goddammit, Sutton, I told you not to touch him."

I barely heard what he was saying, every one of my healing powers called me to the big male sleeping heavily beside me. I pushed myself up, turning to face him. Sitting cross-legged, I held my hands above him and moved them over his massive, muscular body.

"He's suffering," I said, letting Jagger know what I felt, what I saw. "The pain inside him, it surpasses anything he just did to himself." It was like a burning ache deep in his belly that had tendrils reaching up from the top of it, like brambles twisting and stabbing, filling his chest.

"He has a female," Jagger said. "A mate he can never claim."

I looked up at him. "Why?"

"The last time he saw her, he almost killed her."

I bit my lip as tears filled my eyes, because I felt it, that moment, it caused a scar deep inside him. "He'd never do that again," I rasped. "He knows he did wrong. That moment, it tortures him."

"We can't control him, we can't risk letting him free," War said. "And that female, he might not mean to hurt her again, but he will. She's been through enough."

"Can you do something, to make this easier on him?" Jagger asked roughly.

I shook my head. "There's nothing I can do to ease that kind of pain. It's not magic..." I swallowed dryly as the reality of what caused his agony hit me. "It's fate. Stopping it...it's impossible."

Jagger made a rough sound, and my heart thudded in my chest. I refused to look up.

"Can you heal the damage he's done to himself?" War asked.

"I can do that." I got to work while Jag and War watched, staying close just in case he woke. Hounds healed fast, but this kind of damage would have taken time, especially with the pain he carried inside. That kind of agony affected everything in a being, including the physical. "I'll make a potion you can add to his water. It'll keep him a little calmer."

"Thank you," Jag said. "That would be a huge help."

"No problem." My heart was beating furiously in my chest now. Everything that had just happened here, seeing inside this hound and the way being separated from his mate affected him, was getting to me. Did Jagger ache this way?

Did he carry a jagged ball of agony around inside him now as well?

I watched as he dragged Kurgan over to a pallet against the wall. War helped him lift the big male onto it, then Jagger covered him with a blanket.

He and War said their goodbyes and the alpha left. Jagger helped me gather my things, then took my hand again, and led me from the room, shutting the door behind him.

"You were almost hurt," Jagger rasped. "I told you I'd keep you safe, and then—"

"And you did," I said, hating what I heard in his voice. "He didn't hurt me." Jagger was trembling, it was subtle but I felt it. "I'm fine, Jagger, honestly."

He nodded, staring down at me in a way that made my stomach squirm. "Do you really think I'm a warrior?" I asked before I could stop myself. But the things he'd said to me, before I kicked him out of my car, had been going around and around in my head.

"Fuck, yes." His hand lifted to the side of my face, and as soon as he touched me, he released a shaky breath. "You're brave, Sutton, and tough...and so fucking beautiful I don't know what to do with myself when I'm near you."

My heart thumped hard in my chest, and I immediately shook my head. "I look like a monster."

He cursed as his gaze searched mine, sliding over my face, taking in the black veins that pooled below my red and black swirling eyes.

"Fuck, female, the way you look now, so deep in your demon, you look...you're fucking beautiful." His thumb slid across my cheek, tracing one of my black veins, and he drew me closer. "Both versions of you, sunshine, take my fucking breath away."

I shook my head again. How could he mean that?

"You doubt me?" I'd pushed him away, over and over, and it had taken a toll. Feeling Kurgan's pain, his desperate craving for his mate, I couldn't do it again, not right then anyway, not after that, and not with Jagger so close telling me he thought I was beautiful.

I dipped my head, not wanting him to see how much I wanted his words to be true right then. He took my chin, tilting my head back, forcing me to look up at him. "You doubt how much I want you?" He shook his head. "You truly doubt how fucking stunning I find you, all the time, including this version of you?"

"Yes," I whispered. I'd tried to be strong, to own this side of myself, to pretend it didn't bother me. But it did, my whole life everyone had let me know how ugly I was when I was like this, and some had cast me aside because of it. "I'm hideous—"

He pressed his thumb to my lips and growled. "Stop." He tightened his grip on my chin. "You call yourself hideous again, we'll have a problem." He dipped closer, so his mouth was a breath from mine. "You have no idea how much I want you right now, all of you, every fucking version."

CHAPTER NINETEEN

Jagger

Her pretty red eyes widened, and I dragged in a rough breath.

I was trying to hold myself back. Really fucking trying, but then I felt her hand move at my side. She was touching me, setting off really fucking nice tingles down my spine, and maybe I could have maintained my control for a little longer, but then her claws grazed my skin.

"Fuck," I groaned, a full-on shiver rocking me. "Sutton, baby, I'm struggling here. You need to step back if you don't want me to claim that hot fucking mouth."

She blinked up at me, but what she didn't do was step back.

That was it. The only chance she got from me. With a growl, I hooked her around the waist and hauled her off her feet as I shoved my fingers in her soft hair. It was difficult, but I pressed my forehead to hers and took two seconds to remind myself that although she may look like a demon, she wasn't as strong as one, and I needed to be careful with her. I needed to be aware of my strength, because hurting her would fucking destroy me.

So instead of slamming my mouth down on hers, I tipped my head to the side and carefully, slowly opened my mouth over hers. *Oh fuck.* Her warm, soft lips against mine were even better than I remembered. But this time, I slid my tongue inside for a taste. Her little tongue touched mine, and my knees literally went weak.

I tried, I really fucking tried to keep the kiss slow and sweet, but then she tightened her arms around my neck and wrapped her legs around my waist, add to that her wanton little moan, and I lost my mind.

Planting my hand on her round ass, to hold her right the fuck there, I started walking. Every tunnel was imprinted on my mind, every curve and turn and fork. Every crossroad and burning pit. I'd traveled these tunnels for over a thousand years; I didn't need to look as I strode toward the quarters I kept here.

I wasn't going to push her for more than she was ready for, I just needed a little more of her, just a little more.

She moaned against my lips as I rounded another corner, and the scent of her hot, slick pussy reached up and grabbed me by the throat. My mouth watered, imagining my first taste. *Fuck.*

We finally reached my door, and I pressed my hand to it, using my powers to unlock and open it, and carried her inside. She tore her mouth from mine, panting, while I kissed and sucked her slender throat, marking her delicate skin, marking her the only way I could.

What I wanted to do was plant her on the bed on her hands and knees, fist that soft, gorgeous hair, tear her pants off and slam inside her. I wanted to fuck her hard and mark her with my fangs.

I wanted to make her my mate, but Sutton wouldn't thank me for it. Yes, she was turned the fuck on, as hot for me as I was for her, but I didn't need all my emotions to know my female was still hurt by the shit I'd said and done.

Maybe I should stop this. Maybe the best thing for me to do would be to slow this down, keep it to just this kiss, but after seeing her in a room with Tarrant, then working on Poe? Yeah, holding myself back had already tested the hell out of my control. Add to that the shit with Kurgan, having to bring Sutton here, seeing her in danger a second time that night, and my newly developing emotions were all over the fucking map.

I needed more. I just needed her—her scent, her touch, the sound of her voice. Only she could calm the storm tearing through me. Only she had the power to do that.

I laid her on the bed. "Let me get you off," I said as I popped the button of her jeans and slid down the zipper. "Just need a taste of you, sunshine. You gonna give me a taste, baby?"

Something moved through her eyes, and I thought for a moment she was going to say no, but then she lifted her hips so I could tug down her jeans and tossed them aside. I groaned. *Fuck me.* Her pussy was drenched, soaking her underwear. So much so, they clung to her. Desperate for a look, I hooked my finger through the scrap between her thighs and tugged it aside.

"Fuck, baby." I leaned in, dragging my nose along her inner thigh, licking, sucking those sexy black veins snaking up her leg, and breathed her in, teasing us both. "So pretty. Gorgeous everywhere."

I quickly dragged off her underwear. There was no stopping myself, and with a hungry groan, I covered her pussy with my mouth, and finally got a taste of her.

Fucking hell.

The leash slipped, just a little, and my beast's tongue slid from my mouth on the next lick, elongated, broader, so I could tease and taste her the way I wanted to. It wasn't something all hounds could do, but I was old and fucking glad I'd mastered the skill when she arched against the bed and thrust her fingers into my hair with a high-pitched cry.

Holding her wide, I dragged my long, broad tongue over her delicate little cunt. The size and the way my beast's tongue could move meant I was everywhere, the tip teasing her opening while the broader section higher up was pressed to her clit, moving from side to side.

Her thighs shook, and she fisted my hair tighter while her hips churned against the mattress. Wrapping my arm around her back, I lifted her ass off the mattress so I could control her movements and hold her steady. I looked up at her, locked eyes, and slid the full length of my tongue deep inside her.

The red and black of her eyes widened, then fucking rolled back as her mouth fell open on a sexy, dirty-as-fuck whimper.

"*Jagger.*" She tried to move her hips.

I held her still and started fucking her with my beast's tongue, moving it in and out of her pussy while the tip rubbed against the spot inside her that I knew would send her fucking wild.

"Don't stop," she gasped. "*Oh gods.* Oh...oh." Her thighs slammed shut around my head, as she rocked against my face, coming hard for me, coating my tongue with her sweet-as-fuck honey.

When she finally collapsed back, I slowly, carefully

eased my tongue from her pussy, lapping up all of her sweetness before lifting my head. Panting, she watched as I licked my lips, as my tongue returned to a more human form.

"Holy shit." She gasped for breath.

I gripped her thighs and yanked her down the bed. "You want more?" I trailed kisses along her inner thigh, wringing a whimper from her.

She blinked up at me as I leaned over her. "I...this was—"

"The best orgasm you've ever had?"

She squeezed her thighs against me. "No...I mean, yeah, but that wasn't what I was going to say."

I wanted to see her naked. I could control myself. I could strip her bare and not fuck her. I slid my hand up her shirt, and hers came down on mine.

I dragged my other hand down her soft belly, and she stopped me again, a wild look in her eyes. "Sutton?"

She shook her head. "I'm not sure we should have done this. With all that's going on, maybe this was a mista—"

I growled, loud. "Don't you fucking say it."

"Come on, Charming, things are a complete mess between us. Adding this"—she motioned to my mouth—"to the mix while everything is so fucked up is a bad idea."

"Why?" She was wrong. I just had to make her see it.

"Why?" she repeated.

"Yes."

"Because you rejected me, multiple times, and because I don't trust easily...and honestly? I don't trust you. Not yet. I don't know if I'm capable of it. It's not your fault, not really, it's just—the way I am."

"I'm not your family, Sutton. I'm not fucking them. I know I hurt you, baby, and I regret that more than you will ever know, but I'm not them, and I won't do that shit again."

She chewed her lip. "I want to believe you."

"Then get to know me, spend time with me. Let me change your mind." I would never let her go, but if she needed to hear that I would if she chose it, then I'd tell her what she needed to hear. "If at the end of all of this, you still don't trust me, then I'll walk away."

"You don't mean that, and I don't want to hurt you. I saw what Kurgan was feeling. I felt it, the pain inside him. There was other damage, things...power inside him I didn't understand, but being parted from his mate like that had caused a vicious scar inside him that was making everything so much worse, it's driving him mad."

Hearing that, having it confirmed settled like a boulder in my chest. "Kurgan is half my age, damaged in a way that even Lucifer can't heal. What you felt, it won't happen to me. You don't need to worry about that." I was lying. My craving for Sutton would only increase, would never leave me, and I had to hope that spending time with her, trying to show her the male I was, the male I wanted to be, would make her forgive and trust me again, like she had before I fucked everything up.

She bit her lip. "I can't make you any promises right now, Jagger. My life is so complicated. Until Luke is safe and Tarrant is off my back, getting into anything serious with you, it just...it's too much."

"Then we take it one day at a time, yeah? No pressure. Can you give me that?" I asked, trying to keep the desperation off my face and out of my voice. I was willing to die with this female, to have Lucifer take me out when her time came, but I had no idea how to show her that, how to show her just how much she meant to me.

She nodded. "I can give you that." There was still wariness in her eyes, though.

I leaned in slowly, giving her a chance to pull away. She didn't. "Thank you," I rasped and took her mouth in another kiss.

Sutton pulled away from the kiss first, and it was hard, but I let her.

"I need to get back to my place," she said. "Boo's there on his own, and I have product to make for Tarrant. It's going to take most of the night. I need to get it done before my shift tomorrow."

"Okay, sunshine," I said, then stood, taking her with me. "I'll take you home."

CHAPTER
TWENTY

Sutton

"There's somewhere I wanna take you," Poe said when I handed over his drugs.

"Yeah? Where's that?" I was too exhausted to deal with this creep and had to force myself to keep the repulsion out of my voice.

"We have a special event happening very soon. Something reserved for people who have proven themselves to be loyal."

I fought to keep my expression neutral. This could be the break I needed, but I didn't buy his bullshit about loyalty. They'd literally just cut off Luke's finger because they didn't trust me—this was something else. Maybe a way to inextricably tie me to whatever twisted shit they were a part of so I had no escape. "Does Tarrant know you're inviting me?"

His lips twisted. "Don't worry about Tarrant. Once he knows you can be trusted, things will change."

"What things?"

"You don't need to worry your cute little head about that either. Trust me to take care of this." He looked kind of pissed off now.

Trust him? I wasn't sure I'd met anyone more delusional in my life. I curled my lips in a soft smile. "Sorry. I'm just a bit nervous, I guess. So, what kind of an event are you taking me to?" I asked, doing my best to sound excited.

"It's a surprise."

My stomach churned. "Well, I'll at least need to know the dress code. Is this thing dressy, casual, black tie? A girl needs to know these things," I said and huffed a laugh.

He gripped the side of my throat, his hand sliding higher until he was cupping my face, and his eyes dipped to my lips. "Dress to kill, sweetness."

I swallowed, and the sound was audible. "So dress and heels, the works?"

He nodded and leaned in. I wanted to jerk back, to shove him away, but I had to stand there and take it. I had to let him put his mouth on me and pretend I liked it.

While his hands roamed over me, I switched off; while his tongue invaded my mouth, I pretended I was somewhere else. I had to do this. For Luke and all the other people this asshole and his sick, twisted boss were hurting —and because Lucifer had commanded it.

Jagger was somewhere close, watching right now, and I imagined him fighting back his beast while this creep pawed at me. His canines would be extended, his eyes red, every vein and tendon straining with his rage. Knowing someone else was angry on my behalf helped as the seconds ticked by. And after seeing what Kurgan lived with, the pain and longing inside him for his mate that he could never have, I knew what Jagger felt for me was something he had no control over, something no one would ever voluntarily ask for. Jagger said it wasn't the same for him, and the fact that he was staying back and not tearing Poe to shreds now, I guess, proved it.

When Poe lifted his head, I blinked up at him, coming back to myself, and he grinned, looking cocky as hell, obviously taking my faraway look as some kind of befuddled desire.

"Fuck, sweetness, love that look on you." He cleared his throat and dragged his thumb over my lips. "Tarrant doesn't like us fucking around with contractors, shit has gotten messy in the past, but once we bring you into the fold properly and his doubts are alleviated, we can be together."

I wondered why he was being as restrained as he had been. Tarrant ran a tight ship; no fraternization with lowly members of the team, like me. Thank the goddess for that.

"The way you took care of me, healed me, no one's ever done that. I know now you want to be with me too. You're mine, and I want everyone to know it," he said, gripping my jaw tight. "That's why I get so angry when I see you with those hounds. They act like you belong to them." He shook his head and leaned in again. "It's making me fucking crazy, not getting a taste of you. I want you in my bed, witch, and I will do whatever it takes to make that happen." He kissed me again, roughly, then with a growl lifted his head. "I have to go. Our buyer is waiting."

I nodded. "Okay."

"Get a nice dress," he said. "And something sexy for underneath."

I smiled and laughed again. "What's your favorite color?"

"Red."

Of course. How unimaginative. "What night is this event?"

"That's a secret as well. Just make sure you get something ASAP, and be ready to drop whatever you're doing when I call with a time."

"Sounds good."

He gave me another slimy head to toe, then left, getting in a car with Lars and taking off.

I quickly walked to mine, got in and, as agreed, headed straight for home. Jagger was worried someone could be watching, and after what Poe said, being seen with Jag now would blow this thing wide open.

Traffic was heavy, and it took me an extra twenty minutes to get home.

There was no sign of Jagger when I got out of my car, unlocked my door and headed upstairs. As soon as I reached my apartment I knew I wasn't alone, though. The door wasn't locked, but I wasn't afraid, no, excitement burned through me.

I pushed it open. It was dark inside, but I felt his presence more deeply as soon as I walked in and shut the door behind me.

Maybe I should tell him to leave, but when Jagger pressed against my back in the darkness, his heavily muscled arms coming around me, I couldn't do it.

Meeting with Poe, being forced to let him touch me, kiss me, I needed Jagger. I needed his scent and his warmth. I needed him to take it all away.

His lips moved over my throat. "I'm going to kill him, Sutton. I'm going to make him suffer." He rubbed his face against mine, covering me with his scent, drowning out Poe's.

I had to tell him about the event they had planned, but I didn't want Jagger to stop touching me. I needed him more than I ever had.

He nipped my jaw, growling against my skin. "Please, baby. Please let me touch you."

"Yes," I said and covered his hand with mine, pushing if downward.

He shoved it down the front of my jeans and under my underwear, groaning when his fingers touched my bare flesh.

"Watching him touch you, smelling your fear while he put his fucking mouth on you, not being able to do anything to stop it, to protect you, almost drove me to insanity."

His thick rough-skinned fingers brushed over my slickness, then slid deeper. I stepped out, giving him better access to my body. What I was doing for Rune and Lucifer was a risk. I didn't know what was going to happen to me tomorrow, let alone when I went to whatever nightmare Poe insisted I attend. Yes, everything between me and Jag was messed up and confusing, but I realized I wanted this, for him to give me this, because tomorrow wasn't promised.

Once upon a time, I thought I'd get a lifetime with Jagger, then I'd resigned myself to a life without a mate. Now I had no idea what my future held, so this, however long it lasted, wasn't something I could turn away from, not now.

Yes, I would protect my heart.

But I wouldn't turn him away.

I couldn't even if I wanted to, not tonight.

"You feel so fucking perfect, sunshine." His hand slid up under my shirt, and he shoved down the cup of my bra, covering my breast with his huge, hot hand while he teased my opening with the other. "So tight, baby. That's it, work your hips." He walked me forward toward the bed, then bent me over it.

I lifted my ass shamelessly as he positioned me on the bed, my hands and knees pressing against the mattress, then tugged my jeans and underwear down. He stayed close behind me, his lips trailing down my back, then he toyed with my slick opening and, finally, slid his finger inside me, as deep as it would go.

I moaned. "Jagger."

"Rock against my hand, sunshine. That's it."

I did as he said, fucking myself on that one, long, thick digit.

"More?" he asked raggedly.

I nodded. "Please."

He slid all the way out, and when he pushed back in, he'd added a second finger. My pussy fluttered around the intrusion. Biting my lip, I pushed back against him, twisting my hips and trembling from the need building inside me.

"So fucking beautiful, baby. Your pussy stretching around my fingers, your honey sliding down those pretty thighs. Never seen anything more gorgeous, not in a thousand fucking years. Never seen anything more gorgeous as you working that hot fucking pussy for me."

Every dirty, sweet, hot thing he said pushed me closer to the edge. I tried to move faster, but I was shaking too hard. It was as if Jag could read my mind; he hooked his arm around my waist, holding me immobile, then finger-fucked me fast and deep, hitting my G-spot over and over without mercy.

I fisted the sheets and cried out as my orgasm built like a crescendo inside me. Soon my arms gave out, and I buried my face in the covers and screamed, jerking and trembling as I came, for him, soaking my thighs even more.

"Fuck," he snarled, then I heard the clink of his belt, and a moment later, the fat head of his cock was sliding against skin. "Squeeze your thighs together, sunshine, squeeze them for me." He hooked me around the waist, locking me to him. "You're not ready to take my cock, baby, but I gotta feel you around me."

Oh my gods. This was too fucking hot.

I squeezed my thighs around him as tight as I could, and he started thrusting between them while his mouth, his lips, moved over my neck, my shoulder, sucking gently.

"One day you'll wear my mark, right here." He grazed his teeth over my skin, sending a shiver of need through me. "The next time I have you like this, on your hands and knees, when all this fucking mess is over with..." I felt him shudder, and he licked along my throat to my ear. "I'll be sliding into this tight little pussy, Sutton. I'll be fucking claiming what's mine."

My arms nearly gave out again. Everything he was saying was bringing me closer to the edge once more, and with every rough glide between my clenched thighs, he was working my clit. The head of his cock, his long thick, hard shaft was a constant assault on my sensitive flesh.

"Jagger," I gasped. "Oh...shit..."

"You gonna come for me again, sunshine?" he snarled. "Let me hear it, then. Let your male hear you scream his name."

I did. I screamed his name while he held me in place,

not letting up on the constant pressure of his cock against my clit. As soon as I collapsed, he lifted me, spun me to my back and, with my feet on either side of his head, wrapped his arms around my thighs, squeezing them together again and bending them into my chest. He leaned over me, his eyes locked on mine as he thrust faster between my slick thighs.

His canines slid down and his eyes shifted to red as I felt his cock grow thicker. "Jagger...what...holy shit," I rasped.

"You feel that?" His eyes were hooded. "Only you get that, that's only for you. I've been alive over a thousand years, and this is the first time this has happened, because I'm with you, because my body thinks it's deep inside you. Every part of me wants to claim you." He hissed out a breath. "Can't wait for you to take my knot, my perfect little mate," he said, his voice rough. "Locked against me, no choice but to take every drop of come I give you."

His knot? Goose bumps lifted all over me, heat flushing through me at the thought.

"You want that, don't you?" he said as he picked up the pace. "You want your male to make you his." He slammed forward, and hot come splashed against my stomach as he continued to thrust between my tightly clenched thighs until he was spent.

When he finally released me, my legs fell wide, and he came down on top of me, wrapping me in a tight hug. I was covered by him, surrounded by him. He trembled against me, and I wrapped my arms around him as well.

Jagger was gruff, abrupt, often blunt, but then my once emotionless hound would say something that was so hot or sweet or romantic, or gods, heartfelt, that it had the power to steal my breath. But this? I knew hounds liked affection, that they loved hugs, but no one had ever hugged me like this, not for any reason. Jagger held me as if his next breath was reliant on it.

And with every second that passed, I felt my walls starting to crack. I drew in a breath when tears threatened, stinging my eyes. What the hell was wrong with me? Is this all it took? Someone to hold me like I mattered? Was I so broken, so desperate for affection that I could forget everything he'd said and done because he made me feel wanted?

Jagger's phone started ringing, and he growled, his mouth so close to my ear that the rough sounds made me shiver. "That's War's ringtone." I felt his reluctance as he lifted up and reached over the side of the bed to scoop up his phone. His eyes were on me as he lifted it to his ear. "Yeah?"

I made sure to keep my expression neutral. I did not want him to see how deep in my feelings I was after what we'd just done. I wasn't ready to deal with it, not yet. So I smiled up at him, like I always did. Smiling through my fear, or pain, or heartbreak. I'd done it all my life; this was no different.

I didn't really hear what he was talking about—except that he was obviously needed by his alpha—I was too focused on holding it together while those moss-green eyes moved over me. I felt as if he was absorbing me, pulling me deeper into himself, so when he left, he'd be taking a part of me with him. It was a silly thought, but there was no other way to describe it.

He ended the call. "I have to go," he said.

"I got that."

"I want to stay," he added, sliding his hand up the side of my throat, the same spot Poe had gripped me, but this didn't feel like a threat, this felt like comfort. "Just for the record. There's nowhere else I'd rather be than here in this bed with you."

"It's okay, Charming. I get it." It was a struggle just to say that. My emotions were way too close to the surface right now to listen to him say sweet things. I cleared my throat. "I made some calming elixir for Kurgan. The blue bottle on the table. Four drops should calm him for most of the day."

"I appreciate that, baby." He leaned in, pressing a gentle kiss to my lips. "Can I come back, when I'm done?"

This had been more than I could deal with for one night. "I have some more work to do. I'll see you tomorrow, though, right?"

Something moved through his eyes, something that looked a lot like disappointment. "Yeah, sunshine, I'll see you tomorrow." He kissed me again and got up.

I watched him dress, working to keep my breathing slow and even, when in reality I was seconds from hyperventilating.

When he finally shut the door behind him, using his powers to lock the door, I grabbed the pillow and sobbed into it.

What the hell was I doing? Did I want to be with Jagger? *Yes.* Everything in me screamed to be with him, to let him in, and I realized that it wasn't Jagger that I didn't trust, it was the fates who terrified me, who made me want to run and hide and protect myself. They'd hurt me, breaking the organ currently pounding in my chest too many times.

I wanted to trust that Jagger and I could have our happily ever after. He was trying so hard. He believed the things he said to me, the promises he was making, but he wasn't in control of what happened to us, they were.

A childhood filled with mental abuse and abandonment

had altered me in ways that I was only now truly discovering. That damage wasn't easily glossed over, and it wasn't easily fixed.

It wasn't Jagger's fault that his mate was broken so badly, or that the one time I decided to trust myself and what I felt, it had blown up in my face.

I'd been trained by my family never to reach for anything good, because you'd get your hand slapped away every time. Even if I wanted to try to reach for what was mine one more time, and I realized now, I did—I didn't know how.

CHAPTER
TWENTY-ONE

Sutton

I HADN'T HEARD from Jagger since he left the night before and a small, messed-up part of me was relieved. The voice inside me could talk all the shit it wanted. *See? You were right. What you did last night didn't mean anything to him. He just wanted to get off and you're an easy mark. The fates are laughing their asses off at how pathetic you are!*

Except, I knew the truth. Those thoughts were coming from past Sutton—the scared and heartbroken young girl who'd been abandoned and betrayed by the people she should trust the most.

I scrubbed my hands over my face, exhausted. I'd ended up getting out of bed when Jagger left and got a head start on Tarrant's next delivery. I only stopped because I had a shift at the clinic this morning, and now I was home and back at it.

My phone chimed, and I quickly checked it.

Poe: *Be ready in twenty minutes. I'll swing by to pick you up.*

Shit.

I didn't want to do this, not tonight. My poker face was nowhere to be found. But what choice did I have? Also, the fact that Poe obviously knew where I lived sent icy fingers down my spine. Had he been watching me? Did he know Jagger had been here? Was this some kind of trap?

I quickly texted Jagger, telling him what was happening, then rushed to get ready. If it was a setup, Jagger would be there. Nothing bad would happen to me, because he wouldn't let it. I hadn't had time to buy a dress for tonight, but I did own something that could work—it'd have to. I did my hair, quickly applied makeup, then chopped up some fruit for Boo and put it out. I was just sliding on the only pair of heels I owned when I heard his knock downstairs.

Snatching up my bag, I checked my phone as I rushed down to meet Poe. No reply from Jagger yet. *Shit. Shit. Shit.* I had no idea where we were going, and if Jagger wasn't there to follow, no one would know where I was.

He's a hound. He can find you anywhere.

At that thought, I was able to breathe a little easier. Hounds were the best trackers around. He just needed my scent and he'd find me. It was going to be okay. Everything was going to be okay—unless, of course, Poe killed me before Jagger could get to me.

I opened the door, and Poe stood there in a dark suit. His gaze slid over me from head to toe, and I wanted to shrivel in on myself.

"You look good enough to eat," he said and licked his lips.

I forced a smile. "You look good as well." The compliment was like ash on my tongue.

He plucked my phone from my hand, slid my bag from my shoulder, and placed them on the floor inside the door.

"No phones allowed, and you don't need anything else."

Icy fear prickled all over me. "How very cloak and dagger."

He grinned and took my hand, pulling me forward and closing the door after me. I subtly searched the street, the shadowy alleys, and storefronts for any sign of Jagger. Nothing, but that didn't mean he wasn't there.

Poe led me to his car and opened the door for me to get in. I was trapped, with no way to contact anyone, and wasn't sure if Jagger had even gotten my message. Poe could be driving me to my death and no one would know until it was too late.

It was hard, but I shoved all those fears down as deep as I could. I was good at that. Pretending I was okay when I was far from it was my specialty, and tonight I needed it more than ever. "Can you tell me where we're going now?"

Poe glanced my way as he turned a corner. "It's pretty ingenious, actually, I can't wait to show you."

"Oh?"

"There's these old tunnels under the city, part of the old sewer system that was closed off when they replaced it thirty years back. Tarrant's made use of them. It's a bit of a maze, and the interesting part is, there are different ways to get in, depending on which quadrant we're utilizing. Having multiple access and exit points is another way to keep the location secure."

"I'm wearing heels to a sewer?" I made a silly face while my mind spun.

He actually chuckled. "I promise, no sewage."

Poe pulled over on a nondescript street, not one I was familiar with, and before I could get out, he handed me something. "Put this on."

A mask, and he had one as well. I took it. Knowing no one there would see my face was a serious relief.

"Does everyone wear them?"

"Anonymity is of the highest importance. If everyone's faces are covered, no one can be implicated of anything."

My brief feeling of relief slid down my body and out through the soles of my feet. We exited the car and Poe led me down an alleyway. It appeared to be a dead end, but as we neared the end, a small alcove revealed a steel door with a digital key pad. He punched in a code, and the sound of steel sliding against steel sent chills through my veins as the lock disengaged.

We walked through, and when he closed the door behind us, we were plunged into a darkness so complete that I couldn't see my hands in front of my face. I heard and felt Poe do something beside me and a red light came on. We were at the top of a staircase. We descended at least five flights, then he punched another code into a second panel, different from the first one, letting us through a steel door.

This tunnel was much larger, grander, and I felt as if I'd walked into some fancy cellar and not an old sewer. There was even Victorian-style, black iron streetlamps lighting the way. It was almost—charming.

At least until we reached the end and walked into an open area. There was a small stage in the middle of the space, surrounded by chairs, and I could see two other tunnels on opposite sides, one wide open, leading somewhere else, and another with a heavy curtain drawn across it. It was partially open, and beyond it, though mostly obscured, I saw cages. They appeared empty from where I was standing.

My mouth went dry and dread churned in my stomach. "Are there others coming?"

"In an hour, everyone will start to arrive. I wanted to bring you here early and show you around."

I swallowed thickly. "Then why the masks, if we're here alone?"

"Cameras," he said. "We're also here early for the deliveries."

Poe didn't want Tarrant to know I was with him. "Of what?"

He tapped the side of his nose. "All will be revealed. You're one of the reasons tonight could happen, and your skills have ensured these events will continue."

"Me?" I felt sick to my stomach.

"When Luke fucked up, we found ourselves in serious trouble," he said, surprising me by sharing. "We have clients that rely on these evenings. Things could have gotten dangerous if you hadn't stepped up."

Stepped up? They were holding Luke captive and blackmailing me. Poe was utterly delusional. "What should I expect tonight?"

His chest puffed up. "A very special, exclusive auction that I'm tasked with overseeing."

An auction. *Oh fuck.* "That's a…a big deal," I said, trying to stroke his ego and keep him calm. He seemed to be getting more excited by the minute—his eyes were bright and he kept clenching and unclenching his fingers.

He nodded, his nostrils flaring. "It is." His hand shot out, and he grabbed one of my breasts, startling me. The move was odd, awkward, confusing. He breathed in deep, squeezing me almost painfully as he released a shuddering breath.

I didn't know what to do. I was all alone with this crazed demon. If I pushed him away, I could end up dead, but he was hurting me, his hold bruising. His eyes opened, his excitement increasing as he stared down at me.

"After tonight, I can have you," he said, and he actually shuddered. "I can keep you."

What the fuck was he talking about? "Keep me?"

He backed me up until I hit the wall. "Tarrant is... controlling. He likes our undivided attention." He glanced up at the camera, and I realized he'd turned me so his body hid what he was doing to me. "He has ways of knowing if we've...strayed from our path. After tonight, he'll know that you're on our side, and things can be different."

Holy shit. He wasn't allowed to be with me. Tarrant was a fucking twisted weirdo who controlled everything his people did, down to who they fucked, and thank the goddess for that. Poe had risked a lot kissing me at the fights, and Lars was obviously keeping Poe's secret.

He squeezed my breast again, like some inexperienced, grabby weirdo, and I barely held back my flinch.

"You're excited about that, too, aren't you, Sutton?"

I nodded, swallowing thickly, trying to hide the pain he was causing. "Yes, of course."

He smiled, looking relieved, then his gaze darkened. "Fuck, I want to sink my teeth into you..." He squeezed me again and sucked in a rough breath. "Right...here."

His phone rang and he startled, then finally let go of me and held a finger to his lips.

It was hard not to sag in relief.

As Poe listened, his excitement slowly gave way to fury,

even as he kept his tone even and controlled. He had to be talking to Tarrant.

Poe ended the call, shoved his phone in his pocket, grabbed my hand, and yanked me along with him back the way we came.

I jogged to keep up. "What's going on?"

"The auction's been cancelled."

"What? Why?"

"Our biggest clients can't make it, so we've had to reschedule for tomorrow night."

Poe seemed to be regaining his control as we quickly took the stairs and walked out into the alley, but as soon as the door closed, he spun and slammed his fist into the brick wall, over and over again.

I scrambled back while he lost control completely, roaring as he beat the shit out of the wall. Finally, he spun back to me, eyes wild, his usually slicked-back hair messy. I wanted to turn and run; instead, I forced myself to walk up to him, approaching the unstable demon like I would a wild animal.

Carefully, I took his hand, lifting it. "You've hurt yourself." I sent power into him, healing the worst of it, aligning the bones that he'd broken and repairing his split-open bleeding hand, doing whatever I had to, to win his trust.

He let me, watching me closely. "You care about me, don't you, Sutton?"

"Of course," I said, the lie like ash in my mouth. "I'm sorry you're upset."

He grabbed my jaw roughly. "I'm upset, that this, you and me finally being together, has been delayed *again*. I can't take much more. I can't be separated from you much longer."

This was bad.

His phone rang again, and he cursed as he pulled it free. "I have to leave."

"I can find my own way home," I said. "It's fine."

He watched me from under hooded lids for several seconds. His moods, his reaction changed on a dime. He'd gone from excited to furious to whatever this was in minutes. "I'll be in touch," he finally said.

He got into his car and peeled off, and I almost collapsed in relief against the storefront I stood beside.

That's when I realized I had no phone and no way to contact anyone, and nothing was open around me. Putting my head down, I quickly strode along the street, in search of a phone, then spotted a street sign. I was close to Rune's asylum.

I had some things to share with him, then maybe I could get a ride home.

It didn't take long to reach the intimidating building in the center of Seventh Circle, and the demon at the door let me straight in. Rune was waiting with his apartment door open when I stepped out of the elevator.

"Sorry to just show up like this—"

"No need for apologies, lovely." He held his door wide, his gaze roaming over me as I passed. "I like the dress, and the shoes. Is the outfit for me, or is this just a happy accident?"

"I was just out with Poe."

The light and flirty attitude dropped instantly. "You have an update?"

"He took me to some secret lair Tarrant created under the city, it's part of the old sewer system. There was supposed to be an auction there tonight. He made me wear a mask, it's apparently all anonymous—"

The door crashed open. I jumped and spun around as Jagger strode in.

"You could knock, you know? I just had it repaired," Rune said, looking pissed.

But he wasn't the only one. Jagger's anger saturated the room.

"What the fuck?" he said, but his hard stare wasn't on Rune, it was on me. "You didn't think telling me about this outing you had planned with Poe was important information?"

Shit. I hadn't actually told him about the upcoming surprise event Poe wanted to take me to. I'd gotten home to find Jagger in my place, and he'd touched me, kissed me, distracted me.

"I'm sorry. I planned to. And in my defense, he never actually gave me a time or place. It was last minute. I had twenty minutes to get ready before he picked me up."

His nostrils flared, and he looked down at his boots while he breathed heavily in and out, over and over again.

"Jag—"

He lifted a finger and shook his head, silencing me.

I bit my lips together and waited.

Rune sat on his couch, his arm casually draped along the back. "You didn't tell him?" Rune asked me now, brow arched.

"I meant to."

"You meant to?" His eyes darkened. "I don't often agree with Jagger. In fact, I never have. But if you were mine, I would take you over my fucking knee for that shit. Lucifer told you, you were to have Jagger shadow you whenever you were with that fucker, yet you recklessly went to this underground shithole with a demon who is known to be seriously unstable, not knowing what you were walking into or who would be there?"

I straightened. "Now hang on a minute. You and Lucifer were more than happy to toss me into this situation. Jag protecting me was just something he threw on at the end of the conversation to keep the peace. I told you I planned to tell Jagger, but everything happened fast. I did text him tonight as soon as I found out. I'm here, I'm fine, and I'm fucking getting sick of having to answer to overbearing, controlling males."

Jagger was suddenly at my back, his hand coming around and taking my jaw, tilting my head to the side. He dragged his nose along my throat and snarled.

"He touched you, again. Put his fucking mouth on you?" His beast had control of his voice.

"It's okay. Apparently, Tarrant has some rule about fraternization between the demons who work for him and contractors like me. They have to keep it in their pants because of some issues they've had in the past. Poe seems to think once I'm brought fully into the fold, then *we can finally be together*. He seemed to think that me being at this auction would achieve that. When it was called off due to some big buyer pulling out, he lost it, and messed up his hand pummeling a brick wall."

"Is there a new date for this auction?" Rune asked.

"Tomorrow night. I assume the time and entrance to get down to this place will be the same, but I can't be sure of that. Poe said there were many entrances."

Rune sat forward. "Do you know what they're selling?"

"No, but there were cages. Big ones."

"Humans?" Jag said.

Rune's jaw clenched. "If it is, we can send that fucker

Tarrant so deep underground he won't ever see the light of day again."

"If they're messing with humans, the knights will want to be involved," Jagger said.

The Knights of Hell were half angel, half demon tasked with protecting humans and demi-demons like Jack, humans who carried demon blood and special powers.

Rune stood. "Let's not involve them yet, not until we have proof. The last thing we need is them charging in there before I get my evidence to burn Tarrant for good." His gaze slid to me. "This was good work, Sutton. I'm not pissed with you anymore."

"Why, thank you."

He shrugged. "It seems you handled yourself well."

"Yeah, maybe you did," Jagger said. "But don't ever do that shit on your own again."

"I did text you," I said bristling.

"I was in Hell. I was only there for a couple hours, but with the way time moves differently there, I was too late." He curled his arm around my chest. "Won't happen again."

He gave me an affectionate squeeze, and a hiss of pain slipped from me before I could stop it. Jagger froze, and Rune's head turned sharply back to me.

"I'm okay," I said quickly. "It's nothing."

Jagger was pissed enough, I didn't want to worry him more. He turned me to face him, so my back was to Rune, then he hooked his finger in the deep V of my dress and tugged it lower, exposing the swell of my breast where Poe had manhandled me.

Now it was Jagger's turn to hiss. I looked down and the skin he'd exposed was already bruised, and there were clear fingerprints in my flesh.

"Poe did this?" When I said nothing, his gaze sliced to mine. "Poe fucking did this to you?"

"He grabbed me, yes. But that's all he could do. It looks worse than it is. He can't force me to do anything, not when it's against Tarrant's rules."

Jagger's gaze was red now and so filled with rage, it was as if fire danced in his irises as they locked on Rune. "My patience is at its limit, understand me? Asking me to stand back while my female puts her fucking life on the line, while some piece of shit assaults her repeatedly, is too fucking much, Rune."

For once, Rune didn't smirk or say something to piss Jagger off even more. He nodded. "I know, and I know I'm asking too much to continue with this, but I have to ask, because if we don't get Tarrant under control, if he continues to do the shit he is, we risk the gates of Hell closing permanently."

Jagger's head jerked up. "Lucifer said that?"

"Not in so many words, but we both know it could come to that. Lucifer and the angels have been on shaky ground since the drama with his son a while back. They're looking for any excuse to start a war. We've gotten things relatively under control, at least in a way that keeps the angels somewhat happy. But we need to finish this as quickly and as quietly as possible. If humans are getting hurt, there will be no more negotiating. Right now, Sutton is our only way to do that without starting a whole lot of shit, both here on earth and in Hell. Shit is precarious, and your female is the only way we get out of this mess."

I stepped away from Jagger, or tried to. He grabbed my hips and kind of snorted like a deranged bull. I was pretty sure he couldn't release me even if he wanted to by the way his fingers were flexing and the veins were bulging in his forearms, so I stopped trying to step away and placed my hands on his chest. "I can see that you're worried." Massive understatement. He looked seriously feral. "But I am doing this—for Luke, and for everyone else Tarrant has hurt. I'll do whatever I have to, to keep him from hurting anyone else, and if I stop a war between Heaven and Hell while I'm doing it, that's a seriously major bonus."

"Sutton," he rumbled.

"You know I'm right. I have to do this."

"Warrior," he said roughly and slid his fingers through my hair.

My breath caught. "I'm not, I'm just—"

"Yeah, you are."

The silence stretched out and his gaze dipped to my mouth.

I cleared my throat.

"I want to see this place he took you to," he said, thankfully changing the subject.

"The doors are locked with codes and there are cameras." I chewed my lips. "I know a way around the cameras, there's a spell."

"I can get around a lock," Jagger said. "Doesn't matter what kind."

"It's a risk," Rune said.

"No one else was down there when we were. I'm sure of that. If we're going to check it out, now would be the best time."

CHAPTER
TWENTY-TWO

Jagger

I BIT BACK a growl as Sutton sliced an *X* into her palm with a small blade and recited a spell, one that would disrupt the cameras and whatever alarm system they had down there.

I'd stopped by her place before we came here, and she'd changed into dark jeans and a hooded sweatshirt. She wore darker colors more often now. Before I fucked everything up, she'd always worn bright colors that matched all that sunshine that radiated from her.

She curled her fingers into her bleeding palm, and I followed her down multiple flights of stairs until we reached another door.

I lifted my hand and let my power pulse from me, aiming it at the lock and disengaging it.

"This seems too easy," Sutton said as we walked into the tunnels. She'd described them after we left Rune, but they still surprised me. She was right, they were impressive and, from what Poe had told her, vast. "They have to know there are some in this city who could get past these security measures."

"Maybe, or maybe they're that fucking brainless." I scented the air and froze.

"What is it?"

I reached for her. "Fear. So much of it, and pain. I can smell human, Sutton. A fucking lot of it, and something else." I couldn't quite get it yet.

"The cages are this way," she said and tried to lead me.

I pulled her back, holding her tightly to my side.

She looked up at me. "Is someone else down here?"

I scanned the tunnels ahead. "It's the fear. I'm an animal, sunshine, I may be walking and talking like a man, but at the heart of me, I'm all beast. You're my female. Protecting you is a driving need inside me that controls my every thought and action."

She blinked up at me with those stunning fucking big eyes that turned me inside out when I looked into them, that made me want to fall to my knees and beg her to forgive me. I wanted to claim her with a fierceness that was terrifying, and that knowledge caused a pain in the center of my chest for my son. I could stand beside Sutton, I could reach out and touch her, scent her. He would have to suffer with that unfulfilled longing calling to him like a siren, like an addiction, like the sweetest hunger, but for him that hunger could never be sated.

"It's that bad down here?" she asked, no idea where my thoughts had taken me.

I nodded, my gaze on her mouth. I wanted to nibble that perfect lower lip, and I would once we left the danger of this place. "Worse."

Her hand trembled in mine. "This is my fault," she

choked out. "The drugs I made for them, they're using them to hurt people."

I slid my finger under her chin, tipping her head back. "I don't want to hear that bullshit. You had no way of knowing Tarrant's fucked-up schemes went this deep, and judging by the scent in this place, it's vast. The shit they've been doing goes back a lot farther than when they blackmailed you into working for them."

She nodded, those fucking soul-shattering eyes still wide on me. "Okay," she whispered.

She didn't believe me, but she would. I'd make sure she did. "Let's take a quick look around, then get the fuck gone, yeah?"

"The cages are just through there." She pointed to a wide tunnel that was partially curtained off. I quickly led her through the open space, past a small stage in the middle that was surrounded by chairs, and shoved back the curtain.

The cages were large enough to hold two or three people. The scent of fear was stronger here, and my hackles rose as I scented the air again. "Definitely human and something else..." I froze, breathing deeply. "Fuck."

"What is it?"

"Demi-demon." My lips curled. "Tarrant's been snatching demi as well. We're gonna have to bring the knights in on this."

"Why would he be taking them?"

"The demi? My guess, their powers." No, they weren't full-blooded demon, but something happened when mixed with human blood, and their abilities were far more impressive. "For as long as demi have existed, there have been demons trying to capture them to use for their powers."

"So they're auctioning them off here to the highest bidder?" she asked, looking seriously freaked out.

"That'd be my guess."

"Why humans?"

There was a tremble to her voice, but there was no sugarcoating it. "Only one thing that certain demon breeds want humans for...well, two, but I'd be willing to bet money it's the former."

"What? What do they want them for?" she asked hesitantly.

"Food."

She blanched. "They're auctioning off live humans for demons to eat."

"That would be my guess, yeah." Another scent reached out to me and a growl vibrated from my chest. I gripped her hand tighter. "This way."

"What can you smell?" she asked, jogging down the tunnel beside me.

"Hound."

We ran until we reached the end of the tunnel and turned onto another. "We're close," I said as we reached a T at the end. Brick's scent grew deeper.

A growl echoed through the tunnels. I spun left and saw him. He had an iron cuff around his throat, like Kurgan wore, and the chain attached to it was bolted to the wall. He saw me and snarled viciously, baring his teeth and pawing at the ground.

"He doesn't recognize me." He wasn't shifting, and I'd guess he couldn't. He was young, though, and I was still stronger than him, even in human form. If I had to carry him out of here snarling and snapping, I took a step toward him—

"Stop," Sutton cried.

I froze.

"Step back." She pointed to the wall by the tunnel's opening. "Sigils. There and there. I can see more around his collar."

I immediately stepped back. "What kind of magic are we looking at? Can you break through?"

"They're demon, and they're old, powerful. I can feel it. I don't have enough knowledge, but I do know if we go any closer, it would mean certain death for me. You? Well, I'm not sure, but it wouldn't be good." Brick tilted his head back and howled.

"I think the ones on the collar are stopping him from shifting."

Brick pawed at the floor again, then paced.

"We can't get to him. These wards are too dangerous," Sutton said as she took her phone from her pocket and zoomed in, taking pictures of the sigils. "Rune should be able to help us. He'll know how to break through."

I didn't want to leave Brick here, but at least I could tell Dirk and Elena that their son was alive. Tarrant had something planned for him, obviously, whether that was auctioning him off or something equally as fucked up, I had no idea, but for now, at least, we knew he was okay.

Sutton placed her hand on my arm. "The auction's tomorrow. We'll get him then."

I nodded, grabbed her hand, and headed back the way we'd come—

A whistling Lars rounded the corner, carrying bags of meat. He froze—dropped the bags, then spun and ran.

I exploded after him, tackling him to the ground before he'd barely rounded the corner, then dragged the thrashing demon back. I held him down, tightening my grip on the fucker's throat, and scented the air. "He's the only one down here. He can release Brick."

Sutton looked down at him, then up at me. "We have to leave Brick here. If we get him out now, Tarrant will know something's up. He'll postpone the next auction, or move it somewhere else, and we won't get the evidence we need to shut him down."

I hadn't thought of that. Fuck. I kneeled on the demon's chest and glanced up at Sutton. "You're right, but he can still tell us how to drop the ward so we're ready." I gripped the squirming demon's throat. "Tell me how to get through those sigils." Lars clawed at my wrist, gasping for breath. "Speak or I tear your head from your neck."

"There are words that must be spoken and...and a charm."

I squeezed tighter. "Show me."

He nodded, and I lifted him by the throat to his feet. He rushed to the entrance, and I grabbed him by the back of his collar. "You stay at the entrance." If Lars was able to walk through the ward, I wouldn't be able to get to him. "Explain how it works."

He nodded quickly. "Once you say the words, you only have ten seconds to use the charm."

"Do it."

Sutton lifted her phone, recording him as he recited a bunch of words in an old demonic language, then pressed the charm to the sigil closest, the one that was more ornate than the rest.

The demon lifted his hand and demonstrated the ward was down. "Is it safe for me, or just demons?" He looked up at me, and I could tell he was trying to decide whether to lie or not. "Weigh your options very carefully here, Lars. You lie and I survive, you are ash."

"Only those of us with demon blood may pass."

"Is there a way to destroy the barrier completely?"

Fury filled the demon's eyes. "Yes." I gave him a rough shake to keep him talking. "The mother sigil must be broken."

"This one? The one you used the charm on?" Sutton asked.

He nodded, scowling at her.

"We know how to free Brick," she said, then turned back to Lars. "There's another hound, yes? Where is he?"

"I don't know."

"Where?" I slammed Lars against the wall.

"I don't know! Tarrant moves it around. Only he or Poe look after it."

"If anything happens to him, to either of them, you're dead, and it will be slow and painful, motherfucker." I heard the rattle of bags and turned as Sutton...walked over the threshold, through the barrier Lars had dropped, and my heart nearly fucking tore through my chest.

She was fine, unharmed, her demon blood had protected her, but my heart was now lodged in my fucking throat.

"Don't get too close," I called out.

She nodded, carrying the bags of meat closer and stopping just out of Brick's reach. She tossed the meat to him before rushing back to me. "We should get going."

Yeah, I needed to get her out of here before any more demons decided to drop in. I dragged Lars back the way we'd come.

Sutton followed. "What are you going to do with him?"

"Nothing," I said and felt the tension, the fear, drain from Lars. We couldn't make him disappear, but we had to make sure he didn't talk and blow our cover. "I'll leave that for Rune." The demon went wild, fighting and flailing against my hold.

"Don't like that idea, do you, fucker?" I said, then realized the demon had peed himself.

Guess not.

›)》● ((‹

Sutton

As we walked out of the asylum, Jagger curled his fingers around the back of my neck in a possessive hold. We'd just filled Rune in on what we found and handed over Lars. Rune was going to *extract information* from him, his words, and make sure he kept his mouth shut.

Jagger's thumb swiped over my sensitive skin, and the broken, distrustful part of me urged me to pull away, that enjoying the way it felt to have his hands on me made me weak and pathetic—the other part of me, the one that constantly longed for Jagger's touch, purred like a contented kitten and wanted to beg him to keep petting me.

He was quiet as we walked away from Rune's domain, but that hold he had on me was doing all the communicating for him. Jagger felt overly possessive whenever we were around the powerful demon, in the extreme, and as we turned onto another street, one that was quiet, empty, he stopped me with a growl, and spun me to face him.

My heart pounded as he backed me into a short alleyway. One of his arms hooked around my waist in an unforgiving hold, the other hand was at the side of my throat and his thumb slid along my jaw over and over.

"What are you doing?" I stared into his eyes. They looked black in the shadows, and my already pounding heart went wild when he pressed his massive body more firmly against mine. "Jagger?" He was trembling against me, gods, vibrating, a rumbling sound coming from him constantly now.

He dipped his head and pressed his nose to the spot between my neck and shoulder and breathed deeply, and his arm spasmed around me.

"Jagger?" I said again.

"Sunshine," he said low. "I have to do this, okay?" He groaned. "I just...I need a minute."

"Okay," I rasped and realized he needed reassurance, and that it felt so incredibly good to give it to him, to give him what he needed.

He growled softly as he rubbed his scent on me, his jaw scraping softly, his warm lips brushing my throat as that low, constant rumble vibrated from him and through me.

"You were in danger tonight, more than once," he finally said. "The beast needs to be soothed, and scent tells an animal like me everything we need to know. Breathing you in now, taking in your scent without fear or pain, is what I need. Feeling your heart beating against me, your warmth soak into me, is what I need."

Gods, this male was breaking me down more with every moment I spent with him. "You need soothing?" I whispered in the darkness, cocooned in his arms.

"Yeah, baby, I just need to hold you for a little while. Will you let me do that?"

Knowing how much hounds craved touch and how much they loved hugs, I could never deny him that, I didn't want to. "Yes, of course." Another giant piece of my armor fell away. "Is there anything else I can do to help?" I asked, because he was being so vulnerable with me, in a way I never thought he ever would, or was capable of, and I wanted to give him more.

"Can you touch my skin?" he asked roughly. "I need your hands on my skin, sunshine."

Heat flushed through me as I nodded and slid my hands up under his shirt, my palms meeting smooth, hot flesh. "Better?" Now I was having trouble breathing right.

The vibration in his chest increased as he shuffled closer, wrapping his arms around me more firmly, his hands moving over my back. "I can't get enough of you in my lungs," he groaned.

"I like your scent too," I said, because I was surrounded by it, by him, and it was making me lightheaded.

He made a contented sound as he fisted my hair lightly and pressed his nose to it, breathing deeply again. That sound, gods, it had my blood heating and my nipples tightening. He shifted his hips just a fraction, and I felt how hard he was. So impossibly hard.

"Ignore it," he said roughly.

"Ignore the massive hard-on digging into my belly?" I said breathlessly.

"Not expecting anything more than this. So yeah, ignore it. Just having you with me, letting me hold you like this is enough. Not trying to pressure you into anything. I just need you close."

This male was destroying me one word at a time, and before I let myself think too much about what I was going to do, I reached between us and undid his jeans.

"Sunshine?" he rasped against my throat.

"Let me soothe you," I whispered. "Let me touch you." I shoved his jeans down a little so I could free his cock, and I moaned when the hard, hot, thick length filled my palm.

"Fuck," Jagger said, voice guttural.

"Back against the wall, Charming." I pushed his shoulder, and he did as I asked, turning and pressing his back to the brick wall. Yeah, he did what I said because he wanted me to keep touching him, but I was starting to think Jagger would do almost anything for me, anything I asked.

He was too thick for just one hand, so I took him in both and stroked him more firmly. "Good?"

His eyes were on me, glowing in the darkness, and he hooked me around the back of the neck and thrust his hips forward, into my grip. "Fucking perfect." He kissed me then, deep and hard, as he continued to thrust into my tight grip. Always taking over, always the one who needed to be in control.

"You're a control freak," I said against his lips.

"Yeah, but for you...for you I could surrender."

"Just not now?"

He fisted my hair tighter. "No, not now. I feel too fucking volatile right now." He groaned. "Squeeze tighter, baby. Fuck, that's it."

"You're so beautiful like this," I rasped, the words falling from my lips before I knew they were coming.

"Nothing more beautiful than you coming for me, sunshine, nothing."

His breathing grew more ragged, and there was no more talking while he fucked into my grip. He pressed his forehead to mine, panting hard. I was trapped in his glowing stare, unable to look away.

"Please," he choked out, breaking the silence.

That one word, the sound of his voice so raw and desperate, more of that vulnerability, it reached inside me and gripped me tight.

"Please, sunshine," he said again.

I felt it, everything behind his plea, and though I didn't know how to voice the response he wanted from me, I felt that too. I couldn't say it, admit it, to him, or myself, just yet, but another giant piece of my armor fell away, revealing the truth as it shattered to unrepairable dust.

I was his.

His cock grew thicker, impossibly so. He took my mouth in a brutal kiss, and groaning against my lips, he came, shaking and growling for me.

No matter what happened between us from here on out —I belonged to Jagger.

And he belonged to me.

CHAPTER TWENTY-THREE

Sutton

I TRIED to stand tall in the main room of the clubhouse, but it wasn't easy when it was full of huge males grunting and growling with seemingly no ability to communicate efficiently.

And Dirk, Brick's sire, looked ready to punch something. He and his mate wanted their son back and weren't happy that we'd left him there, but they understood why we'd had to. This wasn't just about Brick, or Luke for that matter, it was about all the other people as well, human and demi-demon, that Tarrant had already hurt and the ones who needed help now.

The knight with long black hair and yellow eyes looked my way, and I couldn't stop myself from pushing into Jagger's side.

"You think more of these tunnels are warded?" he asked me.

I tried not to flinch, but as soon as I heard his voice it was impossible not to. The big male quickly glanced away, at least self-aware enough of the effect he had on people. Zenon was scarred and completely covered in ink and, according to Jagger, Lucifer's grandson, and with those eyes it was obvious.

Each of the knights was mated to a demi-demon, which meant they were intense while directing their questions at me. There was also a seriously weird vibe between Warrick and the knight's leader, Chaos. It seemed as if War wanted to cause the other male physical bodily harm, and the knight kind of just ignored it.

"Sutton?" Jag said. "The wards?"

"Oh...sorry." I chewed my lip. "We didn't go any farther along the tunnels, so I don't know for sure. I felt the vibrations of power. I think it's safe to say that, yes, there would be more. We thought it was too easy to get in, and I assume that's because it's the public gallery, so to speak, and needs to be accessed regularly. From what Poe said, there will be a lot of powerful demons in that room auction night. Tarrant would want to protect his prisoners," I said, anger shaking my voice. "I'd bet anything that the other areas are heavily warded with demon sigils as well."

Boo peeked out from under my hair, sensing my volatile emotions. He took in the big males standing around us, then ducked back but remained alert, as if he thought he could actually protect me should I need it. I rubbed his little head with my finger.

Rune straightened. "So, this auction's definitely happening tomorrow, lovely?"

"Yes, that's what Poe sa—"

"Use her name, motherfucker," Jagger growled.

Rune tipped his head to the side. "And what do you call

her?" He tilted his head back and scented the air. "Not mate, apparently."

One minute Jagger was beside me, the next he was grabbing Rune by the front of his shirt and slamming his fist into the demon's face. Rune didn't even swing back, he just laughed, while War and Rome dragged Jagger away.

Every pair of eyes slid my way, and my face heated. Their stares felt like an accusation. Did they think that I was purposely letting Jagger suffer? Probably. I didn't know where to look. Jagger yanked me against his side, and humiliating anger washed through me. I felt my panic rise and suddenly I couldn't breathe. I pushed away from Jagger. "I...I need some space, Charming."

I used the name to soften the blow that I was pushing him away, but I couldn't deal with the guilt on top of everything else.

More unhappy looks were directed at me, and I tried to slow my breathing, even as I clenched my fists. I didn't deserve their judgment. They didn't know me. They didn't know any damn thing about me. "So what's the plan?" I asked, probably a bit too sharply, but my feelings of inadequacy, of being judged in this room full of powerful immortals had taken hold. "Do you even have one, or are we all just gonna stand around while you unzip your pants and pull out a ruler?"

The room went silent, and my face burned hotter. What the hell was wrong with me?

Rune chuckled, probably because I'd accused him of penis measuring before.

"I don't need to measure mine, I know my number by heart," a knight named Rocco said with a big grin on his face.

Chaos shook his head, his lips twitching, while another

knight named Gunner huffed a laugh. Zenon did absolutely nothing.

Chaos turned to me. "We have a plan. The demi in this city are under our protection, and one of our own, James, is missing as well. We want him back, the others too." His gaze slid to Jagger. "And your female's right. We're going to have to get over the past and work together." He turned to War then. "You think you can do that?"

"I can do anything I put my mind to, Chaos. Just don't piss me off and we won't have a problem."

I didn't know their history, but I was over all this male posturing. I didn't know where my courage was coming from, but it wasn't letting up. "Cool. Care to fill me in, since I'm gonna be the one with my head on the block."

"We won't let anything happen to you," Rune said. "We have this under—"

"Don't placate me. Something's already happened, so don't you dare feed me that crap. They cut off my friend's finger right in front of me, and Poe is losing patience. I've had to endure his hands on me, his disgusting mouth, every time I see him."

All the males in the room went on alert, and Jagger's face filled with strain as if he were struggling to control the beast from coming through. I didn't want to upset him, but that was my reality, and it wasn't my job to manage his or anyone else's emotions, new or otherwise.

War studied me. "We know this has been a lot to ask—"

"You have no idea. None. You don't have the lives of a whole lot of people counting on you to be strong and brave, when you are utterly fucking terrified."

There wasn't a sign of judgment on any of their faces now, only anger and determination.

Rune stepped forward. "I promise you'll be rewarded

for this when this is all said and done. Tarrant is going to burn in the deepest pit of Hell for what he's doing."

"I don't want a reward, I just want this over with. What's the plan?"

·)))·●·(((·

Jagger

"What's going on?" Sutton asked, watching as everyone headed to the dens below the clubhouse.

"Movie night." The knights had left and everyone still here was heading down to our common room. There was nothing we could do until tomorrow. I risked taking her hand and breathed a sigh of relief when she didn't shove me away. She'd been unbelievably strong tonight, again proving what a warrior she was. "You wanna stay? Watch the movie?"

She chewed her lip, glancing at the exit. She was going to leave. I couldn't have that, not tonight, not when tomorrow she'd be risking her fucking life for this mission, and not after how upset she'd been during our meeting. If she left, I was going with her, but I needed her here with me in my den. I needed to soothe her the way she had me. I needed to take care of her.

"Fern will be there, and Wills and at least one of her sisters or cousins usually come as well."

She looked back at me. "I haven't seen Fern in a while, I've been avoiding her. I've been avoiding everyone since this mess started."

I tucked her hair behind her ear. "You don't need to hide

shit from her anymore, sunshine. This will all be over tomorrow." I shrugged. "Relic's probably already shared some of what's going on. Why don't you come down, catch up with your girl? Tell her what's been going on?"

I watched the tension drain from her face, and she nodded. "I really want to see her."

"Then let's do it?" Relief filled me when she nodded.

I led her down the stairs to the dens, and when we walked into the common room, everyone was already seated. As soon as Fern saw Sutton, she jumped up and rushed over. Reluctantly, I let go of her hand and watched as Fern took her aside. I couldn't hear what they were saying, but a moment later, they walked out together, no doubt headed to Fern and Relic's den to talk.

I wanted her back immediately, but if this helped, if reconnecting with her best friend made her happy, then I could deal.

I sat on one of the vacant couches, and Relic tossed me a beer. "Good seeing them together. Fern's been worried."

I nodded. He was right, but I couldn't help but glance at the door as I opened my beer. Then the movie started and everyone cheered as bags of chips and candy were tossed around the room.

It was hard, but I forced my shoulders to relax and tried to focus on the movie being projected on the wall. Tonight, Sutton was staying with me. In my bed. And I hoped like fuck she didn't fight me on it, because I needed this, and I knew she did too.

The movie was halfway through when she and Fern walked back in. Both had red-rimmed, puffy eyes. Fern headed for Relic and climbed into his lap. I was about to call to Sutton, but she was already searching me out and, finding me, walked straight over. She climbed onto the couch beside me and tucked in close on her own, letting me wrap my arm around her.

"Okay?" I asked.

She nodded against my chest. "Yeah, I'm good." She tilted her head back, smiling up at me. "Better than good." Her gaze moved over my face and dipped to my mouth, then it shot back up. "Oh, and I put Boo in your den. I made him a little nest in your bathroom, if that's okay?"

"Of course."

She smiled wider, then she turned to the movie. "Oh, I love this one."

I sat there, trying to keep my breathing even as my female lay against me in front of my brothers, in front of everyone in this room, saying without words that she was mine. I stared unseeing at the big screen in front of us, soaking it all in, her scent, her warmth, how fucking right this felt. The way she'd laugh with everyone at certain parts of the movie and squeeze me tighter at others—I *felt* it all. This didn't hurt, though. These emotions didn't cause pain. I wanted more of this feeling, craved more of the way Sutton made me feel.

I thought it couldn't get any better than this, but after I pulled one of the soft blankets from the back of the couch over her, she made an appreciative noise and wriggled closer so she was half on top of me. As I slowly, gently rubbed her back, she relaxed fully, lying against my chest. I had to fight to not fucking shake as my heart thumped wildly. Sutton had to feel it.

Relic tossed me another beer, and I almost missed it because I was so lost in the little female in my lap. He grinned, knowing exactly where my head was, and I couldn't even find it in me to scowl back.

Sutton's hand that had been resting on my thigh slid a bit higher, then back, and just that simple touch had my breath punching from my lungs. Then her hand moved up to my waist, her fingers slipping under my shirt, running over my stomach, touching my skin the way she knew I loved. The muscles tightened, and she made another sound, this one a soft moan.

She lifted up on her other hand then and pressed her face to my throat, her soft hair sliding across my jaw, my chin. I held the back of her head as she nuzzled against me a moment before her lips touched my throat and the soft, sucking kiss she gave me had me fucking gasping.

My brothers, their mates, they made out all the time on movie nights. No one cared, no one paid any attention but, yeah, I'd wondered what it would be like to have that, because I'd told myself I never would. Yes, the reason I should have let Sutton go was still there, but it was far too late for that now. I just hoped when I told her the truth, that she'd still want me.

Then all thought fucking left my head when she shifted, sliding across my lap, putting that perfect round ass on my hard dick, and looked up at me, a sweet, open smile curling her tempting lips, lighting up her eyes.

"Comfortable?" I rasped.

"Best seat in the house," she said.

I cupped the side of her face, my palm against her flushed cheek as a low rumbling laugh fell from me. Her eyes widened, and I didn't blame her. I couldn't remember the last time I'd laughed. I never laughed.

Sutton touched my lips, tracing my grin with her fingers, a look of wonder on her beautiful face. Sliding my fingers into her hair, I pressed my lips to hers, kissing her softly, gently sucking the top, then the pouty lower lip, and it was hard, but I swallowed my moan. No, it wasn't easy, especially when her hand curled around the side of my throat and her tongue darted out to taste me.

I was lost.

Hers.

Only and forever hers.

She curled her arms around my neck, and I held her to me tight, so every part of her body that could be was in contact with mine, and deepened the kiss. I licked into her hot mouth, groaning at the taste of her, the feel of her sweet little tongue against mine. My sunshine wriggled on my lap, and the scent of her hot, slick pussy filled my senses and called to the beast. I didn't want any other male in this room to scent her like this, this was mine, she was mine.

I stood, Sutton cradled in my arms, and strode from the room and into the tunnel, while she kissed along my jaw, my throat, while her hands went back up under my shirt. We finally reached my den, and I shoved the door open and kicked it closed behind us.

I laid her on the mattress and came down on top of her. She wrapped her soft little body around me, kissing the hell out of me, asking for more in every way but words.

She shoved at my chest, and I lifted up so she could yank my shirt up and off, and then her hands were wandering, exploring. It was fucking bliss, perfection. I never wanted her to stop.

"Fuck, sunshine," I groaned against her mouth as I gathered up her shirt and pulled away so I could drag it off.

"I want you," she whispered.

Every muscle in my body locked.

"I want you, Jagger," she said again.

I searched her beautiful face. "What are you asking for, sunshine?"

She blinked up at me in the shadowed room. "I don't know what will happen to me tomorrow—"

"Nothing will happen to you, I won't let it," I growled.

"I know," she said, running her hands over my back, my chest, soothing me with every sweet touch. "But nothing is certain in this life, and all I know is that right now, I need to know how it feels to have you inside me."

She wasn't asking me to make her my mate in truth, and I didn't expect her to, not yet anyway. She wanted me to make her feel good, to give us both a taste of what giving in to this overwhelming connection would feel like. "You want me to fuck you, baby?"

Her entire body trembled beneath me. "Yes," she rasped. "Yes, I want that very much."

I ground against her through our jeans. "As much as we both want that—"

"Don't say no."

I shook my head. "Not saying no. But you know how I'm built. Hounds are big, it takes time to work a female up to that, and even then, sometimes, it's just not possible."

"It'll fit," she said, her eyes bright in the shadows. "That's how it's supposed to work, right?"

"Yeah, that's how it's supposed to work, sunshine." I traced her lovely face with my fingers, and she shivered for me again. "But we have to take it slow." She bit her lip again, questions in her eyes. "What?" I said against her mouth. "Whatever you're thinking, ask."

"How do you...work me up to it?"

Just talking about fucking her had me close to the edge, add in her needy scent and I was surprised I could think at all. "My mouth, fingers, toys."

Her eyes widened. "Toys?"

I ground against her and my hips jerked harder at her

moan. "Because of our size, we can't always fuck a female, so we pleasure them in other ways."

"You have toys?"

There was a look on her face I couldn't read. "Yes," I said cautiously. "A lot of hounds keep a supply of new toys, for those times."

Her gaze slid away.

"Sutton?"

Her pretty eyes came back to me. "When was the last time you had to...use something like that on a female? Did you...were you with that wolf?"

I realized in that moment that my precious, perfect mate was jealous. I didn't ever want her to feel insecure, or less than she was to me. "No, fuck no. Before I met you, I didn't think a mate was possible for me. I didn't even allow myself to believe it when the truth was right fucking there —but my soul knew, my body knew. Since that first day I snatched you off the street, I haven't been with another female. I haven't wanted anyone but you."

"Really?" she whispered.

"Yeah, really. You're it for me. No matter what happens between us, you will only and forever be it for me."

She pulled me down for another kiss, this one deep and wild. Her hands went to the button of my jeans, and she tore them open while I did the same, yanking hers down her legs.

When I finally had her naked, I tossed her thighs over my shoulders and buried my face in her sweet cunt, groaning at the taste of her honey against my tongue as I ate her up. Sutton arched against the bed, hooking her legs around me tighter, and ground her pussy against my face. Perfect. So fucking perfect.

Pinning her down, I pushed her thighs wider and let my

tongue transform into my beast's, long and wide, and slid it deep inside her like last time. Sutton jerked and trembled, coming for me instantly, while she fisted my hair and called out my name.

Lapping her from ass to clit, I lifted my head. She was panting and shaking. "Ready for more?"

"I want you inside me," she said huskily. "I'm ready."

"You're not ready, sunshine, not yet."

"I am... I want—"

I slid two fingers inside her, and she arched against the mattress with a low groan, her thighs quivering as I thrust into her, fucking her slow and deep. Leaning in, I sucked one of her nipples into my mouth and grazed her skin with my fangs. She fisted my hair again and rocked her hips.

"I want you," she moaned.

My cock throbbed hard, the tip weeping for her. I wanted to slide inside my beautiful sunshine so badly. So fucking badly, but she wasn't ready for me yet.

"Can you take more, baby?" I asked, my voice so low and raw, it was almost inaudible.

"Yes, you. I can take you." She reached for me as she said it, her hips churning, her slick pussy coating my fingers.

She was tearing through my control with every needy plea. I slid my fingers out and added a third. She made a keening sound and snapped her thighs closed around my forearm. I leaned forward, forcing her legs wide again.

Sutton whimpered, her head twisting on her pillow, her soft honey-blond hair a sexy mess around her face. "Too much, baby?"

"Yes...no. *Oh gods.*" She lifted her hips, taking my fingers deeper. "Faster."

Fucking hell. She was destroying me one whimper at a

time. I pressed my hand against her belly, holding her steady, and thrust into her, faster, deeper.

Sutton was not just trembling, she was shuddering deeply. She rolled to her side with my fingers still inside her and curled up, gasping as she came for me again.

Leaning over her, I dragged my nose along her shoulder, her jaw, and nipped her ear. "My sunshine," I growled in her ear. "Mine." I eased my fingers from her and kissed her shoulder. "You've had enough for tonight."

She spun to face me, her eyes black and red and swirling. Fucking stunning. "No, I haven't. I want you," she said again.

Whatever control I was trying to hang on to, collapsed. Still, somehow, I didn't flip her onto her stomach. I didn't plant her on her hands and knees and thrust inside her. If I did that, I wouldn't be able to stop myself from mating her in truth. I'd bite her, mark her. I'd make her mine in a way that could never be taken back, and that had to be her choice, when she was ready.

So instead, I lay on the bed, on my back, and crooked my finger at her. "Want you too much. Too much to be careful. So this time, you control how much of me you take."

Her eyes brightened with excitement, and she fucking pounced. My little female climbed on top of me, gripped my hard-as-fuck cock, and positioned it at the opening of her pussy. "Hang on, baby, there's lube—" She sat down so the wide head pushed inside her. "Fuck!" I hissed through my teeth and barely stopped myself from arching against the mattress and pushing deeper.

Her eyes swirled faster as she pressed her hands to my chest and, biting her lip, swiveled her hips, stuffing my cock deeper inside her a little at a time. I was going to fucking perish. Just die of bliss right here underneath her.

"Fuck. Easy," I rasped.

She shook her head, determination on her lovely face. "I want this. It...it has to be tonight. It has to be." Her face was flushed as she leaned forward, wriggling her round ass, trying to work more of me in. Her nipples were dark and tight as fuck, and I grabbed her hip and slid my hand up her back with the other, pulling her forward and sucking one into my mouth.

Her cry sent tingles dancing down my spine. I held her still, forcing her to stop, teasing her nipple with my tongue. Her pussy clenched, fluttering around the head of my cock. "Breathe," I rasped. "Slow down, sunshine. I'm not going anywhere, and neither are you. We've got all night."

I couldn't look away from her red eyes as she looked down at me, panting. "We're doing this, don't try to stop me, Charming," she said, trying to move her hips again.

A low laugh slipped from me, surprising us both for the second time. "Not trying to stop you. You want to fuck me, sunshine? You can ride my cock all fucking night and day if you want to. But if you hurt yourself trying to get to that, neither of us will get what we want."

Her cheeks darkened, but she still fought me, trying to swivel her fucking hips. "I'm not going to hurt myself."

"You're so tight around me, baby. So fucking tight. You need to wait it out, let yourself adjust."

She planted her hands on my chest and looked down at me, her hair falling around her face as she did another little hip roll. "I know what I'm doing." She bit her lip. "I'm not a virgin, Jagger, I know how to take a cock."

Everything inside me seized, my fingers flexing against her, pressing into her flesh as a vicious, growling snarl crackled in my chest and vibrated from the back of my throat. My fingers delved into her hair at the back of her head, fisting, and I pulled her face close, an inch from mine, staring into her wide eyes. "I'm not just some piece of shit with a dick, Sutton. I am your male, your mate. You don't force your body to take my cock, you accept it." Another growl rattled from me. "You submit to it." I shifted her head to the side, dragging my mouth and nose, my jaw along hers, rubbing against her, marking her with my scent.

The beast needed to mark her after what she'd just said, and my voice was pure animal, when I pulled my face from her throat and held that bewitching fucking gaze again. "If you ever talk about another male's cock in this bed, while mine is half inside you, I will spank your lovely ass until you beg for mercy." I nipped her lower lip, forcing a cry from her. "I can assure you, sunshine, you've never taken a cock like mine—"

"Now hang on a minu—"

I brought my hand down on her ass, jolting her forward. She gasped, and her pussy spasmed around the few inches she'd managed. "And just to make things crystal clear, this is the last cock you will ever take."

"What if the fates were wron—"

I slapped her ass again, harder, and this time after she gasped, her entire body trembled. "They weren't, and you fucking know it."

"You can be such an arrogant ass—"

I spanked her again, pulled out, and flipped her to her back, reversing our positions.

"What are you doing? I told you not to try to stop me." She pushed at my chest, trying to shove me to my back again.

I ignored her shoving little hands and her calling me an arrogant asshole and yanked my bedside drawer open.

Grabbing the lube, I squirted some into my hand and rubbed it along my cock, then smeared the rest over her pussy, biting back a grin when she shut up and lifted her hips. "Since I'm superior to any male you've ever been with," I said, snarling a little this time, "I'm going to show you why I'm different, why your male is different, not just in size, baby, but in skill and control." I rubbed my fingers over her slippery pussy, then slid my fingers inside her.

Her look of determination was back. "Go on, then, prove it. Show me."

I didn't know what was going on in her head, but I would get it out of her. Planting a hand on the mattress, I pressed the head of my cock to her tight pussy and pushed in as far as she'd already taken me. She groaned and tried to lift her ass to force in more.

I pulled back, and she growled. "Do it, Jagger. Just fucking do it."

Shaking my head, I pushed back in a couple of inches. "Don't move, Sutton," I said roughly. "You take what I give you."

"You arrogant—"

I pushed in a little more, and her eyes widened, her mouth dropping open. "What were you saying?" I slid out and back, just giving her what her body would allow, easing in a little more each time.

I slid back in, and she stiffened, her hands flying up, slamming against my chest.

"Wait...hang on." She was panting. "It's too much."

I leaned in and trailed the tip of my tongue around a straining nipple and looked up at her. "Breathe, baby. It's not too much. You just need to relax that tight little body for me."

She shook her head wildly against the pillow, panic filling her eyes. "I knew this was too good to be true." She moaned, thrashing beneath me. "I knew the fates weren't finished fucking with my life. This isn't real. They're going to take this away from me too. They're going to make me think you could be mine, then they're going to tear you away again. I know they are."

Fucking hell. That's what she thought? I'd hurt her, this sweet, precious little female. I'd hurt her so badly, she truly didn't trust what we were to each other. I took her jaw in my hand and stopped her from shaking her head, forcing her to look into my eyes. "The fates didn't fuck things up between us, I did. I did that, Sutton, because I was a fucking coward. The fates took me right to you, they did their part, but it was me who destroyed it—"

"No...no." Her eyes were wide, her agony reaching out to me. Her arms went wild, trying to shove me away. "No, I don't get this. This isn't meant for me. You were right, you were never meant for me."

I came down on top of her, stopping her thrashing. "Yes, I fucking was, and you, sunshine, were meant for me."

She gasped desperately. "We don't...we don't even fit together. We're not made to fit together. Mates fit together, they always—"

I rocked my hips and slid deeper inside her. She cried out, her demon claws exploding from the tips of her fingers and scoring my back. I slid out, then made it halfway inside her when I rocked forward again. "Yeah, they always fit, baby, but it's not always easy. They have to work for it."

She stared up at me, eyes glistening, blinking rapidly.

I slid out and back in, taking a little more and wringing another cry from her. "You want me, sunshine?"

"Y-yes," she choked out. "Yes, I want you."

"Then fucking work for it. Don't just give up. Show me how much you want this; how much you want me."

Fire ignited in her eyes and she shoved at my shoulder again, and this time, I gave her what she wanted, falling to my back. Sutton climbed on instantly, straddling me. Taking my cock in her hand, she stuffed herself as full of me as she could, then started working on taking the rest.

I trembled harder with every thick inch she managed.

"This is right, isn't it, Jag?" she said and kept babbling, lost to the fear inside her as she rocked on top of me, trembling and flushed and fucking determined to take all of her male.

My fucking heart hammered in my chest as I watched her fight to take all of me, fight to prove we were meant to be together, to prove I was hers. Then finally, she sat, taking me to the root. The air punched from my lungs, and she stayed there, shaking and rocking.

Her head tipped back, her hands on my stomach, her claws grazing my skin as her pussy clamped around me like a vise, then pulsed, over and over.

"Sutton, baby, fuck." I was going to come, there was no stopping it.

Her head shot up, and she looked into my eyes and moaned my name before she fucking lost it, working me in and out of her tight body, crying out as she went over the ledge, pussy gushing as she came for me so fucking hard.

Gritting my teeth, I held on for dear life as heat tore through me like wildfire, down into my gut and along my shaft, but somehow, I fought back my orgasm until she was spent, then I lifted her off me before my knot could lock her against me, and tossed her onto her back. Gripping my cock, I stroked brutally until I came all over her soft belly and thighs.

She watched me through half-lidded eyes. "I did it," she said huskily. "Jag, I did it. I proved them wrong."

I came down beside her and pulled her into my arms, pressing my lips to her damp hair. "Yeah, you did, sunshine."

CHAPTER TWENTY-FOUR

Sutton

CHECKING THE TIME, I slid on my dress. Poe would be here to pick me up in fifteen minutes. Jagger would arrive shortly as well so he could follow us.

I hadn't seen him all day, well, not up close. Jack had called this morning while I was still in Jagger's bed, still sore and content and sated after what we'd done. There'd been a fire, with multiple casualties, and I'd been needed at the clinic. We weren't equipped for situations like that, not yet and we were always short-staffed.

Which meant Jagger and I hadn't had time to talk, after spending the night together, not properly. There had been food deliveries from him, though, three times during the day, while I'd been working.

He'd also sent messages. The first one, he'd told me he missed me, that he couldn't wait to have me in his den again.

But that would have to wait until after tonight. The hounds, the knights, and Rune and his demons were currently mobilizing, preparing for whatever happened.

I'd left Boo with Fern. I hated leaving him alone so much, but I wanted to make sure he was somewhere safe, with people who loved him if things went wrong tonight.

I opened the bathroom door and walked into my room—and stopped in my tracks.

Jagger stood at my apartment door, leaning against the frame.

"Hey," I said, feeling shy all of a sudden, but it was hard not to. Every time I'd closed my eyes today, I'd heard myself and the things I'd said to him while I'd tried to force him inside me. My face flushed now.

His gaze swept down my body, then back up, and his jaw tensed.

"Are you okay?" I asked, but it was obvious he wasn't.

"I want to touch you, really fucking badly, but if Poe gets even a whiff of my scent, this whole thing is fucked."

I hadn't thought of that. He curled and uncurled his fingers and shifted from foot to foot in those big boots. Antsy as hell. "It's going to be okay, Charming."

His green eyes flashed bright. "Your only job tonight is getting the fuck out of there in one piece, understand me?"

Bossy, blunt Jagger was back, but only because he was worried. "We have a plan. Everything will be fine."

"I know it will, because when the fighting starts or if shit goes wrong, you will run, you hear me? I don't give a fuck about anyone else, not what Rune wants, or Lucifer, none of that shit. You run."

My belly fluttered, and whatever I was going to say fell away when I took in the strain lining his face. "Jagger—"

"What are you going to do when the fighting starts, Sutton?"

"Run," I rasped.

"That's right."

I slid on my shoes. "Poe will be here in a few minutes."

He dragged in a rough breath and his green irises flashed red. "If that fucker somehow manages to survive tonight, I'm going to personally drag him into the pits of Hell. I'll be the one to chain him to the burning stone and make sure he knows nothing but suffering for the rest of eternity."

"Okay," I said, trying to keep him calm. Poe would be knocking on my door any moment, and Jagger was struggling to let me out of his sight, let alone descend into the sewers with a demon who'd made it clear he wanted to make me his—to sit in a room full of powerful demons who had a taste for human flesh.

Scooping up my mask, I walked toward him.

"Not any closer," he said huskily. "You come closer, I won't be able to stop myself from touching you. I won't let you leave."

I stopped.

"Every part of this, letting you walk into danger tonight, letting you put yourself in danger all these weeks, goes against everything in me. I gave you time because I fucked up and you needed it, but when we finish this tonight, we've got shit to talk about," he said roughly.

My heart thumped in my chest. "We do."

"No more being apart, Sutton. I'm done with that."

"Okay," I said, because so was I. I forced a bright smile, shoving all the fear down deep, trying to ease Jagger's as well.

He shook his head. "Don't do that, don't hide from

me. You never need to hide any part of yourself from me, baby, and you sure as fuck don't need to try and protect me."

He saw right through me so easily. Jagger saw all of me, and he still wanted me. I'd been waiting for that my whole life.

Someone pounded on the door downstairs.

"I have to go."

He growled, nostrils flaring. "You fucking come back to me, sunshine," he said, then he stepped back, letting me pass.

I nodded, then rushed down the stairs before everything I was feeling welled up inside me, before I ran and wrapped my arms around him and let him take me away from here.

My stomach churned when I opened the door and looked up at the twisted demon there to take me to their horror show.

His gaze sliced down my body and his lips thinned. "You're wearing the same dress."

"Sorry, I've been busy at work. I didn't have time to go shopping for something different." He wasn't happy, not at all, and fear coiled through me.

"You trying to embarrass me?" he said coldly.

"No, of course not." No one had actually seen this dress—

He grabbed the back of my neck and shoved me toward the car. "Get the fuck in." I didn't know what was going on, but his mood was freaking me out.

Lars sat in the driver's seat and glanced at me in the rearview as I scrambled into the back seat. He was enjoying my humiliation. Either that or he'd already blown my cover and I was being driven to my death.

"Go through East Claymore," Poe said to Lars as he got in, then pulled out his phone and started texting.

We drove for only a short time, when Poe told him to stop. He pointed to a shop, a woman's clothing shop. "Knock on the door, they'll have something for me," he said to Lars.

Lars nodded and rushed to do what he was told. A terrified-looking female opened the door, demon by the looks, and shoved something at him before disappearing back inside.

Lars strode to the car and handed it to Poe, who then tossed it at me. "Put it on."

A dress. It was flimsy, silky, and there wasn't much of it. "I'm okay how I am."

His hand shot out and he jabbed me in the side, knocking the air from my lungs. "Put it on," he said in a now eerily calm voice.

Was he testing me? I had no choice but to do as he said. I worked my dress up over my hips and pulled it off. I felt Poe's eyes on my body, and I desperately tried to cover myself, while I flipped the new dress, trying to get it the right way around. I looked up and Lars was leering at me in the mirror. "Eyes forward, asshole," I fired at him. I may not hold any power in this situation, but I wasn't going to just sit here in my fucking underwear and let that asshole creep on me.

Poe said nothing, watching intently, taking in every scar on my body as if he liked the way they looked, as if he wanted very much to add to them. I shoved the dress over my head and yanked it past my hips. He reached out and ran the backs of his fingers over the silky blue fabric at my side, right over the spot where he'd struck me, pressing on it and making me wince.

"You don't order Lars around, ever, understand? I do. If I want him to look at you, dressed or otherwise, that's my decision. If I want him to do more than look, that's my decision as well." He gripped my throat and shoved my head against the seat, leaning over me. "Say you understand?"

My hand was against his chest, and my power pooled in my palm, reaching out, finding the weak spots in his skeleton, the organs that were the most vulnerable. I wanted to push so badly. I wanted to release all the anger inside me on the fragile parts inside him and crush him from the inside out. "I understand," I said through gritted teeth. My power continued to explore, and I saw every injury and how they happened, his vulnerabilities, mental and otherwise. I saw it all. No, combat magic didn't come easy to me, but this did. I could hurt him this way.

"Why are you looking at me like that?" he said, the anger in his eyes flaring.

"Like what?"

"I don't know..." He held my eyes, searching them. "But I don't like it. I want you, Sutton, and I will make you mine, but I won't put up with disobedience. You betray me, and I will make you suffer."

·))) ● ((·

Poe's grip on me was bruising. I wanted to shove him off. I wanted to force every bit of power I possessed into him and break every one of his bones.

But right then, he was the only thing between me and all the other masked freaks in the sewer.

Jagger's just outside.

I reminded myself of that fact for the hundredth time since we'd walked in here. I searched the room now, and found Lars. His gaze was wide behind his mask, darting around the room. The demon was nervous, and if he didn't calm down, he'd give himself—and me—away.

Rune had kept him overnight. I had no idea what he'd said or done to Poe's bestie, but now he was in the same situation as me—a spy. I'd voiced my concerns to Rune about him talking, but Rune had assured me Lars wouldn't say a thing. He'd had a terrifying look in his eyes when he said it, so I chose to believe him.

I sat silently beside Poe as the auction began. The air buzzed with anticipation and lifted the hair on my arms.

"Excited?" Poe asked, squeezing my hip too hard.

"I'm not sure what's about to happen. You said it's an auction?"

He pressed his mouth to my ear. "Yes, and nights like tonight took us a long time to accomplish." Hatred filled his eyes. "The knights and the hounds have had their boots on our fucking necks for far too long."

"With their laws?" I tried to keep him talking while I scanned the room.

"Yeah, their fucking laws. We're demons; we shouldn't be forced to live like humans. Tarrant's worked hard to make this a successful venture, to make it something the demons in this city could trust, not just by maintaining their anonymity but making sure we don't draw attention from those who want to control and stifle what is only natural." He leaned close again. "Tarrant won't be able to doubt your loyalty after this."

After what? My nerves shot higher, and I had to focus really hard on my breathing.

A voice filled the room through speakers, telling everyone things were about to begin.

The cage in the middle of the room, that I'd seen last

time, was gone, but then the floor began to rise, the top of the cage coming into view. It rose slowly—and I choked down my horror when I saw what was in it.

It took everything in me not to jump to my feet, not to do *something*.

A naked female stood there. She was drugged, no doubt from the ones I'd made, and having trouble holding up her head when the demon standing just outside the cage barked at her to show her face.

The female couldn't lift her head, though, and he shoved the long staff he held through the bars and jabbed it against her hip. It buzzed, shocking her, and she cried out in pain. Excitement filled the room as she slumped to the side. The demon shoved the staff back through the bars to do it again.

Without thought, I fired magic at him, coiling it around the demon's calf and gripping the muscle tight. Cramp was a bitch. He howled, dropping the cattle prod so he could grip his leg.

"Lot number one: This human female is twenty-seven years old. Healthy with optimal fat-to-flesh ratios, and no damage from birthing or previous illness."

The bidding started, and I called my magic back, releasing the demon's leg.

As soon as the highest bidder was announced, the cage descended.

The room was electric, and when the cage rose again, there was a male inside. He wore a steel cuff around his throat, and his head was dipped, eyes shadowed as he scanned the crowd. His fingers were curled into fists, and I could feel power wash from him, over and over, as it battered against the obviously warded cuff he wore, stopping him from hurting anyone in the room.

He was a demi-demon. Was this James? The male the knights mentioned?

"Lot number two. This male demi is twenty-nine years old. Healthy, physically fit, virile, in case any of the females are wondering." Laughter rumbled through the room. "He's powerful, but those powers are unknown. You could say, this lot is a bit of a mystery. We were unable to coax information from him, without damaging him." There was more mumbling, this time sounds of interest of another kind. The mystery seemed to make him more exciting.

The bidding was frenzied, then one after another, humans and demi were displayed for their powers or as a delicacy for the wealthy demons in the room.

"We have one more auction before our showstopper for the evening," the announcer said.

The cage came up, and Poe grabbed the back of my neck, forcing me to stay seated. Luke stood in the cage, trying to cover himself, shivering. He was bruised, gods, he looked broken.

Fury pulsed through me, but I forced myself not to react. Luke would be okay. This was almost over. The hounds and knights would be here any minute.

Poe's grip tightened. "This is how you prove yourself to Tarrant. This is how we can be together. You giving up your friend for me." He'd lost his fucking mind. I hated his guts.

The announcer started talking about him, and several demons in the room sat taller, looking at him more closely. I wanted to scratch their eyes out.

I doubted Tarrant would usually go after a witch and risk the witch's council coming down on them, but because of Luke's mixed blood, they obviously thought they could do whatever the fuck they wanted. They more than likely assumed the council wouldn't care, and they were probably right.

I willed my friend to look my way, to see me. I wanted to give him a sign, anything to let him know I wouldn't let this happen, that we had a plan to save him and everyone else they were holding, but he kept his gaze lowered.

Finally, the cage descended, and I had to bite back the sob trying to crawl its way up my throat—and fight the panic rising.

"We have one more lot tonight, a once-in-a-lifetime opportunity and something you don't want to miss out on. You won't believe what we have for you," the voice said over the speakers. "It's going to take us a few minutes to prepare him, so take the time to refresh your drinks."

A hellhound, or maybe two. They were going to auction off Brick.

That's when I spotted Lars easing back slowly. The prick was getting ready to run. Any minute now, all hell was about to break loose, and he was planning on running the fuck away. Coward.

"We need to talk," Poe gritted out.

Shit.

His hand curled around my arm, tight, and he dragged me to my feet, pulling me toward the tunnel Jagger and I had explored. He pulled me behind the curtain and yanked off his mask. "What the fuck was that back there?" he said and grabbed my throat.

"What do you mean?" I rasped past his tight hold.

He had an odd look on his face. "You were upset when you saw your little friend up there, you tried to hide it, but I saw."

"He's a coven mate. It was a shock seeing him, that's

all." I had to be careful what I said. I had to play into his delusion. "But I see now that you're right. This will prove to Tarrant that he can trust me, with Luke gone, he won't have anything to hold over me."

Poe nodded. "That's right. He'll see that you're working for him because you want to." He gripped my jaw and shoved my mask up, then swiped his tongue over my chin and across my mouth. "I want to fucking take a bite out of you, Sutton, you have no idea how badly."

I wanted to wretch and shove him away, but I smiled instead. "Hopefully, just a little one." I forced a laugh. That was the second time he'd talked about biting me.

Poe didn't laugh, though, he looked at me with so much hunger in his black eyes that I trembled with fear, because it wasn't just lust I saw, it was real hunger, and I got an awful feeling when he said he wanted to take a bite of me, he meant it—literally.

A roar came from the main room, then there were screams and commotion. The hounds, and the knights, they were here and swarming into the tunnel.

Poe looked around the curtain. "What the fuck?" Then he grabbed my arm. "Run." He dragged me with him, and I yanked hard, trying to get free of his grasp. He turned on me, a look of confusion on his face that quickly shifted to betrayal. He dug his claws into my arm. "What have you done?"

I screamed for help.

"What the fuck have you done?" he roared, then he was running, dragging me along with him, while I tried to fight him off.

My magic pulsed hard. "It's over," I said, trying to pull from his hold. "I'm not going anywhere with you." I directed my growing magic at Poe and shoved my hand against his chest. He blocked it, then slammed his fist into the side of my head once, twice—and everything went dark.

I struggled, in and out of consciousness. Poe was running, and I was bouncing over his shoulder as he sprinted down tunnel after tunnel, the sounds of fighting echoing in the distance. I heard him on his phone, he was talking about a hound. Brick.

I tried to rally, to pull on my magic again, but I couldn't stay awake. The next time I regained consciousness, it was from searing pain at my chest. Poe had yanked down my dress at the front and was carving something into my skin.

A sigil. I felt its dark power wrapping around me. I cried out, grasping for my magic again, but it was unreachable, locked behind the demon sigil he'd cut into me. He quickly tied my hands and feet together, then took something from his pocket. He held it up, an evil grin on his face.

The drugs I'd made.

He grabbed my jaw, forcing my mouth open, then shoved several of the pills to the back of my throat before holding my mouth and nose closed. I had no choice but to choke them down or suffocate. I wouldn't overdose, but they would knock me out.

He hauled me off the ground again and tossed me back over his shoulder. Darkness surrounded us as Poe ran, carrying me away, away from Jagger.

I had no way to stop him. The sigil had bound my magic, and the drug was quickly taking effect, taking my fight along with it.

I hung there, limp, as Poe took several flights of stairs, climbing out of the sewer. He pulled me down from his shoulder and, holding me up against his side, walked out onto the street. I blinked several times. We were in a different part of the city.

A car sat waiting, a demon I'd never seen before behind the wheel.

Poe shoved me in the back and got in beside me, then we sped off. I continued to slide in and out of consciousness. When the car finally stopped, we were at Tarrant's mansion. Bringing me here was stupid. Jagger, Lucifer, Rune, the hounds, they all knew this was where Tarrant lived.

Poe hauled me out of the car and rushed into the house.

"What is she doing here?" Tarrant said, eyes lit with fury.

"She's mine," Poe said, voice hard. "She comes with me."

"After what just happened, everything we worked for fucking ruined, and this is what you're most concerned about?" he all but roared.

Poe straightened. "I'm not leaving her behind."

"Do you know who betrayed us?"

"Not yet," Poe lied, covering for me for some reason.

"Could it be her?"

"No."

"Are you sure?"

"On my life."

Tarrant's eyes narrowed, but that seemed to appease him. He was used to Poe's unfailing loyalty, so he was buying the lie. "There will be a price if you're wrong, for both of you," he said, eyes red, his face a mask of horrors.

Poe lowered his gaze. "I understand."

Tarrant snarled, then turned and strode off down the hall, and Poe followed, dragging me along with him. Tarrant stopped at the end and touched something high on the wall. It slid back. A hidden doorway revealing itself as well as a set of stairs going down.

The door slid closed behind us, and Poe half dragged, half carried me down to a small room. Tarrant pressed his hand to the wall, calling to lord Beelzebub, asking him to grant him entrance.

The wall began to swirl, giving flashes of something beyond it, then finally a portal opened, and dread gripped me, shuddering through my body.

The demon blood in me knew instantly where we were going, the knowledge searing through my bones, and gripped my trembling soul. I'd been here before with Jagger.

Hell.

Poe was taking me to Hell.

·))) ● (((·

Jagger

War barked orders, and we surrounded the demons in the sewer. Fender tore the cage from the stage where a naked and drugged female lay, then tugged off his shirt, covered her, and scooped her off the floor. The knights closed in, tearing the platform out of the ground, then jumped down into the lower level to free the other prisoners—and stop any demons still down there from escaping.

I frantically scanned the room, scenting the air for Sutton. It was weaker now, but still tainted with Poe's stench. I followed it, leading me out of the main room.

"Poe has Sutton," I yelled to War and jerked my head in the direction they'd gone.

War signaled Roman to follow, and I burst through the curtain and sprinted into the tunnel. Her scent was much stronger now that it wasn't diluted by others. Rome sprinted after me, our boots echoing off the concrete floor as we turned one corner, then another.

Something zinged over my skin, lifting the hair on my arms and the back of my neck. I stopped in my tracks, my arm shooting out to stop Rome from barreling straight through.

"What is it?" he growled.

"Demon ward."

"Can we get through?"

I shook my head. "You need demon blood to pass unless we break it." Lars had said we needed to destroy the parent sigil to do that. I fucking hoped it worked. I used my blade to gouge through it, attempting to break the seal.

"I can still feel it buzzing over my skin," Rome said and lifted his hand to test it before I could stop him. The skin of his hand immediately bubbled, peeling back and exposing raw flesh.

He yanked his hand back with a roar.

It wasn't the right sigil. I searched frantically but couldn't find it.

"We can't get through."

I sucked in several breaths. Nothing would stop me. I might lose my skin, but I'd heal. "I'm going anyway."

"No fucking way, brother," Rome growled as Relic and Lothar pounded around the corner.

Rome dove on me as I ran for it.

"Stop him!" he roared.

I swung, fighting to get free as Relic and Lothar piled on as well, holding me down.

"You'll be no fucking use to her if you're that badly

injured," Rome bit out. "We'll find her. We will find her, brother."

If that motherfucker harmed her in any way, I would burn everything to the ground to find him and make him pay.

CHAPTER
TWENTY-FIVE

Sutton

I WOKE CHAINED to a stone wall.

Snarls and growls echoed all around me. Poe had dosed me good, then had continued to drug me for at least two days, but it was obviously starting to wear off because I managed to lift my head and open my eyes.

The chamber was huge, set up like some kind of twisted demonic living room. On one side, there were massive couches and chairs, and a huge widescreen TV—and on the other were several apparatuses, some that I assumed were for sex, and others that were obviously for torture, and in the middle, was a fire pit that spat hellfire every couple of minutes.

The huge cavern had openings on two sides, and on one side, a hound was chained at the opening, pacing in front of it, there to stop anyone from coming in. It no doubt was Brick. They'd taken him from the sewers before the hounds could get to him. Beyond him light flickered, and moans of despair and cries of pain echoed in the distance.

The other exit wasn't passable either. I recognized Kurgan instantly, the hound I'd met with Jagger, his inner scars were impossible to miss. He was in his hound form, huge and shaggy and foaming at the mouth. Lucifer said there was a second hound missing, but he can't have meant Kurgan. Not only had I met the wild hound after the meeting at Rune's, but he'd also told War it was someone the alpha didn't know. Which meant there was possibly a third hound being held down here somewhere.

There would be no moving the huge hound, though, no getting close, because if I wasn't mistaken, locked in a cage right beside the entrance he was guarding, was his mate. The small female sat in the middle, her arms wrapped around her knees, trembling, and her face hidden.

They were using her to control him, and she was utterly terrified.

"You better have news for me?" someone roared.

My head snapped back as a door opened across from me, and Tarrant and Poe strode into the main cavern, followed by a huge horned demon.

"I'm sorry, Lord Beelzebub. We have nothing yet."

Oh fuck. This was Beelzebub's home. The terrifying demon spun and grabbed Tarrant by the throat, slamming him against the rough stone. "It's not time." He shook his huge head. "If this comes back on me, if Lucifer finds out what I've been planning, I'm fucked." He roared, then punched the stone beside Tarrant's head, sending shards of stone flying.

I swallowed my scream. The last thing I wanted was to draw attention to myself.

"I want the name of the traitor."

Poe stood beside them, and his gaze slid to me, his eyes wild. He still hadn't told Tarrant and Beelzebub it was me, that I was the one who blew everything wide open. For some reason, he'd decided to risk angering a lord of Hell to keep my secret.

Because he wants you to owe him, to be beholden to him.

I was fucked, either way you looked at it. My powers were still bound. I was in Hell. I had no idea how things worked between realms. Would Jagger still be able to sense me down here? Did the sigil Poe carved into my skin block me from him completely?

"I'm sorry, my lord," Tarrant said, bowing his head in the face of the massive and powerful demon. "I let you down."

"You got sidetracked with your own endeavors. These auctions you've been running, the drugs you have been selling, you forgot yourself."

"I did that for you."

Beelzebub leaned in. "Enlighten me."

Gods, his voice sent terror down my spine.

"Every demon who came to our auctions, who bought and paid for a human, is now beholden to me...*to you*. I'm the only one who knows their identities, and if they were leaked, they would be dragged here to Hell. They don't want that. They owe us. They are allies in the war to come, because they have no choice."

Beelzebub stared down at him, his thick, leathery, muscled back moving in an odd way as he tilted his head to the side. "You have the next phase in place?"

Tarrant nodded enthusiastically. "We have a witch." He pointed at me. "She created the potions we've been testing, to make sure of its effectiveness on as many different humans as we could, to make sure it'll work on a high percentage of them. You see, I had a plan."

Twisted asshole.

"We had another witch duplicate the drug she created, increasing its potency, then produced it in bulk. We have barrels of it now, ready and waiting, more than enough to poison the water supply."

They'd had Luke copy my recipe. They were going to drug the entire city.

"Do you truly believe you can get the task done, Tarrant?" Beelzebub asked. "After your failings? Do you think I should put my future in your weak and incapable hands?"

"I can do this, my lord. I won't let you down, not again," Tarrant said. "This is the only way to shatter the path fate is currently on and set the forgotten prophecy into motion. It's the only way you take Hell, my lord."

"Are you telling me this drug will make the humans offer their flesh to us? It's the only way to redirect the path."

Oh goddess, what they had planned was horrific.

"Yes, I've already seen it happen. It makes them easy to manipulate, to control. I can give you what you need. I can give you that."

They were using my drug to change fate, and to do that they needed something that was so wrong, something so against the natural order, that it caused a major shift.

Humans offering themselves as food to the inhabitants of the underworld would definitely do that.

Beelzebub stood silent for several long moments. "For now, here in my quadrant, we are relatively safe. But if Lucifer discovers who stole from him, he'll know he was betrayed, and it will be only a matter of time before he summons all the lords for questioning. You have two days to set the next phase in motion."

"Thank you, my lord," Tarrant said, slumping when Beelzebub stepped back.

"If you fail in this, you will regret it, Tarrant," the massive demon said, then strode away. Brick moved back, pawing at the ground as the demon strode past and out of the cavern.

"Come," Tarrant said to Poe, then he headed in the same direction as Beelzebub.

Poe strode over to me, closing in, crowding me. "See how I protected you? You owe me your life now," he sneered as he tucked my hair behind my ear, then pulled it hard. "I don't know how long I'll be away, but no one here gives a fuck about you except me. The only thing keeping you alive while I'm gone are the hounds guarding the entrances. If you try to leave, I will come after you, and if the hounds or the demons haven't torn you to shreds, I will."

I rattled my chains. "Where do you think I'm going?"

He smirked and shrugged. "Just reminding you of where you are. You are in Hell, witch, and every demon down here, including me, would love to make you scream." Then he strode away.

Maybe, but if I got free of these chains, I wouldn't be alone. There was no power vibrating through the iron around my wrists. I was marked with a sigil, but my cuffs and chains were not. I wasn't a hound; they didn't think I was strong enough to escape. I turned to the female curled up in her cage. "What's your name?"

She looked up at me, terror in her eyes. "Lenny."

"Hi, Lenny, I'm Sutton."

"Hi." She jolted when Kurgan pressed his snout to the bars and scented her with bared teeth.

"I know you're scared. I am too. But we don't know how long we've got until they come back. If we're going to get out of here, we need to make a move now."

"How? I'm in this cage, and you're chained. And I heard what that demon said, even if we can get out of this cavern, there are more, they're everywhere, and we don't know the way out."

"I'm pretty sure I can get us free, but we'll need to take the hounds with us. Brick's family is worried sick, and Kurgan"—I saw Lenny flinch again—"can protect us."

She shook her head, her eyes wild. "He'll kill me if he gets the chance. He'll kill all of us. He's insane."

The chains were long enough that I could twist, so I faced the jagged rocks behind me. "I've seen inside him, Lenny. He doesn't want to hurt you, that's the last thing he wants. He's in agony over what happened, that he hurt you last time. I think...I know..." I hissed as I scraped my chest against the sharp rocks, tearing at my skin. "If you show him you're in control, if you command him to stand down, he will."

She stood. "What are you doing?"

"Poe carved a sigil into my chest. If I can damage it enough, I can break the bind he has on my magic." Or at least I hoped so.

She watched me wide-eyed, then turned to Kurgan, before her gaze came back to me. "There's no controlling him."

"No one knows we're here, and I don't know if the other hounds can track us between realms. We either make a break for it while we can, or we stay down here, prisoners for the rest of our lives, and suffer in a whole lot of really awful ways." I wasn't trying to freak her out more, but it was the truth.

She bit her lip, trembling again now. "I'm scared."

"I know, me too. But we have to be brave."

She nodded, licking her lips. "Okay. I...I can try."

I whimpered as I scraped my chest against the rocks once more, making another slice in my already damaged skin, and felt the bind finally give way and my magic rush forward. I used the surge of power, sending it into the cuffs around my wrists. I was already bleeding, and the blood strengthened it even more. "Break these binds, set me free, demon iron cannot contain me." Not the best spell I'd ever come up with, but it was all I could think of right then.

I hissed, straining, forcing more magic into the cuffs, reciting the spell again and, finally, they fell away. Blood rushed back, causing agonizing pins and needles to travel from my hands to my shoulders. I shook them out, needing all my strength. I strode toward Brick. He spun, snarling and snapping at me.

"I know you're in there, Brick. I need you to fight the hold on you long enough for me to get that cuff off you, okay?" He bared his teeth. I had no idea if he could understand what I was saying, but I hoped he understood at least some of it.

"Be careful," Lenny said, gripping the bars. Kurgan paced, his low growl so deep I felt it from the soles of my feet to the top of my head.

Searching the ground, I found a sharp rock. I needed to destroy the parent sigil stamped into the collar. I just had to stay alive long enough to break it.

I lifted my hands. "If you bite my head off, you'll be down here forever," I said as I closed in. "If you kill me, you'll be stuck here living with Beelzebub. I know you don't want that."

Brick's head tilted to the side, his lips still peeled back

as a growl vibrated from him. He was going to attack, the demon powers in that iron cuff were too strong. Reaching down slowly, I picked up another rock. I had no idea if this would work, but it was all I had in that moment and time was running out.

Without waiting, or allowing myself to overthink it and chicken out, I tossed the rock and it smashed against the wall. Brick spun toward the sound and I ran at him, leaping onto his wide, furry back and hung on.

He instantly spun around, bucking and snarling, while I clung to the metal around his neck, trying to hang on. Gritting my teeth, and with all my strength and a huge push of magic, I slammed the rock down onto the iron. Sparks burst from the impact. Brick bucked harder, jarring me, my teeth snapping together hard from the impact. I was going to fall off any second, and he would tear me to shreds.

Bringing my hand up again, I slammed the rock down on the sigil a second time. Sparks exploded from the steel again as I went flying, hitting the ground hard and knocking the air from my lungs.

Brick spun around, eyes red, foam dripping from his lower jaw. He prowled toward me, and I scrambled back, trying to get out of striking range. He pounced, leaping in the air toward me. His chain caught him short, yanking him back hard, and as it did, the iron cuff around his throat shattered where I had broken the sigil.

A naked Brick landed hard on the stone floor. He jumped to his feet, swaying to the side, but caught himself, then shook his head wildly.

He blinked down at me, then stumbled again. "Sutton?" He looked around the room, then back to me.

I got to my feet and rushed to him, wrapping my arms around his waist, and he squeezed me tight. "Your brothers, your parents have been so worried about you." I looked up at him and held his strong jaw in my hands. "I've been worried about you."

He tried to give me one of his cocky grins, but it didn't reach his eyes. "I'm okay." He rubbed his head. "The fuckers snatched me out of my female's bed. She asked me over... then..." His brows lowered. "She let them in, she knew them." He cursed. "She served me up to fucking Beelzebub."

"I know and I'm sorry. We'll make sure she pays for what she did, but right now, we need to move while Beelzebub's gone. I need your help to free Lenny and Kurgan."

Brick turned to the huge hound, and Kurgan growled low at him. Brick's head immediately dipped, his beast recognizing a stronger male when he was confronted by one.

"Not sure where that big fucker came from," Brick said, "but he doesn't smell right. The look in his eyes isn't right either. I'm...I'm not sure I can protect you from him. He's a lot older, bigger."

I could see it cost him to say that. I squeezed his arm. "Jagger knows him. The female in the cage is his intended mate. She's afraid, but I think he'll listen to her. I think she could control him if she tries."

"It might work. My ma definitely knows how to get my dad to do what she wants."

"Here's hoping Lenny has the same influence." We rushed to the side of the cage that Kurgan couldn't reach and I used my spell to break the lock. "Are you ready?" I asked her.

"No, but I think we have to try anyway, I'm not staying here." She chewed her lip. "If he kills me, run and don't stop."

That gave me pause. "He won't do that."

"He almost did the first time I met him." Lenny pulled up her sleeve, showing me her mauled forearm. The scar was rough and twisted, the flesh misshapen.

"I don't think he meant to do it. He was confused." I'd felt it, that confusion, his deep regret when I'd sedated him.

Brick cursed, shifting from foot to foot. "That's not normal. We don't do that shit to females."

Kurgan pulled on his chain and roared, the sound bloodcurdling.

"Stand back," Lenny said to Brick, her voice shaking. "He'll see you as a threat."

"Maybe we should leave him here?" I said. "Send his brothers to get him once we're out of danger."

"We need him," Brick said, worry in his eyes. "There are hordes of demons down here, and only one thing will keep them back. Yeah, I'm strong," he said, flexing his biceps, "but one hound, as young as I am, might not be enough to hold them back." He aimed his pretty eyes at Lenny. "You need to speak to him with authority. Hounds love touch, love to be hugged. His aggression will lessen if you touch him."

She paled. "I'm not sure I can."

"You can do this," I said, and hoped I was right. "I was able to calm him once before with my magic. If this goes wrong, I'll try to do that again. While I'm doing that, Brick will hook that chain around his neck. That should slow him down long enough for us to make a run for it."

She nodded and stepped out of the cage.

"Strong voice," Brick said. "With the cuff, he knows what's going on but he's all beast, he can't shift, and everything feels like a threat even when it's not."

That was Kurgan all the time.

"K-Kurgan," Lenny said, turning toward him.

Kurgan pawed at the ground, shaking his massive head, then growled low.

"Speak louder," Brick said. "When my ma uses a certain tone, my dad stops in his tracks. Seen Wills do it with the alpha as well. Works every time."

Lenny nodded and took another step closer. "Stand down," she said and lifted her hands. "That's it." She took another step.

Kurgan lowered his head.

It was working.

But then he leaped, knocking her to the ground. His jaw wrapping around her leg tight enough to draw blood, then he dragged her away from us. I rushed forward, but Brick grabbed me, holding me back.

Lenny screamed, and that only set him off more. He stood over her, gnashing his teeth. He was confused, no doubt by everything that had happened, being taken from his cell, seeing Lenny again, and the strength of what he was feeling around her.

Her hands were planted against his massive chest.

"He doesn't understand what he's feeling," I called to her, my heart in my throat. "The only desire he understands is hunger. That's the only pleasure he's experienced. He doesn't want to hurt you, but biting is the only thing he's felt that's good. You need to speak up, Lenny. You need to show him there are other ways to feel good."

"Stop," she yelled, loud from the force of her panic, then wrapped her arms around his wide furry neck and pressed her face into the side of his. He eased up, no longer snapping and lifted his head. She started singing softly, her voice sweet and trembling. Kurgan stopped snarling completely now and blinked down at her.

She looked up at him. "You don't want to bite me, you want to hug me. See?"

The huge hound dropped, going limp in an instant, lying on top of her, squashing her.

"No," she wheezed. "Get up, Kurgan, now!"

He growled, then whined, then lifted up again. Lenny scrambled out from under him, and he wrapped his jaws around her arm and tugged her back.

"Let go of my arm," she said forcefully. She was shaking, but she placed her hand on his neck. "If you behave, I'll pet you. If you bite me again, then there will be no more hugs for you. Now you need to let Sutton take the cuff off from around your neck."

His glowing hound's eyes slid to me, but he didn't growl or snap his teeth, so I took it as my cue. I walked to him, while Brick fisted the back of my shirt, ready to yank me away if he needed to, and I cautiously, then quickly, scraped a sharp stone over the sigil in the iron, compromising it. It was much easier when I wasn't hanging on to a bucking, foaming hound trying to kill me.

The metal sparked, then fell away a moment later.

Kurgan shifted from huge hound to the massive male he was. His hand snapped out instantly, grabbing the back of Lenny's neck and hauling her into his side.

"Be gentle with her," I said.

She looked up at him with huge eyes.

"My female," he said and dipped his head, pressing his nose to her hair, scenting her. His eyes darkened when they landed on Brick, and he growled again. "Lenny is my female, pup," he said with the beast in his voice.

Lenny looked like she was close to passing out from terror.

Brick lifted his hands. "Your female, brother," he said, then to me under his breath, "Who the fuck is this guy?"

"I don't know. All I know is that Jagger looks after him."

Brick frowned but kept his eyes on Kurgan. "Do you know how to open a gateway?"

Kurgan frowned, then shook his head no.

"Shit." Brick squared his shoulders. "We need to get the females away from Beelzebub, and we need to protect them from the demons."

"Protect, yes." Kurgan bared his teeth. "You're a pup. Weak. I'll protect. I'll kill the demons," he growled.

Brick bristled but was smart enough not to let Kurgan know he was offended. "Do you know the way out of here?" he asked Kurgan.

Kurgan buried his nose in Lenny's hair again. "Yes. I'll take my female to my den."

I'd seen the way Kurgan behaved in his den. He'd seen everything as a threat, but now Lenny had taken control, he seemed to have gone into protection mode, at least when it came to pups and females. I just hoped she could maintain it.

Kurgan started walking, and Lenny limped beside her unhinged mate, her leg bleeding from his bite, trying to keep up. He stopped, snatched her off her feet and held her to him. She gasped in surprise.

"I'll protect you," he said to her, then he kept walking.

CHAPTER TWENTY-SIX

Jagger

THE WOODEN DOOR SHATTERED, splintering to pieces as I exploded through it.

My paws thudded on the rug as I pressed my nose to the floor, breathing in Sutton's fading scent like I had for the last couple of days. Her scent ended here though.

I'd come back to Tarrant's house repeatedly, because I was positive this was the last place she'd been. We'd searched the entire place from top to bottom, same with the sewer. Lars had reluctantly given us the grand tour, but there'd been no sign of Sutton.

Now I was back, and I was going to tear this fucking house apart until I found something that would lead me to her. Fear pounded through me, along with more rage than I knew what to do with. Rune had just found out the reason Tarrant was so controlling with Poe—the last female he'd become obsessed with, a demi-demon who was selling product for them, had been held captive by him—and he'd slowly mutilated and eaten her.

The thud of boots followed me as I raced down the hall. I breathed in Sutton's faint scent, stoking the wildfire raging inside me. But she was alive.

If she wasn't, I'd know. I'd feel it. Mated or not, I would feel it.

Head down, I ran at the first wall, smashing through it, and I kept on going, systematically tearing the house down. Tarrant had completely disappeared. If he was in Hell, I'd know. Our brothers down there would have seen or heard something. Unless he was being hidden from us.

I'd find him, though, then I'd kill him.

My brothers followed my lead, tearing the walls down, looking for anywhere she could have been taken. I turned to the paneled wall at the end of the hall and bounded toward it, exploding through it with a roar—and dropped, landing halfway down a set of stairs. Howling, I alerted my brothers and tore down the stairs into a small empty room.

War, Relic, and Lothar ran in as I shifted, and tilting my head back scented the air. "Brimstone," I said and pressed my hand to the brick wall in front of me. Echoes of Hell reached out to me, shooting up my arm and nailing me in the gut. "Somehow, Tarrant opened a gateway, and did it down here to try to hide it."

War moved up beside me and pressed his hand to the warm brick just as I had done. His eyes flashed red. "Only a lord could have opened a portal for that asshole. No way a hound would have done it, and Brick's too young to have the ability. And Lucifer sure as fuck wouldn't have."

War got on his phone, while I tried to fucking breathe. Pressing both hands to the brick, I squeezed my eyes closed and tried to see her, to find her. Her scent lived inside me, I should be able to track her anywhere. "Why can't I track her? Why the fuck can't I see her?"

"Check it out," Loth said. "More fucking sigils. Powerful ones. Stronger than the ones we found in the sewer. They're designed to conceal. Only a lord could create something like that, something powerful enough to block them between this realm and Hell."

War finished his call with Lucifer. "He's alerting our brothers in Hell and calling in his lords. I told him several of us were heading down."

War, Relic, and the others needed to make sure the females and pups were covered above ground.

"Keep me updated," War said as I lifted a hand and opened a gateway.

I jerked my chin up, then Loth, Rome, Fender, and I walked through the portal and into Hell.

As soon as I stepped through, I tilted my head back and closed my eyes. My world instantly spun, recalibrating—there. Finally.

There you are, sunshine.

"This way," I said, shifted, and ran like hell toward my mate.

·))❯·●·❮((·

Sutton

A naked Brick and I followed the huge and also naked Kurgan, though neither male seemed bothered. Lenny was frozen in Kurgan's enormous arms. She looked terrified, and I wanted to help her, but there was no way Kurgan was going to put her down.

We'd been walking for hours. Every now and then we'd come across a group of demons, and Kurgan and Brick would growl and snarl and they'd run away. So far, so good.

Except for my wound that was hot and weeping. It throbbed as infection set in. I was starting to feel feverish and achy. As much as I needed to tend it, I didn't have any of my supplies. I could use magic to help it, but I was too weak to do that, especially after depleting my power to get free. I needed rest first.

Kurgan headed down another path that opened up into a wide expanse. A forest, but all the colors were wrong. There were clumps of red rock and black-trunked trees with leaves in deep autumn colors, deep reds and browns and burned oranges. There were openings in the forest floor, and every now and then flames licked up from somewhere below, while strange spindly birds with leathery wings perched on ebony branches watching us with red eyes as we passed.

"What is this place?"

Brick shrugged. "Hell is vast, there are many levels, and different climates and landscapes. This is just one forest among many."

I had no idea. "Jagger brought me to Hell, but it looked different. There were caverns and tunnels like the one we just walked out of. How far away is that from here?"

"My sire has shown me a lot of places down here," Brick said, "but we spend most of our time where Jagger took you. That's where Lucifer resides. We're a long way from there now."

"How do you know?"

He placed his hand on the center of his chest. "Lucifer is part of us, even I, born not made like my sire, feel the connection. I know how far away I am from him at all times, and my pack. They feel very distant. I've never been this far from them before."

There was a lost look in his eyes, and I gave his hand a squeeze and didn't let go. He squeezed my hand in return and released a small sigh. My young friend needed physical touch just as badly as his brothers. "If Jagger realizes we're down here, can he open a gateway and come straight to us?"

"That depends."

"On what?"

He glanced my way. "On whether or not he caught your scent before he came through. Without a scent to guide him, or any idea where you are, he'll probably open a gateway in Lucifer's quadrant. If that happens, he'll have to travel on foot to get to you. The gateway takes us between realms, once we're down here we have to walk like everyone else."

"Shit."

"Yeah."

Kurgan stopped suddenly, and I almost walked into the back of him. "What are we doing?"

"Lenny is wounded. I need to tend her," Kurgan said. Lenny's eyes widened with alarm as his green eyes came to me. "You smell sick. The pup will tend you."

Brick looked at me and frowned, then scented me. "He's right, I can smell the infection."

I pulled my shirt down a little to show him the damage.

"Fuck. Why didn't you say something? My senses are all over the place after the shit that happened, but still—"

"It's fine, and you'll need time before you're back to feeling like yourself."

"Suck out the infection and lick," Kurgan said to him.

Brick looked at me, brows lifted. "I'll help you, whatever you need."

Kurgan nodded in approval. "Jagger might kill you, but his female won't be dead."

Brick made a choking sound.

"I'll be okay," I said quickly. "I just need to rest, so I can recharge my magic and work on the infection myself."

Brick puffed up his chest. "I can do it. I can help you. Jagger won't be pissed if I save your life. He will, however, kill me if I let you die because I was too much of a coward to do it."

I couldn't believe he'd ever hurt Brick. He still held my hand, and I squeezed it again. "Let me see if I can do something first, okay?"

He nodded, and we both watched as Kurgan kicked broken branches onto a pile, while still holding Lenny in his arms, then finally aimed one hand at the pile, blasting it with fire and setting the branches alight. At least we'd be warm. Despite the hellfire, the forest wasn't hot, the opposite in fact.

He sat then, still holding Lenny on his lap.

"Put me down now, Kurgan," she said shakily.

"No," he said, shaking his head. "I'm protecting you." He took her foot in his hand and lifted her leg, studying the bite he'd given her. "You're wounded. I'll heal it."

"You caused it," she said. "You caused that wound, and I want you to put me down."

He snarled and gripped her tighter, breathing hard.

"Lenny," I said low, "hounds are emotionless until they find their mates. Being with you will awaken new emotions in him, and he'll have no idea how to deal with it. I know it's hard, but try to keep him calm."

His gaze sliced to me, and he bared his teeth. "She's mine. I protect her. I won't hurt her."

"I know," I said. "You're doing a really good job too. You've kept her safe."

He pressed his nose to her hair. "You're safe, Lenny."

She squeezed her eyes closed. "I know. Thank you."

He lifted her then, sitting her beside him, and grabbed her ankle, dragging his nose along her calf as he growled low, before he started licking.

Lenny shrieked and tried to shove him away.

Kurgan didn't seem to notice.

"Calm," I said to her. "Licking is how a hound heals others."

Kurgan was *focused*. He licked the wound thoroughly and then went back for another round, while Lenny squirmed.

Kurgan made a low, vibrating, repetitive sound and dragged his nose higher along Lenny's thigh.

"No, Kurgan," Lenny said, her face flushing.

He dragged his nose higher still, while she pushed at his head.

"Kurgan," I said urgently. "Stop."

His eyes lifted, and they were glowing. "The scent up here..." He breathed deeply again and made more rumbling sounds. "It makes me..." He licked his lips. "Hungry."

In other words, his pleasure receptors were all fired up. *Shit.*

Lenny shoved him hard. "No! I don't like that."

Brick strode back, carrying firewood, and looked like he was about to intervene, which would have been disastrous.

Lenny quickly started singing, and Kurgan lifted his head instantly to watch her, to listen. Her voice was soft and so incredibly beautiful.

"I think we're good for now," I said to Brick and hoped I was right.

"You should try to sleep," he said to me when he was loading up the fire.

I wasn't sure I could. I was sick, shaking with fever now, and scared. I felt weaker than I had in a long time—and we were literally in Hell. "I'll try."

Lenny stopped singing. "What about demons?" she said from the other side of the fire, now plastered to Kurgan's side. "Will they try to ambush us? If we sleep, they could attack."

Kurgan tilted his head back and *roared*, the sound like a demented lion in bloodlust. We all jumped, then froze. "They won't come now," he said, his green eyes taking in the little female beside him, a look of utter rapture on his face. "And I won't sleep."

She blew out a slow breath, but I could see the pulse at her throat beating wildly. "Thank you," she said.

He looked from her to Brick, a conflicted expression on his face. His jaw clenched, and he looked down at Lenny again, then back at Brick. "Pup," he barked.

"Yeah?" Brick said.

"Find meat. The females need food. Go."

That explained the conflict. He wanted to be the one to get Lenny food, but he didn't want to let her go, or leave her unprotected either.

"I'm fine," Lenny said.

"Me as well."

"You need to eat," he said.

"Not sure if Hell meat will agree with us," I said. "We're not from here, Kurgan. It might make us sick." The birds alone were a breed I'd never seen before, I had no idea what other creatures were out there.

He growled. "Pup, sit down."

Brick cursed under his breath but did as the older and stronger hound commanded.

Kurgan appeared distressed and kept looking down at Lenny.

"I'm not hungry," she said, and I knew she had to be lying because I was starving.

"So where in Roxburgh do you live?" I asked her, trying to stop Kurgan from worrying and possibly losing his shit.

"I'm in Linville," she said, studiously ignoring the huge hound who was again scenting her while a low rumble vibrated from his chest. "What about you?"

"I live in the city. I was with my coven before that, I had to leave, though...to protect them."

She blinked rapidly. "I...I had to leave my family as well, for the same reason, to protect them."

"I'm sorry."

"Me too," she said and she attempted to scoot over and put a little distance between her and her hound. He wouldn't give her an inch.

"You're a shifter, yes?"

She nodded. "Fox."

Her quiet nature made a lot of sense. Foxes were gentle, sweet-natured, and fiercely protective of their loved ones but also tried to avoid conflict. I knew only one other fox shifter. Ren was Willow's familiar, and he had the same gentle yet fierce nature.

I had no idea what the fates were thinking, matching Lenny with such a strong male, but then I'd thought the fates had made a mistake when they paired me and Jagger.

I didn't think that anymore.

All my life I'd felt unwanted. I'd been thrown away. I hadn't even tried to fight it, not once. I'd been so sure I was worthless, so sure I somehow must deserve it, that I took it all. I almost lost Jagger as well, because I hadn't fought. Instead, I'd accepted it as fate kicking me around again, taking on the role of victim, but that wasn't what I was, and that wasn't what they were trying to do. No, the fates had been testing me.

They'd given me a second chance.

To fight.

They wanted me to show Jagger, to show everyone, including myself, just how worthy I was of a happily ever after, and that I was strong enough to fight for what was mine.

And that's exactly what I was going to do.

CHAPTER
TWENTY-SEVEN

Sutton

Brick pressed the back of his hand to my forehead. "You're shivering like you're frozen, but your skin's on fire."

He'd been hovering for a while now. "It's the infection. I just need some sleep, then I can fight it." In theory that would work, but it was impossible to sleep like this.

"Will you let me help you? I think I need to help you now, Sutton."

"I'll...I'll be okay..." My teeth chattered.

"You don't smell right," he said again. "The wound's festering. You need to let me tend it."

He was right. The infection was spreading. Even in my weakened state, I had enough magic that could see it creeping through me, invading, heading for fragile organs and other areas of my body that wouldn't heal so fast or easily. I had no idea what had been on Poe's knife or even on that rock wall I'd cut myself with. It might even cause permanent damage or worse. If I could rest and build my magic back up, I could fight it, but it was becoming obvious that I couldn't do it. "I—I think you might have to. I—I'm sorry, Brick."

"Don't be sorry," he said as he crouched beside me. "I want to do this for you, and for Jag." Still, concern, maybe even a little fear, filled his eyes as he looked down at me.

"I won't let him hurt you. He wouldn't, not for this. Not for helping me."

Brick nodded, but his worry was clear. I was too weak to even lift my arms. "You'll need to unzip my dress so I can pull it down at the front."

He carefully rolled me to my side, unzipped the dress, then eased a strap off my shoulder. When he rolled me back, one of my breasts was exposed, as well as my sliced-up, infected flesh. He flushed, and I wasn't sure if it was embarrassment over seeing one of my boobs or concern over the state of my wound.

"I'll be as gentle as I can. Tell me if I'm hurting you, okay?" he said, then lowered his head.

I was too sick to care that I was exposing myself, and pain didn't worry me, anything had to be better than this. His tongue gently rasped over one of the slices, and warm tingles followed in its wake, his healing saliva instantly taking affect. He didn't linger, doing what he had to quickly and without his body making much contact with mine. When he was done, he draped the fabric of my dress lightly over my breast.

"Best to leave the wound uncovered as much as possible for now," he said.

"Will you lie beside me?" I asked as another icy shiver slid through me. "I can't get warm."

He nodded, then shifted, I was guessing so he wasn't

pressing his naked body against me, and lowered himself to the ground. The young hound pressed his huge, hot body against me, the soft fur of his belly and side against my back.

"Thanks, Brick," I said as heaviness washed over me. A rumbling sound vibrated through his chest and my eyes drifted closed.

⁕

A high-pitched yelp jolted me from my sleep, a commotion breaking out around us.

Jagger loomed over me, his teeth bared and his hand buried in Brick's fur at his throat.

"Let him go," I rushed out as elation filled me. He was here. Jagger was here. His glowing eyes dropped to me, and I realized my breast was exposed completely. "Brick helped me. I was sick. He did what he had to."

"Sick?" Jagger's gaze slid to my chest. His nostrils flared, then he gently covered my chest while still holding Brick down with the other hand. He stood then, lifting Brick with him. "I smell you all over her, pup, start talking."

Brick shifted immediately, but he didn't cower, he straightened. His gaze was lowered out of respect, but he wasn't showing fear. "Poe cut her up, a sigil she had to slice through to break free. Infection took hold, if I hadn't—"

Jagger tugged him forward in a tight hug, surprising us both. "I'm in your debt, brother," he said roughly.

He released a startled Brick, then scooped me off the ground and buried his face against my throat.

"Hey, Charming."

"Fuck, sunshine. I thought I lost you." His big body trembled against me. "I thought I fucking lost you."

"I'll be okay, thanks to Brick." I wrapped my arms around him as tightly as I could, then pulled back sharply. "Luke? Is he all right? Did you find him?"

"Yeah, he's safe. They're all safe, thanks to you."

A snarl erupted around us, and that's when I noticed Rome, Lothar, and Fender. Kurgan looked like he was about to attack. Lenny was held under one of his arms like a rag doll, while his face had partially shifted, fangs extending.

Jagger carefully handed me to Brick. "If you need to run to get her to safety, do it and don't stop."

Brick nodded.

Jagger lifted his hands and slowly walked toward Kurgan. "Put Lenny down. She looks like she's in pain, son."

Kurgan shook his shaggy head.

"Look at her. She's scared. You don't want to scare your female, do you?"

Kurgan's gaze sliced to the other males gathered, and he bared his fangs.

"You need to get back," he said to Roman. "He sees you as a threat. You're all unmated adult males. Brick's too young to be a threat, and I've got Sutton."

Rome and Fender looked confused. "Who the fuck is he?"

Lothar shoved them back. "I'll explain later." Loth lifted his hands as well. "We're not here for your female," he said to Kurgan. "Be at ease, brother."

Lenny wrapped her arms around his thick waist. "Kurgan, stop this," she said, her voice shaky but strong.

Kurgan stilled, the contact from her instantly giving him pause like she knew it would.

"Now put me down."

He growled.

"I'll stay right here beside you, but you're hurting me and you need to put me down."

He immediately did as she said, planting her on her feet, then breathed deep, and growled again when I assumed he scented her pain. He grabbed the bottom of her shirt and tugged it up to look for the source of it. Lenny slapped his hands away.

Jagger stepped forward, ready to intervene, then stopped when Kurgan didn't react to her hitting him.

"It's just a bruise," Lenny said to him.

A look of horror covered his face. "I hurt you."

"You did. You can't hold me so tight. You're much bigger and stronger than me."

His arm around her loosened.

"You okay?" Jagger asked her.

Lenny nodded, then sat, and Kurgan, eyes locked on his female, did the same, holding her carefully pressed against him. "You okay?" he asked, imitating Jagger's tone.

"Yes, Kurgan," she said. "I'm okay."

He looked at Jagger then, as if seeking approval. "Lenny's okay," Kurgan said. "I can be gentle."

"That's good, son. That's really good." Jagger's gaze slid to her wounded leg, it was healing, but an obvious bite, but didn't comment. "We need to go after Tarrant," Jagger said, turning to me and Brick. "You know where they are? We need to find whoever's pulling his strings."

"They're working for the lord Beelzebub," I said.

Rumbling growls rolled from Roman and Lothar.

"You saw him?" Jagger asked through gritted teeth.

Brick's lips peeled back. "Yeah, we saw him. We were being held in his quadrant."

Jagger took me from Brick as we explained what

happened. When we were done, he called Lucifer to let him know.

"He called in the lords. If Beelzebub doesn't know you've escaped, he might go in."

"That fucker's arrogant enough to try," Lothar said.

We headed off, making our way through the forest, Jagger still carrying me in his arms, and every now and then he'd press his nose to my hair and breathe me in, and every time he did, a low rumble vibrated through his chest. "Where are we going?" I asked.

"Somewhere you and Lenny can rest for the night." He pressed his mouth to my ear. "Somewhere I can wash another male's scent off you," he added with a growl.

I pressed my hand to his chest. "Please don't be mad at Brick, he was helping me."

"Not mad at the pup, sunshine, fucking grateful. That doesn't stop the beast from wanting to rub my scent all over you to make sure everyone knows who you belong to."

I fell asleep after that; my body was still fighting off the infection and I was exhausted from being chained to a wall for days.

"We're here," Jagger said, waking me.

I had no idea how long I'd been asleep, probably several hours because I felt rested. A small stone structure loomed ahead through the trees. "It's tiny, how will we all fit?"

He grinned down at me. "We'll fit."

Lothar pressed his hand to the door and the wood glowed red under his palm. The sound of a heavy lock sliding free came next and Loth strode in first, the rest of us filing in after him.

"Holy shit." It opened up to a massive foyer. "What is this, the Tardis?"

Fender grunted. "Something like that."

"It's one of Lucifer's places," Roman said. "He has them all through Hell, so he always has somewhere for him and his handmaids to rest when they're traveling."

Rome, Loth, Fender, and Brick walked into a room that had a pool table and big couches.

Jag turned to Kurgan. "There's a room through there. Go in if you need to check it's safe, then leave Lenny to rest."

"I'll stay with her," Kurgan said.

"You can guard the door from out here."

He shook his head. "I stay with my female."

Lenny touched his arm and immediately got his attention. "I'd feel better if you guard the door for me, please, Kurgan. Can you do that for me?"

He touched her glossy auburn hair that rested against her cheek, rubbing it between his thick, rough-skinned fingers. "I can protect you, Lenny."

"Thank you," she said, then stood back while Kurgan stormed into the room, checked it from top to bottom, then ushered her inside. He walked out then, and after she shut the door, he turned and pressed his hand against it, as if trying to see her, to feel her through it.

"Will he stay out?"

Jagger nodded, a look of amazement. "Lenny seems to have worked out how to control him, at least for now." He tilted his head to a door across from theirs. "We'll be just through there, and my brothers will be watching. If anything changes, they'll be here to stop him."

He opened the door to the bedroom on the other side of the foyer.

"Let's get you cleaned up, then you can rest," he said and carried me into the bathroom. He lowered me to my feet, and I couldn't take my eyes off him as he stripped off my clothes and tossed them aside. "The handmaids have clothes here. We'll get you something clean to wear in the morning."

"I knew you'd find me," I said, letting the last of my armor fall away completely. "I knew my mate would find me."

Jagger stilled, then took my face in his hands. "Always," he choked out.

I smiled up at him as he helped me under the spray.

Jagger thoroughly cleaned me, then, making a rumbling sound in his chest, he lowered to his knees and did what Brick had, but not only licking my barely healing wounds, he sucked on the red and puckered skin over and over again, until I was warm and tingly and felt no pain.

He washed my hair after that, taking his time. His naked body was hot and slick and pressed against me. He was hard, but he didn't seem to be in any hurry, no, he took his time making sure I was clean from top to bottom, and that every trace of Brick's scent was gone. Then he wrapped me in a big, fluffy towel and carried me into the bedroom.

He sat on the bed, pulling me to stand between his thighs, and slowly, thoroughly, dried every inch of me. I slid my hand along his jaw, and his moss-green eyes locked with mine. There was so much behind them. "What are you thinking?"

"Mainly, how beautiful you are, and how fucking relieved I am that you're okay," he said.

"What else?"

The muscle in his jaw tightened. "I'm concerned about

tomorrow, if we can stop Beelzebub, and I'm worried about Kurgan."

"Despite a bumpy start, he's been listening to Lenny."

"He really only shifts in front of me. This...all of this will be a lot for him. This only ends in pain for him. He can't keep her."

I held his pain-filled gaze, that green the exact same color as the wild hound standing across the hall. "You call Kurgan son, is he? Your son?"

His throat worked. "Yes."

I had known there had to be more. The connection between them was impossible to miss. "What happened? Where's his mother? Did you and her—"

"I never met his mother. Lucifer wanted to try to breed hounds from pups, instead of creating full-grown hounds like the rest of us were. He envisioned males like Brick, I guess. More evolved in a lot of ways, and it worked when Relic was created with Lothar's seed. Relic is his success, his only success from that experiment."

"What do you mean?" I rubbed my hands along his shoulders, trying to soothe the pain I saw in his eyes.

"Lucifer created two pups with my seed. One was Kurgan. He was born smelling wrong, something not right inside him, something broken. He was wild, uncontrollable, so much so that he had to be locked away for the safety of others."

"And the second pup?" I asked.

"He died."

"Jagger...I'm so sorry."

He massaged my hips. "The problem was, when they were born, I started to feel. My emotions began to develop, like they have been with you." He gave me a squeeze. "I felt love for my pups, and the pain of losing one and the suffering of the other, was too much. Sutton, it was too much for me to handle after five hundred years of nothing, so I...I asked Lucifer to take those emotions away."

And he'd gone another five hundred years since without feeling much of anything, until now. My heart ached for him. That kind of grief was hard enough for anyone, but to live your whole life not feeling that deeply, then to experience the extreme roller coaster of so much all at once? No wonder he'd asked Lucifer to take them away.

"I told you before, the reason I took so long to realize you were mine was that I didn't think a mate was possible for me. There's a reason for that. I asked Lucifer to stop it from happening for me." He shook his head. "I wasn't looking for it, hadn't allowed myself to feel it, because I didn't believe you were possible."

"You did that?" God, there was so much regret rolling off him.

"After I denied you, after I hurt you, I went to Lucifer and asked what was happening. He admitted that he never did what I asked, that he couldn't. Only the fates made those decisions. I should have gone to you then, as soon as I found out, I should have begged for forgiveness, but I was so fucking scared. I was terrified of losing you because, eventually, I would lose you. You're not—"

"Immortal?" I finished for him when he choked back his words.

He hissed through bared teeth. "Knowing that I'd lose you as well, that I'd spend eternity back in that pain?" He shook his head. "I'm ashamed to admit, I was afraid...so afraid that I hurt you to protect myself."

I slid my thumb along that sharp jawline. "I did the same thing, I refused to let you back in to protect my heart.

We both did that. We both know the pain of losing people we love."

"We do, but the difference is, now you're under my skin, buried deep in my heart, and I'd rather have you for as long as I can than never at all. I can't exist in this world knowing you're in it and stay away from you, so when you're gone, I'll go with you."

I gripped his shoulders. "What are you saying?"

"I made a deal with Lucifer, sunshine. When you go, I go with you."

I shook my head, and he took my face in his hands. "You can't change my mind. It's what I want. I've lived for a thousand years, Sutton, and none of it meant a fucking thing until I found you. Live the rest of this life with me. Don't think about the end, just be with me here, now."

I wrapped my arms around him and kissed him with everything I was feeling, with my whole heart and soul, with all the fire that burned inside me whenever he was near. "I love you," I said against his lips.

He lifted me, turned, and laid me on the bed, coming down on top of me. "I love you, too, my beautiful sunshine." His expression grew serious, his thumbs brushing over my jaw as he looked down at me. "Before we go any further, I need you to know, I can't...I can't give you pups, baby, it's too risky."

He was serious. Didn't he know? "I just want you, Jagger. Nothing else matters, I just want you to make me yours." I wrapped my legs around his waist. "I don't want to go another day, another moment, not being your mate in truth."

"Yeah?" he rasped against my jaw. "You ready to take your male on your hands and knees, baby? You ready to wear my mark on your skin?"

He ground his hard cock against me, wringing a desperate whimper from my lips. "Yes, I'm ready. I want that, more than anything."

One moment his big body covered me, the next he'd lifted up, taking me with him, and flipped me onto my front.

He hoisted my hips up, then bent over me, his mouth at my ear. "I'll make love to you, baby, I'll make you come all night long. I'll worship this sweet, soft, perfect little body until the day we die, but tonight, right now, I'm going to fuck you, Sutton. I'm going to make you mine like the animal I am needs me to."

I shivered. That's exactly what I wanted. I wriggled my ass against the hard, hot length resting between his tight stomach and my ass. "Do it," I demanded.

I'd transformed, a red haze shifted through my sight, my black nails sliding from the tips of my fingers and digging into the mattress. He rubbed his face, his jaw over my throat and shoulders, marking me with his scent as he slid his fingers deep inside me.

Gasping, I rocked against his hand.

"That's it, sunshine. Nice and wet for your mate. You're gonna take all of me, aren't you, baby?"

All I could do was whimper and nod as those thick fingers thrust into me faster, hitting the spot inside me that made my eyes roll back over and over. "Oh fuck."

"Give it to me."

I cried out, coming all over his fingers, and as soon as I stopped clutching wildly, he slid his fingers free. A moment later, I felt the thick head of his cock at my entrance and I squirmed, wanting him inside me so badly.

"You ready to take my knot?"

"Yes, I'm ready. I'm so ready."

He chuckled low and sexy. "Better dig those claws deeper into the mattress, sunshine."

I shivered with excitement.

"Breathe," he said in a rough voice, pushing the tip inside me. "Relax that pussy and let your male in."

I did. I breathed in through my mouth and out my nose, and on every exhale, I forced my body to relax, and Jagger pushed a little more, filling me deeper, claiming me more and more with every inch he took.

He groaned. "You feel so fucking good, you're gripping me so tight. Fucking hell, I hope you're ready 'cause I need to fuck you now, baby, before I lose my damn mind."

I pushed back, taking the last inch inside me in answer, a needy cry bursting from me.

Jagger's arm immediately snapped across my chest, locking me in place underneath him, holding me immobile, then he slid almost all the way out, making me shudder, and slammed back in, growling against my ear.

I cried out.

"Fucking made for me." He grunted and did it again, thrusting deep. "Every inch of you was made for me, my beautiful sunshine."

With every thrust, my body accommodated his. I was impossibly wet and each thrust took me higher, driving me to heights I didn't know were possible. The feeling was too big, too good. I felt as if I were losing my mind.

"More," I groaned. "Harder, faster."

Jagger cursed viciously and gave it to me, slamming into me, claiming me in a way we both needed. He slammed deep one more time and I screamed, coming around him. He snarled as his cock grew bigger inside me.

I tried to rock forward, but I was locked in place by his knot. He hooked his arm around my waist, holding me to him, not giving me any room to move, and swiveled his hips.

"Ready?" he asked huskily.

"Yes." I was so ready.

His fangs sank into my shoulder, marking me as his, and I came again so hard that my arms gave out. I was stuffed so full of him, while his thick cock pulsed inside me over and over, flooding me with hot seed until it slid down my thighs and dragged out my pleasure.

I lost track of how long I floated in that space of unimaginable bliss, but, finally, he wrapped his arm around me and fell to the mattress, holding me close to him.

"You did so fucking good, baby," he said as he gently licked the bite mark he'd given me. He nuzzled my throat. "Fuck, my bite looks good on you."

I reached back, grazing my claws along his hip, and loved the way he shivered. His cock was still hard, but his knot finally released me, and he gently eased from my body, more of his seed sliding out with it.

"I'm sorry, sunshine. This time you had to take my knot, but I'll sort something out for next time. Is there something witches can take to prevent pregnancy? Human males can have something done to stop them from impregnating their females, maybe I can—"

I turned and placed my fingers over his lips. "I want to have babies with you someday, Jagger."

Pain filled his eyes. "I told you, my seed, it's no good. I'd never want to watch you suffer while our pup dies in your arms. I could never do that to you. And Kurgan, with how wild he was—"

"Kurgan's situation, the pup you lost, I know it had to be so incredibly painful, but that was different, we have no idea what will happen if we have a baby together."

"I want to protect you from that pain," he said roughly.

"You can't protect me from everything, Jagger, and if we do have a baby born with challenges, we'll face it together, and we'll love them anyway. We'll help them the best we can."

There was pain in his eyes, a wariness. Jagger wasn't convinced, not yet. He didn't say no, though, he pressed his mouth to my forehead and wrapped me tight in his arms.

"We're in this together," I said against his chest. "Whatever happens in the future, we face it together."

CHAPTER
TWENTY-EIGHT

Jagger

"Wake up, sunshine." The last thing I wanted to do was wake my mate and pull her out of bed. What I wanted to do was stay under the covers with her all soft, sated, and wrapped around me. But that would have to wait.

Sutton blinked up at me slow and drowsy. She frowned. "Why are you out of bed, Charming?"

My heart thudded in my chest. I pressed a kiss to her still puffy lips and forced myself to keep it quick.

"I'm sorry, baby, but we've gotta get going. Beelzebub's been spotted, and we need to get to him before he takes off."

Her eyes widened, and she shoved back the covers, looking around frantically for her clothes.

I pointed to the clothes sitting on the end of the bed. "They're Roxy's. They should fit." Someone knocked on the door. "Come out when you're dressed," I said to her and forced myself to walk out of the room.

Rome, Fender, Loth, and Brick were waiting, a mix of concern and violence on their faces.

"Beelzebub ignored Lucifer's summons, so why the fuck is he sticking around?" Loth said.

Rome crossed his arms. "No idea, but if that prick escapes before we can get to him, we may never find him."

He was right. Beelzebub could move between realms easily and quickly and Hell was vast. There were places he could hide. Either way, tracking him wouldn't be easy. "Lucifer won't let him get away with this betrayal."

Loth scowled. "We can't give him time to regroup and then come back and attempt a takeover."

"Whatever cards Beelzebub's holding have to be fucking good ones," I said. "He has to believe he has a chance at overthrowing Lucifer or he wouldn't have made a move in the first place."

My brothers' rumbles of agreement filled the space as I headed over to Kurgan. "You give Lenny the clothes, son?" We'd found some for him and Brick as well.

He nodded, his gaze locked on the door his female was behind.

"You get any sleep at all?"

He shook his head. "Lenny needed to be protected."

"You feeling solid? You got a handle on your control?" He'd done better than I ever thought he was capable of. I tried not to let hope fill me, but it was hard not to.

"I won't harm her again," he said roughly, then his gaze dipped to the floor. "I bit her leg, but I healed it."

That hope fizzled, and I patted his shoulder. "That's good. Healing her was good."

"She'll stay with me now," he said, nodding to

himself. "My den is strong, I have water and meat, a comfortable pallet for her to sleep on. I can protect her better there."

My fucking heart clenched. He didn't understand why that was impossible. Knowing the pain ahead of him, knowing that he would again have to suffer the rejection of his mate because he couldn't be the male she needed, fucking killed me.

The door opened and Kurgan instantly stepped forward, startling Lenny. He grabbed her around the waist before she could step back.

"Control, son," I said. "Give Lenny some room."

He grunted and released her but didn't step back, looking down at her in a way that would be unsettling for anyone, especially a tiny female, but if we tried to pull him away from her, it would make everything a lot worse.

"You doing okay?" I asked her.

Kurgan turned to me, then back to his female. "You doing okay?" he asked before she could answer me, in an almost perfect imitation of my voice.

She blinked up at him. "Yes, thank you." She gave her answer to Kurgan and stepped forward. He didn't move. "You'll need to let me past."

He instantly stepped back but touched her hair and dipped his head, breathing in her scent as she moved by.

The door across the room opened and Sutton walked out. She was dressed similar to Lenny, in a pair of leather pants and jacket. It acted as a lightweight armor. My gaze skimmed down her sweet body as she strode toward me.

"Ready," she said, then looked over at Lenny. They exchanged a look, and Sutton nodded, offering her a reassuring smile.

"Take the front," I said to Loth, Rome, and Fender. "Me,

Brick, and Kurgan will take the rear." I looked to my son. "We'll shift and carry the females."

His eyes lit up. He liked that idea.

Lenny spun to me. "You want me to ride him like a...a freaking horse?"

"I'm faster than a horse," Kurgan said, puffing up his chest.

"We have to move fast," I said, feeling bad for her, but there was no other choice.

Sutton took her hand. "I know it's a lot to ask. All of this has been a lot, but Jagger won't let anything happen to you. None of the males will...especially not Kurgan."

She lifted her chin and nodded. She was a strong female, stronger than I thought she was, and brave.

Kurgan shifted, exploding into his huge beast, and it was easier than I'd seen him shift in a long time. With shaky hands, Lenny gathered his clothes, and when Kurgan lowered for her to climb up, she did without much hesitation. Thank fuck.

We strode from the building, and the rest of us shifted. Sutton grabbed everyone's clothes and climbed on my back.

"Grip on to Kurgan's fur. It won't hurt him," she said to Lenny, then we took off, exploding through the forest.

>)>●(((

Sutton

I clung to Jagger as he tore through Hell. Kurgan ran beside him, Lenny pressed low, gripping on to his fur with white knuckles.

We'd ridden hard for a long time and had left the forest

a while ago. We were now high on a cliff above a river that glowed red.

Jagger slowed, and Lothar made a low chuffing sound ahead. Jagger returned it with one of his own. They'd seen something.

Beelzebub must be close.

Jagger dropped to his belly and reached back with his snout, touching my leg, telling me to climb off. He made a series of throaty sounds to Brick and Kurgan and used his snout to give me a shove toward them.

I did as I was told, standing beside Brick as Lenny scrambled off Kurgan's back, but she stayed close to him.

That's when I heard the snarls.

We all turned, looking across the wide chasm to the other side of the river. Beelzebub had a chain fisted around his massive hand, wielding a whip with the other. A hound with pale gold fur was attached to it. He growled and shook his head wildly, fighting with everything he had. He was smaller than the other hounds I'd seen and finer boned. A pup? It had to be, but he was strong, and Beelzebub was struggling to control him.

Jagger leaped ahead of his brothers and sped off. There was a bridge ahead, and Jagger tore onto it, his brothers following, running at full speed, toward the demon lord on the other side.

Beelzebub saw them and a gateway flashed opened behind him.

"Holy shit," I choked as he tried to drag the hound toward it.

The smaller hound dug in his paws, his claws scratching the stone. With a roar, Beelzebub flung the hound against the wall, then yanked him toward him, gaining some ground.

Jagger and his brothers were closing in, snarling and growling with bared teeth, determined to save the hound and drag the lord back to Lucifer. Beelzebub roared again and, biceps bulging, dragged the hound closer, then he threw out a hand, aiming for the bridge. The hounds leaped as the black ropes at one end gave away. Jagger, Rome, and Loth made it, but the massive demon lashed his whip at Fender, knocking him back. He fell, barely catching the edge of the cliff.

Lenny grabbed my hand. "Oh no."

Rome shifted and dove for his brother, but it was too late. Fender fell, plummeting into the burning river. I screamed and rushed to the edge, watching as Fender was washed away—as something huge and scaled thrashed in the water and went after him.

There was nothing they could do. Rome bounded off the ground and raced to help Jagger and Lothar. The small hound was still fighting for his life. Jagger leaped for Beelzebub, and the demon had no choice but to let go of the chain attached to the small hound and dive through the gateway, escaping. It instantly snapped closed after him.

Lothar tore off along the cliff, I assume going after Fender, while Jag and Rome approached the small hound.

"There's another bridge a couple miles that way," Jagger called across. "We'll meet you there."

Brick gave me a nudge and lowered to the ground. I climbed on his back, and we took off again. I looked back as Rome approached the hound, hands raised, then we rounded a corner and I lost sight of them.

Brick and Kurgan sprinted along the cliff, and I searched the river below for any sign of Fender and Lothar. When we rounded a corner and the next bridge came into view, I sat a little higher, frantically looking for any sign of life.

I saw Lothar first, then I saw Fender. He was lying on his back, panting hard. Loth stood as we approached. I jumped off Brick's back and rushed to Fender, calling on my magic so I could treat him, and dropped down at his side. "Oh gods. I thought you were dead." I searched his body, hovering my hand over him, down past his hips, to his legs, and flinched. The right one stopped just below the knee and was perfectly cauterized. My gaze shot up to his. "Your leg."

He gave me a pained grin, gritting his teeth and shaking. "There's more than a few bitey things in that river, babe."

"Will it...can it grow back?" Hounds were immortal, and they could heal from almost any injury.

"The burning river can't touch us, can't penetrate our skin or hair, the same as hellfire, but an open wound's different. As soon as the Vysan took my leg, the river sealed the wound and killed the ability for it to grow back."

"What if we opened the wound?"

He shook his head. "It will grow as far as the stump I have now, no further."

"I'm so sorry," I rasped and took his hand in mine.

He grinned again, but it didn't reach his eyes. "I'll live."

The thud of someone coming across the bridge echoed off the cliffs, and I spun around. Jagger strode toward us, naked and glorious, Rome following, holding the smaller hound in his arms, and by the looks of the pup's back leg, it was probably broken.

I stood and rushed to Jagger, flinging my arms around him. "Are you okay?"

"I'm good." A strange look shifted over his face. "But we might need your help...with her."

"Her?"

My mate actually looked shaken, and I realized the same expression was mirrored on Rome's face.

"The hound's a female?" I said.

He dipped his chin.

"But I thought...you said there weren't any female hounds."

He turned back to the small hound in Rome's arms. "There aren't...weren't."

Rome carefully lowered her to the ground, and I sat beside her. "I'm Sutton. I'm a healer, and if you'll allow me to, I can fix that broken leg."

She bared her teeth, but there wasn't much fight behind it. She'd worn herself out.

"We need to get this collar off her," I said. "The goddess only knows how long she's been trapped in her animal form."

Rome moved closer, and the pup's chest heaved with exertion as she snarled at him. He made a soft sound in the back of his throat. "Easy," he rumbled.

She kept her teeth bared but stopped snarling.

"You need to damage the sigil to get it off."

Rome took the massive knife that Brick handed him, and the smaller hound tried to jerk away. Rome grabbed the thick iron collar, stopping her, and steam rose from his hand, followed by the scent of burning flesh. He barely flinched, just made that low, soft sound again as he worked the blade over the parent sigil, breaking the lines and the demon magic.

Not releasing her, he handed the blade back to Brick, then tore the collar off. Sparks burst from it like they had when I'd removed Brick's and Kurgan's, and Rome tossed it over the cliff and into the burning river.

She shifted instantly.

Rome blinked down at her, his nostrils flaring. She was curled up, covering herself. Her hair was the same gold as her fur and streaked with a deeper brown. It covered her face.

Rome held out his hand to Brick. "My shirt." Brick tossed it to him, and Rome laid it beside her. "You can put this on."

Her hand shot out, and she grabbed it, holding it to her chest.

"Let's give her some privacy," I said.

They quickly did as I said, turning their backs. "Can I help you?"

"Yeah," she said huskily. "Please."

She pushed herself up to sit and we got the shirt on, covering her, and the males all turned back, looking at her with obvious stunned expressions. I quickly did what I could for her leg, and she barely made a sound when the bone snapped back into place. I pumped her full of healing magic, letting it flow through her, and saw the scars inside her. She'd come close to death once, very close.

"How does that feel?"

"Yeah, good. Thanks."

Jagger held out his hand to help her up. She looked at it but didn't move.

"This is Jagger, the alpha's lieutenant. He's a good male. They all are. No one here will hurt you."

"Jagger?" she rasped.

"Yeah," he said and crouched low.

She tilted her head back, looking up at him—and Jagger froze. His eyes flared, then he shot to his feet. Kurgan eased closer as well.

"What's going on?" I asked, looking between them.

She struggled to stand, and Rome helped her get to her

feet, supporting most of her weight. "My eyes, you recognize them?"

Her eyes were stunning, unusual, like nothing I had ever seen. Bright pale gold that shone like the real thing, surrounded by moss green and ringed with a deeper shade.

Jagger paced away, then back, closing the space between them. "You died."

She huffed out a strange laugh. "Everyone thought I did, but it turned out I didn't. Uncle Lucifer thought not telling you was for the best."

Uncle Lucifer? That wasn't something I ever thought I'd hear.

Jagger growled viciously. "Where did he hide you?"

"I was brought up by the handmaids. I've lived with them my whole life."

"What's going on?" Loth asked. "You know this female? And how the fuck does she even exist?"

She turned to him. "My name's Zarriah, but I go by Zuri. I exist because Jagger here sired me. Though, I'm guessing he thought I was a male?"

"I had no idea," Jagger growled. "You were covered, and I...I assumed..." His throat worked.

Holy shit. The pup he thought he lost—and she was standing right there in front of him. I reached out and took Jag's hand.

Zuri turned to Kurgan next, who had moved closer still, pulling Lenny along with him. "And going by your scent, I'm guessing you're my brother." She held out her hand, and Kurgan took it and lifted it to his nose, scenting her as well. "The handmaids told me about you," she said gently. "I'm happy to finally meet you, Kurgan."

He made a sound similar to Rome, a soft throaty chuffing, then looked at Jagger. "She needs to be protected."

Jagger's jaw was like granite. "Yes, son, she does."

"I appreciate the offer, but I can look after myself."

"What did Beelzebub want with you?" Lothar asked her.

She shrugged. "No idea, but can we all agree that he's a giant asshole?" Then she glanced up at Rome. "Thanks for the shirt. I might need your help to walk for a while yet."

He grunted, then swung her up into his arms. Kurgan growled and Jagger stepped forward, then Rome bared his teeth at both of them.

Jagger sucked in a steadying breath and visibly shook out his shoulders, then jerked his chin up at Rome and put his hand on Kurgan's shoulder. "Be calm, son, Zarriah's safe with Rome. You have Lenny to look after, and I have Sutton."

Kurgan nodded, then tugged Lenny closer.

We headed off after that, and I squeezed Jagger's hand. "Are you okay?"

"No, and I won't be. Not until I get some answers."

Lucifer had lied to him. Again. Of course, he wasn't okay. "I'm so sorry."

He stopped and tugged me to him. Then he lifted me off my feet and pressed his forehead to mine. "Thank fuck I have you by my side."

He kissed me, then put me back on my feet, and we headed for Lucifer's quarters, and going by Jagger's red eyes and granite jaw, it wasn't going to be a happy reunion.

CHAPTER
TWENTY-NINE

Jagger

Roxy opened the door, her gaze sliding over each one of us, then landed on Zuri, still being carried by Rome, and her eyes widened, filling with relief.

"Who is it?" Lucifer called from behind the wooden door.

We'd walked for hours, finally making it to Lucifer's quadrant of Hell, and I wasn't leaving until I got some fucking answers.

"The whole gang's here," Rox said and pushed the door open, letting us in.

Lucifer sat on his chair, his cat, Mini, sitting on his shoulder. He looked up as we strode in, his gaze slicing to Zarriah instantly, then flying back to me.

He placed Mini on the couch and strode over to her, taking her face in his hands. "You're okay?"

She nodded. "I'm fine. Beelzebub had me chained and collared like a dog, and I couldn't get away."

Lucifer reached out to take her, and Rome looked to me, not relinquishing her until I gave him a nod, something that obviously pissed off Lucifer, but I didn't give a fuck right then.

"Everyone but Jag, go with Rox." He tilted his head to the dining room that was always stocked with fresh and plentiful food. "You all must be hungry."

"Sutton stays," I said. "Anything you have to say to me, you can say in front of my mate."

Lucifer's yellow eyes darkened, but he inclined his head. "Fine."

He handed Zuri back to Rome, and Roxy took her hand as everyone left the room. The doors were closed behind them, leaving the three of us alone.

"You told me my pup died, that my *son* died. Instead, I had a daughter, and she's very much alive and well." My fists clenched, and it was hard, but I held myself back when all I wanted to do was plant my fist in his fucking face. "You kept my daughter from me for five hundred years." The handmaids' quadrant was inaccessible to anyone except those they allowed in. If Lucifer didn't want her found, that was the best place to hide her.

Lucifer slid his hands in his pockets. "She may have been created with your seed, Jagger, but she was my experiment. Zarriah was always mine."

"But Kurgan is mine? The experiment you deemed unsuccessful?" I bit out. "I have taken care of him his whole life, and you've ignored him."

Lucifer's eyes flashed. "I have never forgotten him, he's one of my children, like you all are. With how unstable you were after—"

"After you made me believe my pup was dead? Yes, *my lord*, you are correct. I was lost to emotion." My fangs had elongated, my eyes now red.

"And I took it away for you. I allowed you to raise Kurgan—"

"You arrogant, fucking—"

"Watch your tone," Lucifer said, low and deadly. "You are my child, and I love you, Jagger, but I will not tolerate disrespect."

Sutton squeezed my hand, her fear reaching out and wrapping around me. It was enough to get my anger in check, or at least prevent me from doing something stupid.

I would give him a few home truths though. "Respect goes both ways, and you have shown me none."

Ursula stood. She'd been sitting in the corner, and I hadn't even seen her there. "Okay, everyone needs to take a breath." She strode across the room and stopped beside Lucifer. "You owe Jag," she said to him. "You know you do."

He turned to her, fury in his eyes. "The fuck I do."

"He's right. You lied to him. You made him think his pup died and let him think he was the reason. You let him think he was defective, Lucifer."

His jaw clenched. "You know I had my reasons."

She shrugged. "Your reasons don't mean shit to Jag."

"What reasons?" I bit out. "What reason could you possibly have for doing what you did? Is it something to do with why Beelzebub took her? How does Zuri play into his plan to overthrow you?"

Lucifer slid his hands into his pockets. "That's not something I'm willing to share at this juncture."

I growled.

"But I suppose Ursula makes some sense." His gaze slid

to Sutton, then back to me. "I do owe you. Tell me what you want, and I'll give it to you."

Hot rage throbbed through my veins. "That won't change what you did—"

"Don't be a fucking idiot," Ursula said to me, her head tilting to Sutton. "Tell Lucifer what you want."

It hit me, hard, exactly what I could ask for, what I could have. "Immortality, for my mate."

"Fine," Lucifer said, his yellow eyes darkening. "Anything else?"

His tone was dripping with sarcasm, but I took advantage anyway. "I want to get to know Zuri. I want her to spend time above ground and to stay at the compound whenever she wants."

"No—"

"Please, let me."

Lucifer spun around as Zuri walked back in, and he shook his head. "No, it's too dangerous. I just got you back. I won't risk you being taken again."

"It was the hounds who saved me. You can't tell me they aren't capable of protecting me. Besides, they're my pack. I have a pack." Her eyes brightened. "I've felt their absence my whole life. I belong with them."

He shook his head. "You can spend time with the hounds below ground."

"I want to get to know Jagger, and I want to leave Hell. You've kept me down here since I was born. You need to let me go."

"One of us will go with her," Ursula said.

"You're supposed to be on my side," he fired at Urs.

She shrugged. "I am. I'm also on Zuri's side. She's been coddled far too long. Let her live a little."

"Fuck. Fine, but if anything happens to her—"

"It won't."

His gaze came back to me. "We cool?"

Not by a long shot, but I'd have to be. "We're cool."

"Good, now tell me what you know and how I can find that fucking traitor Beelzebub."

"Tarrant made moves above ground, setting up Beelzebub's takeover," I said and explained what they planned. "Beelzebub escaped through a gateway before we could get to him." Lucifer knew what that meant as well as we did. He wouldn't be easy to find.

"First things first," Lucifer said. "Stop those morons from killing thousands of humans and setting the fucking angels off, then bring Tarrant to me. I want him alive."

Which meant that Poe was fair game.

Good, because that fucker was mine.

›)》●《‹‹

Sutton

Jagger looked up from his phone. "Rune thinks one of his scouts spotted Tarrant. We need to go." His hand tightened on mine as everyone headed for the door.

Before we reached it, though, he stopped, blocking Kurgan. "You have to stay here, son."

He studied Jagger, then the massive hound pulled Lenny tight to his side. "I'll protect Lenny in my den."

Pain slashed through Jagger's eyes as Lenny tried to pull away, looking alarmed.

Lucifer stepped forward. "Kurgan and Lenny will stay here with me and Zuri until you finish this," he said, holding Jagger's gaze, then looked back at Kurgan. "You can watch me build Fender a prosthetic. I have something stunning in mind."

Fender was on the couch behind him, Ursula at his side. She punched him in the arm and called him a fucking pussy, which I assumed was her way of comforting him, going by his rough laugh.

Lenny was shaking her head when Roxy bounded over. "We'll have fun, promise."

Trying to take Lenny from Kurgan now wasn't an option. The hound would fracture, he'd need Jagger with him, and Jag was needed above ground.

I took Lenny's other hand. "We'll be back as soon as we can. Everything will be okay."

She nodded, but terror filled her eyes as Jagger led me from Lucifer's quarters, the other hounds with us.

We rushed along several caverns, then Jagger opened a gateway. Only Lucifer could open one close to his quarters. But when we stepped through, we weren't in the city, we were just beyond it.

It was dark and Rune along with several of his demons were there to greet us. Warrick stood beside them.

"What's going on?" Jag asked.

"We followed their trucks from a warehouse just beyond Seventh Circle," War said. "They're loaded up with barrels."

"It's poison," I said. "They're going to drug the water system in an attempt to control the humans in the city."

Rune's hands curled into tight fists. "That would explain why we're by the river."

A short field stood between us and the large building on the other side. The sound of rushing water came from somewhere close by. A water treatment plant. They were going to dump the drums in at the source. There were several huge trucks, and I spotted at least a dozen demons moving around outside, hauling barrels. There had to be more in the building.

"Would they really have enough in those barrels to poison the city?" Rune asked.

"More than enough." I wrapped my arms around myself. "If the drugs in those barrels gets in the water, it will poison the whole system."

"Tarrant's working for Beelzebub," Jagger said to his alpha. "Beelzebub got away, though, and he's angling to overthrow Lucifer. This is part of his plan. His demons will take over the city, make humans their cattle, and cause an all-out revolt here and in Hell. He mentioned some forgotten prophecy, that they need humans to willingly offer their flesh to start some alternate path, then Beelzebub can take over."

War bared his teeth. "That fuck isn't taking over this city."

There were grunts and growls of agreement.

"Tarrant may look like a weaselly piece of shit, but he is Beelzebub's nephew," Rune said, his face a mask of hatred. "He's more powerful than he looks. He and I, we're closely matched, if you can, leave him to me."

Jagger nodded. "Lucifer wants him alive, so try not to kill him. And Poe? He's mine."

War and Rune didn't argue, then Jagger turned to me. "Stay here with Brick. I want you safe."

"I can help. Let me fight," Brick said, stepping forward.

"You're needed here," War said and gripped his shoulder. "Jag's trusting you to protect his female."

Brick puffed up a little, nodding to his alpha.

I had no desire to throw myself into the middle of this, but worry filled me. I couldn't lose Jagger, not when we finally worked things out, not when he was finally mine. "Promise me you'll be careful," I said to my mate.

"I promise." He leaned down and kissed me hard.

Then the hounds, along with Rune and his demons, used the shadows to move in and surround the huge building.

I watched with my heart in my throat as Jagger, War, and Rune stormed the building from the front. Rome and Lothar had gone around the back with several of Rune's demons—for tonight, at least, they were working together.

Shouts broke out inside the building, and the demons outside ran in to see what was going on. The sound of fighting grew louder—things breaking, screams, roars.

A moment later, a dark figure ran from a side door. "Did you see that?"

Brick followed my line of sight. "Someone's trying to get away. Fuck."

"There's two of them." Only they weren't running away. They'd jumped into one of the trucks yet to be unloaded and were backing it up to the edge of the river inlet. "They're going to dump the poison into the river. We have to do something."

"Stay here," Brick said, then he bolted across the field toward them.

As I watched, Brick yanked the driver from his seat, and they attacked each other. I couldn't see the other demon, he'd raced around the side of the truck. I had to do something before he got in, finished backing it up, and dumped the barrels in the river. I couldn't physically fight him, but maybe I could slow him down.

With no other choice, I sprinted as fast as I could across the field, calling my magic forth as I ran, letting it swirl and grow inside me to heights I'd never been able to get it before. Brick was snarling. He'd shifted, and his jaws were locked around the demon's leg, shaking him hard, while the demon—oh gods, it was Tarrant, stabbed at him with a knife.

I threw out a hand, forcing my power into his shoulder, wrapping around it, searching for the weakest point, and forced it out of the joint. Tarrant screamed, and a bloody Brick dug his fangs deeper, shaking him harder.

Poe ran around the side of the truck and was headed for the driver's side. I dove for it, bounding up and onto the seat and yanked the keys out of the ignition. I would not let these fuckers hurt anyone else. Poe grabbed my jacket and jerked me back. I hit the ground hard, and I gasped for breath, but managed to quickly scramble to my feet before he could advance on me.

He smirked. "Give me the keys, Sutton. Now."

I shook my head and, lifting my hands, let my magic dance across my fingers. "Stop where you are. I'm warning you."

"What do you think you're going to do, you fucking traitor?"

With a growl, I tossed the keys as far as I could and they landed somewhere in the long grass edging the clearing, then I straightened my spine. "I'll break every fucking bone in your body, one by one."

His eyes flashed with fury, but he laughed, and it grated down my spine.

"Try it," he said as he strode toward me.

I aimed my magic at him, but he didn't slow. It didn't touch him.

Poe tore his shirt down the front, revealing his chest, and the same sigil he'd carved into me. "You can't touch me."

I was screwed.

I turned to run, but it was too late. He dove on me, knocking me to the ground. Flipping me to my back, he grinned down at me. "Gotcha."

Brick screamed, a sound like I'd never heard before coming from the hound. Shoving my forearm against Poe's throat, I spun to Brick. He was battered and bleeding from deep wounds all over his body. I threw out my other arm, to fire my powers at Tarrant, to stop him from hacking into Brick—but Poe grabbed my wrist pinning it to the ground.

He shook his head. "No you don't. Now you get to watch the pup die. It's what a traitor like you deserves."

Growls and snarls filled the night and Poe lifted his head, and bared his teeth.

The hounds, they were coming.

"Tarrant," Poe yelled, getting his attention.

The demon stopped his attack on Brick, and turned to the hounds barreling down on us. He didn't look worried, though, no, he smiled. Brick went flying, hitting the side of the truck and staying there, suspended, bleeding and barely conscious, while Tarrant lifted his hands, calling out words in a demonic language.

The hounds slammed into an invisible barrier, and were tossed back with snarls and growls. They rushed back, and Jagger shifted into his human form, slamming his fist into the invisible wall between us. He was standing so close to me, I could clearly see his face, and how it was contorted with rage. He slammed his shoulder into the barrier next and roared. But it was no use, Tarrant's shield was too strong.

Tarrant closed his eyes then and called to Beelzebub, asking him to open a gateway.

Poe grinned at him, then down at me. "It's almost time to go. You're not getting away from me again. Never again."

I stared into his black eyes. "I'll never be yours," I said, fury burning through me. "Do you want to know why?"

He gripped my wrists so tight my hands were going numb and my bones were close to breaking. Hissing, he lowered his head, so close his nose touched mine. "Enlighten me."

"I already belong to someone else," I fired at him. "I'm mated, to a hellhound. I'm mated to Jagger."

His face turned bright red. "You're lying." He shook his head. "You're fucking lying."

"You can't smell him? His scent's all over me. It's inside me." I grinned up at him, it was hateful, gleeful. "And no matter what happens, he will come for you. No matter what you do or where you take me, he will find me, then he'll make you scream."

Poe yanked the neck of my shirt to the side, checking for Jagger's mark and finding it. His eyes flared, and he shrieked, the sound like nothing I'd ever heard in my life.

He grabbed my throat and hauled me off the ground, choking me.

All the hounds had shifted now, all of them in their human forms, and they held up their hands, palms out. Battering Tarrant's power, weakening the barrier, firing hellfire at it. I saw then, as the fire hit it, a shimmering wall. It trembled, thinning.

Jagger would get to me, I just had to stay alive. My sight washed with red, and my claws burst from the tips of my fingers. Thrashing, I clawed at his fingers around my throat, at his wrist as he carried me toward the edge of a cliff, high above the rushing, furious river below.

"You know the saying, don't you, sweetness? If I can't

have you..." He jerked me forward and pressed his mouth to my ear. "Nobody can."

His arms tensed, about to toss me over the edge into the freezing river, but I dug my claws deeper, hanging on to him, and swiped with the other hand, shredding the skin at his chest, destroying the sigil there.

He slammed his fist into my side and tried to shake me off, but I refused to let go. If I was going over the side, he was going with me.

Gasping from exertion, I aimed my magic at his ankles, and with a cry, I snapped one, then the other. He roared and collapsed on the ground, almost sending us both over the edge. My legs dangled, and I scrambled to find purchase. Using my claws, and Poe as an anchor, I dug them into his skin and crawled up his prone body.

Poe swiped his own claws at me, trying to dislodge me, but I refused to let go. I slammed my power into his elbows, wrenching them the wrong way, and bone burst through skin. I didn't stop, I crawled over him, the way he had me. "You don't get to die, asshole, not yet."

"You fucking bitch," he hissed. "You fucking whore. I'm going to—"

I grabbed his jaw and broke it. He screamed, and I stared into his furious, hate-filled eyes. "You will never force a female to endure your disgusting touch ever again. You'll never blackmail another female into accepting your revolting kiss out of fear for the people she loves. You'll pay for what you've done, for all the people you hurt."

Poe flailed on the ground and I kept a steady stream of my power pumping into him, keeping him broken, while I looked up, meeting Jagger's furious stare. He was so close, but I couldn't reach him. The barrier still stood. It shuddered, but remained intact.

Then a bloody and ash-covered Rune strode forward, joining them, and with a bloodcurdling sound, he aimed his power at Tarrant. Brick dropped to the ground. With Rune's added strength, Tarrant wasn't able to hold him up any longer.

Brick struggled to his feet, then with a growl, he leaped. He knocked Tarrant down, and with a vicious snarl, wrapped his jaws around Tarrant's throat.

The barrier shuddered.

Poe suddenly bucked beneath me, and I fought to hold him down. I hissed. "You're not going anywhere."

I was lifted away suddenly, dragged off Poe. I thrashed, trying to fight.

"It's me, sunshine." Jagger wrapped me tight in his solid arms. "It's over, baby. You did it."

I looked around me. The barrier had collapsed, the fighting stopped. Brick was leaning against the truck, naked and bleeding, and War stood over Tarrant, while Rune used his power to bind him. Ash floated through the air, from the demons who hadn't survived the fight, but Rune and the other hounds all seemed okay.

Jagger held me close, and I wrapped my arms around his neck and buried my face there. "Thank the goddess you're okay."

"Seeing you lying here with Poe, fuck." He growled. "I thought..." His throat muscles worked. "Can smell your blood, sunshine, how badly are you hurt?"

"Just some scratches, a few bruises." I lifted my head. "I'll be okay, but right now I need to help Brick."

Jagger didn't put me down; he carried me to the younger hound and only then lowered me to my feet. I treated him while Jag and his brothers gathered the drums and set them all on fire.

War had several of his brothers come in their trucks to take us back to the clubhouse, and when they arrived, Jag helped me into one of them with Rome and Lothar.

"Wait at the clubhouse for me, sunshine," he said.

"You're not coming with me?"

"Not until I know Poe and Tarrant are where they belong." His eyes turned red. "Killing him would feel so fucking good, but knowing he's in the deepest pit of Hell, suffering every moment of every day, right alongside Tarrant feels even better." He pressed a kiss to my lips, then shut me in. I watched as he strode over to Poe, grabbed him by the throat and dragged him to the gateway War had just opened.

Then the hounds stepped into Hell, taking Tarrant and Poe to live out a fate worse than death.

CHAPTER
THIRTY

Sutton

I WOKE when Jagger wrapped his arms around me, pressing his mouth to my shoulder, right over the mark he'd given me.

Boo chattered from his spot, hanging off the wall light across the room, saying his hello, then promptly went back to sleep.

I'd tried to stay awake, but I was exhausted and somehow had drifted off. Jagger smelled like soap, his hair damp, but I could still smell brimstone on him.

I turned in his arms and pressed a kiss to his chest, then placed my hand there. "You're in pain." I could feel it as if it were my own, an agony that had been there a very long time. "Zuri?"

"Yeah," he said roughly. "Things could have been so different, in so many ways." His throat worked. "But what's fucking me up the most right now? Watching Kurgan lose Lenny all over again."

Oh gods. "What happened?"

He stared ahead blindly. "I used the potion you gave me, a sedation dose, and put some in his drink. There was no way we'd be able to get her away otherwise. He lay there, watching War lead her away, unable to do anything. I fucking felt something shatter inside him, Sutton, I'm sure if it."

"Do you think Lenny would visit him occasionally?"

He shook his head. "She doesn't want to mate with him, and I don't blame her. She's been attacked by him, kidnapped by fucking demons, and used as bait to keep him sane. She's terrified of him." He shook his head. "No, seeing her, spending more time with her, then losing her over and over again would just be fucking cruel."

I slid my hand up the side of his neck. "Do you need to go to him? If he needs you—"

"He doesn't want to see me right now." There was another wash of pain. "He told me to leave. Zuri's with him."

I blinked up at him. "Really?"

His eyes and his mouth softened. "She has this way with him." He swallowed thickly. "His sister talked to him and he calmed. She's powerful, baby. I can feel it. Fuck knows what Lucifer has planned for her, but it has to be something big if he kept her hidden, if Beelzebub took her from him. She's the key to something, I just don't know what."

"We'll figure it out," I said and pressed a kiss to his jaw. "And until we do, we'll show her what life can be like out of Hell. You have an eternity to get to know her."

His hand slid to the side of my face. "And now, I have an eternity with you, my perfect, precious little sunshine."

"I still can't believe it."

"Believe it," he said and kissed me.

It was soft at first, but it didn't take long before I was desperate to deepen it. Jagger kept it slow, though, only deepening the kiss when he finally rolled me to my back. He licked into my mouth, sucking gently on my lips, driving me crazy with need.

"Jag, baby…please."

He gripped the shirt I was wearing, his, and dragged it up and off. "You don't have to beg, sunshine. The way I need you tonight, I won't make either of us wait." He dragged my underwear down my legs and tossed them aside, and I wrapped my legs around his hips. "That pussy wet enough to take your male?"

"Yes," I rasped. I was always ready for him.

He slipped one big hand down between us, sliding thick fingers over my pussy, grazing my aching clit and teasing my opening. He growled. "Fucking dripping for me, female." He gripped his cock and pressed the head against me. "Relax that pussy for me."

I did. I'd do anything to have him inside me, right the hell now. He pushed forward, the head filling me, but he didn't stop, he kept coming, filling me in one slow, smooth movement. I arched against him, moaning from the pleasure of being claimed by my mate.

"Yes, oh gods, yes."

"You feel so fucking good, baby."

I was spread wide under him, and he pinned me down with his chest, kissing my neck, my jaw, rubbing his against me, marking me, surrounding me with all that was Jagger.

He started moving then, claiming me deeply, in a way that was earth-shattering. I could only take it, pinned as I was, one slow, deep, soul-shaking thrust at a time. I clung to him, my claws grazing his back as I trembled from the power of the orgasm building in steadily increasing waves inside me.

Jagger felt it, too, and he groaned. "You gonna come for me already?"

"It feels too good."

"Yeah, it fucking does. You're gonna take me with you, Sutton." He fucked me harder, faster. "Fuck, baby, you're gonna take me with you."

Then he was locked inside me, his knot holding me in place as he swiveled his hips, driving me wild. "I want it," I cried out a moment before I threw my head back, my orgasm unfurling, flowing through me one intense wave after another. My pussy clamped down on him, pulsing along with the heavy throb of his cock as he came inside me. "Yes," I whimpered. "Yes."

Still locked together, Jagger wrapped his arms around me and rolled to his side, holding me to him.

When I caught my breath, I pressed a kiss to his chest. "I never thought I'd ever have this. I still can't believe you're mine." I looked into his gorgeous green eyes. "You're my family, Jag." I smiled. "My Prince Charming."

"I never thought I could feel this way, but you made it so. I was so fucking scared to feel, but you brought me back, you made me feel safe enough to feel everything." He kissed me gently. "I fucking love you so much, sunshine, my beautiful mate."

I wound my arms around him. "I love you, too."

Then we lay in the darkness, wrapped in each other's arms, and for the first time in a long time, there was no fear, no panic that I might lose him one day, that he would leave me.

No, the fates knew exactly what that were doing. They'd led me to this moment.

Jagger would always love me, and he would never let me go.

EPILOGUE

Jagger

I CURLED my arm around my mate's shoulders as we stepped through the gateway from Hell and onto the clubhouse parking lot.

"I'll go back in a couple days," Sutton said, pressing her hand to my chest.

"Okay, sunshine."

She'd just finished a healing session with Kurgan. I wasn't sure there'd ever be any improvement, not without Lenny, but she insisted on trying. My mate was compassionate and powerful, and I couldn't help but hope.

Zuri had been spending a lot of time with him as well. He was calm with her in a way I'd never seen before. She read to him and was teaching him to read as well. He could write his name, Zuri's and Lenny's as well. He could also draw. His sister had given him charcoal and pastels, and now his stone walls were covered in images, scenes, places

I'd never seen and had no idea where he'd come up with them. Lenny's name was everywhere.

The guilt was hard to deal with. Why hadn't I done that for him? Why hadn't I tried to give him more? But, then, I wasn't sure anyone but Zuri could bring out that side of Kurgan.

We walked into the clubhouse, and Sutton made a little shriek of delight. "She's here!"

Zuri stood with Ursula and smiled wide when she spotted us. It was her first visit, and my heart fucking filled to bursting when she strode over and hugged Sutton. I didn't want to force her to hug me, but I really wanted to pull her into my arms and breathe in her gentle, fresh scent. To me, she smelled similar to Kurgan, and it ignited my protective instincts.

Finally, she turned to me and opened her arms. Thank fuck. I pulled her against me, hugging her tight. "Glad you're here, Zuri," I said against her hair, breathing her in. As soon as I had her scent in my lungs, the beast rumbled in contentment. My mate and my daughter were here with me, safe.

When she finally stepped back, she smiled up at me. "This is..." She bit her lip and looked around the room, and I realized every one of my brothers was staring at her. "Overwhelming." I'd filled them in, but seeing a female hound was still a shock.

I looked around the room and growled low. My brothers quickly looked away.

Sutton laughed low and grabbed Zuri's hand. "I think your sire's feeling a bit protective."

I turned back, and that's when I realized what Zuri was wearing—the shirt I'd wrapped her in when she was a baby. I gave the sleeve a tug, my throat tight as fuck. "You still have it."

She looked down, running her hand over the worn fabric, then up at me and smiled. "It's my most treasured possession."

Then Rome was there, Fender with him, and I quickly cleared my throat. Lucifer had made Fender's prosthetic from bone charred in hellfire. It'd taken Fen a few weeks, but he was walking good on it now.

"Hey," Zuri said to them, her cheeks turning pink.

They both pulled her in for a hug, and Sutton squeezed my hand when she heard the growl rattling in my chest, silently telling me to calm the fuck down.

Ursula clapped her hands. "Right, enough reunion time. We need a drink, preferably a beer."

"I'm not sure you should have alcohol," I said to my daughter when Urs grabbed her hand to pull her across the room.

Ursula stopped, turned back to me, then threw her head back, letting loose a loud, throaty laugh.

"I'm not exactly a pup," Zuri said, grinning up at me. "I've also lived with handmaids." Her gaze slid to my brothers. "I could probably drink Roman here under the table."

He grinned. "Big words, babe, for a short-ass, but you're on. You got yourself a bet."

Then they were all headed across the room to one of the tall tables.

I watched her go, so beautiful and warm and bright. "She's beautiful, isn't she?" I said to Sutton.

"She looks like you."

I wrapped my mate in my arms. "I need to keep her safe, sunshine."

"You will." She gave me a squeeze. "And when you can't

be with her, she has the handmaids, and they won't let anything happen to her."

"Lucifer has something planned for her, something big, I can feel it."

"And she has us now, all of us," Sutton said.

I cupped my sunshine's face and stared into her gorgeous eyes. "Do you have any idea how much I fucking love you?"

"I think I have an idea, Charming." She grinned. "Now how about we go hang with your daughter?"

"Yeah," I said, grinning back. "No fucking way I'm letting her try to outdrink Roman."

Sutton laughed as the music was turned up, and we went to join them.

⋅⟩⟩▶●◀⟨⟨⋅

Hell: Lucifer's quadrant

Roxy

Tarrant screamed as I peeled the skin from his back. Blood covered my hands and was splattered across my face. I fisted his hair and jerked his head back. "You ready to talk?" He said something, and it sounded all lisped and garbled. "Pretty sure he said he doesn't know anything," I said to Lucifer.

Lucifer stood on the other side of the room, yellow eyes glowing. He was shirtless, covered in as much blood and gore as me. He'd let his mask slip, his true face twisted with fury, his black horns curled back and glossy. He was beautiful like this. Luci was beautiful in any form he took.

He strode forward and crouched in front of Tarrant, and

the demon tried to jerk back. "This could all stop. All you have to do is tell me where Beelzebub is."

He shook his head and tried to speak again. More blood bubbled from between his lips and dripped down his chest.

Lucifer rose. "We'll leave him for a day to recover, then try again."

"I don't think they know, Luci," I said. Poe hadn't given us anything either.

Lucifer snarled. "I need to find that fucker—"

Someone knocked on the door.

Startling, I turned toward it. No one disturbed us in here, and if it was a handmaid, they'd just walk right in. Lucifer didn't seem surprised though.

"I think you're right, Rox," he said, his eyes red and bright with fury. "Which is why I've called in some help."

A familiar scent hit me before I even opened the door. "Why is Lothar here?"

"He's our best tracker." He held my gaze. "And you're my best warrior."

I flinched. I couldn't help it. "What have you done?"

He cupped the side of my face. "You know I wouldn't put you in this situation if I didn't think this was the only way."

"Luci—"

"Open the door, Roxy. We'll talk more about this later."

My heart slammed into the back of my throat, and I forced myself to walk to the door. I thought I'd gotten over it, or at least I'd learned to live with the past, but I was seriously struggling again, and I didn't know why. A cold sweat coated my skin, even as fluttery wings took flight in my belly. Shoving down the wild emotion pulsing through me, I straightened my spine, plastered a huge smile on my face, and opened the door.

Lothar stood there, tall and handsome, and, like always, I wanted to climb his massive body, wrap myself around him, and never let him go. I also wanted to cause him significant bodily harm. "Loth, hey," I said, giving him a dose of my usual bubbly self.

His gaze slid down my body, taking in Tarrant's blood smeared on my skin, and his nostrils flared. "Rox, how you doing, sweetheart?"

He took a step closer, about to pull me in for a hug, like he always did, like the hounds did with any of the handmaids. But lately, I found that too difficult as well.

I stepped back quickly before he could touch me. "Good," I said and motioned for him to come in.

He frowned, not missing a thing, of course. "You still pissed with me, Rox?" he asked, a small teasing grin on his lips.

I wanted to fist that sexy beard, yank his head down and sink my teeth into his lip. Instead, I laughed. "I'm never pissed at you, you know that."

"Getting a look at you now, Rox," he said, taking in my bloody state again, "gotta say I'm fucking glad about that."

"Brother," Lucifer said to Lothar. "Thank you for coming at such short notice."

"Not a problem. What's going on?" Loth asked.

"We've tortured Poe and Tarrant for several weeks and still we don't know where Beelzebub is. My lords say they haven't heard from him, and I need him back, where I can keep an eye on him. I'm sending you and Roxy to find him."

My heart slammed in my chest. Lothar didn't even raise an eyebrow. He nodded. "When do we leave?"

"In the morning. You could be gone a while, so make sure to pack accordingly."

He jerked up his chin. "You think Beelzebub stayed away from Hell?"

"Possibly. It might pay to visit the other quadrants first, though."

Loth lifted his chin, then turned to me. "Catch you in the morning, Rox?"

Seriously? Fuck my life. "Yep," I said, keeping my voice upbeat and giving him what he expected—happy, goofy Roxy—when what I really wanted to do was punch his perfect mouth, then lick up the blood and kiss his face off. "See you in the morning."

Lucifer studied me when Lothar left. There was love in his eyes, so much of it, because he did love me, like he loved all his creations. But revenge burned even brighter, and there was nothing more important to him than getting Beelzebub back and retaining his positon in Hell—as it should be.

And I was here to serve him, always. Still, he had to know. "This is a bad idea," I said.

Lucifer's face shifted, his mask coming back down, and he slid his fingers through his hair, straightening it. "What's the worst that could happen?"

Lothar could remember.

He could remember everything.

THANK YOU!

I hope you loved Jagger and Sutton's story!

Lothar and Roxy's book is next in:
BAD BLOOD

Also by Sherilee Gray

Hellhound Heat:
Bad Demon

Bad Magic

Bad Blood

Blood Moon Brides:
Blood Moon Bound

Blood Moon Heat

The Thornheart Trials:
A Curse in Darkness

A Vow of Ruin

A Trial by Blood

An Oath at Midnight

A Promise of Ashes

A Bond in Flames

Knights of Hell:
Knight's Seduction

Knight's Redemption

Knight's Salvation

Demon's Temptation

Knight's Dominion

Knight's Absolution

Knight's Retribution

Rocktown Ink:

Beg For You

Sin For You

Meant For you

Bad For You

All For You

Just for You

The Smith Brothers:

Mountain Man

Wild Man

Solitary Man

Lawless Kings:

Shattered King

Broken Rebel

Beautiful Killer

Ruthless Protector

Glorious Sinner

Merciless King

Boosted Hearts:

Swerve

Spin

Slide

Spark

Axle Alley Vipers:

Crashed

Revved

Wrecked

Black Hills Pack:

Lone Wolf's Captive

A Wolf's Deception

Stand Alone Novels:

Breaking Him

While You Sleep

About the Author

Sherilee Gray is a kiwi girl and lives in beautiful New Zealand with her husband and their two children. When she isn't writing sexy contemporary or paranormal romance, searching for her next alpha hero on Pinterest, or fueling her voracious book addiction, she can be found dreaming of far off places with a mug of tea in one hand and a bar of chocolate in the other.

To find out about new releases, giveaways, events and other cool stuff, sign up for my newsletter!

www.sherileegray.com

Printed in Dunstable, United Kingdom